Leofwin's Hundred

By J. J. Overton

Book one of The Grid Saga

Second Edition

For Sandra, David and Chris

Acknowledgments

Grateful thanks to the following:
Sandra Horton for her patience and support, David Horton for his help in tightening up the novel, Toby Knight, Pauline Weston and Heather Harper for their beta reading. Thanks also to Andy Docking, an adventurous helicopter pilot, for his beta reading and information about flying. Lastly, thanks to Chris Horton and Connor Horton for their much-needed encouragement, particularly when the problems of writing loomed large.

1

803 AD, ANGLO-SAXON ENGLAND

A cheer roared into the storm from those waiting on the jetty as the dark silhouette of a vessel appeared through the driving rain. The ship had a fierce black-painted carving of a bird high on the prow, and it went by the name of Raven. With a great swell running, it took skilful seamanship to manoeuvre the ship to the landing stage beneath a sky black enough for the end of the world.

A passenger who had changed his name to Eadmund Wigstaning was leaning over the gunwales. He was thickset, of tall stature, with black hair and a beard. Although his complexion was swarthy, there was a green pallor about him. Wigstaning clutched a leather bag under his arm to keep the top out of sight. It was an unusual bag for the time since its closure was by means of a zip fastener. The bag contained gold coins stolen from a Frisian trader, and during the theft, Wigstaning had narrowly escaped with his life.

Two brothers owned the first of a waiting line of wagons. Soaked to the skin and miserable they nudged their horse forward, hoping to pick up freight for transport to the middle shires. Wigstaning hailed them. In a few halting words, he explained that he had to get to Heanton in the Arden. They discussed money, and he showed them three gold coins, which sealed the bargain.

As they made their way along the track heading north below the overhanging trees of the Forest of Anderida the brothers whispered about their passenger. They had attempted to make conversation with him but lapsed into silence because of the lack of response. When Wigstaning did choose to speak they recognised only a few of his words, and he spoke them with a peculiar accent from the front of his mouth.

To the brothers the passenger was like the forest, quiet and menacing, but Wigstaning was going to pay them well so his moodiness was worth tolerating. During the whole journey, he gave them no reason to suspect that his real name was Theodore Uberatu, or that he had travelled much further than anyone who encountered him could possibly have imagined.

After lodging for the night, Wigstaning directed the brothers to take him onward to Heanton in the Arden, a village near his destination in the Kingdom of Mercia. Taking the north western route out of London, they made their way along the street called Watling, heading toward a track that would take them through the Forest of Arden.

* * *

As they neared Heanton, the sky showing through the canopy of leaves became black and threatening. The brothers thought it was odd how, with the onset of a fierce thunderstorm, the mood of the passenger lightened. He pointed to his destination in the distance, a hilly part of the forest known as Leofwin's Hundred, where the House of the West Wind lay.

The brothers became nervous as they drew near to Leofwin's Hundred because of the superstition associated with it. They whipped their horse into a brisk trot as they guided the wagon along a track by Shadow Brook. The turgid water was almost overflowing its banks and carried debris with it from the forest. Uberatu stood unsteadily in the swaying wagon, flicked straw off his clothes and said some words the brothers found unintelligible. He laughed for no apparent reason, and out of habit he pulled up his sleeve and checked the time pulsing by on his digital watch.

Uberatu stepped down from the wagon and handed the brothers their payment. He pulled up a hood to shield himself from the driving rain and after crossing the stream on stepping-stones he headed off through the trees.

The brothers turned the wagon and urged the horse into a gallop. When they were approaching the wayside inn in Heanton where they intended to stop for the night they could see a bluish glow reflecting off the rain-soaked wall. They peered back through the rain in the direction of the House of the West Wind and saw vague blue lines of light rising into the darkening sky.

There was fierce lightning that night and thunder echoed over the forest. Seven people in Heanton in the Arden claimed to have seen the blue lines rising into the sky that they said were similar to lightning, but rather than a jagged downward flash, the lines curved gracefully up into the heavens from the depths of the forest. When they told the innkeeper what they had seen, word spread quickly. The priest, grasping a holy relic and glancing nervously into the forest, lost no time in going to see them.

The centuries passed. Leofwin's Hundred remained a place of superstition and a haunt of wild creatures. Only a few individuals who had the extra courage and an enquiring mind went to the House of the West Wind, and sometimes whilst there, they caught sight of beings who looked only vaguely human . . .

2

THE PRESENT DAY

The SHaFT rescue team were in black fatigues, skin blacked-up, sweeping the area through night vision gear. Dearden moved to ease his muscles. After five hours of observation, a pattern had developed in the movements of the guards he was watching. Four were patrolling the grounds of the house at regular intervals, and every half hour two heavies in suits entered a room where Dearden could see the two captives tied to chairs. He recognised the Home Secretary, only last week Lorna Durham had questioned him on the television news. Tied to a chair by his side, his wife looked knocked about, with her hair awry and a livid bruise below her right eye.

"Ready?" Dearden whispered through the comms. At his side, Templestone checked his Smith and Wesson. Twenty yards to the right, Mitch Doughty slipped the safety off his Colt M1911 and Matt Roberts, ex-commander RN who had gone wild, unsheathed his Bowie. They confirmed they were ready. The suits went out of the room and the guards started patrolling the grounds. Dearden gave the call to go.

Two days before the start of the SHaFT mission the Prime Minister, who was new in office, had been enjoying a coffee before he went to the House of Commons for question time. He was reviewing the list of improved statistics in health care to answer the opposition's charge of his party's failure when his private secretary burst into the room. He was usually solid and steady, well mannered, but not this time.

"We have a situation," he said, and showed the Premier two sheets of paper he took from a brown envelope. There were letters cut out of a newspaper glued to the sheets of paper. The message demanded money for the release of the Home Secretary and his wife, and there were conditions attached threatening their lives. The PM absorbed the details of the message. As he read, the colour drained from his face. It was the first major challenge of his time in office. He usually thrived on challenges, but this was a challenge too far.

"I think you should make the call. In my opinion, you don't have a choice."

The Premier nodded. He went to an alcove on the far side of the room. His predecessor had explained about the special telephone, but the new PM never dreamt he would have to use it.

"It's a scrambled line, for dire emergencies only," the outgoing premier told him. "Those you would call always accomplish what they set out to do, they are part of the MoD but they operate with total anonymity." Although the outgoing premier was on the opposite side of the political divide, he was sincere when he gave the incoming PM his advice.

The new man's hand clasped the phone and he paused. Three problems made him indecisive about making the call. The first, it was government policy not to give in to terrorists or kidnappers. Second, the roughly assembled letters of the demand warned him to keep the information to himself. If he divulged the situation to law enforcement the Home Secretary and his wife would die, and more hostages would be taken. The final problem was one of self-sufficiency. He had not risen to the position of Prime Minister by depending on others. His method was to issue policy not to beg for help. The ticking of the long-case clock on the wall was pressing in on him, and he lifted the phone. A few seconds went by and then a man with a cultured voice responded. There was a lengthy conversation. When the PM put the phone down the SHaFT Operations

Commander on the receiving end of the call, Sir Willoughby Pierpoint, picked up another phone and spoke to Jeremiah Dearden, a bright star in the hierarchy of SHaFT. Pierpoint gave him the go-ahead for a rescue mission.

The Home Secretary and his wife never knew who rescued them. There had been silenced shots and scuffling noises before the door was broken in and then four men covered from head to foot in black stormed the room. They used bolt cutters to cut the captives' chains and gave them firm commands to follow. Dearden led the way, handgun held high, followed by the Home Secretary and his wife with Templestone guarding the rear. Mitch Doughty and Matt Roberts stayed behind in the shadows, waiting to deal with the rest of the kidnappers.

After the mission, Dearden sat in the apartment above the stained glass studio started by his father. It was always the same routine. He would analyse how the operation went. There would be quiet music, subdued lighting, no visitors. If the doorbell rang, he wouldn't answer. People who needed to contact him knew his phone number. Sometimes during the quiet hours, he would recall previous missions and compare outcome against the strategy. Occasionally he remembered how it all began between him and SHaFT. At the time, Dearden was working with Arthur Doughty at his stained glass studio in Leamington Spa . . .

* * *

Arthur Doughty, a Geordie from Newcastle upon Tyne, sometimes had a visitor, Sir Willoughby Pierpoint, a tall man with a military bearing. He and Doughty would go into a little-used room at the back of the studio. They would lock the door and there would be a low murmur of conversation.

After a while Pierpoint would leave and Doughty would

warn the others in the studio that he was going away. Sometimes it would be for a few days. Occasionally it would be for weeks. One time when he returned his arm was in plaster and he had a freshly sown scar dangerously close to his left eye. The injuries invited curiosity but Doughty was silent about what had happened, which made those who worked for him all the more curious.

Dearden vividly remembered one particular day in 1993. He was in his early twenties and nothing seemed insurmountable until someone pounded the knocker on the studio door. It was a police sergeant bringing news that Dearden's father Maxwell had been found dead in Leofwin's Hundred, the forest near Dearden Hall Farm. The subsequent inquest determined that the cause of death was unknown.

It took Dearden months to work through the numbness of the loss. He felt anger gnawing deep inside. For his mother's sake, he tried to inject normality into the fractured family life but it was difficult and it caused Dearden to develop a hard, defensive edge. One day it exploded onto Arthur Doughty. It was an uncharacteristic burst of anger, which started with something small. Dearden couldn't remember the reason when he reminisced, but he had stormed out the door and headed toward town. As he came to the river, he felt free but after he walked along the bank for a while, the weather changed. Dark, sombre clouds drifted from the south-west, and with them, Dearden's mood darkened and he regretted his outburst and went back to the studio. He apologised to Doughty, expecting the older man to fire him but Doughty said nothing. He unlocked the door to his private room at the back, called Dearden over, and led the way in.

It was an odd, Spartan sort of room. There was a variety of objects hanging on the walls and on shelves about the room. A stained glass panel set in a window frame in the outer wall let in a blaze of coloured light. There was a shield motif in the centre with a bull's head looking out and to the left and right were emblazoned a pair of rampant lions facing centre.

Doughty invited Jem to sit and went to a cabinet at the side of the room. He took out a bottle of Courvoisier and two glasses and poured an equal measure into each one. Then he took a bottle of rare 1938 vintage Amandio's Old Tawny Port and added a measure into the Courvoisier.

"I keep this for special occasions, give it a try, it's smooth and has great depth."

Dearden wondered what was coming. It was an odd prelude to being fired and the offer of a drink threw him. He sipped the liquor and felt the warmth spreading inside.

"Port and Brandy, it makes the heart rejoice and smooths the edges. I'm a great advocate of it." Doughty put his glass down. "There's something I want to discuss with you."

Dearden avoided Doughty's direct gaze.

"I liked your challenge earlier on, and what I also liked was that you had the guts to come back and apologise."

"But—" and then Dearden was at a loss for words.

Doughty nodded. He was always straight, a good man to work for. "I felt things pressing in myself a few years back, and I needed time out." The amazing thing had been Doughty's perception. He had hit the spot.

"Time out would be impossible. I'll have to get involved with the business now dad's not here."

"There is a way out . . . get a manager. I know someone who's ready for a change, he's an all-rounder with stained glass and he could manage the business for you." Doughty sat back in his chair. "There's something else. Your show of strength earlier convinced me to talk to you about an organisation I'm involved with. What I am going to say must never go beyond this room. Listen, and afterwards, if you want to get involved

I'll tell you more. If you're not interested, forget everything I'm going to say. You've probably seen Sir Willoughby Pierpoint come here occasionally. Pierpoint and I were in the Special Forces together."

"Really . . . what did you do?"

"It's what we still do. We run an organisation called SHaFT. There are only a few of us involved, we're a very select military group, and only the highest level of government knows of our existence." Doughty had Dearden's attention. "SHaFT is an acronym for the Shock and Force Team. We conduct missions in pursuit of justice anywhere we're needed, there are literally no boundaries."

"None at all?"

Doughty was silent. He moved to the wall and, almost reverently, touched some of the objects, moving from one to another. Many of the objects were ordinary, an early mobile phone, large and cumbersome. A riding crop, and by it a black riding helmet. There were other items in glass showcases. In one of them, there was a Fabergé egg exquisitely decorated in gold and enamel sitting in an equally beautiful egg cup.

"What you see around the room are mementoes of some of our missions. The Russian government gave us this egg after a mission in Russia at the height of the cold war. A rogue double agent and some men he recruited had the Kremlin held to ransom with a nuclear bomb. On the quiet, both the Russian and the American presidents approached us to go in and sort them out. We did, and the egg was a token of thanks from the Russian President. The Americans thanked us and gave us money. Jem, the missions could fill an encyclopaedia, but not one of them will ever be in the public domain."

"So you're like the SAS."

"There are similarities but the SAS is too well known, too public. We are so covert that our presence is deniable at any point. There are no paper trails or notes in meetings, all telephone calls are high-level encrypted."

Dearden looked at the legend under the stained glass shield, Nos Successio Procul Totus Sumptus. Doughty saw where he was looking. "In English, the motto says We Succeed At All Costs. Do you see the bull in the centre of the shield? He stands for power, the lions each side stand for courage. The scales above the shield stand for justice."

The words of the legend ran through Dearden's mind, Nos Successio Procul Totus Sumptus. We Succeed At All Costs. He asked Arthur Doughty to tell him more.

*   *   *

Doughty's son Mitchell and Jem Dearden became inseparable friends after an initial period of mutual loathing and bloody combat in a park at the side of the river running through Leamington Spa. They became involved with SHaFT at the same time, and the organisation filled a large part of Dearden's life after his father's death.

There was a time of intense training, some of it under live fire conditions at Kineton Base in incursion scenarios around mocked-up aircraft and houses. Dearden spent months learning survival techniques in the jungles of British Columbia and over a period of time he became a formidable opponent for anyone who crossed him. He could use any type of weapon or no weapon at all. The missions he had been involved with and his sharply honed skills brought him respect from the men of SHaFT and a commission to the rank of Captain.

In 2003, an event took place that forged his character still further, gave him a harder edge. He became acquainted with a girl named Jackie Mason. She telephoned the studio after buying an old townhouse near the centre of Knowle. She wanted to get the Art Nouveau leaded glass panel in her front door restored to its original condition.

Dearden ran weekend residential stained glass courses, which were a great success. Participants who didn't live locally enjoyed a stay at The Barley Mow, a public house on the bank of the Grand Union Canal. Over a number of weekends, the students would learn how to cut glass into intricate shapes and join the pieces together using lead and solder. The idea appealed to Jackie's sense of creativity and she wanted to restore her door panel herself, so she signed up for the course.

Dearden visited her house to remove the panel and temporarily board up the hole left in the door. She was waiting for him and there was an immediate rapport between them. A few weeks later, the course started, and when the first weekend was over, they went for a meal together. The relationship felt right immediately, and after a few months, plans were in place for them to be married in the summer.

Earlier the same year Dearden's mother Philippa re-married. It was strange to see David Hilton in the place where his father had been but he came to terms with it, and occasionally he visited them at their home in West Fleet, on the coast of Dorset.

* * *

In early June, Dearden was working in the studio behind a bow-fronted shop window. He had seen Jackie the night before and they had made more wedding plans. He put his soldering iron in its rest when he heard sirens in the distance. Glancing up he saw two police cars hurtling up the main street followed by an ambulance. He was on the pavement as a silver coloured Vauxhall Cavalier raced past in the opposite direction. He memorised the registration number. There were blue lights further up the main street. Looking back on the situation, he remembered the awful sense of foreboding that made him run up the road. He could see a woman lying in a pool of blood with a police officer supporting her head. It was Jackie. She had been in the wrong place at the wrong time putting money in the bank for the wedding. The bank heist left her on the ground with a bullet in her chest and Jem Dearden cradling her in his arms watching her eyes growing dim as her life ebbed away.

After the death of Jackie Mason, Dearden threw himself deep into the affairs of SHaFT. He left his family business in the hands of the manager, Lloyd Perkins.

3

The insistent ringing of the doorbell startled Dearden awake. He went to the door and opened it to a police constable and a female police Sergeant who asked if he was Jeremiah Dearden. His first thought was that something had happened to his mother. He asked them in and showed them his driving licence to prove who he was.

"I understand you've got an uncle named Francis Rawdon Dearden." Jem nodded.

"I'm afraid there's some bad news." Starting uncertainly, and then finding resolve, the woman sergeant told Dearden about the death of his uncle. She said that a postman delivering mail to Dearden Hall Farm had found his body.

The funeral took place on a Monday, which started bright but deteriorated into lashing rain and gloomy skies. Beforehand, Dearden looked in the mirror and shaved off the growth of his overnight beard. He was looking older, he thought. The carefree face had gone, his face looked more determined, the lines around his mouth more obvious. His right eye was bloodshot. It wouldn't be long before it healed and matched the other one that was pale blue. Some who met up with Dearden thought his eyes were piercing and incisive. The interpretation depended on context. His friends thought his eyes were warm. His enemies thought they were merciless. He brushed his hair. At least it didn't need dying, it was still auburn and full.

Dearden's mother and David Hilton travelled up from West Fleet for the funeral. They and Jem represented the family. A scanty group of neighbours turned up out of a sense of duty. Francis had made more enemies than friends by his bad-tempered isolation. After the funeral, the family met at The Barley Mow in Knowle. They dried out around an open fire.

A few days later mail dropped through Jem's letterbox. Turning the volume down on the Agnus Dei from Jenkins' Armed Man, a Mass for Peace, he went to retrieve the mail. There was a letter marked Private and Confidential. It had a Warwick postmark. He thumbed the envelope open and saw the letterhead of the family solicitor.

> *Dear Mr Dearden,*
>
> *We understand you are the nephew of the late Francis Rawdon Dearden. We wish to give you our sincere condolences over your loss.*
>
> *After enquiries, we have concluded that you are the sole remaining relative of the aforementioned Francis Rawdon Dearden. We wish to meet with you to discuss information of interest to you concerning the disposal of your late uncle's estate.*
>
> *Please contact us at a suitable time to make an appointment to meet with our Mr A. Sharkey, whereupon he will inform you of the details regarding the above information.*
>
> *Yours sincerely,*
> *Cynthia Burroughs*
> *pp. Mr A. H. Sharkey.*

* * *

Two days after receiving the letter, Dearden arrived at the solicitors.

The grey-haired Andrew Sharkey beamed with delight as he told Dearden he had inherited Dearden Hall Farm near Hampton-in-Arden. He gave him a bunch of keys, a number of which were large and not modern, and he told him there was money, a great deal of it. When Dearden left the solicitors, he was feeling dazed but elated, and he rang his mother down in Dorset.

She squealed with delight. "So there is some fairness after all. I always thought the old goat would leave everything to an animal charity. I'm glad I was wrong." So was Dearden. Within the hour he swung left off the B road rising toward Hampton-In-Arden. There was a private drive that he recognised from childhood, and he stopped the Range Rover to unlatch a five-barred gate with a large sign saying *PRIVATE, Trespassers WILL DEFINITELY be Prosecuted.* His uncle had not wanted visitors.

He drove into a gravelled courtyard riotous with weeds and pulled up in front of outhouses attached at right angles to the main building. He switched the engine off and birdsong replaced the exhaust noise. Dearden looked around, taking in the setting.

The house was large. It was a back-to-front sort of building with the outbuildings on the side of the front entrance and its weathered stone implied it was ancient. It was still as he remembered from visits with his mother and father when he was young, but years of disinterest and lack of maintenance had taken their toll. Some of the windows were rotten and green algae crept up the wall on the northern side.

The west-facing main entrance door was solid, without a window, and an old covering of paint was peeling off. When he turned the key, the bolt slid out of the jamb with a grating noise. He pushed the door open and stepped through the round-topped arch of the entrance into a large square hall with a stone floor worn smooth by previous inhabitants. The air smelled musty so he left the door open. Off the hall ran a wide stairway leading to rooms above. Intense beams of sunlight filtered through the windows, picking out carved woodwork in sharp relief against the deep shadow.

Dearden felt an affinity with the building he recognised from childhood and knew he would grow to love it. Doors led off the entrance hall. One of them opened onto a great hall of baronial size at the far end of which was a massive fireplace built with stone blocks.

There were other rooms on the ground floor, a library, a kitchen where copper saucepans still hung on hooks from a beam, and there was a room with a full-sized snooker table covered with an overlay of dust. Dearden climbed the stairs and walked along the length of a corridor with windows overlooking the courtyard. He passed by six bedrooms and four bathrooms and at the end of the passage he stopped and looked out of a window. The outbuilding wings he looked out on must have been added later, maybe in Regency times judging by the multi-paned windows.

Dearden went back outside to look at the outbuildings built onto the wings of the main house and walked by some stables. The split doors were open and swinging in the breeze. He shut and latched them. Further on there were a granary and storage rooms with a hayloft above them. He crossed the courtyard and opened a door to a room with small chimneystack above it. He heard a flutter of wings as birds disturbed by his intrusion escaped through the chimney above a blacksmith's forge. The smithy's tools, festooned with cobwebs were still on hooks screwed into boards on the walls. The top of the anvil was smooth, a shining signature to the smithy's work. Dearden rubbed his hand on it and it felt slick with the oil the blacksmith smeared on it to protect it before he left for the last time.

The next room contained a cider press, and a number of large barrels lined the walls. Standing at the door Dearden could smell the scent of apples and yeast still hanging in the air and it reminded him of a long childhood autumn spent at the house. In the holiday from school, he met Cozette, the neighbouring farmer's daughter and he fell in love with her for two whole long weeks of boyish love. He smiled at the memories and slowly shut the door on them.

He turned to face the forest. Leofwin's Hundred seemed much larger than he remembered from that autumn. It spread out in front of him to the left and right. He could see the detail of the trees at the outer edge. Some were tall and had huge girth and he could hear their foliage rustling in the breeze.

Dearden walked to the fencing around the perimeter of the forest and leant on a wide gate beyond which a track disappeared amongst the trees. A large padlock secured the forest from unwanted entry. Fastened to the gate was another no trespassing notice. The track was inviting, slightly dark where the trees gathered over it but it would have to wait.

A wide stream was flowing noisily out of the trees through a gulley to his right. Dearden eyed its course up and saw where it entered a culvert taking it underneath the track he had driven down to the house. On the other side of the track, it meandered across a small field over rocks and boulders as it coursed downhill. In the valley, he could see where the stream joined the River Blythe, which wound through marshy land toward some lakes further afield.

Dearden made his way back to the house and in the courtyard, he sat on a bench with cast iron armrests that he remembered from when he was young. The green paint had faded and was peeling after years of weather and the varnish on the wood was flaking. He sat on the bench last when he was eleven years old. His first job would be to paint the bench again. It was so many summers ago but, in his mind, he could still hear the laughter echoing around the courtyard the time he helped his father paint the cast metal ends and got more paint on his hands than on the bench. He vowed to bring the laughter back again.

Dearden rang Mitch Doughty to tell him about his turn of luck. Doughty had gone into the building trade a number of years previously,

"What, you've got the big place?"

"None other, I'm there now. It needs a lot of work. Can you come and see what needs doing?"

* * *

Doughty had finished surveying the outside and was squatting on the floor in one of the bedrooms making notes on his walk-through to assess the internal restoration. Dearden left him to carry on and spent some time going from room to room, examining them in detail. He came to a door at the far end of the landing running along the western wall before it turned left into the north wing above the outbuildings. The hinges creaked through lack of use as he pushed the door open.

It was a large room with built-in wardrobes and cupboards. A bed stood against the wall opposite the window, its mahogany headboard was dusty after years of neglect. He went to some half-drawn curtains on a pole with a writing desk in front of them and slid the curtains open disturbing cobwebs and dust. He looked through the window and saw the forest; low at first and then higher where it became more distant.

There was a swivel chair pulled out from the desk as if the owner had left the room a few minutes before. Its arms and seat were padded leather, worn and discoloured with use. Dearden knocked the dust off and sat down. He saw some words carved into the woodwork on the front edge of the desk. He dusted the carving with his hand and looked more closely. It was his father's name, and there was a date, carved into the wood in a childish hand, *Maxwell Dearden, 1953*. Dearden gazed around the room. It must have been his father's bedroom when he was a boy and his study when he was a young man, probably until he left home to get married. Jem and his father had been close and as he touched the carving, his fingers lingered on it.

He pulled the drawers in the desk open one by one but found nothing in them apart from old items of stationery, some pencils, a slide rule, and an A4 pad with some scribbled notes dated 1973. He recognised his father's handwriting. Judging by the date, his father had written the notes on one of his visits to the hall after he was married. Dearden began reading.

I have conducted research as planned after the phenomena occurred again. It must have been Leofwin who I saw, all the clues point to that. He was a contemporary of Leofric of Mercia, possibly his brother, he was an earl, and he looked magnificent. I must go back into the forest to see if the events occur randomly, or whether something specific triggers them. The makers must surely have planned such a complex mechanism to operate in a more controlled way.

Dearden laid the pad down on the desk and contemplated what his father had meant when he wrote about Leofwin and the complex mechanism. The writing in the next paragraph was untidier. It was as if his father had some reason to put greater urgency in the information he was recording.

Went into Leofwin's Hundred again this morning. It was stormy so I had to dress in waterproofs. The weather got worse but I was able to get into the building again to shelter. I think the great crystal in the centre of the room has something to do with what happens. The outer walls become transparent, but I have no idea what causes it. I looked outside through the binoculars and focussed on the great hall. I saw the Saxon again. It was then I noticed the keystone set into the arch had writing cut into it, a date, 1063.

I must attempt to go through the door to the world outside, but if I do I might be opening Pandora's Box. There are so many uncertainties. This is doing none of us any good, particularly poor Philippa who must wonder where I keep going. I will tell her when I know for certain. I am tempted to cover the entrance at the bottom of the hill up again and forget the whole thing, but the damn place has a grip on me.

Reading the notes forced a memory to surface. Jem remembered an occasion when he was young. His father said they would go for a walk in the forest and had hoisted Jem onto his shoulders. It seemed to Jem they walked for ages. His abiding memory was of sunlight shining through the leaves of the trees and the soft green grass of a clearing. It was magical. The image was still vivid even though he must have been only two or three years old at the time. His father was wearing Wellingtons and was whistling a tune softly on his breath as they went. They forded a stream, and afterwards, they came to a place that his father said was an engine house.

Curiosity aroused, Jem pushed back in the chair, its castors squeaked from lack of use. He crossed the room to the cupboards. There was nothing in the bottom one, so he stood on a chair to reach the top cupboard. It smelt musty and was full of books. There were piles of textbooks, reference works large and small, some of them leather bound with gilt edging, and there were diaries with year-dates on the covers. Dearden began to remove the diaries and put them in two piles on the desk. Something had lodged in his mind to do with the A4 notepad in the desk drawer. He went to the desk and re-read the notes. He found what he was looking for, the phrase, I saw the Saxon again. It was odd, and he wondered what his father meant by it and what he meant by covering up an entrance at the bottom of a hill.

Doughty appeared at the door with a tape measure. He saw the books on the desk.

"Going to have a fire?"

"No, far from it. These books are something to do with research dad was involved with. I'm taking them home to see what the old chap was up to, his diaries are here as well."

"Did he talk about what he was researching?"

"Not that I can remember, but according to the diaries there was something going on in the forest over there. It's called Leofwin's Hundred."

Downstairs in the great hall, an immense fireplace dominated one end of the room. There were logs and kindling, and old newspapers in a galvanised bucket, and very soon, Dearden had a fire blazing. The damp and chill in the room started to lift as flames roared into the chimney void.

A large rectangular table with the patina of years of polishing and burn marks on the surface was at the end of the room near the fireplace. Carved oak chairs around it were in a state of disorder and crumbs and dishes from a bygone meal were at one end of the table. Dust covered everything. Dearden couldn't understand why his uncle allowed the house to become neglected. He could have had someone live-in to help him keep the place up to scratch.

Ignoring the dust Doughty put his notepad on the table at the end nearest the fire and drew up a chair. Dearden sat beside him and put the diaries on the table ready to take to his apartment.

"It's good news for a place this old," Doughty said. "The outbuildings are straightforward; we can deal with those later.

Most of the problems in the main house look worse than they are. Some of the windows are rotten and need replacing. The walls are a yard thick and they're strong. Overgrown plants are growing close to the building. They've got to come out because they're causing damp to penetrate the walls."

"I'll take care of that," Dearden said.

As Doughty's voice droned in the background, Dearden's mind wandered back to his father's hurried notes about covering up the entrance at the bottom of a hill. He moved the writing pad and glanced at the passage again. He recalled no mention of such a place from his childhood. There was the recollection of the walk into the forest when his father said about an engine house, but he had said nothing about research. Doughty was still talking.

"—and if we get those jobs done you'll have a good start in preserving the building. There is a problem in one corner where there is minor subsidence. The house is on a rocky outcrop, and where the northern wall meets the wall on the eastern side, the outcrop falls away. It's only by a few inches, but it needs underpinning."

"Do it, Mitch, when can you start?"

4

After a few weeks, Doughty had converted one of the outbuildings on the southern side of the courtyard to living accommodation. Old plans for the farm referred to it as the Malt House and Frieda and Gil Heskin who Dearden hired as his housekeeper and handyman had moved in. It was a time of comparative peace for Dearden as far as SHaFT was concerned. Others came on board in the organisation and took the strain. Younger ones had to learn the ropes and Dearden took more of a backseat from operations and did some teaching. Occasionally Pierpoint would ring him if there was a difficult mission and Dearden would disappear into his father's old room to plan the logistics for surveillance or infiltration.

"Going again sir?" Frieda Heskin would ask.

"I am. Pack the usual items."

"Does that include the Beretta, Mr Dearden?"

"It does," he might say, or "Not this time," and she would ask no more questions, she was discrete that way. Dearden would go to Kineton Base where he would fly or take other transport to the action zone. He was glad SHaFT missions weren't a dominant feature of his life anymore. He had more time to work on the house, and he enjoyed doing that.

Doughty made great progress with the building restoration and after an intense few months of work, Jem had the interior sorted out. He had sandblasted the exposed stonework and painted plasterwork with lime-based emulsion. Dearden spent most of his waking hours dividing his days between working on the house and on stained glass at the studio in Knowle. Came the time when work on the house tailed off, which gave him time to spend reading his father's diaries. He sorted them into chronological order and started with the earliest, 1959, which was when his father was fifteen.

On the flyleaf was the youthful heading, 'This is the diary of Maxwell Dearden of Dearden Hall Farm, Hampton in Arden, Warwickshire, England. 1959.'

Jem opened it to the first entry.

> *January 1st, 1959.*
> *It has been snowing for days on end. The drifts are half way up the wall to the windows. It is quiet outside and the snow has covered the fields and the trees at the back. I am going out for a walk into Leofwin's Hundred to see what it is like with the covering of snow. More tomorrow.*

> *January 3rd, 1959.*
> *Did not write an entry yesterday. I am not into the routine yet, but will get better with it. The snow is v deep. The trees sheltered the pathway into the forest where I went for the walk. Logs blazing on the fire in the Dining Hall where I am writing this and the wind is blowing a gale outside. Saturday Night Theatre is about to start. It should be good. It is a dramatisation of The Kraken Wakes.*

> *January 4th, 1959.*
> *Sky looks more settled and the Sun is trying to break through. The weather forecast on the radio said a thaw should start tomorrow with clear sunny spells and rising temperatures.*

The diaries continued in this style, but sometimes whole weeks went by without an entry. Jem found the reading addictive. He was learning more about his father than he had ever known when he was alive. Max Dearden had a sensitive side he had hidden from his son and Jem wished he could have been part of it.

As Dearden read the diaries, he could see that the many entries up to the one of August the 20th 1970 described the life of a young man learning his trade and then his time living at Dearden Hall Farm. The September entries introduced a theme, which became recurrent. His father became fascinated in one particular part of the forest. Jem was surprised his father mentioned nothing about it to him when he was a child.

September 3rd, 1970.

I was working at Compton Revel Manor today. All of the stained glass in the library is in a sorry state of repair and will need restoring in the studio. I had a break for lunch and looked at the books in the library. Surprised that I found one about our home. The author, someone named Nathaniel Devenish, called the place Dearden Hall, not Dearden Hall Farm. The date of printing was 1724, and the title was Leofwin's Hundred, Time and Ley-Lines, a Naturally Occurring Phenomena of Magnetism and the Augmentation of Them. I looked through the book and read some directions Devenish gave into the forest.

Take the track passing through the forest by way of the Old Hall. Go thirteen hundred and forty paces down the forest track to the ancient oak given the name Old Jack. Once there, turn a sharp right through ninety degrees of the compass, walk on and cross the stream given the name Shadow Brook at its deep cutting by way of stones set in. Follow the bank with the stream to the left, looking to the right until the House of the West Wind is seen. It is atop a hill that has good height.

Dearden was intrigued about what the House of the West Wind might be and he set out early next day with sandwiches in a rucksack to see if he could find it. The first thing he was aware of was the feeling of solitude in the forest and then how dense it was with undergrowth. There were vague paths, the runs of wild creatures, and the tree canopy created dark places where fungus grew and fallen wood was rotting. Dearden stopped occasionally and listened, to see if he could hear the sound of Shadow Brook to give him some sense of direction.

He came across a grassy glade and ate his sandwiches. He looked at his watch. Two hours had gone by. He hadn't found what he was looking for so he decided to make his way out of the forest. He gauged his direction from the Sun and went roughly north-northeast, and eventually came to the boundary of Leofwin's Hundred a few hundred yards from the five-barred gate near his house. He felt frustrated not finding the House of the West Wind, but decided to look again when he could find time in his schedule.

In the evening he picked up the 1970 diary again and continued reading from where he left off. The remaining months contained descriptions of his father's walks into the forest. They were becoming obsessive. He always walked to the House of the West Wind, and he wrote about wanting storms to occur. Then at the start of the 1971 diary, there was a change of theme. It was a poignant entry.

> *February 3rd, 1971.*
> *I have met the most beautiful girl. Her name is Philippa Grainger. She and I are so alike. We mostly have the same interests and the small things where we differ are of no consequence. I love those differences, and I love the girl.*

Jem felt as though he was intruding into the private lives of two people he loved, but despite that, his urge to read on persisted. There was now a long time between each entry. It was understandable under the changed circumstances. His father had found interests that were more important. After a gap of well over three months, the entries resumed. They were especially poignant.

April 19th, 1971.
Phil and I find it increasingly hard to be apart, and we have decided to get married next month.

Then his father reverted to the old theme in the same entry.

I am intrigued with what Devenish writes and must go to the building in the forest once again to try to get inside it and find out its purpose. At times, the forest near the House of the West Wind seems far from normal. It has an indefinable presence. Sometimes, when the weather is bad, a luminescence arises from the building in the form of lines reaching up into the sky.

May 28th, 1971.
Philippa and I were married last Saturday. Best day of my life and it can only get better.

A sentence or two later there was a return to the old theme.

Went into the forest and examined the area around the hill. There seems to be a pathway leading into the sloping escarpment because it is solid a few inches below the surface. I shall dig there. It could be a lot of work for nothing, but I am sure Augustus will help. He is very interested in the site.

Dearden wondered who Augustus was, and what his mother thought of the escapades into the forest. He would ask when he saw her next. The next entry was short and to the point.

June 11th, 1971.
It seems as though Nathaniel Devenish was right after all.
The events are random and unpredictable. This is contrary to
my original thinking, that there is purpose in what is
happening at the House of the West Wind. It is very
disappointing. All of my reasoning about the building has been
mere supposition and a total waste of time.

Dearden could tell his father had been deeply disillusioned.
There was a gap of two months, during which his father
regained enthusiasm and then the writing became optimistic
again.

August 5th, 1971.
Today, while I was walking in the forest the phenomenon
occurred again. The weather became thundery so I rushed to
the building to shelter by its wall. I feel sure the events to do
with House of the West Wind have a connection with
atmospheric electricity. I was surprised that the door was
unlocked and I was unprepared for what I found inside the
building. To say it was out of this world would be an
understatement. There was a great crystalline structure in the
centre of the room. It was like the hub of a wheel. I shall call
the building the Hub; it's shorter to write than the House of
the West Wind.
On the far side of the room, stairs were leading
downwards. There was a locked door halfway down so I have
no idea what lies below. I must excavate the base of the hill to
see if there is another way of getting into the lower parts of the
building. I do wonder how old it is. There is no clue to its age.
It was present in the forest in 1724 when Devenish wrote

about it. He also said that the building 'Goes beyond living memory.

As the days passed by Jem enjoyed the mix of physical work around the hall in the mornings and reading the diaries in the afternoons. He opened the 1971 diary again and as he was reading it, he came to an entry that stood out above all the others. Jem wished he could have been with his father to help him.

October 22nd, 1971.
We are getting tools into the forest ready for the excavation. We will soon know what lies below.

October 24th, 1971.
Excavation started with Augustus helping. He has brought his son, Theo, along. He is a young lad of eight who seems introverted and sullen. First, we dug down vertically into the soil for seven or eight feet where the face of the wall enters the soil on top of the hill. No foundation material was present, so we are unsure how deep the building penetrates the hill. Most likely it goes to the forest floor, where I think we shall find the foundations. We will attempt digging into the base of the hill where I found the pathway. It must lead to a door. I tried to get Francis involved. Another pair of hands would make all the difference.
October 25th, 1971.
The work is backbreaking and slow. Francis stops by occasionally. He spends a short while looking at us working but does not help. I have never known anyone so idle. The forest lies on undulating land, but the hill with the House of the West Wind blends into the surrounding land, and it is impossible to see it from the road, which is some distance away.

I do not want anyone to know what is going on. If the Hub became public knowledge all sorts of scientists and cranks would descend on us.

It is difficult to say how long it will take to dig into the hill and reach the wall. There is a great air of expectancy and because of what Devenish said, and the presence of the pathway, we are confident that we shall find a lower entrance.

While we were working the best of coincidences occurred. Stormy weather had persisted for a few days. It had been a sultry sort of day until a breeze sprang up pushing dark cumulus before it that developed into a thunderstorm. A glow in the form of flowing lines began to curve upwards from the building, rising way up into the heavens. We agreed afterwards about other lines of luminescence high above which formed a grid visible in our peripheral vision. The lines reminded me of the Aurora Borealis, and when they died out a smell of ionised air was present, as though an extremely high voltage had discharged. Maybe the Hub is an electronic component in its own right, part of a colossal electronic circuit. It is an intriguing thought.

Dearden put the diary down and rubbed his eyes. He had been trying to read but was drifting in and out of sleep. The hour was late. He stood up and stretched. He made a coffee, which revived him, and he continued reading. The entries in the diary became less frequent as the year went on but there was far more detail in each entry.

November 2nd, 1971.

Our excavations have reached the wall of the building. We were soaked to the skin and it continued to thunder. The effort was worthwhile because we found a door set into the building. It was made of a hard type of metal. As we cleared the last remnants of soil away from it, we turned the handle and pushed the door open. We had no idea what we would find inside the place. I must admit we were all nervy, including Augustus who is usually steady in most situations. The air was fresh as we entered the large space within. As we crossed the threshold, a gentle background light shone so we didn't need the torches we brought with us.

Opposite the entrance, there were stairs leading both up and down. Going up the stairs to the next room, we could see a collection of many objects, most of which were alien to us and quite repulsive. We stayed in the room for a while to examine what was there, and then we carried on upwards passing through the next room, which had a number of seats, large by our standards. They were facing toward the outer wall. The single seat at the front had a panel in front of it with buttons that had symbols on them. I don't know if it was my imagination with being in such a strange place, but I am sure I saw a shadow from someone behind us on the wall at one time.

On the next level up, we saw structures that were unlike anything we had ever seen before. The crystal was there in the centre of the room, immense and dark in colour, almost opaque. Internally it was coruscating with vague fiery colours and shapes darting back and forth, giving it the appearance of life. A cradle supported its lower end, and the crystal disappeared into the ceiling. About halfway up the crystal, there was a metallic looking ring with coils wrapped around it, and great leads curving up and joining the circular outside wall where it joined the ceiling.

We carried on up the stairs and came to a door on a half-landing. The catch released with the lightest touch and we found ourselves at the highest level. I recognised the room at once as the one I had sheltered in from the storm. The upper part of the crystal was there, coming through from the room below. Augustus Uberatu, who has a scientific background, said that he has never seen its like before.

There was the smell of ionised air throughout the building, and a low-pitched humming noise rose in its intensity when lightning flashed outside. A remarkable thing about the topmost level was that the circular wall and ceiling had become transparent. There was no indication of that from outside. Looking through the wall, we could see a panoramic view of the surrounding countryside. It had changed beyond recognition. My feeling was that the building and its surroundings had come into an altered state.

Augustus was interested in the array of equipment on all the floor levels because of his background of science. We contemplated the building's use and its age. Back in the seventeen hundreds, Devenish must have wondered about its age too, because, in his book, he recorded interviews with local folk who he had questioned, and all agreed that the building had always been in the forest.

That first time we looked out from the topmost level there was bright daylight outside apart from directly overhead where the thunderclouds were gathered. The scene defied logic. There were far fewer trees directly around the building but the trees of an immense forest now stretched to the far horizon. From our position on the hill, we had a view to a settlement straddling rising ground about half a mile away. At the end of the settlement, there was a large building with a fortified wall surrounding it that was made of wood with a stone foundation. Smoke was rising from a fire near a man who was working on some large timbers

Then another man came through a gateway in the outer wall. It took him a while to come close enough for us to see some detail. He was carrying a sword and its surfaces flashed in the sunlight. He looked like the images I had seen of a Saxon warrior. Augustus was most excited about this and muttered some words in German, which was strange because I had always thought he was Argentinean.

Inside the Hub, from the room we had entered at ground level, there were the stairs leading downward. We ignored those because there was so much else to see. We still have no idea what lies below but at some point, we will have to explore. What other marvels will we find down there?

Jem closed the diary for the night. He was absorbed by what he was reading but confused because the information in the diaries was absurd, as though his father had lost touch with reality. It was an uncomfortable thought because he didn't want his father's memory tarnished. That was the tipping point. As the evening progressed, Jem became determined to investigate the phenomena himself. As soon as the intensity of the restoration work of Dearden Hall eased off he would walk into Leofwin's Hundred again to see if he could find the Hub. He thought it unlikely the diaries were describing actual events but he couldn't get away from the fact that his father had been a rational man through and through. The way he had written the diaries gave everything the ring of truth.

* * *

The interior restoration work of Dearden Hall Farm was finished by the spring of 2007. Doughty had finished the underpinning on the north-eastern corner and had fitted the last of the new windows in place. Dearden had moved in, and as farming had not taken place on the estate for many years, he renamed the house 'Dearden Hall'.

Not long after he moved in the phone rang, but there was no response from the other end apart from hearing someone moving about, and then the phone went dead. At the time it didn't concern Dearden too much. It could have been a mistaken call, and he forgot about it.

Mitch Doughty converted the Smithy into a stained glass studio and Lloyd Perkins, who was managing the business, moved into one of the two apartments above it. Doughty suggested that some machine tools he bought in a bankruptcy sale would be better at Dearden Hall than standing greased up in his warehouse by the canal in Long Itchington. He partitioned the studio off and installed the machines into a workshop so that he could make items of tooling, or spare parts for his building plant.

Dearden showed Doughty a sketch of a project he had in mind involving an enclosure with strong eight-foot high wire fencing. It had a hut with a door opening into the enclosure and another opening into the courtyard. He was secretive about its purpose.

* * *

A backlog of stained glass work had developed. Once the move from the apartment and studio in Knowle had taken place Dearden and Lloyd Perkins attacked the backlog of work in the new studio with urgency. Maxwell Dearden's diaries went onto the back burner.

After a couple of weeks, the anonymous caller rang again. It was much the same as before with the background noises, but this time he could hear someone breathing on the other end of the line. It irritated Dearden when the caller rang for a third time two days later with the same creepy anonymity. The calls came every few days and Dearden became more unsettled about them. He tried to force them to the back of his mind. The caller appeared to have an agenda but didn't say what it was, or reveal his identity.

After a few weeks of restoration, there were some gaps in Dearden's workload. He was able to put building restoration and orders for stained glass to the back of his mind. It seemed appropriate, now he had decorated his father's old room, to use it as his pad. He installed a computer with a router for broadband, as well as easy chairs and a bed. It became his inner sanctum.

Dearden had left the diary he was reading bookmarked. He opened it and found the next entry, December 18th, 1971. It was another poignant entry. What it said reached deep into his psyche.

December 18th, 1971
Phil and I have had a beautiful son. We chose a name for him ten minutes after he was born. Jeremiah. We will call him Jem.

There was a long passage of time separating the December 1971 entry to the next one and there was no explanation for the gap. Maxwell began by writing about a decision he and Augustus had come to about not having any interface with people in past ages because it added too many complications. In the same paragraph, Maxwell had written about a growing rift between him and Augustus Uberatu. Augustus is not listening to reason, Maxwell wrote, but there was no further explanation about what had taken place between the two men, but apparently, they had parted company.

The timeshifts, as Maxwell described the events when the outside world changed, became further apart, and the last entry in that diary was startling in its simplicity and its message.

July 18th, 1985.
I have covered up the lower entrance. The implications of leaving it open are too great and I cannot allow the risks involved to affect

my family any longer.

The year in gold leaf on the outside cover of the last diary was 1992, seven years after his father said he had covered up the lower entrance, and the year before Maxwell died. In 1992 Jem had been a twenty-one-year-old working for Arthur Doughty. He opened the cover of the diary reluctantly. In one way he wanted to know what it contained, but wondered whether he ought to leave the past and his father's memory alone. The diary won and Jem turned to the first and only entry. It was out of place in the book. An April date on the first of January page. The writing was more mature and had lost its earlier tightness but it was still clearly recognisable as his father's hand.

April 11th, 1992.

After all these years I have a hankering to go into the Hub again, but the uncertainties hold me back. Jem is OK now and can look after himself respectably. He has grown into a fine man and he's doing well with Arthur Doughty. Art is a good man; he'll keep his eyes on Jem.

I have seen one of the tall slender shadowy figures near the outskirts of the forest. It's almost as if he wants to contact me but something holds him back. That makes the two of us who are reticent. I was right to cover the entrance back up and draw down the curtain on trying to summon up the courage to speak to the Anglo-Saxon. We aren't ready for what may be opened up.

Signing off,
Maxwell Dearden.

Jem was puzzled. There was so much information to absorb in the diaries, and the talk about timeshifts, shadowy figures and the Anglo-Saxon was intriguing but unbelievable. Nevertheless, since trying and failing to find the Hub when he went into the forest a while back Dearden still felt drawn to follow up on his father's investigation. Like the poles of a magnet pulling inexorably together, the forest, and what was within it were drawing him. As soon as he could get away from his busy work schedule to be able to devote a couple of weeks to the task he would go into the forest again to see what was going on. In the meantime, he would snatch a few hours to do some research into the history of his family and its connection with the forest.

5

Dearden was uncomfortable when he mentioned his thoughts to Doughty. His fear was whether the series of events in the diaries were a symptom of his father losing his mind, and Dearden wanted to protect his memory.

"I think there's something basic you've forgotten," Doughty said.

"That's not surprising with so much weird stuff going on. What have I forgotten?"

"Nathaniel Devenish. Your father wrote about having had similar experiences to Nathaniel Devenish." Dearden caught Doughty's line of reasoning that the events Devenish wrote about in the seventeen hundreds were remarkably similar to those his father experienced. They gave credence to what his father wrote in the diaries.

"Did your dad say what happened to Devenish?"

"No, and the Devenish book isn't in his collection."

"You should try Amazon for a copy."

* * *

They were sitting at the breakfast table next morning. Doughty, pen in hand, had started on a crossword puzzle in the daily paper.

"I'm going to Warwick later on," Dearden said.

"Oh yeah,"

"I'm going to the County Record Office to do some family history research," Doughty didn't appear to hear.

"On the way back, I'm calling in at B.W. Breeders at Offchurch."

"Mmmm . . . what do they do?"

"Breed Wolves."

"What are you going there for?"

"To get a Wolf."

"You're joking . . . aren't you?" Doughty heard that and looked at him critically.

"I'm not joking. That's why you built the enclosure. A wolf will do well with the forest nearby. I've always wanted a wolf."

"Well let's hope it's not a free thinker who decides to return to the wild."

"You have to know how to handle them, and tuition comes with the wolf."

"Wouldn't an Alsatian be easier to manage, they don't look too different to wolves, do they?"

"An Alsatian does resemble a wolf . . . there's a bit of wolf in every dog."

"OK, now here's one for you. Do you think that's true with a poodle?"

* * *

Dearden arrived in Warwick with Gil Heskin driving the Range Rover. They pulled up outside the County Record Office where Dearden had pre-booked his research session. Heskin dropped him off and carried on to a local builder's merchant with a list of materials he had to get for Doughty.

Dearden went in and a pretty research assistant gave him a demonstration of how to load a microfiche and view the images on it. He had no particular plan, other than to try to find records of his family history and details of Dearden Hall and Leofwin's Hundred.

The assistant led him to some shelves labelled The County of Warwickshire, General Information. He browsed the archival works and other records transcribed from handwritten originals into typed records. Dearden came across a

Warwickshire Topography subsection and spotted The Warwickshire Arden, Past and Present by N.P. Trickett, and Warwickshire Legends, by George M. Gresham. He took them to his desk to look at later.

The 1871 census records revealed where the Dearden family split to one male line, his great, great grandfather, and two female lines. He was able to follow the male line back to the 1841 census and then he turned to the parish records. Two generations further back became tricky because of the ineligible handwriting. For a change, and to give his eyes a rest, Dearden tried a different tack. He asked the assistant for advice about where to find more information and she suggested he should try the Private Accessions Index.

"The PAI is an index where you might find records of specific events that happened to individuals or families."

In the index, Dearden found a reference to a document relating to a Thomas Bradnock who,

> In 1486, received an annuity for life from Lord Henry Dearden of Dearden Hall in the county of Warwickshire.

There was a cross reference to a document relating to the trial of Thomas Bradnock. On the PAI card, there was a brief summary of the trial. It revealed how, in April 1486, Bradnock appeared before magistrates for poaching in Leofwin's Hundred. The next PAI card in the series confirmed Bradnock's discharge and noted an annuity provided for him and his immediate family for the rest of their lives by Lord Dearden. There was also mention of a Green Man, who was in some way involved in the trial. It was an interesting but vague lead. He wanted more detail and the assistant suggested he should refer to the original documents at the Public Records Office at Kew.

Dearden had a contact in London, Commodore Peter Aldridge RN retired, who did voluntary work as a guide at the National Maritime museum. Peter wouldn't mind going to Kew to look into the records of the Bradnock case, he liked that sort of challenge. Sitting at the desk by his microfiche reader Dearden thumbed through Warwickshire Legends. He came to chapter five, The Legend of the Green Man, and it surprised Dearden that the book described the Green Man's association with Leofwin's Hundred. Dearden thought it had to be significant that The Green Man was the name of the public house in nearby Hampton-In-Arden.

At twelve thirty the assistant announced that the record office was closing for lunch, so Dearden gathered his notes together and went outside to where Heskin was waiting in the Range Rover.

They arrived at B.W. Breeders in Offchurch. The owner was a weathered, dark-haired man with reddish-brown skin who went by the name of Anders Wiseman. He spoke slowly and had a deep voice with the remnants of an American accent.

"We do not let our pups go to anyone. We had to run a few checks before we rang you back, Mr Dearden. There are some unscrupulous people about and it is important we do the checks. You have a nice home."

"How do you know that?"

"We checked your place out. Your wolf will enjoy the forest once you have trained it." Dearden was ruffled.

"If you've been there you must have been pretty damn quiet," he said. "How come I didn't see you?"

"That is what we are good at, Mr Dearden. You see, I am a Native American, and we can blend into the land so people do not see us. Amongst my people, I am known as Chief Red Cloud. You can call me Red. This here's my wife. Her name is Possum Chaser. They are our Lakota Sioux names."

Red led the way to a number of large log stumps set on end and sat on one. Possum Chaser sat on the ground at his feet and he indicated other logs close by for Dearden and Heskin. They chatted for a while about land and forest and rivers. Red told them how his great grandfather used to chase herds of Tatanka on the Great Plains.

He produced a pipe out of his top pocket and slowly loaded it, looking into the bowl as if he was gazing into something real significant. He took out a box of Swan Vestas and lit up, sucking until the tobacco smouldered. It smelt pungent. Dearden declined when Red offered him a pull.

"Mr Dearden, we walked through your forest to see that it was suitable. You would not have seen us because we move like the shadows. Tell me, do you know that other men are sometimes walking around in your forest?"

"Are there now . . . do tell me more," Dearden thought of the spate of odd phone calls.

"There are four who are occasionally there together, but mostly there is one."

"Are you sure?"

"As sure as the River Avon flows through Stratford."

Possum Chaser had been sitting quietly on the ground at Red's feet listening to the conversation. She nodded that they were sure, and suddenly she stood up. "Red, let's show Mr Dearden and his friend the litter." She knew what her husband was like when he got into conversation. Sometimes he just went on and on and she wanted to get down to business. She tugged his sleeve briefly as a come on and then made her way over to a large one-storey building made of wood in the style of a log cabin. Dearden saw she was petite, only about four foot six, but well-shaped. Red stood up from the stump he was sitting on and indicated to follow her.

"I will tell you about the men in your forest later, Mr Dearden." They caught up with Possum Chaser as she opened the door and they went through. Dearden looked around the room.

"We work together with our wolves and our wolves work with us. Sometimes they surprise us," Possum Chaser said.

In the far corner was a wolf, who Possum Chaser said was *Wah-hen' Koh-pay Shahn of Offchurch*. She had her pups around her, and she stood as the people drew near. Dearden noticed the intensity of the wolf's eyes and Red warned him to keep his distance.

"Her name in English is Arrow, but we give them all Lakota names. Shortly Arrow will come and investigate, she is protective of her litter," Red's face became stern. "What I say now is important. Do not look her in the eye. You must let her fit you into the pack. By not looking her in the eye, you will be showing her she is the boss. For raw power she is. When she comes to you, slowly offer her the back of your hand. She will become familiar with your scent. Do this and all will go well."

There were five pups in the den area. One stood out because his colouring was different and he was bigger than the others were. Possum Chaser saw Dearden looking at the larger pup.

"Have you heard of the runt of the pack, Mr Dearden?"

"The runt's the smallest of the litter—"

Red interrupted, "This one used to be the runt but now look at him. He has passed all the others. See his black colouring? That means he'll be real big. He won't stand no messin'." Red looked at Dearden to see if he was taking in what he was saying.

"He'll be an Alpha Male, he will lead the pack," Possum Chaser said, as she looked at the pup affectionately.

"He's the one I want," Dearden said. It hadn't taken him long to make up his mind. The creature had gangly legs and large paws, similar to a large domesticated dog pup. The resemblance ended there. Dearden noticed its eyes. The young wolf looked him in the eye and Dearden fancied he felt communication across the boundary of species.

"He is *Nazunspe Cik'ala Shahn of Offchurch*. That is Lakota Sioux for Tomahawk. This is Tomahawk Shahn of Offchurch, but I don't think we ought to let him go."

"Why not?"

"Why not Mr Dearden?" Red looked him straight in the eye. "Because sometimes he might just go on the wild side."

6

Royal Leamington Spa was the place where Theodore Uberatu chose to live. Argentinean by birth, he was the son of a Nazi Obersturmbannführer named Augustus who fled to Argentina's hinterland in 1945 as a young man to escape the wrath of the Allies. Augustus shed his German surname and blended into the surrounding populace with the name Uberatu, and formed a relationship with a beautiful, dark-skinned Hanera girl.

She had fled from the attentions of her tribal medicine man down the Brazilian Pira-Paraná, into Argentina. The young woman had first stolen the medicine man's heart and then, fearful of her safety after some abuse, she stole his dugout and courageously made the river trip alone.

Uberatu senior saw the semi-naked young woman pull into the shore of the trading post he owned. She came into the store and looked longingly at the wicker baskets lining the shelves that were full to the brim with food. Augustus Uberatu satisfied her hunger, and with doubtful motives, offered her some accommodation above the store. The result of his help and her vulnerability was that she formed an attachment to him, which grew into love on her part. The Nazi based his relationship on possession of an object of beauty, as he might do with a painting. After a while, his young wife bore him a son who they named Theodore.

Augustus Uberatu had been involved in weapons research under the regime of the Third Reich. He had a brilliant mind and researched the nature of matter in pursuit of $E=mc^2$ coupled with uranium 235. Questions about the nature of time followed those of matter, and Obersturmbannführer

Uberatu pursued the answers relentlessly. This sometimes brought him into England through a quiet cove in Cornwall to see a Cambridge don who was a Nazi war-prize studying particle physics. When the Allies cooled down in their clamour for ex-Nazis, Augustus stayed in England and settled with his family in the county town of Warwick.

Augustus' son Theo was above average height, swarthy in the face, and had a bushy black beard with intense deep-set eyes under a mass of black hair inherited from his mother. He inherited none of her beauty or charm. His actions were sometimes bizarre, and it was noteworthy that he would never look others straight in the eye. Because of that, people avoided him. They felt he couldn't be trusted.

Taking the lead from his father, Theo took an interest in the fringe sciences. He put a lot of effort into studying things that might be, rather than things that are. He also inherited his father's personality flaw in that he had no conscience.

Theodore had a dog he had named Snarl. The dog was a young but full-grown Bull Mastiff when it roamed into his life as a stray by way of shitting in his garden. It was a dubious start, and afterwards, Uberatu took delight in chastising the dog, ill-treating it with vigour, but then the dog wised up and became vicious with everyone, but to a slightly lesser degree with Uberatu. There was no subtlety in the relationship, Uberatu had the food and Snarl wanted it. From Uberatu's point of view, Snarl was an always-available sparring partner.

They lived at number twenty-two Stephenson's Terrace, which was an end terraced Georgian townhouse in Leamington Spa. From the outside, the house looked compact, but it was spacious inside. On the ground floor, there were two reception rooms and a large kitchen. There were four bedrooms on the first floor, two in the attic with en-suite, and there was a basement.

Anyone walking by the houses in Stephenson's Terrace had a view into basement rooms through windows set behind tiny belowground courtyards separated from the pavement by wrought iron railings. A wrought iron gate set in the railings opened onto steps leading down to the small area where people sometimes put potted plants.

Some of the basement rooms had been modernised as expensive kitchen diners. At night, passers-by would see the occupants cooking meals, or eating in pleasant surroundings. Other basements had become an extra sitting room, while still more were untidy, the dusty resting place of generations of family surplus and forgotten toys.

Unlike some of his neighbours, Uberatu didn't want to be seen, so old damask curtains the other side of grimy glass closed off the view into his basement. Passers-by had to remain curious.

Malcolm Reed wanted answers. He was Theo's next-door neighbour, and he had become determined to find out what was going on in the subterranean room. Down there in the evenings, for the six months since Uberatu moved in, there had been whirring and humming noises that Malcolm found intrusive. Added to that, and winding up his overwrought mind to near-bursting, was a large dog, which barked persistently for hours on end in the back garden.

Malcolm didn't have a good tolerance level to noise. His favourite pastime had been to lie on a sun lounger in his garden in the warm summer evenings reading a book, but ever since the man moved in next door, noise invaded the evenings. He had to do something about the problem, so he decided to investigate the disturbances. He waited until it was dark, on an evening that felt right.

He went to The Clarence, a public house not far from

where he lived, and chatted to old Pop Wesley sitting in his usual corner. Malcolm had a double whisky to bolster his courage. He was nervous, and there was still time to forget Uberatu and the noise, but the problem would persist if he didn't do something about it.

He drained the whisky and walked down the road. There was no one around when he stopped outside the Uberatu place. It was in a dimly lit part of the street, which suited what Malcolm had in mind.

He peered down into the darkness in front of the cellar. There was a gap between the curtains down there, and through the gap, he could see a colour similar to dim fluorescent lighting. The troublesome humming noise was coming from something the other side of the curtains. It rose in pitch, stopped, and then began again cyclically. The light between the curtains dimmed and brightened in time to the noise. He fancied there were vague blue lines of light coming out of the basement, but he put them down to nervousness playing tricks with his eyes.

Malcolm slipped the latch of the gate in the railings. It creaked when he opened it. He paused, and then stealthily made his way down, conscious of the noise of his trainers on the steps. Below the level of the pavement, the noise from The Clarence had become a whisper. He was nervous as he looked around the lower level, but other than a dim light through a gap in the curtains, he could see nothing, there was only the disturbing darkness.

Malcolm got close to the window and tried to see into the room through the gap. There was some machinery, but he couldn't see much of it because of the grime on the window. He pressed his cheek to the glass to see more clearly.

The curtains suddenly jerked open and there was the hairy face of Uberatu, pressed against the glass the other side, looking like a gargoyle. Malcolm fell back with a startled noise. He tripped over a large plant pot, which fell over and broke, shattering the quiet of the evening.

The face at the window was the stuff of nightmares and Malcolm's courage fled. He stretched his hand into the darkness feeling for the bottom step and scrambled to his feet. Nearby in The Clarence, someone was on the piano rattling out boogie-woogie, determined the neighbourhood was going to like it. Then there was a pattering noise on the pavement above. It was dark up there so Malcolm couldn't quite see what was going on.

Driven by rising panic he fumbled up the steps, and when his eyes drew level with the pavement, in the dim light from a street lamp up the road, he saw a pair of large paws. His gaze travelled up the legs and fixed on the bared teeth of Uberatu's Bull Mastiff, Snarl ready for some blood sport.

The river Leam ran dark and deep three hundred and fifty yards from Uberatu's house before plunging noisily over a weir, where Victorian cast iron footbridge crossed the river. The bridge was convenient for people with things they needed to get rid of in the river on a moonless night. A clandestine figure up to no good could dart in and out of the black shadows and hide amongst the shrubbery of the public gardens before offloading his surplus into the river. Uberatu went to the footbridge with a wheelbarrow and the heavy thing it contained covered by a blanket. It splashed into the darkness of the raging water of the weir.

A few weeks passed. In Stephenson's Terrace, The Clarence was hosting a quiz night. The locals sat at a table near the bar, discussing things they thought relevant. One of them mentioned not having seen Malcolm Reed for a while.

"Come to think of it I haven't either. He used to come in

for a pint every night and a bit of a read," Jane Stubbs the barmaid said, joining in the conversation as she collected empty glasses and crisp packets.

"Probably gone on a cruise," piped up old Pop Wesley from his corner, not realising how close he was to the truth.

* * *

The Warwickshire Echo landed on the mat inside the front door of number twenty-two. Uberatu, in his weekly ritual, sat in the easy chair scanning the pages for items of interest. Snarl was looking at him expectantly. Uberatu saw a name he recognised from the past, and his heart skipped a beat. It was Compton Revel Manor in Shipston on Stour. Local auctioneers were advertising a forthcoming sale. It was to include,

Antique furniture made by Chippendale and Hepplewhite, and various choice pieces of Elizabethan and Jacobean furniture. There will also be other items of general and scientific interest including rare and out of print books having early scientific themes.

Uberatu sat bolt upright.

The connection with the forest near Hampton in Arden started back in 1970. Theo's father, Augustus, was in The Barley Mow, a seventeenth-century coaching inn in Knowle. A man, who turned out to be Maxwell Dearden, had come in looking flushed and agitated but with a huge grin on his face. The pub was crowded and Maxwell came over and asked if he could share the table with Augustus. Uberatu senior had agreed, with annoyance at the disturbance at first. Maxwell mentioned about having finished some work at Compton Revel Manor, where he had seen some very interesting old books. Then Maxwell talked about an ancient building with peculiar properties in the forest attached to his family home. Augustus' scientific background and curiosity made him immediately interested. After that meeting, nothing would ever be the same again. As the cast of a dice determines the outcome of a game, Max and Augustus' conversation determined how things would be for the world in coming generations.

*   *   *

When Augustus arrived home, he was in a state of wild excitement. Theo was seven years old at the time and he remembered how difficult it had been for his mother to calm his father. The memory was vivid because of his father's excitement. He had grabbed Theo's dark-skinned mother and danced around the room with her in an abandoned sort of way. Not long after that, Augustus started disappearing for days at a time.

When Theo was older and had come out of university with a respectable degree in physics, his father explained what was going on in the forest. "It has to do with the dimension of time," he said, in an undertone. Augustus wanted to revisit The Barley Mow with his son to tell him about the time when Max Dearden drifted noisily into his life.

A few days after that evening in The Barley Mow with his father, Uberatu senior came out of the forest with a cardboard box full of oddly shaped objects. Augustus tried to assemble the parts, which included a crystal about thirty centimetres long into a working machine, but when he switched on the amperage drawn blew the main fuses into the house.

Augustus raged for an hour, during which his wife hid in the coal cellar and Theo escaped and roamed the local common until past midnight wondering how to please his father.

Augustus was disgusted with himself and the machine he was trying to build and turned his attention once again to the great machine hidden in the forest. When Theo arrived back home his father's dangerous mood had cooled. He was waiting for his son to return, and gave him a winning smile as he came uncertainly into the house.

"Imagine this Theodore, if we go through that building in the forest together we'll be able to rob some of the ancients and come back to our own time laden with their riches. It'll be better than working." He slapped his son on the back and they laughed until their sides ached. Theo's mother heard the laughter and came back in from the coal cellar.

After that evening, Theo and Augustus had times when they went into the past together and other times when they went alone. Three times Theo went back to the other age alone and buried his haul before he returned. It was better than money in the bank.

Theo remembered the time when he went back into the past and impersonated Eadmund Wigstaning, the king's messenger. That was a triumph. When he encountered Wigstaning near the House of the West Wind, the man wouldn't keep quiet. He seemed frightened and kept on bleating in that unintelligible language. Theo Uberatu was doubtful about using the gun, but he had to do it. Good job it was fitted with a silencer, but he cringed when he thought of the folly of taking his shoulder bag with the zip fastener to that bygone age. It could have been a fatal mistake; a dead giveaway that weird things were going on. Shortly after that excursion in 1991, his father died and his mother disappeared. With Augustus' death, most of the knowledge about the ancient building and the processes inside it died as well, but the experiences lived on strongly in Theo's mind.

He couldn't believe his luck when he read about the auction.

There was a chance the book Max Dearden told his father he had seen at Compton Revel could be included in the sale. If he managed to buy it the contents would help him understand more about both the machine in the forest and the machine his father had started building that he was trying to finish in his basement. He was frustrated with his progress. It seemed he was going five steps forward with the machine, and four and seven-eighths back.

Theo walked over the ornate stone bridge that crossed the River Leam at the end of The Parade. He was heading to a room at the back of a Regency building called the Pump Rooms, which was right next to the river. He went down a narrow path between the building and some railings to prevent people slipping down the steep scrub-lined bank into the river. A notice was pinned to the door advertising a meeting. Uberatu went into the room where a group of people calling themselves the Weir Club drifted together in fortnightly meetings. Therein, they discussed the latest finds in the field of the fringe sciences.

When Uberatu arrived, he detected an air of latent excitement. He was convinced that a huddle of people in one of the corners of the room was talking about him because they kept looking in his direction. He approached as near as he could without appearing intrusive and listened in. Sure enough, they were talking about the auction at Compton Revel. He got the impression they intended to go and do some serious bidding and it made him slide into one of the foul moods that gripped him at times.

He sat on a chair in a corner of the room, trying to work out what to do. As the invited speaker droned on with his talk, Uberatu's mind wandered again to the times he used to have with his father. He was having more of the episodes these days where he heard his father's voice in his head, mostly talking about the forest. His foot tapped a staccato rhythm on the floor that he made sure everyone could hear. They were startled when he leapt up and shouted wild abuse at them. Those sipping wine near the door spilt it when they parted quickly as he approached them with a wild look in his eyes, and he slammed the door so hard on his way out that its Georgian frame rattled.

The mood he sunk into lasted through the following day and then he decided to phone an acquaintance who called himself Raegenhere. Three years back they had met in a field doing some metal detecting, and they hit it off immediately. Creeping over the field by the light of a shaded torch, they learned about each other. Raegenhere found out Theo Uberatu had a scientific bent when he spoke about the peculiar process he was working on in a remnant of the old forest near Hampton in Arden. In turn, Uberatu discovered Raegenhere was rich when he visited the man's home that he called Dracasfeld. Behind a massive door locked by round, concealed bolts that slid out from the edge, was a breath-taking collection of artefacts that astounded Uberatu. After Uberatu mentioned how he and his father acquired some ancient gold, Raegenhere was aware that the way they came across the artefacts had the ring of credibility. Uberatu had shown him some exquisite pieces, which he claimed he and his father had taken from a Saxon treasury. A few weeks after they first met the men formed an agreement because of the amount of money involved, based on the satisfaction of greed. Raegenhere would fund Uberatu's research projects and Uberatu would ensure that Raegenhere had a hefty cut of the spoils.

Uberatu phoned Raegenhere and told him about the forthcoming auction of the books, in particular the book Maxwell Dearden told his father about when they were in The

Barley Mow, written by Nathaniel Devenish. Raegenhere agreed to fund the purchase and didn't put a cap on the outlay.

"Do it, get the book," Raegenhere said. "If it'll help us get the apparatus in the forest working cost doesn't matter. But remember this Theo, you're on twenty percent, I'm on eighty."

* * *

Theo was on his way to the public house where he would stay the night before the auction. In his enthusiasm to get to Compton Revel he drove too fast for the winding country lane he was on. In the darkness ahead, failing to see where the road divided to left and right, he went straight on and hit a stout oak post holding a five-barred gate. His head hit the steering wheel.

Theo was lying on a sagging settee with a loudly purring cat perched on his chest when he regained consciousness. His head was aching abominably and as he touched the lump on his forehead, he winced and wondered where he was.

"Ah, you've woke up then," someone out of sight said.

"Just about. Have you got a paracetamol for this headache?" Typically, there wasn't a please with the request. Uberatu's head was pounding. He remembered something about a gate. "Look, where's my bloody car?" He shoved the cat off and tried to stand, but his limbs felt like jelly and he sank back onto the settee again.

"Car's still down by the gate you smashed into. If I was you, I'd sit tight. You're in no state to walk, let alone drive." The voice faded into the background as Uberatu became unconscious.

He awoke with the Sun shining full in his eyes. He grasped the back of the settee before moving further. He walked unsteadily outside into a farmyard toward the sound of hammering which made his head throb with each blow. The farmer was bending over the front of the damaged car knocking the offside wing into shape. It was creased, but away from the wheel.

"You'll have to go slow," said the farmer when Uberatu insisted on leaving. "There's a wobble at the front offside I can't put right."

When Uberatu arrived at Compton Revel, the auction had been under way for a few hours. His foul mood had returned and his head was aching unmercifully. He picked up an illustrated catalogue. The auction had commenced with early scientific and electrical apparatus. The books would follow, eighty-five of them in seven lots starting with lot 63, *two books in the category of Early Reference Works on Magnetism and Electricity, the first by Nathaniel Devenish, the second by Charles Smythe* . . . Uberatu asked a woman sitting at a desk with an open ledger the number of the next lot for auction.

"Lot 127 sir, A Jacobean carved oak chest having a mythological theme."

"So I've missed the damn books . . . who bought them?"

"I'm afraid I can't tell you, Data Protection you know, sorry." She carried on writing in the ledger, ignoring him. Uberatu wondered how much more crap would come his way. First crashing the car, because of that, missing the sale of the books, now this damn woman with her data protection.

The hammer fell on the next lot, and an assistant came from the room with the details of the sale, which the woman at the desk entered into the ledger. She was uncomfortable with the man standing by her and put her arm around the writing to hide what she had written.

Theo had an idea how to see who had bought the books. The sales clerk became attentive when he whispered in her ear.

"See that guy with a red jacket?" she looked to where he was pointing. "I just saw him pocket something out of that cabinet with the silver in it." She stood quickly. In her haste, she knocked her coffee over, and its contents pooled across the desk.

"Oh dammit," she hissed. Ignoring the spill, she strutted into the saleroom to tackle the man Uberatu pointed out.

He spun the ledger round through the pool of coffee, flipped the page back, drew his finger down to Lot 63 and read the details. Somerton's Books, Rugby. Leaving the ledger in the coffee, he walked to his car with a smug grin on his face.

Uberatu had a delayed reaction to his accident. He languished in bed next day until late afternoon when Snarl began whimpering for food. Theo went downstairs and filled the dog's bowl with scraps from the butcher.

He phoned Somerton's about the books. His telephone manner was abrupt and put Mrs Somerton on edge. "We have some of the books from Compton Revel, but we already have a customer for them, he's viewing them tomorrow."

"I'll pay double."

"I'm sorry, but we've promised first refusal to another gentleman. If he decides not to buy I'll get in touch with you." Mrs Somerton asked Theo for his name and phone number. He gave it reluctantly and swore in a vulgar way. "Well really," he heard her say before he slammed the phone down. He hoped the slamming damaged the old woman's hearing. He swore loudly and Snarl glanced at him warily while gulping down the remains of the offal. Theo's head was aching so he went back upstairs and sank into the softness of his mattress.

When he woke up his head was better but he was still in a vicious mood because of his bad luck with the car and the uncertainty about the books. Snarl sensed the oppressive mood and growled defiantly from his old blanket when Uberatu shouted at him to be good as he left the house. The journey was slow because of the wobble on the wheel. With the rhythmic beat of the wobble, Theo heard his father's voice again. This time it was telling him about how he came across his barn on the edge of Leofwin's hundred.

It was in 1970, a few months after his first meeting with Maxwell Dearden in The Barley Mow, when Augustus learned about the barn on the edge of the forest. He was reconnoitring the territory around Hampton in Arden. The hedges on each side of the road were tall, and the mud covered road became narrow where it passed by the entrance to a farmyard on the left. What he had seen through the opening was a swathe of dense broadleaf woodland. With a shout of exultation, he skidded to a halt a number of yards further on. He reversed back to the farm entrance and peered up the lane. He compared the woodland he was looking at to his Ordnance Survey map and couldn't believe his luck. He was looking at the boundary of Leofwin's Hundred where it was over half a mile away from Dearden Hall.

There was a small stone building at the edge of the field near the trees. Augustus drove up the muddy track and parked on a patch of hard standing near the door, which turned out to be unlocked. A shepherd had probably used it at one time because there was chimneystack at one end with a fireplace beneath it. The building needed repair, but it would be ideal for what he had in mind. The field could be his back way into the forest and the House of the West Wind, and it would be out of sight to the people living at Dearden Hall.

Augustus drove up another track to the farmhouse and pulled up near to the door. Before he got out of his car, he checked for dogs, and then went to the door and knocked. There was no response so he knocked louder.

"Alright, alright I heard you," a voice called from inside.

The door opened a touch and an elderly man with an unshaven face blinked in the strong sunlight.

"Good afternoon, sir," Uberatu led off with a slight bow and added a click of the heels from the days of the jackboot. "Sir, the field down the road," he pointed, "I want to buy it."

The man's mouth fell open in surprise and he opened the door fully. The final demand, before legal proceedings commenced for the settlement of the bill for the heifers he bought, had dropped through his letterbox two days previously. Paying for repairs to a newly developed leak in the roof of his house was going to have to take precedence over the heifers, but he didn't know where to turn to for the money.

The farmer, Dennis Twigger, had been feeling embattled and now this strange looking angel had come bowing and clicking to his door offering money for the field that was full of rocks too close to the surface. Once he tried barley, and the following year wheat, but both years gave a meagre yield. Now he only used it for grazing, and he had plenty of grazing land.

"How much?" Dennis asked the stranger

"Get it valued."

"OK, come in." Dennis couldn't believe his luck.

Within a month contracts changed hands and Augustus had his hidden way into Leofwin's Hundred. It was to serve him and his son well in future years. He had the barn renovated. It was basic but they spent idyllic hours there.

Theo snapped out of his reverie. He was on edge by the time he arrived near the bookshop in Rugby. The mole at Dearden Hall had called him on his mobile phone to say Dearden was on his way to the bookshop as well. Theo parked his car in a side street in view of Somerton's and saw Dearden as he was going in through the door.

7

Dearden persuaded Red Cloud to part with Tomahawk. He got the impression he was taking on an animal version of a Sherman battle tank because of the warnings that came with the creature. He arrived back home with the young wolf on a leash. Dearden told Doughty he was going to have the Wolf in the house as well as in the enclosure to get him used to people. He would give visitors health warnings like, *Offer him your hand to sniff, but don't try to stare him out, or he may go for your throat.*

They had settled down in the great hall in the evening, and Dearden was reading the local paper. On page five, there was a picture of a Warwickshire manor house and below it a name from the past, Compton Revel. He began reading.

An auction took place yesterday of some of the effects of the late General Sir Walton Spiers Greswold MC, DSO, of Compton Revel Manor in the county of Warwickshire. Buyers came from as far afield as Atlanta in the U.S and Christchurch New Zealand and the sale helped the General's heirs to offset the crippling costs of running a large country estate. The library was of special historical interest, and various book dealers bought the antique books released for auction.

"Mitch, this may well have come at the right time."

"Oh yeah, what is it?"

Dearden showed Doughty the newspaper article. Doughty read it and handed the paper back.

"Did you see that the sale could have included the Nathaniel Devenish book?"

"That would be remarkable, but I guess stranger coincidences have happened. What will you do?"

"Get on the phone first thing tomorrow. I'll phone around and see if I can find who bought them." He looked at his watch, 6:35 p.m. Maybe tomorrow he would start to understand what his father had been involved with in the forest.

The three antiquarian bookshops in Stratford upon Avon drew a blank, so Dearden rang the ones in Warwick, after that Leamington and then Coventry, all of them without any luck. He rang the second to last on his list, Somerton's Books, in Rugby, and described the book he was looking for. The woman who answered told him the book had recently come in, and that it was extremely rare. He asked her if she would give him the first option to buy it, and she reserved it for him.

* * *

The Range Rover pulled into a car park near the back of the parish church in Rugby town centre. Dearden walked in one direction through the churchyard and Heskin toward High Street where he was going to pick up some stained glass supplies. He kept quiet about his call in Windsor Court. Heskin rapped on the door. After a minute, there were slow footsteps within. The door opened and Heskin stepped through into the dark interior.

Dearden arrived at Somerton's Bookshop and pushed the door open to the sound of a jangling mechanical bell. An elderly woman was sitting behind a counter reading.

After an explanation of who he was, she put down her Anna Karenina and led him up some uncarpeted stairs to the room where she kept the rare books.

"The Devenish work is a choice volume," she said. Dearden thought she might be trying to inflate the price, but gave her no reply. Shelves surrounded the room upstairs and there were two wide alcoves each side of a chimneybreast with a glass-fronted cupboard in each, filled with leather bound books. Mrs Somerton stood on tiptoe and reached for a fully leather-bound volume in Royal Quarto. The author's name, Nathaniel Devenish, was in gold leaf on the spine. She took the book to a large table in the centre of the room and gave Dearden a pair of cotton gloves to wear. The bell on the outer door rang and she went downstairs to deal with the newcomer.

Dearden pulled out a chair and sat down. The book was in exceptional condition. Scanning it briefly, he could see where Devenish described in precise detail the date and time of each occurrence at the House of the West Wind. He started his book with the preamble that,

> *The electrical and magnetic disturbance had truthfully occurred in the sight of witnesses thereto,* and he attributed the disturbances to,
> *The presence of the lines of strong magnetic flux in similarity to those described by Mr Isaac Newton, which exists in many places throughout this our Kingdom and possibly throughout the whole of our earth. They are given the name Ley-Lines and some hath their origination from the building called from ancient times The House of the West Wind. An engine lies at the centre of the House and it doth cause unusual happenings.*

There were detailed records of an excavation Devenish had undertaken in an appendix at the rear of the book. Dearden closed it carefully and took it downstairs. He heard the customer downstairs moving about in the back room.

"I'll have the Devenish book, but have you got any books on Warwickshire traditions and folklore?"

"There's a section on Warwickshire just through here." She showed him to the room at the back and pointed out the shelf in one of four tall bookshelves parallel to each other that were in semi-silhouette because of the strong light from the window.

The section on Warwickshire was in the centre aisle. It was a row of books filling up three feet of the shelf. He spotted a copy of 'Warwickshire Legends', the same book he saw at the County Hall in Warwick. As he took the book off the shelf, his eye shifted to the gap between the top of the books and the shelf above. Looking at him through the gap was a pair of dark, deep-set eyes set in a swarthy face. Dearden said afterwards to Doughty the face was malevolent, and he felt targeted. He instinctively raised his defence level.

The anonymous phone calls came immediately to mind and he wondered if he had met the caller. If the dark-eyed individual intended to cause trouble, and that was what Dearden picked up, he wanted to take the problem outside for old Mrs Somerton's sake, so he took the Warwickshire Legends to the counter and paid for both the books.

The bell clanged behind him as he left the shop. He walked slowly at first, seeing if his exit drew the individual after him. Inside the shop, the dark-eyed customer came from the back room and faced Mrs Somerton, who had picked up her Anna Karenina again.

"Why did you sell the book to the man who just left?" the individual asked in an oddly quiet, cold voice. His attitude was more frightening than if he shouted, but he just stood there confronting her. Mrs Somerton's pulse raced. People usually treated her with respect.

"Come on, tell me you stupid old woman," he was still quiet. She recognised the voice as that of the rude man who phoned the shop late the previous day. He was getting too close and he raised his fist to hit her. She tried to speak, but the words locked up in her throat.

* * *

Mrs Somerton's daughter Pamela, who did all the donkeywork replenishing stock for the bookshop, used to display prowess at throwing the hammer when she was at university studying philosophy, English language and literature. She had the ideal athletic build for the hammer, and in her university days, she had represented the sport at county level.

Pamela had gone to see Mick Tunbridge, who phoned about some books he inherited from his grandfather. After a few well-placed questions over the phone, she decided the books would be worth viewing.

Tunbridge was a Heavy Metal fan, and the books from his grandfather were to do with travel in the early nineteenth century. The books didn't interest Tunbridge, but travel did and their sale would help pay the cost of tickets for the concert by The Grunge, over in Berlin, in the park opposite the Reichstag.

Mick had the books lined up on a table and Pamela could see the majority were only fit for the two for a pound table outside the shop. Three of the books were very desirable. The first was a quarto volume in half leather called *Travels in the Interior of Africa, to the Sources of the Senegal and Gambia*, written in 1820 by G. T. Mollien. The others, a two-volume set, *Recollections of Italy, England and America* by F. A. Chateaubriand, printed in 1818, were full leather bound, and valuable.

Without telling the punter she had mentally categorised the books as very fine, she made him an offer. They haggled, and eventually were both satisfied. The three heavy volumes were in Pamela's leather bag slung on her ample shoulder.

She smiled to herself as she left Mick's house. She managed to get the books for a song, but never in her wildest dreams did she imagine how soon they would come in useful. It was when she was on the side of the road opposite her mother's bookshop that she saw the diminutive figure of her mother cowering as she looked up at a large black-bearded man standing over her with his fist ready to hit her.

Pamela sprinted over the road dodging the traffic coming at her from both directions with horns blaring. The two-hundred-year-old bell clanged as she ran into the shop and swung the weighty volumes in the leather bag as she used to do with the hammer. She grunted with the effort and the books landed on the shoulder of the attacker, who yelled with surprise and pain and clutched his shoulder. He turned to face her. She approached him quickly, her eyes small with fury, but he dodged her and ran from the shop, cursing as he went.

Dearden caught a reflection in an angled shop window. The man in the bookshop came out quickly and looking around, caught sight of Dearden. Dearden quickened his pace and saw in another window that the follower's pace was matching his. The man was holding his shoulder, grimacing. Dearden noted the weakness to exploit when he got to Windsor Court. He increased his speed down the High Street to gain valuable seconds and took a left into the blue-bricked archway. He sprinted through the passageway and into the court where it widened out and reached a pallet loaded with bricks he had seen when he left Gil Heskin. Dearden pushed his parcel of books under the pallet and ran back to the alley where he waited for the follower.

Dearden looked at the brightly sunlit floor waiting for the man's shadow. It came into view. A mental calculation of the seconds left for his follower to turn the corner, 3 . . . 2 . . . 1 . . . then the man's bulk filled the passage. Dearden launched himself and grabbed the man's beard. Yanking it down hard with his left, he struck out with a hard right to the man's injured shoulder and then went in with a left to his solar plexus. The man doubled up and sank to his knees gasping, trying to put a hand on his shoulder. Dearden grabbed the man's arm on the injured side, levered it behind his back and frog-marched him out of the court toward the graveyard surrounding the parish church.

The graveyard was a stark Victorian affair where there were mausoleums and dark, moody statues contemplating eternity. There was nobody about above ground so it was an ideal place for an interrogation. There was a flat sandstone slab, and Dearden shoved the man towards it. He resisted so Dearden put on more pressure.

"I'll get you for this Dearden," the man grunted through gritted teeth and stumbled.

"You know my name then. Try this slab for size. Get on belly down before I break your arm." Dearden forced the arm to the point where he felt resistance. The man yelled and scrambled onto the slab. Dearden sensed someone behind him too late, he half turned, and then there was a savage blow to the back of his head.

Dearden tried to focus on Heskin, who was shaking him into consciousness. Heskin's face was turning in circles above him.

"You've been out for a while Jem, you had me worried, what happened?" Dearden tried to think through the pain in his head.

"I was being followed when I left the bookshop. I was finding out why when I was hit from behind." Heskin helped him to stand and steadied him. "He was a shifty-looking character, and he knew my name. Must have had an accomplice." Dearden felt the back of his head and winced.

"Did you see anything, Gil?"

"Nothing. Anything been taken?" Dearden checked his pockets and shook his head. He was unsteady and needed help to get to the pallet and retrieve his books. They took it slowly on the way back to the Range Rover. Dearden's head felt sore and his ego prickled as he thought of how he had allowed someone to get him from behind. He ought to have realised the evil looking guy would have had an accomplice.

8

Dearden was back home and shaky on his legs. His vision was working independently from the rest of his body. Doughty had gone home to Warwick and Dearden fought nausea to ring him. He explained what happened.

"Folks seem to have a serious interest in you," Doughty said.

"Don't I know it, Mitch, but it's the forest they're interested in, not me."

"The hill, you mean?"

"The building on top of it. The opposition made themselves known after I got interested in it."

"What do you want to do?"

"Nail them. Find out what they want. I think the person to help us is Red Cloud. When Gil and I first met him in Offchurch, he warned us there were people snooping in the forest."

* * *

There was no reply from Red Cloud when Dearden phoned him. As night drew on his headache eased and he switched the television on for the local news. The name Somerton's riveted his attention to what the news item. A view of the shop in Rugby came on screen. The newsreader was detailing how Pamela Somerton foiled a raid on her mother's bookshop and that, although still in shock, the elderly Mrs Somerton said that she would be open for business again next morning come hell or high water. Dearden switched the television off. In the morning, he would phone Mrs Somerton to see if she could give him any information about the identity of the raider.

He leafed through the Devenish book, scanning it to get a feel for its contents. It took a while for him to grasp the archaic language, but what became obvious was the similarity of the events that had happened to both his father and Devenish. Dearden's mood lightened. Devenish's writing gave weight to the events his father wrote about.

Jem came to the concluding chapter where Devenish described covering the lower entrance up again and then, for reasons he didn't explain, he stated he would never go back to the House of the West Wind because he nor any other man was ready for the device within. It was difficult for Dearden to comprehend why both Devenish and his father would have gone to the trouble of excavating, only to cover the work up again.

With the interest the old building was inviting, forced Dearden to go into the forest to try to find the old building again, so he took a walk with Tomahawk who he was allowing to roam free. He followed the directions given by Nathaniel Devenish and came to an immense oak tree that must have been the one the writer called Old Jack.

Dearden followed an overgrown path heading toward the sound of running water, most likely the Shadow Brook Devenish mentioned. After a few minutes, he came to the bank of a fast flowing stream carrying forest debris in its wake. Two moss-covered logs lashed together with rope served as a bridge. He trod carefully as he crossed the torrent but Tomahawk crossed at a reckless pace.

Dearden recalled Devenish' words, to turn left after crossing Shadow Brook, so he followed the bank of the stream for a while and took an obvious path to the right. It ended at a thick patch of undergrowth. He hacked through it to the other side, where the path continued. He put Tomahawk on the leash, and in a short while, they came to a place where the trees were thinner. In front of them was the steep side of a tree-covered hill. Dearden could see the outline of an Ivy-covered building at the top. He urged Tomahawk forward and they walked around the base of the hill, looking for evidence of excavations.

In that moment, walking around the base of the hill, Dearden decided to carry on with the investigations where his father left off. The forest and the building were getting under his skin and he needed answers. He made up his mind that he wouldn't adopt his father's approach and write a day-to-day account of events. He knew he couldn't keep that up, but he could make careful observations and use military style planning to find out what was going on. He would try to enlist the help of Red Cloud. The Native American would help him locate the intruders, and when he found them, he would extract an explanation of what they were hoping to achieve by trespassing on his land.

* * *

Dearden rang Mrs Somerton. He asked if she could give him any information about the individual who threatened her, explaining that the same man had followed him after he had left the shop and he wanted to know why. Dearden didn't tell her about the fracas that followed. He preferred to forget that.

"I am sure he wanted the book I bought from you. Did he mention anything about it?"

"No. But I do know he was desperate for it. You see, he rang the day before you came in and said he would pay double for the book. I remember his voice so well. He was far too insistent you know, and I remember he had a foreign sounding name."

"So he gave you his name, what is it?"

"I'll tell you in a minute." He heard her pull open a drawer and turn some pages.

"Here it is. Uberatu . . . yes, his name is Theodore Uberatu, but he wouldn't give me his address." Before Dearden he rang off he told the old lady that if she ever needed help, to ring him.

*   *   *

Dearden raised his level of awareness because the opposition was getting serious. He went about his everyday tasks without any change, but underneath he was ready for action. He walked over to the studio each day to look in on Lloyd Perkins, and a few days after the graveyard incident in Rugby the phone rang and Dearden picked up. It was Peter Aldridge phoning from London.

"I looked at the original documents about Bradnock's poaching episode. I needed help reading it because the language was Anglo-Norman, so the people at the National Archives put me in touch with a chap called Bob Selby. He makes a study of Anglo-Norman and he was pleased to help out."

"Did you find anything new?"

"Yes. That your name isn't Dearden."

"What do you mean?"

"Well, I managed to trace the transcription of the legal proceedings against Thomas Bradnock when your ancestor got involved. In the original document, he signed his name as Henry de Arden. Your family name has been anglicised to Dearden over the years."

"That's interesting. Dearden toyed with the name for a second or so. Did you find anything out about the poaching?"

"I did. In the hearing, the court absolved Bradnock of all blame over the alleged poaching incident. The document attests to Bradnock's right to an annuity paid annually for the duration of his life, or the life of his spouse, whoever lived the longest. But get this, because of his faithful and honest service,

Bradnock was also given the post of Keeper of Game for as long as he was able to do it, and he had a tithe cottage for life too."

"So Bradnock had an unexpected change in fortune?"

"Too right. He had a job for life, a place to live and an annuity. He was rich beyond belief for someone of ordinary birth."

"What was the catch? Did Bradnock have something on Henry de Arden?"

"There wasn't a catch. Lord Henry looked after this man and his family because he felt obliged to repay a loyalty to the man who, even though he was wrongly accused, remained loyal to him. Bradnock didn't even kill Henry Dearden's deer when he and his family were desperate for food."

"But why did Lord Henry feel so strongly about it?"

"I'm coming to that. I had permission to go downstairs with an assistant to poke around in the original records. The document we needed was in a cardboard box. It was full of information about the de Arden family. Most of the records in the box were mundane statements of account and documents to do with the day-to-day running of de Arden Hall.

"I thought I had come to the end of the line, but right at the bottom of the pile was what I had been looking for. The document describes the way your ancestor, a nobleman, dealt with someone who had little in the way of social standing. Because Lord Henry wanted to ensure there wouldn't be any doubt about Bradnock's innocence. He wrote a personal record of events in his own hand."

"He must have had a good reason to do that."

"He did. You said you read about a Green Man, at Priory Park, remember?"

"And I wondered what that was about."

"It's all in the record. The Court proceedings show

everything was stacked against Bradnock. His innocence hinged on him seeing a running figure dressed in green, and that was the reason he had his bow drawn, he was ready to defend himself, not kill a deer. The Keeper of Game, who came across Bradnock with a longbow drawn in the forest, did not believe him.

"Now we come to the crucial point. Lord Henry was well aware that the man in green had been in Leofwin's Hundred before ever Bradnock saw him. The document in the bottom of the box was an attestation written in de Arden's own hand, about seeing the Green Man in the forest two weeks before Bradnock's encounter with him.

"Immediately before Henry de Arden's signature are the words, *written by mine own hand*, and after his signature, his personal seal pressed into red wax authenticated it."

"Is there any mention about what Henry de Arden claims to have seen?"

"That's where Bob Selby helped because the original writing was difficult to understand. He said that de Arden described giving precise directions into Leofwin's Hundred. He mentioned going past something called Vieux Jacques and Shadow Brook. Then he described meeting a swarthy looking black-bearded man in green clothing. Which appears to be where the local Green Man legends began. Henry de Arden challenged him, and could only understand a few words of the reply. De Arden then wrote about the individual being like a man possessed, in a great hurry and pointing to the hill further on in the forest."

"Where does all that leave us?" Dearden asked.

"It leaves you knowing that unusual events in Leofwin's Hundred were testified to over five hundred years ago."

"And now it looks as though at least four people over a period of five hundred years have had similar experiences with the House of the West Wind."

They rang off, and Aldridge wondered what the hell was the House of the West Wind.

* * *

Dearden walked Tomahawk into the forest. The wolf had grown as large as his Alaskan Black Wolf sire and his colouring was an intense black. Red Cloud had been right when he had said he's gonna be big. It was a long walk and Dearden's thoughts turned back to Jackie Mason. A number of years had passed since she had died but he still felt the loss keenly. As good a companion as Tomahawk was, Dearden would have preferred Jackie's company, but the wolf was steadily gnawing his way into his heart.

It was 5:15 when they returned. Dearden settled Tomahawk in his pen and felt tiredness pricking the back of his eyes. He asked Frieda Heskin to rustle up a meal and sat in front of the fire with the Devenish book. Later he tipped out a double measure of Courvoisier, into which he poured a measure of Port. He toasted Arthur Doughty, who had introduced him to the drink. Then he had another, and yet another, before drifting off into a restless sleep.

The dream was intense. He was in a forge and the huge Blacksmith, who had a rugged face and thick-lensed glasses, was hammering red-hot iron into shape. Sparks were flying. In the heat of the forge, white hot by the action of the bellows, the man's face started to distort.

The dream's location changed to a dreary looking cemetery, in which moss covered granite headstones were scattered amongst discoloured marble statues. The statues were weeping marble tears for the dead that lay in the earth beneath them. Dearden dreamed that he saw a shadow creeping toward him from where he was lying on a sandstone slab in the cemetery.

He woke up sprawled out on the bed in his father's study. He was sweating profusely and his heart was hammering as if he had been in combat. He hadn't even remembered coming up the stairs. The light was off but the curtains were open and the full moon illuminated the room with its pale light. There was a sound from outside so he went over to the window. The Moon picked out the scene in deep shadow and silvery light.

Tomahawk was unsettled and moving about in his pen, snarling viciously. Immediately alert, Dearden struggled into his jeans and a tee shirt, grabbed his Beretta, took the stairs two at a time and ran through the great hall, out into the night.

He caught sight of a shadowy figure running across the car park away from the studio to a trail bike. Its engine roared into life and as Dearden gave chase it hurtled through the open gate, its back wheel spitting gravel.

The wolf darted to the wire fence of the pen with his teeth bared, snarling as he tried to get to the intruder. He leapt onto one of the boulders placed as landscaping and Dearden saw Tomahawk silhouetted in the light of the Moon against the backdrop of the forest.

The studio door was open. Filing cabinet drawers had been ransacked, and paper and tools were strewn all over the floor.

The morning after the break-in, while it was still dark, Dearden phoned Mitch Doughty who took a few seconds to understand what was going on. He suggested that Dearden should straightaway phone the police.

"Come on, Mitch, I'm not doing that. All I'd get is a crime number, and telling them about the burglary would make them nose around in the forest and they could come across the Hub. I have to keep it hidden from the outside world until we find out what's going on here."

Doughty said he would be on his way over within the hour.

After ringing off from Doughty Dearden rang Red Cloud. When the answer-machine clicked in he briefly explained what was going on and asked for Red's help to track down the intruders in the forest.

After the phone calls, Dearden felt more on top of the situation. An enemy in plain sight was one thing, but when they were out of sight in the forest, to flush them out would need cunning, which the Native American could certainly supply.

He looked at Tomahawk. "Well boy, what's going to happen next?" The creature's gaze at him was intense and unwavering.

* * *

"So Uberatu's behind the break-in?" Doughty suggested.

"I think so. Going by his performance in Rugby I'm sure he wants the book I bought."

"Any idea why?"

"Not yet, but it looks as though he's heard about Devenish and the House of the West Wind and he's determined to get in on the act."

Red Cloud and Possum Chaser arrived in a Ford Transit later that day. They had come home after a few days away and listened to the message Dearden left. Red heard the tension in Dearden's voice and took it into his head that they should come and stay for a few days to give some assistance. They were in the great hall discussing how best to deal with the rising level of threat.

"We have left the wolf pack in the care of our neighbours," Possum Chaser said. "They are Romani, of the Old Clan and have the name, Hicks. They live on our land in one of their caravans with a round roof."

Red Cloud interrupted her. He spoke slow and with authority. "Jem, remember I told you I went into your forest before you bought Tomahawk? I said I saw tracks of four men. They were clumsy men. They came early in the morning and left evidence. I was in the forest before the Sun and I missed the men by minutes. Dew was on the grass, and when the Sun came I listened to the earth and found footprints where the grass was bent over. Two big men and two small men had been there. A big one spends more time in the forest. He has a den where there is rotten wood, which he drops from his shoes. Possum Chaser and I will search for these men. They will not see us; we will be like shadows." Red grabbed a rucksack, and they headed off into the forest.

9

Over the next three days, they scoured the forest for the intruders. Late on the third day, Red Cloud called Dearden on his mobile. He told him where he was in relation to Shadow Brook, and asked him to come as quick as he could.

Dearden and Doughty found him in a small clearing.

"You came like two stampeding buffaloes," Red whispered, "You must learn to be quiet." He pointed to the ground and showed them where it had been disturbed. The grass was bent over and bruised, and it bore the vague shape of footprints.

Red indicated a leaf almost covering an object shining in the early evening light. He lifted the leaf, exposing a gold ring. Dearden picked it up and examined it. At both points where the bezel blended into the circle of the ring there was an oak leaf, and on the bezel itself was the representation of three standing figures in close-fitting clothing. One of them was female.

Dearden put the ring deep in a pocket of his combats then got down on his hands and knees to examine the area.

"You will not find anything more here Jem, I have already looked," Red Cloud whispered close to his ear. "The evidence points to one of your four forest jokers losing this ring. He found it and realised he had lost it, and the four different pairs of shoes that have trampled this place in many directions tell us they were searching for it. The ring looks old. It is probably valuable."

They walked past the Hub on their way back to Dearden Hall. Red Cloud led the way and using the sound of Shadow Brook for directions he hacked through the untouched undergrowth with a machete. They came to a grassy path that they followed. Red suddenly halted and held his hand up for them to stop. He looked at the side of the path and then got down to examine the ground.

"The footprints here are telling me that one of the four men is a heavyweight, but not tall, his footprints are deeper than the others, but he wears small shoes. Another man is in a hurry because he has long strides. He is also impatient and keeps striding out in front of his companions as if he is trying to get somewhere fast. Then he stops and moves about in one place so the others can catch up with him. A third one is an ex-military man because his strides are precisely controlled and when he stops, he stands still, listening to his surroundings." Red read surprise on the others' faces.

"My friends, you are wondering how I know about those men. I let the wilderness talk to me. The wilderness is my friend. I was going to tell you about the fourth man. He says one thing and does another. He is a riddle."

"What makes you say that?" Dearden asked.

"His footsteps go all over the place, first in one direction and then another. He is not in control of himself. My friends, you must be careful. The mixture of these men is dangerous."

Red Cloud spent a lot of time in the forest over the next week but found no further sign of the trespassers. Dearden had a CCTV system installed with cameras placed at strategic points around the house and grounds and the track leading off into Leofwin's Hundred. He felt more equipped to handle whatever threat the four skulking in the forest may throw at him.

Doughty left for Coventry, where he would be working for a few days, but he said he would be back as soon as the work was finished. Red Cloud and Possum Chaser had to get back to their smallholding and the wolf pack, but they told Dearden to call them day or night if he needed help. With his colleagues gone, Dearden spent more time in the forest with Tomahawk.

The level of work in the studio was picking up and Dearden decided he must enlist another pair of hands to keep up with demand. He didn't want to go back to working full-time himself. Bill Templestone came to mind. Templestone, called Priest by his SHaFT colleagues because of the Temple in his surname, came from Temple Balsall in Warwickshire. He worked with Arthur Doughty in his military past, and afterwards with Doughty in his stained glass studio.

Bill, in his late sixties but looking years younger, had remained a good friend, and Dearden thought he would be the perfect choice to help with the studio and as a backup around the property because of the threat from intruders. Ex-SAS, and a member of SHaFT from its early days, Bill could defend the place with vigour. If he were free, Templestone would be able to dip in and out of the workload in the studio, help guard the place, and be good at it too. When Dearden phoned him, Templestone agreed immediately, saying that he would be over ASAP.

Dearden saw Templestone's classic Morris Minor Traveller draw to a halt at the entrance to the car park. He remembered, as a young man, being in the same car with Templestone driving at sixty when Bill lifted his knees up to the steering wheel to control the car's direction. He took a Senior Service out of its packet and lit it. *Look no hands*, Bill had said. At times, he could be crazy. Dearden didn't wait for his old colleague to announce himself over the intercom. He pushed the button to release the gate and the black Morris Minor with its shooting-brake bodywork came into the parking area.

Jem welcomed the greying, square-jawed Templestone into the studio. "Good to see you again Priest," Dearden grasped his elderly friend's hand affectionately.

"Likewise, Jem," Templestone's gaze circled around the room. "This is a nice set-up," he said, and then his voice got serious. "Are you sure you're OK with me using the place over the studio?"

"It's part of the package, but how will your daughter feel about you moving out?"

"She's alright with it. Becky's new bloke's moved in, and he's trying to push me out. I might look old and quaint now, but for two pins, I'd deck him. I need to get out to keep the peace."

"Better here than deck the new bloke. Bill, you're very welcome here." Templestone pulled a chair out from a bench and sat.

"You said you've got some serious goings on here, I'm curious."

Dearden told Templestone about the recent occurrences. Then he showed him his father's diaries. At first, the older man was silent, and then humour flickered across his face.

"If it was someone other than you telling me this I would tell them to get their brain sorted. Are you sure it's not some idiot playing on a local legend?"

"I've been down that route, Bill. For a start, there are intruders here who mean us harm, and there are a wealth of documented facts going back five hundred years to back up events going on in the forest. I need to find out what's happening, particularly since dad was involved. I think he was in too deep for his own good."

"He never mentioned anything to me,"

"I'm not surprised. I heard nothing about it when I was a kid. He was secretive about everything to do with the forest. Bill, I'm in too deep to give it up now."

"Have you made any plans?"

"I'm tightening security, that's priority. I'm not doing it in an obvious way because I want to lull them into making a false move, and then I'll nail the bastards."

"Are you involving SHaFT?"

"It'll have to get a lot worse before I do. At the moment I'm OK with it."

"It's unusual one of those guys got the jump on you."

"What happened in Rugby?" Dearden's eyes narrowed. "I must be getting older, I wasn't quick enough. If I get hold of him he'll wish to hell he hadn't jumped me."

Templestone remembered Dearden using the same tone of voice when the two of them were on a mission in Tierra del Fuego. It looked as though there was no way out after the ambush, but Templestone had seen that same steely look of resolve in Dearden's eyes back then. Templestone had been impressed. It looked as though the drug cartel was going to win. He sometimes remembered how glad he was back then to be on the same side as Dearden.

They had been given an hour to make their minds up. Join the drug operation or get shot. It was Dearden's sixth mission. His father's death had changed him. Templestone remembered that almost overnight Jem was no longer the carefree youth he had come to like. He had become a complex character with a big heart and a lousy temper. Art Doughty took him under his wing and taught him the three R's. Risks, take them when there are no more options. Run, run with your instincts, ninety-nine percent of the time they are correct. Rage; use it in a controlled way. It is a venomous tool, but it gets the job done.

They were in a cave, tied hand and foot. Dearden had struggled to his feet and shuffled over to a sharp projection of rock. He turned his back to it and started laying into the rope with a will, sawing it up and down as if demented. He cut himself on the rock but took no notice. Fifteen minutes later, the rope parted. It didn't take long to free his feet and then it was Templestone's turn. Another five minutes and Priest was free. In the semi-darkness, lit by the dwindling light from outside, they waited for the enemy to come back.

When the hierarchy of the drug cartel returned they were armed but that was of no consequence. Dearden and Priest were out of the cave in seconds with the cartel leaders dead on the floor. They located a petrol store and after lighting an improvised fuse, they ran to a Robinson R22 chopper. A quick check revealed the keys were in and it was fuelled, damn the pre-flight checks. With Priest at the controls, they were airborne and away, leaving the drugs operation in burning ruins.

* * *

Templestone unpacked his cases in the flat above the studio. Dearden was reading in his father's old room in the manor house and he sneezed again. By evening it was worse, which was precisely what he didn't want when there was so much to do. He was running a temperature and had a severe headache. He had a fitful night's sleep, and by the morning, he was coughing. Gil Heskin called the doctor, who called in after morning surgery.

The doctor diagnosed influenza and wrote a prescription for an antiviral medication. During the following hours, the fever was persistent and Dearden drifted in and out of sleep, dreaming of a snow-bound landscape where the figure of a huge blacksmith with a black beard drew nearer with lumbering steps.

In the nightmare, Dearden tried to run but he couldn't make his feet move quickly enough. A short distance in front, he saw a building with an open door through which the fierce flames of a forge blazed. He had to get into the shelter of the forge to get away from the figure in black who was catching up with him with outstretched hands. Dearden woke up sweating profusely. He drank a glass of water with paracetamol and Ibuprofen and then drifted back into an uneasy sleep.

He was aware of Gil Heskin looking in on him and keeping the water refreshed at the side of his bed. Two days went by and he woke up with the Sun shining full on his face. He felt considerably better. He swung his legs out of bed and pulled out the clothes he wore when he went walking with Tomahawk. A walk in the forest with the wolf seemed attractive. The fresh air would clear his head.

Dearden decided he would try to make it a long, fast walk, to sweat the remains of the fever out. He got Frieda Heskin to rustle up some bread and cheese, which he put in a rucksack, along with a container of meat scraps for Tomahawk, his medication, and two bottles of water.

The day started fine, but the light had developed a watery look so Dearden put a poncho in his rucksack and headed off into the forest with a machete hanging from his belt. He planned to go through the region that had already been searched, and then onward into the unsearched area.

Half an hour into the walk, Tomahawk growled and disappeared down a winding trail through the dense undergrowth. Dearden called but there was no response. He hacked through patches of nettle and brambles to widen the trail, spraying yellow fluorescent paint on trees as he went.

As he made his way deeper into the forest, the western sky began growing dark with rain clouds. The weather forecast had not been good, but with the day of freedom coming after feeling unwell and months of work restoring the Hall, Dearden decided to walk, whatever the weather. The air warmed slightly and a breeze disturbed the foliage above, and then the first large spots of rain penetrated the leaf canopy.

He continued to chop at the undergrowth but he was feeling increasingly hot, and a wave of dizziness came over him, the same as it had a few days previously. He was sweating and the headache returned. He heard the rain intensifying above and the trees were no longer a protection so he slipped the poncho on and pulled it down as far as it would go.

He had to carry on to find Tomahawk, so with an effort of will, he followed the disturbed foliage, and shortly heard the sound of running water ahead. The rain was lashing the overhead canopy with increasing ferocity and runnels of water began to flow toward the sound of the stream. Finally, up ahead, he heard Tomahawk growling. Dearden moved toward the noise, brushing the rain out of his eyes, and saw the wolf in a clearing with his hackles raised and teeth bared in an ugly snarl. A few feet in front of Tomahawk, backed up against a tree, was an over-weight man whose dirty looking clothes were soaking wet. His eyes were wide with fear.

Dearden eyed the man suspiciously and called Tomahawk to his side. The wolf ignored the command so Dearden repeated it with more force and pointed to the ground at his side. Tomahawk's ears drew back and he slunk back to Dearden, where he sat watching the man. Dearden hooked the leash onto the wolf's studded collar.

"What are you doing here? This is private land," Dearden challenged.

"I'll tell you if you back the animal off," the man said, looking at Tomahawk.

"The wolf's got more right to be here than you, this is my forest and my wolf. I'll ask you again, what are you doing here?"

"I was out for a walk and got lost."

"Didn't you see the notices? This is private woodland."

"Yes, but I'm in KWOFA,"

"What's KWOFA?"

"Keep Woodland Open For All, but I didn't expect it to be

open for wolves."

"So it was stupid of you to come past the private notices wasn't it? This forest is private, that's why the notices are on the boundary. Have you got any identity?" The man fished in his pockets and found a driving licence. As he handed it to Dearden, Tomahawk bared his fangs.

"Steady boy," Dearden commanded as he studied the licence. His eyes were watering and he wiped them on the back of his hands. He saw the man's name was Antony Beggs.

"Is anyone with you?" Dearden asked, thinking there might be another three of them, but just after he spoke there was an intense flash of lightning, and the thunder was instantaneous. Dearden was temporarily blinded and deafened, and his arm jerked as Tomahawk lurched forward on the leash. By the time Dearden recovered his besieged senses, Antony Beggs had run.

Dearden looked around through watery eyes and sneezed again. It crossed his mind to let Tomahawk off the leash to hunt the man down, but Tomahawk off the leash with the man on the run would have a bloody outcome. He pocketed the driving licence. He had contacts who would check out the details. Chances were that Beggs was the overweight man of the four Red Cloud said were roaming the forest.

Dearden looked around for Beggs, and as he did so, he noticed a pale blue glow coming from rising ground further on in the forest. Despite feeling feverish, he forced himself toward the light up ahead. As he walked, the rain became torrential and started to seep down the front of his neck inside the poncho.

Dearden reached the hill and could see a soft radiant glow through the trees surrounding the building at the top. There were four vague lines at ninety degrees to each other curving up into the sky, while another rose vertically from the centre of the structure. He scrambled up the hill, barging his way through thickets of soaking shrubs and closely growing trees with Tomahawk following on the leash and reached the top.

The feverish symptoms were returning with a vengeance, and as he peered upwards trying to understand what was going on, his head was unsteady and he felt nauseous. In his peripheral vision, he fancied that the lines were part of a huge grid high up, and the Hub had drawn the Grid down.

Dearden re-focussed on the building. It appeared to be moving because of his unsteady vision, but through the rain-soaked ivy covering most of the wall, he could see the outline of a door. He hacked at the vegetation on one side of the door, and at the top and bottom, and then, exhausted, he hinged the curtain of foliage to one side. He could see a handle and he levered it downward and pulled. Nothing happened. Pushed, and the door swung open. He cautiously went inside with Tomahawk, both of them dripping water. He shut the door against the driving rain and sat on the floor.

The room was pleasantly warm and lit by a soft radiant glow and it revived him slightly. What first struck him was that he could see the forest because the walls and ceiling were transparent, exactly as he read in his father's diaries, and there was an immense crystal in the centre of the room. On the far side of the room was the spiral stairway leading downwards.

Dearden stood and, with Tomahawk following, he walked unsteadily to the transparent wall and looked out on an astounding scene. He rubbed his eyes, trying to clear his vision to make sense of what he saw. The sky above the Hub was still full of thunderclouds, but the surroundings outside were completely different to those he had left the other side of the door. The valleys were deeper, the hills higher, and he could see an immense broad-leaf forest extending to the far horizons. He wiped his eyes again and sneezed.

Dearden thought he might be hallucinating. He put his

hand to the transparent wall to steady himself. It felt warm and solid. To his left, he could see a long winding area cleared of trees that straddled a wooded hill. On its highest point, as if the builders were trying to get it closer to heaven, was a small stone church with its square tower encased in wooden scaffolding. There were houses clustered around it and a track curved around the church before continuing downhill. At the foot of the clearing was a large stone manor house, which looked much like Dearden Hall before the addition of wings and outbuildings. A tall wooden stockade built on top of a stone wall of dull red Warwickshire sandstone served as protection. Set in the wall, between stone pillars connected at the top by a rounded arch, were a pair of stout double gates, which opened into the manor grounds. Dearden could see writing on the keystone of the arch. He wasn't able to focus on it from where he was standing, but he assumed it was the date 1063, that his father had seen.

Dearden could see a rutted well-used lane leading up to the village. Branching off it was a narrow track heading in the direction of the House of the West Wind, where he was standing. He placed his hands on the window to support himself and thought how surreal the situation was. He looked further afield beyond the manor house where a river glinted in the subdued sunlight. It meandered through fields separated by dry stone walls. Further to the right beyond the river, Dearden could see where the forest gave way to marshy ground bordering some lakes.

He looked back to the village on the hill, where there were buildings each side of a rough winding cart track. There were wooden dwellings, mostly with thatched roofs, and a few buildings of stone with a covering of wooden shingles.

A movement caught Dearden's eye from the direction of the manor house. A man had come out of a low building attached to the large house. He stopped abruptly and turned, looking in Dearden's direction. The man appeared transfixed to the spot before suddenly running toward a little girl with long blond hair, similar to his own. It was striking how they were dressed in an ancient style of clothing.

Dearden recalled his father's hastily written words on the A4 pad, *The Saxon, I've seen him again.* He glanced at Tomahawk. The wolf gave him confidence, grounding him in a situation that seemed unreal. Dearden turned, and facing the doorway, he pulled the hood of his poncho tight for warmth.

"Come on boy," he croaked to Tomahawk. "Let's see what this is about." Dearden picked up the leash and walked to the door. He pulled it open and the change of atmosphere made him sneeze again, but it was cool and refreshing as he stepped through the door and shut it against the outside weather. Normality ended, because a huge crystal, alive with fiery internal movement, dominated the centre of the room.

10

The master mason, named Athelstan Rúmedlíc because of his large frame and his generous nature, placed the mallet and chisel on the rough stone next to the one he was dressing for the new defensive wall. He rubbed his arms and gratefully accepted the horn of beor.

He looked around the building site and saw the great hall with its new covering of slate from Wales. His men had worked quickly, hammering each piece into place on the massive roof timbers and now they had gone to Coufaentree to work on the granary attached to the castle.

The addition of the defensive wall and the change of roof covering from thatch to slate improved the great hall immeasurably. Athelstan lifted his eyes to the church on the hill with its incomplete square tower showing above the trees surrounding the village clearing. Word was that the building work started by his father would commence again before long. It had stopped when the old earl died, and the money set aside for church building had to be used to fight the Danes.

The middle part of Mercia was a good, fertile land, and Athelstan was glad he had returned to Heanton in the Arden to live. He had done well at Wintan-ceastre, where his skill was valuable in strengthening some of the lower parts of the cathedral showing signs of wear. Some of the money he had accumulated enabled him to buy one of the houses on a bend at the side of the track running through Heanton, where he lived with his wife and children.

They settled into village life after the bustle of Wintan-ceastre, and the other forty-seven villagers and the fifteen smallholders accepted them. The priest, who lived in a hovel near the church, had called on them and they shared a meal with him. After that, he visited them occasionally. He was grateful for the warm surroundings and showed himself to be a mild-tempered man, but inside the church, he was a different character who preached fiery sermons about avoiding the old religion.

Athelstan climbed the steps onto the defensive wall enclosing the land of the manor house to get a better view of the finished roof. The Sun glinting on the river in the nearby valley caught his eye. He owned a field near the river that had cut its way through the soil and the clay of the lower lying fields, in places reaching bedrock. Buying that field had turned out to be a mistake. The exposed rocky outcrops formed natural obstacles to the river, so that the water, in times of spate, gushed fiercely along its course. At those times, the river could be cruel and flood the surrounding land. Sometimes it rotted all the crops the village were growing ready for use over the wintertime.

A flock of crows arose from one of the trees beyond the river, where there were lakes and marshland and nothing grew apart from sedge grass in great, dark green tussocks. It was a wild place, the haunt of crane, moorhen, geese, and swan.

The large stone manor house was the seat of Earl Leofwin of Mercia and entry to it was through thick oak gates, which, were to be kept shut against the brooding forest. Athelstan returned to the stone he had been working on. It was to be the keystone in the arch above the gates. He moved the winch, grasped the stone with the metal claws and turned it over. after drawing his design on the face of the stone with charcoal, he selected a narrow chisel and cut his monogram for future generations to see that he was the stonemason who worked on the wall, and then he cut the date, 1063.

* * *

Earl Leofwin, with two armed men, rode out of the forest into the compound after meeting his brother Leofric in Tamoworthig. Leofwin owned a great tract of the forest in which he hunted. He called the forest after his own name, and as a sub-division of a county, known at that time as a *Hundred*, it became known as *Leofwin's Hundred*.

Leofwin glanced at the sullen sky. The rain that had lashed the land for a week was easing. He was glad about that because people were suffering from the damp and the cold. They had moved their beasts to higher ground in case the pastureland was flooded by the river.

As he neared the great hall, Leofwin turned to look at the forest. He felt uneasy because the forest looked far from normal. Dark and ominous-looking clouds were forming over the hilly part. Leofwin slid from the saddle and handed the reins to Ienur, his groom. A warm breeze ruffled the hair of the two men. The older man, Ienur's, was wispy and thinning, Leofwin's hair was thick, the colour golden, like ripe corn. They made their way to the stables.

Ienur looked at the dark clouds over the forest "There's a storm coming soon, my lord. We must get the horses under shelter."

"Do it straight away . . . I don't like the look of it." Leofwin affectionately rubbed the muzzle of the horse he called Brannling and left the groom to his work.

He was making his way over the sodden earth to the great hall when he saw light from behind him reflecting in the wet stonework of the building. Turning, he saw a strange vision in the sky over the place further in the forest where the trees were higher than the rest. He called urgently to the men who had ridden in with him and shouted for them to follow him, ready to use their weapons against whatever threat lay in the forest.

The last time such an event occurred was a number of years ago in the cold winter months. Leofwin had been unable to get into the forest in time to see what was happening. This time he was ready. He was on edge after the heated discussions with the nobles in Tamoworthig, so a hard run to find out what was going on in the forest would stop him dwelling on the cobweb-like affairs of state.

He was startled to see his children running around the large pond toward the boundary wall where the gate was still open leading into the forest. The little girl, Blythe, followed by his young son Ingwulf, was running along the track toward the trees in the direction of the light. The girl was chuckling, with her arms outstretched and her hands open, as if trying to grasp the blue colour rising into the sky.

Leofwin had never threatened his children with ogres and misshapen beasts of the night like some parents did. There was no need to threaten them with untruths.

"Your grandfather and I have sometimes seen lights coming from the hilly part of the forest, it happens every-so-often," he told his children when they could understand, preparing them for the next time it happened.

Tales and superstitions about the forest abounded. Often, parents who lived in the forest lands told children who misbehaved, that, if they did not mend their ways the Green Man would come and take them. They would squeal and become contrite, but they would grow up looking over their shoulder, scared of the forest and of its darkness. A lane cut through Leofwin's Hundred. It cut many miles off a journey taken on the old Roman roads running around the outside of the forest. Travellers could use the shortcut as long as they did not trespass into the forest. Nevertheless, travellers seldom used the short cut through Leofwin's Hundred because of the superstitions. There was talk of folk unlike normal men, seen on occasions by those who dared to venture along the narrow tracks of Leofwin's land in the course of their work.

One of the lanes passed close to the building in the heart of the forest that local people called *The House of the West Wind* because when a wind arose, most times it funnelled through from the direction of the building in the forest to the west of Heanton. Some even thought that the building caused the winds to blow.

The Westerlies had forced some of the trees into oddly stunted shapes that twisted up to the light in a way that made the trees near the House of the West Wind look threatening, and assume the shapes of beasts. To add to the superstition, moss and hoary lichen, which shivered when the wind blew, covered some of the trees on their sheltered side and gave the trees a look of elemental life.

"Blythe, Ingwulf, come quickly," Leofwin called the children, fearful they would get to the forest before he caught up with them. They slowed down and he reached the girl and grabbed her around the waist, picking her up. She was still giggling, thinking it was a game. Then he caught up with his son and, after scolding him for running to the forest without permission, he held his hand firmly and ran with both children back to the safety of the house where Aelfryth, his wife was waiting. Leofwin, looking unusually concerned, told her to take the children inside and make sure they stayed there. Then he ran into the great hall for his sword and began to buckle it on as he rushed into the manor grounds past Aelfryth.

"What's out there?" she called.

"Later . . . I'll tell you later," he shouted, buckling his sword on tighter as he ran toward the gate with the two who were ready to go with him. Aelfryth was looking in the direction of the forest when the heavy gates slammed shut behind her husband, and she saw the gathering clouds. She felt uneasy and went quickly into the house to protect her children.

Leofwin and his men were soon running down the cart track in the forest. They veered down a badger trail at the place where a tall oak tree was growing and eventually came to a fast-flowing stream where it coursed through a gulley. They leapt over it at its narrowest point and ran along the opposite bank toward the area where the blue light was gradually fading.

They came out of the dense undergrowth into an area where the trees grew thinly. A man was standing there, as if waiting for them, at the foot of the hill. There was a wolf, big and black sitting at his side, its eyes were focussed on them. Its hackles stood high and it growled deep in its throat. It stood as they drew near, snarled and made as if to lurch toward them. The man muttered a softly spoken command and tugged on the tether attached to a studded collar. The wolf responded and sat back at the man's side with its ears laid back.

"Keep the wolf covered," Leofwin said to the man on his right, and he walked up to the stranger on the side away from the wolf. He drew his jewelled sword from its scabbard and saw the man look down at it. Leofwin thought how unusual the man's clothes were. His coat was plain and had only a hint of places for the arms, and there was so much material that the detail of the man's figure was lost. His legs were protected from the weather by breeches from the same material as the coat. They fitted loosely over some green boots that flexed when the man moved. The stranger had a bout of sneezing, which made Leofwin and the other two men back off.

It was the first time for many years that anyone had been as close as the three Anglo-Saxons were to the House of the West Wind, and never had a person met with any who came out of it. Leofwin stretched his hand to the stranger's arm and felt it. He withdrew his hand quickly as the wolf stood and snarled again, showing its vicious fangs. The stranger relaxed his stance and pulled on the leash again. Other than his odd clothes, Leofwin thought the man did appear to be real, not some hobgoblin or phantom of the forest, as some would say he was.

Leofwin asked the stranger where he came from; unaware he was using language separated from that of the stranger by a thousand years of adaption. Leofwin's question received a puzzled look. From Dearden's point of view, the language had similarities to English but with longer drawn-out vowel sounds and with some Germanic intonations mixed in.

Leofwin replaced his sword into its scabbard. He looked the wolf full in the eyes and it moved forward to the full length of its tether, baring its teeth again. The stranger spoke to the creature and it drew back. Despite the feeling of threat from the man and the wolf, Leofwin had admiration for this man who had a wolf for a companion, but he was not prepared to trust him.

"Why are you on my land?" Leofwin asked, raising his voice. The stranger shrugged his shoulders and did not answer. He was still calm, but the barrier of language was creating tension. Leofwin decided on a different approach.

"Come with me. Come." He gestured and stepped back a few paces. Leofwin expected the stranger to follow. The man shook his head, wiped his bloodshot eyes, sneezed again and the Anglo-Saxon retreated a few more paces with his men. The plague started with sneezing and then collapse, but this man seemed firm on his feet. Then the stranger from the House of the West Wind tapped his chest and pointed to himself.

"I am Dearden," the stranger said, "I am a friend, my name is Dearden," he tapped his chest again for emphasis, *Dearden*, he said. The Anglo-Saxon understood it was an introduction and did the same as Dearden. He tapped his chest to indicate himself.

"I am Leofwin," he said but barely were the words out of his mouth when a jagged bolt of lightning struck a tree nearby with a deafening thunderclap, which rolled into the distance. A deep humming noise came from within the hill and the faint blue lines sprang skywards again from the House of the West Wind, curving upward through the swirling black clouds and backlighting them to the sound of thunder.

"I must be going," the stranger said, pointing to the top of the hill. Leofwin picked up the word *going* and together with the man's pointing, understood it to mean *gán*.

"*Eow gán,*" Leofwin replied, gesturing the man away toward the hill. With obvious urgency, the stranger, Dearden, tugged at the leash and the wolf followed. They reached the top of the hill and the man pushed the door open. He turned to look at Leofwin before going back into the building. He lifted his arm in a gesture of farewell and shut the shining door behind him.

11

Dearden made it into the Hub just in time. The humming noise that had been rising in pitch reached a crescendo and then began cycling down. The noise was coming from somewhere below, causing the air to vibrate, and it made his head feel worse. He sat on the floor. The room was still gently lit and pleasantly warm. Although he felt feverish, Dearden understood what his father meant when he had written *the damn place has a grip on me*. He wished they could have shared the moment together.

Why the phenomenon was happening was a different issue. He tried to think the event through but there was an overload of information. He felt ill and confused. His mind contemplated the possibility of a genetic glitch in his makeup and that of his father, where a fantasy of the mind passed through the male line of the family. The only alternative was that the event was real and somehow there had been an adjustment in time, enabling him to talk to Leofwin, the Anglo-Saxon.

The immense crystal had shades of purple and fiery red moving restlessly back and forth within its depths. Tomahawk was looking at the crystal as the internal light swirled. Dearden saw the movement reflected in the wolf's eyes. The scene through the transparent wall was changing. He stood unsteadily. When he came back into the building from meeting Leofwin, he had still been able to see the altered world through the wall, with the Anglo-Saxon men watching what was going on from the base of the hill. Now the world of trees outside was morphing, twisting and turning upon itself chaotically.

Most of the dark cloud soon cleared and all trace of the

Anglo-Saxons and the vast forest landscape had disappeared. Although there had only been a fleeting contact with Leofwin and his time, it had a profound effect on Dearden, and he yearned for a return to the bygone age. He tried to focus on something, anything out there that wasn't moving, but with the increasing dizziness, he failed to see the three figures standing at the head of the stairs behind him. They were curious about the Earths, rarely had they had the chance of being so close to them, and they silently surveyed Dearden, and Tomahawk sitting at his master's side. Tomahawk turned, looked at the three and stood as if to go toward them. They stepped quietly down the stairs and opened a door that led into the depths of the building. There was a faint click as the door closed behind them.

Dearden turned quickly at the sound, but saw nothing. He shrugged his shoulders and tugged on the leash. His mind was in a state of overload with all that had taken place. He needed to get out of the place and think, to try to set events in order. Tomahawk glanced back at the stairwell, and then followed to the outer door. It clicked open and they crossed the threshold into the twenty-first century. Dearden's legs felt weak and he leant on the doorframe for support. He closed the door. Inwardly he was on a high more exhilarating than anything he had experienced before, but the experience drew a mix of emotions that were draining. Coupled with that, he felt feverish again and it was a great effort to get to the base of the hill on his feet.

He stumbled a few yards to an ash tree, sat down heavily and leant back against it. He managed to thread his foot through the loop of Tomahawks leash. Feeling exhausted he closed his eyes and quickly drifted into a feverish sleep.

He had a dream where he was lying in bed and three tall slender people approached and looked at him. They were discussing him in a language that sounded melodic. One of them bent down and touched him with something. The three of them walked away and a great sense of peace descended on him.

* * *

Templestone was worried. He had seen Jem walk off into the forest with Tomahawk. He thought it had been far too early for Dearden to be out after his debilitating bout of 'flu. Jem always expected too much of himself. He had been gone for hours and the weather had turned bad. Templestone had a fatherly interest in Dearden, so he slung on a jacket with a hood to protect himself against the weather, and walked down the track into the forest. He was certain Dearden would have gone toward the Hub, so that was where Templestone headed.

On the boundary of consciousness, Dearden became aware of a rank smell and then something wet sliding over his face. He opened one eye a fraction in case he had to force himself into action. Tomahawk was standing close, his muzzle up to Dearden's face and the creature's tongue slid over his cheek.

"Faugh, your breath stinks. Clear off." He pushed Tomahawk aside and reached into the rucksack for a bottle of water. The box of antiviral capsules in foil dropped out. He felt a lot better for the sleep, but he broke one of the capsules out of the foil and swallowed it with a swig of water. The box and the information sheet from it dropped to the ground. The wolf moved a couple of paces closer and looked at the water bottle. Dearden aimed it at his mouth and it was squirt-gulp just as Templestone appeared through the trees.

"Am I glad to see you? You've been away hours."

"Have I? It doesn't seem that long. I must have fallen asleep." Templestone picked up the blister pack of medication and the information sheet for the tablets.

"I had a weird dream." Dearden scrambled quickly to his feet and tried to recall the images.

"It was after I went into the structure up there to shelter from the storm. The door was open. After a minute or so, I came back out of the door with Tomahawk and things had completely changed outside. It was insane how it had changed. I met some people, talked to them, but they weren't from our time."

Templestone frowned and tried to keep up with the rush of words.

"I could see my house from inside the building, but it was different, Dearden Hall was smaller than it is now, and there were no outbuildings. The stonework was new. Then I came back out of the House of the West Wind. I was feeling bad . . . had to rest. After that, I dreamt three creatures came to me. They weren't quite human, they were taller, thinner. They went away and now I feel great, more aware than I've felt for ages."

Templestone could see Dearden's recent pallor had gone but the irrational flush of words had the older man worried. He glanced at the information sheet he picked up from the floor and read,

Side Effects are; palpitation, dizziness, headache, hallucinations.

"It says here that one of the side effects of your medication can be hallucinations—"

"No," Dearden snapped. "No Priest, hallucinations my arse, it happened I tell you, Tomahawk was with me," he looked down at the wolf as if expecting confirmation.

"You need to rest up Jem, let's get back now." Templestone took hold of Dearden's arm in a fatherly sort of way to help him, but Dearden shook it off. He knew Templestone didn't believe him. Why should he believe he had accessed some other place in time through the building on the hill? Dearden thought his father must have had the same problem with the people he told.

When they arrived back home Dearden went to his room and got his father's A4 pad out of the drawer. Locating the place where his father had written about seeing the Saxon again, he wrote down the details of what happened to him while it was fresh in his mind. One thing was certain. After the day's events, he knew that his life would never be the same again.

Dearden put the pen down and sat back in the chair. It occurred to him how sharp his vision was. The fever had completely gone. The sudden improvement in health was unusual. He glanced at the clock on the wall and made a mental calculation. It was over five hours since he set out into the forest. He looked out of the window at the trees bordering the forest moving in the breeze.

He picked up the pen again and, as he wrote, serious concerns came into his mind about what he was getting into and where it would lead. Neil Armstrong's *One small step for man, one giant leap for mankind,* came to mind. On the exploratory level, the process in the forest could dwarf the Apollo 11 mission into insignificance, and in that, there was a problem. If he continued, would the genie pop out of the bottle and plunge his life and everything else he knew into chaos?

Dearden closed the writing pad. He needed to talk about the event, sensibly, rationally. He could confide in Mitch Doughty. His old colleague wouldn't jump to conclusions. Mitch would take what Jem had to say at face value. Yes, he would ring Doughty and ask him to come and talk things through. Now he had written up the event in detail he wanted to relax. The atmosphere at The Green Man up in the village would be therapeutic.

* * *

Dearden walked into the lounge where Ken Tillman was pulling a pint for a customer Dearden didn't recognise.

"You OK, Jem?" Tillman got a glass and went to the pull for Abbot Ale. "Pint?"

Dearden was on a high and only half listened to Tillman telling him about a local group he hired for the coming Saturday.

". . . Charles Dexter Ward and the Imagineers, they're getting a large following dressed up in Victorian gear, so if there is an old stove pipe hat in that place of yours, drag it out and shake the moths off. The more come here the merrier it'll be."

He would normally chat to Tillman. This time he wasn't in the mood. He took his drink to a table in an alcove near the back of the room. Difficult thoughts crowded in. His perspective of time was under threat and he had to sort it out. Instead of time being the solid, immutable pathway, measured by the ticking of a clock, with events experienced in a forward progression, time had become fluid, with even the past brought within his grasp. He looked at the heavy beams in the ceiling that were black with age and winter fires. He saw the marks of an adze in the surface and thought of the workman. He could never again look at work produced by an ancient artisan, without thinking of the man who produced the work. He stayed for an hour and drank enough to make the room spin. He laughed loud enough for it to echo when he got outside The Green Man and wondered if he ought to go into the forest now and get the three unusual beings to cure his current dizziness.

Dearden walked unsteadily home down the drive leading to the security gate. He fumbled with the keypad and the gate swung open. It had been a long and unusual day. Apart from being a little drunk, he was aching and tired. He went into the house, avoiding Frieda Heskin's gaze as he walked by the entrance to the large kitchen. He went up the stairway to his father's study. Stretching out on the bed, he remembered nothing until the next day.

* * *

With the phone in one hand and a cafetière in the other, Dearden poured a strong black coffee and told Doughty what happened at the Hub. After initial disbelief and Dearden's bad tempered response, Doughty suggested that he should inform one of the universities specialising in experimental physics so they could look into it.

"I've got some ideas about what to do next, but I need to talk them through with you face to face, not over the phone. I can trust your opinion, Mitch. I don't want to involve anyone else." Doughty thumbed through the schedule in his diary.

"OK, give me three days and I'll be with you."

"Before you go, Mitch, do you have any equipment for testing high tension electricity?" Dearden thought the humming noise in the Hub sounded similar to an electrical sub-station.

After the call, Doughty sat still for a minute, all humour gone. He was worried about his friend's state of mind. Dearden seemed to be convinced that the building in the forest was a gateway to another place in time.

Later on in the day, the Warwick Times came through Doughty's letterbox. It carried the front-page headline;

UFO incident in skies near Solihull,

There was a strange sighting in the skies during yesterday's heavy thunderstorm. It was seen by Mrs Tracey Carter, a local resident, and also, long-serving Police Sergeant, George Farley, who reported the following;

'*There were some vague blue lines rising into the sky over Hampton in Arden. In the same part of the sky, high up, a small patch of dark thundercloud was moving as if there was a fierce wind up there. I could see the lines in my peripheral vision for a short while, as they curved upwards. Then they vanished as fast as they came.*' Sergeant Farley reported the event as it happened. When other officers arrived in a mobile incident unit, they saw nothing out of the ordinary.

Mrs Carter, out with her mother for afternoon tea in Balsall Common, said she was certain that what she saw in the sky was like nothing she had ever seen before. The event remains a mystery.'

Doughty put the paper down. He had an unsettled feeling in the pit of his stomach. Events in Hampton in Arden were taking an ominous turn.

12

Doughty finished the roofing work in Coventry sooner than expected and arrived in the evening a day and a half after Dearden's phone call. His Land Rover was packed full of equipment. There was a chill in the air so they drew close to the blazing fire in the great hall with Templestone, who was asleep in a wing chair,

"How are you feeling now?" Doughty asked over a coffee.

"The flu, you mean? I'm fine, back to normal. But coming out of the building in the forest I felt rough, and then I recovered, very quickly."

"What's been going on in the forest? Come on Jem, we know each other, tell me straight." Dearden seemed quite rational as he told Doughty what happened when he went from the building into what he seemed convinced had been a totally altered landscape.

"There were some men at the foot of the hill. I exchanged names with their leader, Leofwin." Dearden told Doughty about the great forest and the rustic look of the nearby village. How he had returned to the present and had a vivid dream about three beings who came out of the old building he called the Hub. "What do you think Mitch?"

"Well, if it really did happen, there's something very odd about the Hub. There's a large impossibility factor about the whole thing. You're saying you went out of the room you went into a few minutes before and the landscape had completely altered. Come on Jem, there must be another explanation."

"There's a first time for everything."

"Sure, but think it through, you need evidence. How would you *prove* those events happen at the Hub to a court of law?"

"I could video it."

"You could. Apart from that, there's another question that needs an answer, so try to forget what happened to *you* for a minute or so."

"That's difficult."

"It might be, but bear with me. Who made the building in the first place?"

"I've no idea." Dearden stood as logs settled in the hearth, sending a shower of sparks into the void of the chimney. He put more logs onto the glow and sat back down, looking at the shapes created by the flames as the logs began to burn. Both men were deep in thought, and it promised to be a long night.

Doughty broke the silence. "When I packed all the gear up to bring here, I included another item you didn't ask for. I thought it might be useful because of the dodgy characters in the forest, and your attack in Rugby." He reached into a pocket of his combats and took out his Colt M1911 and a box of cartridges. He checked the safety catch was on and loaded the magazine.

"I had a similar thought," Dearden went to the Jacobean sideboard. He unlocked a steel lined drawer. "I hoped I wouldn't need this, but I'm not so sure now." He took out his Beretta and laid it by Doughty's Colt on the side table.

The next morning was dry and bright. All trace of the bad weather of the past few days had gone. Dearden was chatting in the studio with Bill Templestone and Lloyd Perkins, updating them with recent events in the forest. Perkins was sceptical and said he didn't want to get involved. Templestone was different. He was intrigued with what was going on.

Dearden's suggestion further intrigued him. "With the opposition that's showing up, I need someone as capable as they are to help protect the place. Will you ride shotgun Bill?"

"That I will, but how about the gun?"

"Easily sorted, come with me." They walked over to the manor and down some worn stone steps to the rooms below. Dearden pressed the combination on a keypad, which released deadbolts in the edge of the door, and they went on through into one of the rooms where there was a large steel gun-cupboard.

"Take your pick." Templestone chose a revolver he recognised, a Smith and Wesson 38 with a six-inch barrel. It might be clunky, but it was a reliable weapon. He had taken it on a number of missions, and it had helped him out of some tight corners. He opened the chamber, spun it to check it was empty, and then snapped it shut. He raised the weapon in a two-handed stance. Its weight was familiar.

"It would work better with cartridges." He held out his hand, and Dearden gave him a box of fifty.

With Tomahawk on a leash, Dearden and Doughty went along the track into Leofwin's Hundred. There was evidence of the passage of vehicles, but the narrow ruts and peaks were grassed-over and compact. Doughty kept an eye on the thick undergrowth crowding in on each side of the track. It might have been the age of the place and its untouched state, but although the day was warm he felt a chill of uncertainty.

"Jem, can you feel it?"

"Feel what?"

"Difficult to say, but it's as if we're not alone."

Tomahawk was still on the leash and restless. He slowed down and stopped, looking to the left. Dearden checked in that direction but it seemed clear. He pulled on the leash, drawing the wolf closer, and walked on.

After a while, Dearden pointed to a massive oak tree a few yards ahead. "That's *Old Jack*. We're going to the Hub along

Devenish's route, and Old Jack's one of his route markers."

"It's big, how old is it?"

"No idea, but it was mentioned as a landmark they called *Vieux Jacques* in the 1485 Thomas Bradnock documents."

They made their way past the great oak and headed for a fluorescent mark Dearden had sprayed on a tree further on. He slashed at the undergrowth with his machete, widening the path, and Doughty followed behind, clearing the remaining vegetation.

They came to Shadow Brook and crossed the stream on tree trunks lashed together with rope. All was quiet other than the sound of water coursing over stones and fallen branches. They followed the bank of the stream to the left, and eventually came to the base of the hill.

Dearden pointed to the top of the hill, to the structure visible through thickly growing trees and undergrowth. "That's the Hub. They used to call it the House of the West Wind."

"You could easily miss it, with the trees growing so thick," Doughty said. He could just discern the building. "It looks as though it could have been a Motte and Bailey,"

"It's not one of those. The tower of a Motte and Bailey used to be a wooden structure. The building up there is stone."

They made their way around the semi-circular perimeter. The face of the hill ascended at a steep angle from the forest floor to a height Doughty estimated to be about fifty feet, where it flattened to a plateau continuing into the forest toward the west.

They scrambled up the slope and Dearden made his way to the door. He pulled out the stake he used to keep the covering of ivy in place, pushed it into the ground through the loop of Tomahawk's leash, then grasped the handle and tried to undo the latch, but it was solid.

"It opened easily last time," Dearden said.

Doughty tried the handle himself. "It doesn't open now, what's different?"

"There was torrential rain, and lightning close by."

"The static could have released the latch."

"Could be possible. If static is what unlocks the door it would explain why dad was always on a high when he came back from the forest after a thunderstorm. He would be soaked to the skin but elated. It was bizarre."

"So we wait for bad weather." Doughty looked at a patch of the wall he could see and rubbed the surface with his hand. He took an old Jack-knife from his pocket and scraped the surface of the wall with the spike. He looked at the effect on the wall, examined the end of the spike, and frowned.

"Look at this," he showed the spike to Dearden. "This knife might look as if it came out of the ark but it's made of the best quality high carbon steel. There's not a mark on the wall but it's worn a flat on the spike."

As he looked around from where he was standing Dearden noticed an area of forest floor that stood out because the growth was stunted compared to the rest of the lush undergrowth. The area was roughly parallel. He pointed it out to Doughty and they went down to examine it.

Doughty measured the width of the area. "Two metres wide." The tape measure snapped back into its case and Doughty scraped the soil away with his boot. It revealed a hard surface underneath. He bent down and examined the area more closely. The material was the same colour as the building on the hill. "It looks like a pathway," he went further from the hill and scraped the forest floor with his boot again. The soil came away and revealed the hard material below.

Dearden traced where the path went toward the hill. "Dad spoke about this in the diaries. Look at the side of the hill in line with the path. The ground's lower there. It must have sunk where he filled it in after the excavation."

"So what do you suggest we do next, dig?"

"I think so. We'll dig our way into the Hub in line with the path, and you've got the JCB to do it with."

"I thought you might suggest that."

* * *

Tomahawk was lying on the rug in front of the fire in the great hall. Dearden wanted to get him used to mixing with people. Doughty put his Jack Daniels down on the side table and continued with the crossword puzzle.

"Recklessly bold or daring",

"Who is?" Dearden put his notebook down on the floor.

"Eight down, what's a word for recklessly bold or daring?"

"Audacious," Templestone called over, although he found crossword puzzles irritating, and avoided them like the plague.

"Thanks, audacious fits."

Dearden picked up the copy of George M. Gresham's *Warwickshire Legends* he bought from Somerton's and thumbed down the list of chapters. He turned to the one called *The Green Man of Arden* and scanned the first paragraph.

"Listen to this," he said to the others.

The Green Man of Arden differs from other Green Man legends, in that he is not connected to paganism, as are most of the other worldwide legends of the Green Man. Evidence points to the Green Man of Arden having had his beginnings in Saxon times. There was a story that developed into a song about two warlike travellers who appeared in the forest from a land a long way off over the wild sea.

The words of the folk-song say that,

They were dressed in green garb, strange all over from head to foot, leaves were their hair, their thighs were as thick as trees, and their faces were a glowering green.

Another verse of the song says they were,

Tormented and forever hurrying, and must go into the forest while lightnings abide.

The legend grew, and people became afraid to enter Leofwin's hundred. Over the years, there have been tales of similar Green Man appearances in that part of the forest, and it became a place to avoid."

Dearden read on silently. He turned the page and came to the next chapter called *The Golden Maid of Maldon.* He thought it of no consequence and turned a few more pages to the next chapter, *The Lights of Leofwin's Hundred.*

Doughty finished the crossword puzzle and put the paper down. He picked up his notebook where he had been planning the excavation of the Hub. He ran his ideas through with Dearden and Templestone.

"We'll have to use ground penetrating radar to find out what's below ground on the hill before we start digging. I haven't got the equipment, but I know who has, Julia Linden-Barthorpe, I think we need to get her involved."

Templestone heard what they said. "It would be good having Jules around," he said, with amusement in his eyes.

13

Julia Linden-Barthorpe was using a trowel at the bottom of an eight-foot deep trench in a dip between one of the Burton Dassett hills. It was an ongoing exploration of an area rich in archaeology, which had produced a wealth of Roman and Saxon artefacts. The data would take at least two years to analyse and write up. Wilf Sheldon was at the top of the trench, cup of tea in hand, waiting for Julia to come up the ladder to collect the warming brew.

It was muddy in the trench. When she appeared she presented a sight that was both dedicated and comical. Her soft brown eyes flecked with gold were what people noticed first, and her skin, tanned to the colour of honey by the outdoor work in the summer, added to her beauty. She was a lithe thirty-two years old with lustrous auburn hair. The soft feminine exterior belied the person at the core. She was a black belt Godan, a fifth Dan Shotokan Karateka and lethal with it. Her strength was how she controlled her explosive nature.

Her mobile phone rang as she was stepping off the ladder. It was Jem Dearden and he was in an unusual state of excitement. They kept in contact every few weeks, enjoying each other's company over a drink or a meal, but without romantic attachment.

Dearden gave Julia a brief explanation about the old building in the heart of Leofwin's Hundred. The thought of a new dig grabbed her attention. Dearden asked her if she could lay her hands on some geophysics equipment to do tests on land surrounding the monument-like structure.

"I have my own Geophys, and I'll bring some other equipment I think we may need, but tell me more."

"At this point, all I can say over the phone is that you won't be disappointed, but I'll tell you everything when you get here, when are you free?"

"Come on Jem, what are you hiding?"

"Sorry, Jules, I can't tell you over the phone, but I promise I'll reveal everything when you get here."

"I'm curious about the need for secrecy," while she spoke, she calculated the state of her Burton Hills dig. "OK, I'll be with you in four days."

* * *

Shortly after her mother died, Julia Linden-Barthorpe, in her early twenties, had moved back into Moat Field Cottage with her father. She had returned after a spell away from home while she gained her degree with first class honours in archaeology and forensic science at Exeter University. By the time she was twenty-nine she had fast-tracked to a professorship. She found it easy because she loved history and the detail of forensics. She was in her element uncovering artefacts of the past from the earth and piecing together the lives of the people back there from the clues they left behind. Julia achieved results that were legendary and by the age of thirty-two, she was a recognised authority in her field of study.

Moat Field Cottage lay in the shadow of Kenilworth Castle. The Earl of Leicester made sumptuous additions to the castle to make it fit for the Queen, Elizabeth Tudor. He had dwellings built outside the castle's stern outer wall for the artisans and labourers needed for the everyday running of the castle. This included Moat Field Cottage.

Julia's father, Alex Linden had turned the cottage over to her and there was plenty of room for father and daughter to have their own space. From the vaulted cellar below the cottage, Julia ran L-BarX, which was devoted to the excavation and study of English social history from Pre-Saxon through to Saxe-Coburg-Gotha. Developed from her studies was a working knowledge of the Anglo-Saxon language.

'Linden-Barthorpe Archaeological Explorations', was affiliated to the British Museum, and her extensive body of work and sound research methods led to her work being funded by the museum and the National Lottery Fund. Private individuals and other museums that recognised the benefits of her research kept L-BarX financially buoyant and the income stream ensured there was a healthy profit.

In Moat Field Cottage, there were two vertical oak beams with a waist high wall between them. Julia and her father had discussed what to do with the gap above the wall and decided that a stained glass panel based on a Tudor theme would look good. She found Dearden Stained Glass online. They were only twenty minutes away, so she decided to try them.

When she walked into the studio in Knowle, a flyer stuck on the door advertising weekend residential stained glass courses attracted her attention. The idea appealed to her so she signed up and went along.

Dearden found her attractive, but he was determined not to get romantically involved with any other woman. Jackie Mason still occupied a large part of his heart. Jem Dearden began to trust Julia after it became obvious that she had a strong sense of justice he admired. It was during one evening when they had driven out for a meal in Stratford. The background music was quiet, and they were sitting at a table out of earshot of other diners in the candle-lit restaurant. Unusual for Julia, there were gaps in the conversation.

"What's on your mind, Jules? You don't seem your usual self." She looked down at the table avoiding his direct gaze, and toyed with the saltcellar, saying nothing. Dearden knew there was a problem. He put his hand on hers and squeezed. He wanted to reassure her.

"Jules, tell me, I can handle it, whatever it is." She looked up at him and—unusually for Julia—he saw tears welling up in her eyes.

"Sometimes I hate this bloody world." Dearden looked around the room, the other diners had not heard her outburst, but she understood Jem's warning to keep her voice down.

"I feel so helpless sometimes," she said quietly.

"Why?"

"If I was able to . . ." at that point the waitress appeared.

"Is everything alright with your meals?" she asked.

"Fine . . . it's just fine," Dearden was distracted. "It's good, thanks." Julia looked up but said nothing. The waitress moved away and the candle flame fluttered.

"You were saying *if you were able to* . . . what else were you going to say?"

"I was on a dig in Cornwall about a year ago. I was glad when it was over, but because of the circumstances back then I've kept in touch with the people who owned the land. I've tried to help them out."

"Why?"

Julia went on to tell Dearden about a man who had found a Celtic artefact in his garden.

"The owner of the house, George Underwood, had been digging an area for a pond and he found a gold chalice. The British Museum became involved and they called me in to do the work on their behalf. We dug trenches and found a hoard, gold coins, amulets and other objects. They were worth a fortune. George and his family would have been set up for life."

"That sounds great, so what happened?"

"Their next door neighbour happened." Jules was twisting her table napkin into a tight coil. The memory was obviously painful. A tear fell onto the table and Dearden gave her a handkerchief.

"Go on then Jules, explain, if you feel able to," he squeezed her hand.

"Years before George and his neighbour were born there had been a disagreement between two of their ancestors over ownership of land bordering their properties. The dispute did not go to law because the two people agreed to differ. They agreed to share the use of the land and it carried on that way until recent years. George's neighbour must have heard about the discrepancy, but he was rich and didn't need the land. Then he heard about George's find and out of sheer bloody spite and greed, he went to see his lawyers and told them to prove his ownership. It turned out to be a long and protracted affair that went through the courts for months."

"And the decision swung in the neighbour's favour," Dearden concluded.

"Yes. It was a ruling under some ancient bylaw. Oh, it was legal all right but it was so unfair. The court granted ownership of the land to the neighbour. Along with the land, he got ownership of the treasure. George was a trespasser on the land. He and his family got nothing, other than spiralling debts. Today I heard that he has committed suicide. It happened two days ago and his wife is distraught." There was a catch in Julia's voice. "George left a note. He said that he had failed everyone he loved, failed in his responsibility to his wife."

"And you felt like you wanted to kill the bastard next door."

"Yes, but that's not the answer is it?"

"I'm not saying it is. I'm talking about how you felt."

"I felt powerless."

"What would you have done if you could have stepped into the situation?"

"I would've made sure *real* justice took place. George's

business was failing. He was a victim of a downturn in trade, but the business had been in his family for five generations and he felt he had caused its collapse. When it did fail the family's livelihood went with it. Any spare cash they had went to pay creditors. Proceeds from the hoard would have lifted them out of the situation that had become dire. I knew it was bad, but I didn't realise exactly *how* bad. Now it's too late." Julia held her head in her hands, quietly sobbing.

Dearden put his hand out to her. She took it and he squeezed. She gave him a weak smile and said she wanted to straighten herself up, so she went to the powder room. Dearden called the waitress for more wine.

When Julia came back she looked more her old self. She looked at Dearden and could tell he had something on his mind. Julia knew him well enough to wait for what he had to say. She was glad of his company but glad of the break in conversation. He looked at her as she pulled out her chair to sit down. "There is something I need to tell you," he said. "It won't help with the situation in Cornwall, but it could give you the chance to help fight injustices in the future. In the short term, it could help settle your mind." He remembered Arthur Doughty's explanation about the SHaFT motto under the stained glass shield. Getting involved with SHaFT had helped him through the grief after his father died. Dearden asked Julia the same question Arthur Doughty had asked him.

"Do you know what 'Nos Successio Procul Totus Sumptus' means?"

"What the hell does it matter what Procul . . . whatever it is, means?"

"It has to do with an organisation that ensures justice is done when all other methods are failing. It isn't a perfect way of resolving problems, but it balances the scales in favour of justice—" which was how Julia first became aware of SHaFT.

Initially, she was involved in an advisory capacity to do with forensics until she proved she was able to keep everything confidential under all circumstances. After a while, she took on a more active role and since then there had been times when her input had been vital to the success of a mission.

* * *

At the top of the trench, she grasped the cup of tea. Its warmth seeped into her hands, chilled from working in the shade and damp at the bottom of the trench. She had been brushing centuries of debris from a gold clasp in grave number three.

When Jem's phone call came through Julia thought at first that he was drunk because he was stumbling over his words. The lucid but short conversation that followed convinced her Dearden wasn't drunk but was desperately excited about a building in the area of forest he owned near his house.

Two days after his phone call, Julia was reading the Warwickshire Herald when a small article on page five about lights in the sky caught her eye.

Dearden picked up the phone. It was Julia.

"I've been reading the Herald, Jem. What on earth is going on around Hampton in Arden?"

14

Julia Linden-Barthorpe's Jeep Grand Cherokee pulled up at the electronically controlled gate and her voice came over the intercom.

"Come on through Jules," Dearden pressed the button and the gate opened. He hoped he could convince her that his encounter with the Anglo-Saxons had not been fanciful. He was unsure about Doughty and Templestone. He felt they might be humouring him. All four tyres locked as Julia pulled to a halt in the car park.

Dearden put Tomahawk in his run on his way to meet her. She climbed out of the 4 x 4 and eyed the Wolf up suspiciously, as she stepped to the rear of the vehicle. She opened the tailgate and lifted out a trolley with three wheels and a cradle.

They hugged briefly. "Good of you to come, Jules, it's great to see you."

She smiled. "You asked for Geophys, we've got this instrument on trial." She lifted out a control box and placed it in position on the trolley. "It's Ground Penetrating Radar. This other instrument is a magnetometer. It uses the Overhauser effect so it's very sensitive," she lifted up the long instrument that had a shoulder harness. "It'll help us do the subterranean mapping."

"Thanks for your help, Jules. I'll bring you up to speed with what's happening after Frieda shows you to your room. We'll have a walk into the forest later so you can get a feel for the Hub, and we can start in earnest tomorrow."

Dearden helped her take some heavy toolboxes and padlocked packing cases out of the back of the Jeep. She stopped and squared up to him.

"When we were on the phone the other day you told me you had a break-in. There's valuable equipment here, is it going to be safe?"

"No worries on that score. I've had electronic security installed on the doors and windows. Bill Templestone's here with his Smith and Wesson for company and Tomahawk's close-by too." They were walking by Tomahawk's run. The wolf sensed there was a stranger about and was eying Julia up. "We're taking no chances, Jules. No one will get in now."

* * *

Dearden was waiting for Julia in the great hall with Mitch Doughty. When she came into the room, they stood. Templestone gave her a wave from the armchair.

"Jules, it's good to see you," Doughty said. "If Jem turns out to be right about what's happening here, welcome to the strangest place on Earth."

She shrugged her shoulders. "I reserve judgement about how strange it is."

Dearden had the books and written records out on the table, and he moved from one to the other, pointing out the details of the events in Leofwin's Hundred in chronological order.

"This is difficult to believe." A smile flicked across her features. Then she frowned. "You seem to have plenty of evidence." She picked up the copies of the Private Accession Index cards relating to the trial of Thomas Bradnock.

"That court hearing took place here, in this hall in 1485," Dearden pointed out the words about the House of the West Wind. He picked up the Devenish book next.

"Devenish tried to rationalise what causes the phenomena and put forward theories about Ley-Lines."

"That's fanciful. Does he put forward any proof?"

"No, it was pure supposition, but the useful thing about Devenish is the record he left about his personal experiences with the House of the West Wind. He refers to excavating it with the owner of the Hall." They moved on to the Warwickshire Legends book and Dearden opened it to the chapter on The Green Man. "The Green Man is a common link through some of the events, although how he fits in I don't know." Julia read part of the chapter Dearden underlined. They moved along the table to where he had put some of the diaries. There were bookmarks in the relevant pages. Finally, he picked up the A4 pad and pointed out his father's hurried writing, where he wrote '*I Saw the Saxon again.*'

"That was written shortly before dad's death." There was silence in the room as she read the information, moving from one record to another.

"Fascinating, but the whole thing sounds pretty surreal. Do you expect me to believe all this?"

"I know how it must sound, but I'm telling you I went into the House of the West Wind when it activated and I saw the Saxon. I even talked to him . . . as best I could, that is. I talked to Leofwin, Jules. I swear it's true."

"Come on, Jem, do you think I'm stupid enough to believe that bullshit? It's impossible." She had a hint of a smile on her face when she looked at Dearden. She expected him to laugh, but she could see he was deadly serious.

"I'm finding what Jem's saying difficult to accept as well." Doughty cut in. "But what I keep coming back to is the evidence here," he indicated the documents and books on the table. "It's not simply what Jem's saying. The evidence goes back hundreds of years, and over those years, different people have testified to similar events that have occurred in Leofwin's Hundred independently of each other. That tells me that what Jem is saying will stand up to serious scrutiny."

Dearden changed his approach. "The inside of that building is astounding. It's full of electronic gear centred on a huge crystal. There's a stairway leading to a level below, but a locked door bars the way down. After my father excavated the entrance at the base of the hill, he wrote about finding interconnected levels inside."

"Alright, let's go along with what you're saying for a minute and assume that this transfer in time actually happened. Do you know what triggers it?"

"I don't know for sure," but according to all the records, and what I experienced, there's always dark cumulus about when it happens, thunderheads—"

"Which are loaded with electricity. So to have any chance of seeing it working we can assume there have to be the same weather conditions."

"That's what Mitch and I concluded. And another thing my dad suggested was that the building comes into a ready state under those conditions. It changes from passive to active. He came up with various ideas as he tried to make sense of something alien to his experience. He even suggested the building could be an electronic component in its own right, part of a colossal electronic circuit."

"There are all sorts of imponderables that come to mind with this Jem." Julia was mentally exploring the possibilities. "It looks as though your dad was *more* than interested in the place in the forest. He was in deep, maybe too deep and it turned his mind in some way. Are you letting the place get to you, the same as it got to him?"

Dearden shifted in his seat. He was uncomfortable with Julia's question. She had no right to call his father's sanity into question. He felt himself heating up.

"Next point, the illness you had, influenza. You had a fever with it. It is possible you hallucinated or constructed the event in your mind because you *wanted* it to happen. After reading the diaries your father wrote it could have been wish-fulfilment, you were close to him."

"Don't be stupid, I don't work like that."

"You might not normally, but you'll have to think this through and explain it rationally and with evidence if you want to justify what you say happened."

"There's another possibility," Doughty interjected. He wondered how to put over what was on his mind.

"Go on, what is it?" Dearden asked.

"You told us your dad was trying to make sense of something that seemed alien. Is the building in the forest exactly that; *is it alien?*"

"Hold on Mitch," Julia cut Doughty short. "No assumptions. We'll take this one step at a time and we haven't eliminated the earthly options." She smiled. "I want to see the place, and then we'll run some tests and see where the results take us. After we've done the tests we'll form our conclusions, but not until."

"OK, anything else?" Dearden was getting impatient. He stood up.

"Yes, there is," Julia said. "If you want me in on this we must work the way we do at L-BarX, that is systematically, and you'll follow my lead. Are you alright with that?"

There was muttered agreement.

"We've talked enough," she said, "Let's go and look at it."

*　*　*

Dearden pushed the ivy covering the door aside. He tried the handle. It didn't move, applied more force, but it was solid.

Julia was looking around the site, weighing up the logistics. She took her mobile from her pocket and took photographs of the site then stood there, thinking. Then . . .

"This is the plan. We will have to clear the site and fell some of these trees so we can use the Geophys. If the electrical storm did unlock the door, we need a repeat of the same weather. I'm not convinced about your leap into history, Jem, but on the archaeological front this find is too important to ignore."

"I had a feeling you'd be impressed."

"I am, and here's what I propose. I could stop at your place until we find out what's going on. It is likely to take some time, and it's best for me to be on hand. Wilf Sheldon can take care of the dig at Burton Dassett for a while."

Dearden had been hoping she would stay. They scrambled down to join Doughty and Templestone by the path at the base of the hill.

"How far do you want this investigation to go?" Julia asked when they were together.

"Wherever it leads, we'll follow," Dearden said. The mood was upbeat. Doughty wanted to see inside the building, and Templestone said it was about time he had some excitement back in his life.

"Good. Then I'll organise the archaeology, but we need to clear the site before we can make a start."

"I'll do that," Doughty said. "I'll get Matt Roberts to bring the equipment over in the morning. We'll get started by nine."

"And I'll ride shotgun. I have the very efficient tools to do it," Templestone tapped the Smith and Wesson that he had tucked into his belt in a very well-practiced way.

The receiver jangled into life on Uberatu's surveillance gear in Stephenson's Terrace. He cursed it for startling him but his mood changed as he listened to Doughty asking someone to bring chainsaws and other machinery to Dearden Hall.

"We need it here early in the morning Matt, and we need your help here as well."

Uberatu became attentive and his mood lightened. Things

were moving in the forest and he felt he could make progress after months of inactivity. Dearden and his cronies were getting construction machinery and test equipment on site. Uberatu wondered what they would uncover.

He glanced at Snarl, who growled deep in his throat. The phone call from the Hall ended and Uberatu stood up abruptly.

"So this is it," he said to the dog. There was a responsive wag of the tail. "The game's afoot," Uberatu gestured wildly to his sparring partner, "Cry havoc and let loose the dogs of war."

* * *

Dearden was in the forest, widening the track with a chainsaw soon after dawn. He had felled a number of trees along the track by the time Matt Roberts arrived in a Daf CF75 truck loaded with equipment on wooden pallets ready for the site clearance. Doughty and Gil Heskin loaded Doughty's Land Rover with chainsaws and other equipment for the ground clearance, and then they moved the vehicle yard by yard along the track as they widened it. It was hard going, hacking years of undergrowth away to widen the track through the wildwood, but they set too with a will. They reached the landmark tree, Old Jack, and pushed onward to Shadow Brook.

The bridge over Shadow Brook, which was a small river, rather than a stream as the name suggested, needed widening to get the Land Rover to the other side. Dearden hammered in heavy iron spikes each side of some newly added logs from the tree felling, and Doughty drove the Land Rover over them slowly. Once it was on the other side, they carried on widening the track where it followed the course of Shadow Brook. After three days work, they stood in the clearing at the base of the Hub with the Land Rover.

* * *

Some distance away, blending in with its neighbouring trees was a noteworthy oak, not as large as Old Jack, but it was still impressive. In the seventeen-eighties, lightning had struck it, and the trunk had split. In the years afterwards, rot had set into the trunk. Over the years, worms and beetles ate the soft, rotten parts of the tree back to the heartwood, and it survived. The bark re-grew inside and out, and it fed the luxuriant leafage of the tree that had become cavernous.

Uberatu was sitting on a collapsible seat inside the tree. He had fitted the interior out over the previous months as an observation post so that he could keep his eyes on the progress of work at the Hub. He fitted a couple of shelves to put tools on and a camping stove with a double burner. There was a small portable heater for warmth. A Camping Gaz lantern hung from a hook screwed into the timber above gave comfortable light. Aware that the portable appliances could cause oxygen depletion that would kill in confined spaces Uberatu fitted a terracotta pipe to act as a vent, which he held in place with puddled clay from the bank of Shadow Brook. He drilled a small hole through the trunk to keep an eye on what Dearden was doing.

Theo visualised himself sitting in the heart of the oak, covered from head to foot in ancient timber. He was an oak, his limbs were the mighty boughs of the tree . . . he stunk of it and was at one with the forest. He practised trying to make his breathing and heartbeat reduce to a sentient level, to become at one with the tree surrounding him.

Getting in and out of the tree was a tight squeeze, but it did make him feel secure. To disguise the entrance Uberatu devised a canvas sheet onto which he had sewn a thick plug of camouflage. It looked like moss covered tree bark, and it blended in perfectly with the other trees in the area that had moss and lichen that moved in the breeze on their eastern side.

Once inside the tree he would place the plug into the hole using locator bolts and hold it in place with wing nuts.

One night he had stayed after dark. It was a full moon and the Dearden crew had gone away. Uberatu undid the bolts holding the mossy cover in place, ready to go back to his barn. He took one last look at the hill through his spy hole and what he saw gave him the creeps. He stood back and rubbed his eye. He hoped they were saplings he had seen. He looked again. Three very tall figures were standing at the foot of the hill. They seemed to be conversing. They looked green and ethereal in the moonlight, and after they turned to face the tree where he was hiding, they began walking toward him with long loping strides.

Uberatu's heart lurched. What would have been a cry of fear stayed silent in his throat. He pulled the cover away from the entrance, placed it back quick and ran, gasping and making whimpering sounds as he ran, catching his flesh on twigs and brambles. He didn't care about the pain of the thorns, he just ran. He got to his car where he had parked it at the side of his barn, fumbled with the key and headed for Leamington Spa at a speed far too fast for the narrow roads. It took him days to get over the fright and muster up the courage to go back into Leofwin's Hundred. He vowed never to say anything to anyone about the incident. He felt ashamed of his fear and found it difficult even to look Snarl in the eye. In his mind, he couldn't shake the vision of those three things walking toward him.

Came the day when all hell broke loose. Uberatu, still rather fearful, was looking through the spy hole. He was watching four people clearing timber from around the base of the hill. He was sick of the noise of chainsaws that had grown steadily louder over the past three days. Then they arrived at the hill. They even had a stump grinder, which added to the mayhem as it sprayed chippings like a snowstorm.

Uberatu had a deep-seated headache caused by the noise. He wished one of them would chop his leg with a chainsaw. He imagined he had a zapper that would make one of them drop his chainsaw and take a foot off. He held the zapper out in front of him, aimed it at the wild looking man named Roberts who walked like Robocop. Uberatu plunged his thumb down on the imaginary button, *psssss-thwack*. He half expected to see the man fall to the ground, bleeding. He went for Dearden next.

Things looked as though they were coming to a head, so Uberatu called Otto Fengel and Antony Beggs on his mobile phone and whispered to be ready to move as soon as he gave them the call to action.

* * *

Doughty turned off the stump grinder and removed his boots to empty the wood chippings. They took off their ear defenders and Julia clambered down from the top of the hill where she had been running tests on the building. She had discovered that the external structure consisted of two different materials, that had a minute colour change compared to each other. They were sandwiched in alternating layers. Julia sat on the ground making notes and then she relaxed with her legs drawn up and her arms curled round her knees. She had reached a conclusion with her calculations. What she discovered was difficult to believe.

Mitch Doughty was sitting at Julia's side, looking over her notes. "The hardness level of the building is at the top end of Moh's scale," she told him. "Moh's scale is how gemologists grade the hardness of gemstones. I tried scratching the wall with an industrial diamond, but it had no effect other than to wear a flat on the diamond. Do you know what that means?"

"I do know diamond is the hardest known substance."

Doughty looked up at the others, who had gathered round, realising that Julia had completed the tests. Doughty thought Julia's colour was paler than normal. She repeated the question for the others' benefit.

"The material that building is made of is *harder* than diamond. Have you any idea what that implies? Think it through, it's important."

"Could be that a technical group have built it on the quiet and not let on," Matt Roberts suggested.

"There are problems with that," Julia reasoned. "The first problem is that the building is ancient and well documented. Another thing, until recent years it would have been impossible to develop and produce such a material. Even now, it would be impossible to manufacture it in the quantity as we see here. We must not forget that Leofwin's Hundred has been in Jem's family for generations. No outside agency has interfered in this area for close to a thousand years."

"It could have been built by an early civilisation in human history," Dearden conjectured.

"Let's go along with that argument for a minute. If this technology represented the industrial expertise of a society, there would *have* to be more archaeological evidence for it, and there isn't." The conversation faltered briefly as she thought about an incident in the past. "Could there be a third possibility?" The silence was heavy. "Come on, what *could* be the other option? Mitch mentioned it a few days ago. I shot the idea down in flames because we had no evidence at the time. Now we've done our tests and found the material the Hub is built of is artificial, hi-tech, *and* ancient, so what is the other option?" Julia was getting them to work it out for themselves.

"Come on, what is the remaining alternative? You mentioned it the other day, Mitch. Which of the three options is more probable? All of them sound far-fetched but one has to be less far-fetched than the others are. Which one would you go for?"

As she waited for the answer, a memory from another dig came to mind again. Matt Roberts jerked her back to the present.

"You say there's a complete lack of archaeological evidence anywhere about this material. You're the archaeologist, you should know. On that basis, I'd say the option Mitch mentioned the other day is more probable. The alien one."

"OK, Matt. Good reasoning. Any of you heard of Occam's Razor?"

"It's something to do with probability."

"Yeah. The Occam's Razor principle states that if you've got two theories, both explaining the observed facts, you should use the simplest as the truth, however unlikely the fact until there's more evidence to the contrary."

Matt Roberts took the reasoning forward. "So you're saying that, because there is no more archaeological evidence of the material the Hub's built of, the most likely option is that it must have come from an extra-terrestrial source."

Dearden was the first to speak. "That comes as no surprise. When I came out of the Hub the fever I had just vanished. I have a vague memory that some form of humanoid life came and helped me, so they're probably still about. Look, a lot's gone on today, I suggest we need a break. Let's get back to the Hall and chill out. This evening we'll analyse what we've found so far, and decide where we're going with it."

"Sounds good to me." Doughty wiped the sweat away from his eyes. "I'll finish the site off with the stump grinder tomorrow."

There was a buzz of excitement in the great hall. Templestone had uncorked a quality wine and had filled the glasses. Julia, whose scepticism had disappeared, was explaining to Dearden how she intended to tackle the archaeology at the site. "Whether or not it happened like you said when you went into the Hub is immaterial, Jem. The building itself warrants a complete archaeological investigation but the historical context of the material opens up a complex issue. I'll do a paper on it after I've done some research. All the textbooks will have to be rewritten." She thought of the satisfaction of researching the virgin territory of the site, the accolades that would follow after publishing the results.

"You are not going public," Dearden left her with no doubt.

"What do you mean, not going public? This is a major find. We *can't* keep the wraps on it."

"We can, and we will."

Julia stood up abruptly, her face flushed. The other three looked at what was going on. Julia and Dearden each had a strong case to argue, one for publicity the other for secrecy. Jem beckoned her out of earshot of the others.

Julia faced him with her hands on her hips. There was a temperamental side to her that sometimes got out of hand.

"Go on then, speak." The others looked over. Doughty shrugged. He knew Jules.

"You're right, of course." Jem tried to be rational. "The building in the forest is tremendously important, but let me outline some details you're not aware of."

"Go on then. They'd better be damn good details or I'm out of here."

Over the next hour, Dearden cautiously, tentatively, won her over, and then they rejoined the others. The session went on long into the night until sleep called, and they drew down the curtain on the day's events.

15

During the night, Tomahawk was pacing about in his run. Dearden was sleeping light and he heard the wolf growling. He took his Beretta with him and went to investigate. The Moon was shining through the windows of the upper floor corridor where the bedrooms were located. He rapped lightly on Doughty's door. A few seconds later Doughty appeared, also with his pistol.

"Anyone would think there was a problem," Doughty said, looking at Dearden's Beretta. They felt their way downstairs, heading for the outside. On the way, Dearden turned off the master switch for the security lights and they crept over to Tomahawk's run. He was standing by the wire, his black form blending into the night, apart from his eyes, shining yellow in the moonlight.

"Shhhhhhh," Dearden offered his hand up to Tomahawks muzzle from the other side of the wire. The creature settled. "Impressive or what?" Dearden whispered.

"Yeah, and I'm glad he's on our side."

Dearden shone his torch into the run and picked out something red on the ground. Tomahawk was near the lump as if protecting it. Dearden felt a cold chill and ran to the door, fumbled with the lock and raced into the enclosure, shouting. Doughty followed, slamming the door shut as he got inside the wire. Dearden faced Tomahawk, who was snarling, and he stepped between the wolf and the meat.

"Go," he shouted, and louder, "Go, move it!" Dearden was unnerved by the situation. Red Cloud warned him against what he was doing, but he stared Tomahawk out, and then, in submission, the wolf crouched to the ground with its ears laid back. Dearden picked up the meat and felt a sticky substance on it as he threw it out of the enclosure.

"The bastards tried to poison him, we were only just in time," He slipped the leash onto the studded collar and tugged the wolf out of his run. Dearden was silent as they walked back to the great hall, and once there, he found it difficult to settle. The anger kept coming back, and with it, the desire to get hold of those who tried to poison Tomahawk. He poured whiskies, and he and Doughty talked long into the night. They slept downstairs, with Tomahawk on the rug in front of the fire.

Dearden still smarted next day when he remembered the events of the night. If they, whoever *they* were, wanted to play dirty, he could too. He decided to keep quiet about what happened. Dearden didn't want to create an issue over the security of Julia's equipment stored in one of the outbuildings. She could be volatile and the situation could blow up way out of proportion.

* * *

There was an upbeat atmosphere at the site. Matt Roberts started placing the tools back on the trailer after Doughty finished with the stump grinder. Julia scanned the area that was ready for the sweep with the Magnetometer. She went to the top of the hill on the south-west corner of the search grid and walked forward, looking alternately at her path and the screen of the instrument suspended at waist height.

Reaching the base of the hill, she moved half a metre sideways to the next virtual grid line and walked back up the slope. The sweep carried on in this way for the next twenty-three minutes. It was slow and tiring and she was puzzled. There should have been a reading developing on the screen as she walked, representing differences in the magnetic resonance of the soil below ground. Usually, Julia would be able to interpret the readout in terms of historically disturbed and undisturbed soil.

The reading that was developing was different to anything she had seen before, and it puzzled her. It was completely off the scale, dark grey right across the screen. The result indicated a residual magnetic resonance at levels she had never experienced before. Julia heard the cooling fan kick in and felt the case of the instrument. It was far hotter than it should have been, so she switched it off, and made her way down to the base of the hill.

"Take a look at this," she called to Dearden, "I've never had this type of result before."

"What does it mean?"

"There's a powerful magnetic field present. We'll have to get inside the building to see what's going on in there, and I need to get this checked out," she tapped the screen.

Doughty came over, brushing debris from the stump grinder out of his hair. "That's the last one done, Jules. We can start digging as soon as you're ready. I've got the JCB fuelled up at the yard ready to roll."

"OK, get it here as soon as you can, this promises to be very interesting." The odd result of the magnetometer reading puzzled Julia. She rang Frank Dryesdale of Dryesdale Electronics saying there was a problem with the Magnetometer and she needed to get it checked urgently. Within the hour, an engineer arrived from the lab at Warwick University Science Park and met Julia at the hall. He tested the circuitry and upgraded some of the components on the assumption that the instrument had not been designed to cope with a magnetic field as powerful as the one Julia was trying to measure. The engineer also fitted a more powerful cooling fan as an added precaution.

Julia resumed the sweep and the result confirmed that the high magnetic resonance she picked up previously was a permanent feature of the hill. It also showed that the soil, apart from the region where the previous excavations had taken place, and a small local area where there was a dip in the surface, had lain undisturbed for a length of time geological in scale.

The Ground Penetrating Radar needed a crew to operate it because of the difficult terrain, and Dearden and Doughty steadily let the trolley-mounted instrument out on a rope down the face of the hill. Matt Roberts walked behind, guiding it, with Julia calling out directions to keep the instrument on the virtual survey line. After each downward sweep, they hauled the instrument back to the top of the hill, moved it a half metre increment, and repeated the process.

The GPR survey of the hill had been strenuous work, and after they finished they rested. Julia connected the instrument to her laptop and downloaded the results. Unprocessed data began to show up on the screen, but with poor resolution.

She called the others over. "Now for the magic." She clicked an icon on the screen with the name *Gridiron* under it. They watched as the unprocessed image dissolved and gradually started to re-build in a smooth graphic form that developed the shapes within the interior of the Hub. There were floor levels visible, a spiral stairway, and the outline of objects they could only guess the purpose of, solidifying behind the shadowy mass of the outer wall where it lay below ground.

The results showed the cylindrical building continuing downwards through the hill to the forest floor. The pathway they had found led to the outer wall below ground level in the hillside. Tantalisingly she could discern an entrance at the end of it. Julia panned the results and stopped with a sharp intake of breath as she viewed the second-floor level. There were many different shapes in the room, but one stood out. Sitting on a chair was a shape similar to one she had come across previously below a burial site in Wiltshire. She panned away from it quickly. Dearden and the other two men hadn't noticed it and she was careful to avoid the level where the unusually shaped skeletal remains lay. Julia saved the results and minimised the screen and then the others drifted off with chainsaws to log the trees they had felled which were lying about the site.

Julia thought back to when she had found the hidden room at the dig in Wiltshire by accident. She was working in the chamber by herself when one of her gold and diamond ear studs had dropped off. It had landed in the sandy soil and the more she probed for it the more it sank into the soil. She went topside for a metal detector.

When she had scanned the soil, the signal was far greater than she had expected it to be from an ear stud. She remembered how, as she dug, the anticipation grew about what could lie below, and how her heart rate had quickened. It had been a memorable moment. One that usually only occurs in archaeology once or twice in a career. She had gone out of the chamber to where her team were working and told them she had come across a detail that was fragile and they were not to disturb her.

To be doubly certain she would not be disturbed, she had put a rope across the entrance with a red 'No Entry, Work In Progress' sign hung on it, and carried on digging. She had found the earring but the signal from the metal detector persisted so, with some difficulty due to the sandy nature of the soil, she had dug down still further.

The shiny metallic plate she found was unexpected. Clearing the soil away from it, she lifted the plate and saw a flight of steps, which she descended into a lower chamber. A soft glow giving adequate light came from the walls. She guessed it could have been a control room, but it was like nothing she had ever seen before. In the middle of the room was a large chair, and in the chair was a skeleton sitting in front of a panel with keys similar to a computer keyboard. The skeleton was large and humanoid, but definitely not human.

Julia had examined the remains and the rest of the room. She took photographs and made extensive notes. Dating was imperative so she plastic bagged a small item from the chamber before she re-sealed it and covered it with soil. She had wanted to ensure the chamber's secrecy until she felt able to handle the challenges its revelation would bring. She remembered trying to put the find to the back of her mind because of the uproar it would cause if it became common knowledge.

The complex moulded object Julia had taken was made of a form of moulded plastic and had no apparent purpose. She had it carbon dated and it turned out to be far older than any manufactured object ever found, and it matched nothing previously discovered. It excited the curiosity of the technician who conducted the dating, but she managed to swear him to silence by threatening to make public some details she had overheard about his private life. Afterwards, she locked the object in her safe at Moat Field Cottage and kept the presence of the lower chamber secret from everyone, apart from her father.

* * *

She scrutinized the image of the second floor. What she could see on the screen at the Leofwin's Hundred dig was similar. It seemed they had migrated from the larger site in Leofwin's Hundred, and had a presence in Wiltshire.

Julia turned to see if anyone was about. Dearden and the others were still working on the felled trees by the clearing.

She had to handle what was inside the building with caution.

The skeletal shape arranged on the chair matched what she had found in Wiltshire. Compared to a human skeleton it was tall, with a large cranium. There was a small chest with two longish arms. A spine continued to a small pelvic region, from which protruded two long legs. Nearby she could see a different skeleton. Its cranium had a long nasal protrusion, following the vertebrae down the spine there was a thorax, from which two arm-like appendages protruded, and then there were the bones of another region with four legs, which made the whole skeleton vaguely insect-like. It could be an animal companion, she thought, maybe like a dog to a human. Whoever it had been, sitting on the chair in the second level of the Hub, had an affinity for creatures not of their kind.

Julia felt uneasy about the issues the skeletons in the Hub raised. It would be difficult for archaeology and science to accept the intervention by an alien race sometime in the Earth's past, which was why she had covered up the Wiltshire find. She did not want to upset the balance. It crossed her mind that similar issues could be why Maxwell Dearden and Nathaniel Devenish had covered their excavations back up. She moved the image on the screen because she sensed Dearden and Matt Roberts coming toward her. Whoever went into the building first would have to be prepared.

She pushed a memory stick into the USB port and saved the results of the Gridiron program.

"What do we do now?" Roberts asked.

"After a few more tests we go back to the hall. I need to write the results up."

Julia held a meter used for testing residual electrical charge an inch away from the wall of the Hub. A powerful positive charge was present and holding. The unusual electrical nature of the place had to be by design, she reasoned, but its purpose was not apparent. Her knowledge of electronics was insufficient to understand what was going on.

* * *

"Jules, what were you doing with that gadget you were holding up to the wall?" Doughty asked later, from the comfort of his chair in the great hall.

"It tests electrical potential and it's telling me the Hub has an unusually high positive potential. I'm wondering what we are dealing with."

"Yeah, more questions have been raised than we've got answers for," Dearden said.

"How shall we start the dig, Jules?" Doughty asked.

"We'll excavate where you found the path, wide at first and as we progress toward the entrance we'll narrow the trench down. It'll need shoring up, and we'll form a timber roof for protection against a cave-in."

"I hope we can open the door when we get to it."

"There is always uncertainty with a dig, but where there's a door there's always a way to get to what's on the other side."

Over the course of the evening, the logistics of the dig were finalised, and Dearden had a rising sense of anticipation. The following morning would see the project his father started and left incomplete, moving forward once again.

16

Matt Roberts arrived with the JCB at 8 o'clock in the morning, and within half an hour of him pulling into the yard, he had driven the machine to the bridge over Shadow Brook. He backed the front wheels off after Doughty shouted a warning when the logs started to spread under the weight. There was no option but to spend time strengthening the bridge to make it more permanent.

Matt Roberts shuttered the bridge, and with the logs as a resilient core, they mixed and poured quick setting concrete. While they were waiting for it to set, they continued to prepare the site at the Hub for excavation. The ground sweep of the forest for the intruders Red Cloud warned them about continued.

Julia had come to terms with keeping the Hub out of the public domain. After all, she had done the same with her Wiltshire find so she had no real grounds for complaint. If Jem *had* experienced what he claimed and the Hub was the gateway to another place in time the potential would be enormous. If they could get hold of it, power hungry individuals or government agencies would exploit its potential for military use. The trespassers in the forest were intensely interested too, and after internal turmoil where Julia had to rethink the basis of her work ethic, she decided that Jem and the others were right to keep the place secret from the outside world and have their firearms ready for use.

It was four days before they were confident that the concrete slab over Shadow Brook had set and gained maximum strength. Matt Roberts drove the JCB up to it, gunned the engine and gently drove onto the bridge as dusk was falling.

There was no movement, so they planned to excavate next day.

Matt Roberts assigned himself the task of patrolling the area in camouflage gear, keeping his wild hair in control with a bandana. He had a favourite knife, a Bowie he called Mavis after a previous girlfriend he ditched because of her sharp and destructive tongue. A set of throwing knives completed his arsenal. Always selected as part of a SHaFT mission if there were jungle incursions, Roberts was a master of survival because of his knowledge of the environment, and his stealth.

Roberts reasoned that the trespassers would gravitate toward the Hub because of their apparent interest in it, so the method he devised for patrolling was to circle it low and silent at a respectable distance so that any threat would be between him and the Hub. From the undergrowth, where he was invisible, he could place one of the throwing knives close enough to an intruder to make him surrender without spending too much time thinking about it.

Uberatu was aware of Dearden's added security, and he was uncomfortable with the increased presence of Dearden's team around the House of the West Wind, so he took most of his tools out of the oak tree hideout. It was a temporary move and as he fastened the camouflaged cover in place, he decided to return to it at night. Back in the basement at number twenty-two Stephenson's Terrace, Uberatu rang the phone number of an acquaintance. After a few rings, the person answered in a vaguely foreign accent.

"All right, I will see you later, and I'll pick Beggs up on the way," the man said, after a brief discussion.

Uberatu put the phone down and redialled. It was a number Antony Beggs had given him a few days before. He outlined his plan to the man he phoned, who was known as the Monkey.

If there were a difficult job to do with trees, arborists across

Warwickshire would contact the Monkey to help them. With no fear of heights, he would skip from bough to bough, chainsaw ticking over ready for use as it swung on a lanyard at his side.

"It will have to be done at night, do it on the quiet, and I'll pay you well."

"When's the full moon?" asked the Monkey.

"Are you suggesting I'm a lunatic?" Uberatu growled, taking the Monkey's question far too personally.

* * *

Matt Roberts was coming to the end of another stealthy circuit of the Hub. As he crept low to the ground, he saw something glinting in the sunlight a few feet ahead of him. When he got to it, he saw it was a screwdriver with a yellow and black handle.

He studied it, wondered what it was doing there. There was no tarnishing so it had not been in the open for long. He crouched further to the ground looking around defensively in case it was a trap. There was no one around, only Jem and the others working over at the Hub. Roberts saw a group of hazels, five of them coppiced at one time in a tight bunch near a patch of brambles. Elm and oak trees were there in profusion, one of the oaks was large, not as big as Old Jack, and it was an odd shape.

Roberts could see that at some point in its history, lightning had struck it, but it had recovered and it was healthy. At first glance, he thought it was two trees growing out of the same massive trunk. Its shape was abnormal, so he went over to it keeping low to the ground, his eyes moving rapidly, taking in the surroundings and alert for movement.

He crept around the tree, looking at the crevices in its gnarled trunk until he came to the fissure caused by lightning.

Something embedded in the trunk caught his eye and he moved closer to examine it. It was a bolt with a wing nut on it. The dull colour of the metal made it blend into the tree but Matt Roberts' keen eyes quickly picked out three more bolts with wing nuts. A vague, ragged line in the bark traced its way from wing nut to wing nut. Roberts grasped one of the nuts and tried undoing it but it was too tight. He silently made his way to the Hub.

"Jem, got any pliers?"

"Yeah, hold on."

"I think I've found where the opposition have been hanging out, come and look."

Roberts indicated with a finger to keep quiet, and they walked the forty or so yards to the tree. Roberts pointed out the wing nuts and loosened them with the pliers, then spun them off. There was the stub of a sawn-off branch projecting from the trunk. Roberts grasped it and pulled. A cover made to blend in with the bark of the tree came away, exposing a cavernous space inside the oak. Dearden took a torch from his pocket and shone it into the cavity.

"They've been right on our doorstep all the time," Dearden exclaimed, as he shone his torch around the interior. The beam picked out a covered peephole drilled through the trunk in the direction of the Hub.

"Cunning devils." Roberts felt faintly envious of the work inside the tree as he squeezed into the earthy smelling interior after Dearden. He saw tools hanging on nails knocked into the bole of the tree and there was a box of tools on the earth floor.

"We've spent enough time here. We don't want to let them know we've found the hideout." Dearden backed out of the oak. "Let's get the cover back on."

"OK, but how's about we set up some countermeasures when we've sealed it up," Roberts explained his plan to

Dearden. It was a simple idea, and it had to do with a plant.

Matt Roberts had an encyclopaedic knowledge of flora and fauna that enabled him to survive in the wild. He knew what was edible, and what could prove fatal in seconds. During one of his circuits of Leofwin's Hundred, Roberts had come across a clump of Giant Hogweed, Heracleum Mantegazzianum. He noted its position, intending to tell Dearden to get rid of it because of what would happen to anyone who touched it.

Roberts spoke to Templestone about his plan and they waited until after dark. Roberts wore thick combat clothing, goggles and rubberised gloves to handle the plant. With Templestone standing guard, Roberts circled the Hogweed with a sharp spade, the same way he would circle an opponent with Mavis the knife before he started to dig the plant up.

They carted the Hogweed back to the hollow oak in a wheelbarrow then Roberts dug a hole for it, positioning it in such a way that the foliage would need to be pushed aside to get to the wing nuts holding the cover in place on the tree. They watered the plant in, scattered fallen leaves around it, and stepped back to admire their work.

* * *

As Doughty drove the Land Rover into the forest at the start of the next day's activity, Templestone, sitting at the back and still bleary eyed, sniggered as he told Dearden and the others about the night's events. They arrived at the clearing and after they offloaded the gear from the trailer, Julia pulled a number of context cards out of her rucksack.

"We write the details of a dig on these cards for reference. If there are any questions about finds, we can refer back to the context cards to get answers that are traceable back to the source. In our case, position of artefacts"

151

Dearden looked at the top of the hill and felt a thrill of anticipation. A thought crossed his mind that they were about to cross a frontier they could regret and that it might be better to leave the building untouched. After initial enthusiasm, his father Maxwell, and Nathaniel Devenish before him filled their excavations back in and left the old building alone. Dearden wondered if they had been afraid of what they found inside, and had covered the entrance back up to keep whatever they found locked away.

Roberts had a metre wide bucket on the JCB to make quick progress. During the initial stages of the dig, he centred the excavation on the ancient pathway. The soil was of an open texture, so he had to widen the trench to prevent collapse into the working area, and soon came to the point where the sides of the trench needed shoring with timber.

Five metres out from where they expected to come to the wall the finds started. The first became visible when a slice of soil fell away from the face of the trench and revealed the circular base of a large earthenware object. Matt saw Julia waving her arms and he opened the cab window.

"Back off, Matt! Back off." Roberts heard Julia yelling from her position on the hill where she was watching the progress. He stopped the excavator with the bucket poised in mid-air and Julia scrambled down to where Dearden and Doughty were carefully removing soil from the object with their hands. She went to a toolbox and came back with an assortment of trowels and brushes, and got the others to move aside. The base of the earthenware object was large. Julia forced herself to steady her hands, which were shaking with nervous excitement.

"Take it easy with this sort of find, it could be fragile. Take the soil away as if you were handling a land-mine." She stood up and took photographs then recorded the location on a context card, measured from virtual datum points.

They eased the object out of the soil. It was a large earthenware container about eighty centimetres long with a wooden plug sealing the opening. It was heavy and came out without damage. Its contents rattled as they gently placed the container on its base away from the dig. The plug was too far inside the neck of the container to get a grip on it, so they decided to open it when they got back to the Hall. Julia went back to where the earthenware jar had been lying and saw the glint of metal in the hole.

"Can we have a torch here? There's something else." Dearden took the torch from his pocket and shone it into the hole. A fine tracery of metal and the glint of gemstones shone in the torchlight.

"If I'm not mistaken that's gold set with carnelian." Julia recognised the style. Roberts revved up the engine of the digger. "Matt, back off!" Julia gestured for Roberts to move the JCB away. He gunned the engine and reversed the machine into the clearing, switched off, and scrambled up to where the others stood around the finds.

Julia had the torch and shone it on the object in the hole.

"What do you think it is?" Doughty asked.

"I'm not sure. There's something else in there too." She took a camera out of her pocket and photographed the metallic object and a small ivory coloured mass about an inch long lying below it.

"Looks like bone, could be a phalange. With any luck, the rest of the skeleton will be here." She stood up from her cramped position. "Welcome to my world guys. Its spades from now on, then trowels and brushes. This is where the hard graft starts."

Dearden's mobile rang. He had to go to the studio.

"I'll keep you informed," Julia called, as he walked off down the track back to the hall.

She brushed more soil away and while the metallic object was still in-situ, she ran some tests on it. It was gold, of the highest quality, and the brushing revealed the pommel of a sword inlaid with semi-precious stones. She brushed the hilt clear, and then the hand guard where there was finely chased detail that looked like winged lizards. She brushed more soil away and revealed some characters she recognised as Anglo-Saxon Runic, engraved into the blade, which was partly withdrawn from a scabbard. It took her a second or two to get her mind into gear and keep the surge of excitement down.

"This sword was a gift to someone. They often used to name their swords in Anglo-Saxon times, particularly if they were valuable. This word says *Aelfrythsgiefu*, it means Aelfryth's gift."

"Who did Aelfryth give it to, do you know?" Doughty asked as Julia wrote a description of the sword and its position on a context card.

"Aelfryth gave it to Earl Leofwin. She was his wife. It must have been a treasured possession." She went back to the task of easing the weapon from the soil. "This is really rather odd." She examined the scabbard, which was made of hardwood, with gold facings. "This wood should have rotted years ago. I can understand the gold surviving with no deterioration, but not the scabbard." Julia took a soil sample for testing.

She brushed the artefact off. "Let's have a look at the sword, the blade should be eaten with rust, unless. . ." Against all her instincts and ingrained training, she grasped the hilt and pulled the sword from its scabbard. Its metal rang as the blade bent slightly and then whipped back straight. "Yeah, the soil conditions are abnormal to have preserved this." The Eastern Damascened blade was exquisite, with a design of iron, fused into the steel of the blade with the art of an ancient sword maker's craft. Below the guard was a symbol Julia recognised as the tree of life, the taproot ran down the length of the blade. It was a handsome weapon. Julia took Aelfrythsgiefu to the top of the hill, and when she was there, she lifted the sword to the sky, testing its perfect balance. Dearden came back into the clearing with Tomahawk as Julia lifted the sword.

"It's Aelfrythsgiefu," Julia shouted down to him. "Earl Leofwin's sword." Sunlight flashed on the blade. Dearden was puzzled as scrambled up the hill to where she was standing. When he drew near to her, she brought the sword down with the point toward him and the stones decorating the pommel glinted in the sunlight. She replaced it in its scabbard and laid it on the ground. "All ready for use again, as good as it was when it was buried. That's weird."

"I've seen the sword before, Jules, it's the one Leofwin drew on me." Dearden looked at the detail, the pommel with its carnelian cabochons and filigree was unmistakeable. It was the sword the Anglo-Saxon threatened him with a few days ago, and now it was lying on the ground dusted with the remnants of soil. He could still picture Leofwin replacing the sword in its scabbard, and he recalled a detail that was insignificant at the time.

Julia bent to pick the sword up again.

"Jules, leave it. Listen to me, this is important." He put his hand on her shoulder and she straightened up.

"On the other side of the pommel from the one we can see now, there is a stone that should be identical to the one you can see. It is red, and should be rounded, like that one." He pointed at the uppermost stone.

"The stone on the other side of the pommel is damaged. Half of it is missing. There is battle damage on the guard as well. Deep cut marks where another blade has struck it. There are three of those marks, two are parallel to each other and another one crosses them at roughly thirty degrees. Look at it and tell me what you see."

She picked up the sword, turned it over. She looked at the semi-precious stone and then at Dearden. "How the hell did you know that? Unless . . ."

"Unless I had seen it before. Hallucinations my arse. I've been telling you all along, I *have* seen this sword before, and I *did* see the Saxon, *and* my father did." Dearden looked triumphant.

* * *

Julia was carefully brushing soil off the skeleton, removing it from above and around the bones. She left the remains resting on a cushion of soil underneath them. She came to the disarticulated skull, lying in an un-natural position in relation to the vertebrae.

"What's this?" Doughty, at Julia's side, pointed to a round hole in the forehead with inward splintering. He shifted it so that Julia could see the damage.

"The hole's too small for him to have been struck with a pike." She picked the skull up carefully, with reverence, intending to place it correctly at the top of the spinal column. As she lifted it, there was a light rattling noise from inside and something dropped to the ground with a light thud.

Julia looked at the object as she would an opponent in unarmed combat. Dearden saw the uncertainty in her eyes.

"Jem . . . a bullet isn't in context below those Anglo-Saxon artefacts."

"And now we've got a murder scene on our hands." Dearden pulled Tomahawk's leash. The wolf was showing too much interest in the bones.

"It may have been a murder scene at one time, but these bones are historic, and that's the problem." Julia shivered. She looked behind her. The forensic side of her mind was in denial.

"It's not a murder scene now. The magnetometer proved this soil has been undisturbed for a thousand years. So *how* was this person shot with a modern bullet, and buried all those years ago?" She pulled her coat around her as a cold breeze blew across the clearing.

They worked for another hour around the skeleton, and then stopped for the day. Matt Roberts stayed on to guard the site overnight. Roberts was a loner, happier in the open than inside. He would find a strategic place to hide up and catnap, with one eye open, ready for action.

* * *

Later in the evening, after moving the long table out of the way in the great hall, the earthenware container was on a plastic sheet on the floor. There was a cloth nearby, a bucket of cold water, a hair dryer, and a coil of thin rope. Dearden and Doughty were there, and they had set the camcorder up on a tripod and arranged some studio lights and a diffuser around the container. Doughty switched on the camcorder as Julia drilled a pilot hole into the centre of the plug, and then she screwed in a substantial hook.

"Now the rope," she tied one end to the hook and handed the other end to Templestone. "Jem, see the cloth over there? Soak it in the bowl and wring the surplus out will you."

He passed it to her and she tied the cold cloth around the top of the earthenware container, then she picked up the hair dryer.

"Why the hair dryer?" Dearden asked.

"Don't hassle, let's see if it works."

Templestone whispered into Dearden's ear. "She'll shrink the wooden plug by applying heat. It'll be in an expanded state with the moisture in it now. The wet cloth'll stop the earthenware shrinking."

Julia switched on the hair dryer and directed the hot air over the wooden plug. Steam started to rise and the top surface of the wood lightened in colour as moisture in it dried out. A slight crack appeared between the wooden plug and the earthenware.

"Mitch, hold the container while Bill pulls the plug."

Templestone pulled. Nothing happened.

He pulled a bit harder and with a loud pop, the plug came free from the container and they all moved in, trying to see inside it.

Julia sniffed the air, getting close to the rim. "Smell this," she held the plug up.

Templestone sniffed, "Pure turpentine."

"Yeah, the inside's been kept bug-free by the resinous atmosphere. Can we have more light here?"

Doughty brought the studio lights closer.

"Let's have the camcorder here."

Doughty shifted the tripod closer and aimed the camera down to get a better view of the interior. Julia looked into the pot. It looked three-quarters full of golden objects, some inlaid with semi-precious stones. Their beautiful brilliance reflected the photographic lights. Julia knelt and reached inside the jar.

"Mitch, are you getting this?"

"I am. Camera's rolling."

"Then take a look at this."

Like a conjurer on a stage of magic, Julia brought out piece after piece of the finest jewellery, laying it on a cloth Dearden had grabbed from the sideboard. There were exquisite pieces of jewellery, golden platters, the precious metal incised and chased with mythological designs. There were knives, coins and objects with fine filigree inlaid with carnelian and agate.

Julia was exuberant, "This is even better than Sutton Hoo, everything's intact," she commented to the camera as she reached in and removed the next item. She held it close to the camera and laid it on the cloth with the other treasures. "There is no damage on any of this, and it's definitely Anglo-Saxon, see the runic designs?" She picked up an exquisite bracelet and held it up to the camera. She reached deeper into the jar and brought the next item from the darkness inside, and dropped it as if it stung her. The back of her hand went to her mouth and the sound she made was a mix of fear and surprise as she looked at the black plastic casing and five letters spelling out the word *Nokia*.

"Now that's a real challenge, Jules. Are you sure the soil was undisturbed?"

"Of course I'm sure, do you think I'm stupid? The equipment I used is state of the art, and it was set up correctly before you ask."

"So how did the mobile get there?"

"It looks as though they had a visitor back then wouldn't you think?" The group were used to seeing Julia sure of herself, sometimes a trifle arrogant. She sat down and looked at the others in turn. The room had gone quiet.

Dearden picked the mobile phone up from where Julia dropped it. He tried the switch.

"That's not surprising." He went to a cupboard and rummaged through a box of spares. He pried the back from a similar Nokia phone, fitted the battery into the one from the earthenware vessel, and connected it to a charger.

It took a little while, but then the phone lit up and Dearden flicked through the menu.

"Is there anything?" Doughty asked.

"There is, it's working." He held it up for them to see, then went into the menu looking for the contacts. He found the 'my number' setting and opened it up.

"Bingo, here's the owner, someone named Otto Fengel."

Templestone wrote the details down as Dearden read them out.

Julia continued easing each bone from the earth. She was putting the remains that she had numbered and photographed in a padded box that lay on the ground. Dearden was helping, and at the same time trying to reconcile himself with the latest bizarre event. With his mobile phone in the treasure hoard, the man named Fengel must have shifted back in time, but how had he done so, and when?

Mitch Doughty and Roberts were digging forward by hand, adding more shoring to the sides and top of the trench, making a tunnel as they went. It was hot with the heat of work lights in the enclosed space, so they worked in twenty-minute shifts with ten-minute breaks in between. Templestone was sitting behind a heavy crate at the entrance with his Smith and Wesson.

Julia finished extracting the last bone of the skeleton from the earth, laid it with the rest and she and Dearden went to the dig and shared the work. Nothing of interest was unearthed at first, apart from pieces of pottery and fragments of clay pipes, presumably discarded by workers who had helped Nathaniel Devenish with his excavation. As they dug further in, they came across a few shards of the material used to build the Hub. Julia wrapped and bagged each one after numbering them and recording their GPS referenced positions. As soon as she had time to spare, she would take them to Charley Ludgate at Warwick University Physics for analysis.

* * *

In the basement at twenty-two Stephenson's Terrace, Uberatu was sitting in front of his computer screen gazing at the forest scene. He tried to zoom in on what was going on. The Monkey had been busy the night before. It had been a full moon and in the ethereal light, he had worked quietly and efficiently. The result of his work, disguised high up in the twisting branches of an elm tree was a miniaturised high-powered video-cam, focussed on the hill and the clearing. It had all-round manoeuvrability and Uberatu was able to control it with a small joystick on a handset from his basement. A powerful amplifier lying in the heart of a decaying log transmitted the signal from the camera on the elm tree to Uberatu's basement.

But there was a major problem. The wooden shelter erected over the excavation was hiding what was going on with the dig and he might just as well be blind.

"What a waste of damn money," Uberatu shouted at Snarl. "The Monkey's installed a blind bloody video-cam." The dog wagged its tail.

"If you go down to the woods today," he sang wildly out of tune to Snarl. He put his coat on, "You're sure of a big surprise. And you can stop wagging your damn tail." The malice in his voice matched the wild look in his eyes.

He hated the wooden structure they were building and wanted to destroy it by fire. He imagined flames scorching the people thrashing around inside. He hated everything. He needed to hit something and looked at Snarl, who recognised the symptoms. The dog's doleful eyes were unflinching, and it growled a savage warning.

17

"Who's it going to be?" Dearden asked the group sitting in the great hall. They agreed on the need for more manpower, but the concept of temporal shift wouldn't have to disturb whoever they chose.

"Leon Wynter," Mitch Doughty suggested. Those gathered discussed his merits, and when they agreed he would be the best choice Dearden rang him.

Leon, 'Lee' Wynter was Afro-Caribbean. He had dreadlocks and an inbuilt sense of rhythm. If music was about, he bounced to it. Like all his SHaFT compatriots he had a deep-down sense of justice, and the temperament to hit hard to get rid of injustice, no questions asked.

When Leon was ten his parents moved from the West Indies to the United States searching for a better life.

They had relatives who lived in the Bronx, and the ten-year-old Leon's introduction to New York was by a diet of Bronx gang and drug culture. He avoided the drugs, and experience taught him which gang to join to be top of the action. At the age of eighteen, he joined the US Navy and four years later, he was a Navy SEAL.

After ten years of front-line and covert action, Wynter wanted a change. He left the Navy and the United States with an illustrious but clandestine military career behind him. He ended up in Warwickshire in the UK with an English girl he met while backpacking around Europe. One day he was motoring through Knowle when he bumped into Jem Dearden.

Dearden had been pulling out of the parking space by the side of the studio. Wynter was driving down the Warwick

Road. They met in the middle with both vehicles dented. There was a heated exchange followed by unarmed combat. Two police officers stopped what could have ended up nasty when they walked out of a local store and cooled the situation down. Dearden and Wynter agreed to differ. After the circle of onlookers drifted away, the two protagonists grinned at each other and drifted into The Barley Mow. They forgot their differences over a drink and soon became firm friends. A few months later Dearden introduced Wynter to Arthur Doughty and SHaFT.

With Wynter's experience, and his ability to think in three dimensions, he was an ideal addition to the team Dearden was building to deal with the Leofwin's Hundred situation. Wynter should be able to adapt to the fourth dimension, the temporal one if the need arose.

The Mini Moke pulled up at the gates, the sound of Rap from its 1200-watt Vibe Slick Boomers was plastering the air with the joys of sun and beach.

"Leon's here," Doughty shouted as he caught the beat threading its way into the workshop where they had drifted in ready to commence the day's plan.

Dearden pressed connect when the intercom buzzed from the gate.

"Yo, bro," came the introduction in New York Bronx from the outer end.

"Yo, Lee, come on in my man." Dearden entered into the spirit of things. Lee's presence always lightened the mood however tense the situation. The booming grew louder as the diminutive vehicle with its large presence careered into the gravel car park and came to rest near the studio door.

It was seven months since they had last been in touch. The event had involved SHaFT and a call for assistance from *Y*

Wladfa Gymreig, the Welsh Colony in Argentina. Terrorists captured some of the community and they were holding them to ransom. A four-man SHaFT unit, Dearden, Doughty, Wynter, and Alan 'Gren' Mills landed at night on the mainland near Puerto Madryn. Wynter was in his element as Finisher in the mission. His Afro-Caribbean skin made him blend in during the latter part of the night operation to save the wives and children of well-known government officials.

Wynter found languages easy. Although loud on the outside, his personality was one of quiet reserve when needed. He brushed up on Welsh before the operation and it came in handy at the last minute when he whispered instructions to the huddled bunch of captives in the darkness at the back of the cavern. They all made it out alive, and then Wynter had gone back in to make sure the kidnappers would never kidnap again.

He was uncertain about the events in the forest.

"You sure it's on the level, man?" he asked when they told him what was happening. "You sure there's no woojies there?" he asked Dearden.

"It is physical, Lee, nothing psychic, if that's what you mean. It's weird but there's scientific evidence to prove it."

"So you reckon you could visit your great granddaddy's granddaddy from years back?"

"Looks like it's possible, but there would have to be strict safety measures to avoid a paradox," Julia said.

"Kiss my ass." Wynter smiled in disbelief.

Matt Roberts looked serious. "Lee, this stuff really is happening. We wouldn't have wasted your time, or ours getting you here on false pretences."

"S'pose not. OK Jules, you're the sensible one of this bunch. What do you think? Is it some government thing, some left-over secret weapon thing from the Second World War?"

"It's not. There's proof the Hub is hundreds of years old at least."

Wynter looked at the ground, smiling. They could tell he was unconvinced. Templestone knew how to persuade him.

"Leon, if what they're saying turns out wrong I'll personally give you a grand." Wynter looked up sharply. He could tell Templestone was serious.

"You're on, my man." He grabbed Templestone's outstretched hand to cement the deal. "That's what I like to hear, Priest, the promise of cash. OK Jem, what's the plan?"

"We carry on digging, tomorrow at nine."

* * *

They were inside the tunnel early. Wynter and Doughty were removing soil from against the wall after inserting the final pieces of side and roof timbers. Wynter swapped his shovel for a trowel and Templestone was still at the entrance to the tunnel with his Smith and Wesson on display in case anyone challenged them.

Wynter's trowel rang as it hit metal, and a patch of silver material shone in the floodlights as soil fell away. Dearden took over and worked urgently at clearing the remaining soil away with Matt Roberts bucketing it out of the tunnel until a door fully eight feet tall was exposed. Inscribed into its surface was lettering, script-like shapes that glinted in the floodlights.

"I don't recognise those characters. They're like nothing I've come across before." Julia moved in to get a better look." Dearden was brushing the soil away from a latch set into a hollow in the door. Julia tugged his sleeve. "Are you sure we're ready for this?" she asked quietly, so the others couldn't hear.

"Dead sure." Dearden sounded upbeat.

"There are no precedents." She thought about the enormity of going through the door. "Jem, what's happening in this place is crazy, just be careful."

"Come on Jules, think of the possibilities of seeing the fossil before it died," he said. She smiled. "Anyway Jules, there's too much of *me* invested in this. I must go inside to find out why Dad covered the entrance back up."

"OK. But before you go inside there are some precautions you need to take, let's get some kit together." She went to the clearing and picked up a box with *First Entry* written on the lid.

18

There was a fresh breeze blowing across the clearing. It was pleasant after the heat from the lamps in the tunnel. They gathered around the First Entry box.

"A word of warning. There's something in there you may find disturbing."

"Now the lady tells us," Wynter said.

"It showed up in the GPR sweep. When you get inside, be prepared for something radically different. I don't want to colour your judgment, so I'm not saying anything else." She unlocked the military looking First Entry box and took out a yellow hand-held unit.

"It's a GasTect 'Sniffer'. This gizmo will detect any type of abnormal air conditions." She gave it to Dearden and opened an aluminium case.

"This is an NBC suit. I know you are familiar with these, but this one is different. It does the usual toxic environment protection, with twenty minutes of safety guaranteed, then ten minutes un-guaranteed. It's the best in its field, with two-way audio and visual comms built into the helmet so we'll be in touch throughout the entry. We'll see what you see, and hear what you say, so remember to give us a commentary as you go through. We'll do a full audio-visual recording of the entry session." She handed him the suit.

"All that's way over the top," Doughty said. "Max Dearden went into the Hub and he was OK for years afterwards."

"It's not over the top. Believe me, we need to know exactly what's in there. Remember, we're doing it the professional way. This kit will give us a full analysis of the atmosphere in the Hub. I want to know what I'm breathing when I go into it."

"How long will it take to analyse the sample?" Roberts asked.

"Five minutes at the most. This is the plan. Matt, you help Jem get suited up and check his life support systems. Jem, once you are inside, shut the door and go one level up or higher if possible. You must get well away from the newly let in fresh air unless there's an airlock inside. Wait five minutes for the alarm to sound that will tell you the sampling is complete. After that, come back to the entrance, place the Sniffer outside, then go back in and shut the door. I'll run the analysis through the computer. I'll tell you the result over the comms. If there's no toxicity, we'll join you inside."

"What if it's not OK, Jules?" Wynter asked. "If the atmosphere's toxic, do you have a scrub-down unit?"

"Yep." Julia reached over and removed the contents from a yellow plastic drum on the trailer, and started to set it up.

Dearden was suited up and in the tunnel facing the door to the Hub. He reached for the handle. It moved easily downwards. The others heard him breathing on the two-way unit and they had a view of the door through the helmet video-cam, on a laptop that Julia set up.

"Here we go." He pulled and then pushed. The door wouldn't budge. "Oh shit . . . that's the second time I've forgotten that. After all this bloody effort, it's the same as the one at the top, locked solid."

"That's all we want." Julia snapped the laptop shut. She was annoyed and frustrated. "It's obvious when I think about it . . . we need the same conditions that were about when you got into the place."

He nodded. "Don't blame yourself, Jules. I should have remembered; the atmosphere was loaded with electricity. We need the lightning again." Julia nodded. She sat on the ground and leant against the wooden shuttering at the entrance to the tunnel. She looked about ready to give up.

"So we'll have to wait," Dearden said. He came to where Julia was sitting and put his hand on her shoulder. "So be it, Jules. One thing's a fact; this place won't go away in a hurry." He tried to lighten the disappointment, but she shrugged his hand off.

Doughty checked the weather forecast on his mobile phone.

"Cloudy for three days according to the Met Office. Temperature is high for this time of the year; then it says it'll be changeable with light rain and raised temperatures." There was no indication of the weather they needed.

Tempers frayed during the prolonged wait, and then after five and a half weeks Matt Roberts, who had been working with Doughty re-roofing the stable, came into the workshop. He broke the news about the long-range weather forecast.

"Six days' time, thundery showers, let's hope they've got it right." The mood in the room immediately lightened.

On the day the forecast had predicted rain, they awoke to dark skies. The rain was heavy and the temperature warm. They had a hurried breakfast, put on heavy weather gear, and went to the Hub in an upbeat mood.

They met Roberts who had bivouacked in the tunnel. There was a fire going near the entrance, and he was roasting a rabbit on a twig for a spit. The clearing was saturated, and water was draining in the direction of Shadow Brook, which was almost overflowing with turgid, fast-flowing water carrying debris from the further reaches of the forest. There was thunder in the distance, getting nearer as the sound rolled over the countryside. Dearden suited up again with Matt Roberts' help and they tested the internal support systems while Julia and Doughty rigged a decontamination unit.

Templestone checked his Smith and Wesson and stood at the entrance to the tunnel.

Lightning flashed and thunder came from the near west. Dearden, waiting at the door with the GasTect Sniffer, tried the catch. The door moved easily and silently inward.

Dearden entered cautiously and looked around, checking the locking mechanism on the inside of the door before shutting himself in. He could see the mechanical bolt working, so he pushed the door and it clicked shut. A soft glowing light coming from the walls illuminated the room.

"No torch needed." He put the one he had with him on the floor. He checked the temperature. 21° centigrade. The conditions inside the building, with comfortable heat and lighting, made it seem as though the previous occupants had recently left. He couldn't shake the feeling that something was present, and looked behind him to make sure he was alone.

"Jules, is any of this familiar to you?" Dearden walked further into the room, the camera in his helmet picking up the way he was going.

"Why would it be?"

"I was wondering."

Viewing the scene on the laptop outside, they could see the room clearly. Banks of doors with inscriptions on them lined the wall. Some of the characters looked similar to those on the entry door.

Julia's voice came through the earpiece. "Jem, make sure you carry the Sniffer well away from the entrance."

At the far side of the circular room, Dearden saw the spiral stairway about which his father had written. He went over to it. It went down, as well as up. Looking downwards, he was unable to see any detail past where the stairs curved to the left. He carried the Sniffer up to the next level, where his entry wouldn't have disturbed the atmosphere appreciably.

He reached the top of the stairs and placed the instrument on the floor. Transparent freestanding cases of different shapes and sizes occupied the room. Dearden looked around. "This level goes way back into the hillside, the room is oval, and it's big. Looks as though it's some sort of collection, it's full of exhibits." He walked along an aisle at the centre of the room; looking at the exhibits that he passed so that they were seen through the camera in his helmet.

Julia's voice through the intercom startled him. "Five minutes are up. Get the results from the Sniffer down here. Carry on with your walkthrough afterwards." Dearden retraced his steps to the entrance with the instrument and put it outside. He shut himself back in and went up the stairs to continue the exploration from where he left off.

Outside, Julia was following his progress with rapt attention. "Go to the part nearest the outer face of the hill." Dearden knew why she was asking, and he made his way to the exhibits on the outer edge. He saw that some of them contained the strangest of objects, some non-organic, but some that had been alive.

Attached to each case were labels with extensive information, written in the script that was on the outer door. Portrayed at the bottom of each label was an arrangement of different sized spheres, different on each showcase he came to. Below the spheres, in tabular form were four separate lines, each with multiple characters. Dearden stopped in front of one of the cases and moved closer, to make the finer detail picked up by his camera visible on the screen of Julia's laptop outside.

"Good image, more of those please."

Dearden walked to the circle of cases parallel to the outer wall facing the clearing. "Which way, Jules? I should be above the lower entrance now."

"Go anti-clockwise. The objects I want you to look at aren't far away now." Dearden walked around the outer wall and approached a showcase that was larger than the others were, and markedly different. Intricately worked detail embellished on the framework made it stand out from the other cases. He could see that three of the sides were matt and opaque, but the fourth side he was coming to was catching the light, and it would be transparent.

He stopped at the front of the case and stumbled backwards, his heart began racing. He had similar reaction years before when he was a child. Some kittens had been born at the farm but there was a problem with one of them. The creature was born with two heads. It was mewing pitifully and the young Jem had nightmares about it for months afterwards. Not that the figure exhibited was hideous, like the kitten was. The exhibit was *different*, like a parody of a human, stretched out and disproportionate. The head was too large, it was tall and thin, but most different to a human being was its light green skin colouring.

The being was sitting in an elaborate chair, looking up and forward as if into the distance. It was pointing. Dearden followed the direction of the outstretched arm. On the outer wall near the ceiling was a plaque on which there was a symbol of two spheres with irregularly placed smaller spheres around them. Below that, there were three lines of symbols, and there was a fourth line double-spaced below them.

"OK, we've seen that. Move on will you," Julia's voice sounded unsteady.

There was a skeleton in the next showcase. It looked like a species match to the fleshed-out pointing figure. Its large orbits were black and vacant. Similar to the previous exhibit, the skeletal one was pointing to the plaque on the wall.

He looked over his shoulder. "Are you guys getting this? Have you ever—"

Julia's voice interrupted.

"You've done thirteen minutes, get out now," but he wanted to see more, and went to the next showcase. It was a different skeleton this time, large, the size of a small pony but insect-like, the thorax had two limbs and the abdomen had four. The spine curved upward where it joined the thorax as if the creature walked on the four limbs and used the other two independently. It was like a scorpion but the head was high rather than the tail. Dearden moved past case after case containing creatures and objects, some of them in bizarrely landscaped settings.

Another particularly remarkable exhibit showed a plant-like object that had short stubby legs and a bud-like appendage in place of a head. It appeared to be moving through a jungle-like landscape, and seen through the tendrils of foliage, low in a purple sky, was a triple sun in the process of setting.

"That one's surreal," Dearden heard Templestone say to the others through his earpiece. Time was passing too quickly, and he headed to the stairs. He wanted to see what was up there. As he climbed the stairway, he realised how high each step was.

From the top of the stairs, he could see screens on the wall with seats facing them and in front of the seats were panels with keyboards.

"This looks like a control room." When Julia heard Dearden's comment, it forced a memory to return. When she found the subterranean room in Wiltshire, she thought that it looked something like an aircraft's flight deck. The uneasy feeling she had those years ago came back, and she shivered. The discovery did not fit into any archaeological context. Right or wrong, that uncertainty, with an added measure of fear, had been the reason she decided to cover up the entrance to the Wiltshire vault and try to forget she ever found it. The problem was, it had come back in large measure to haunt her.

* * *

Dearden placed the GasTect outside the door and Julia checked the results. The atmosphere inside the Hub was purer than outside. The only irregularity was a fractionally higher ozone level to normal. She told Dearden, and he immediately stripped off the NBC suit, opened the outer door, and breathed the cool air in. He had been sweltering inside the suit.

Templestone stayed guarding the entrance. He saw Doughty go in through the door and turned back to face the forest, scanning the area for movement. They couldn't afford to drop their guard. His turn to go into the Hub would come later.

"High tension current, if I'm not mistaken," Julia said to Doughty, sniffing the air as soon as she was inside. The smell of the ozone in the building took her straight back to a time with her father when she was in her teens and her dad repaired the vacuum tube television.

"Don't touch that, even when the mains are disconnected," her father Alex warned as he pointed to a transformer connected by a flying lead to the cathode ray tube. "If you touch that before residual current is drained it could kill you." It was a warning she remembered. Strange, and sometimes beautiful she thought, how a scent could transport you back to something that took place a long, long time ago. Whenever she smelt wallflowers, it took her back to the mass of wallflowers outside Moat Field Cottage the year before her mother died. She sniffed the air again. There was definitely high-tension electricity present.

19

It occurred to Templestone that eventually the door would lock again due to the passive activity of the Hub draining the current provided by the electrical storm. He hammered a wedge into the latch, which held it open and allowed them continual access. This raised a security issue because of the interest the intruders were showing, so Templestone suggested they try welding shackles to the door for padlocks and heavy-duty chains. The welding worked and he fitted a high-carbon steel chain and a top of the range tamper-proof padlock to the shackles. "Let them try and get past that," he said, and stood back to survey his work.

Dearden set up sensors that would activate video cameras with infrared capability, one aimed at the tree the intruders were using as a hideout, the other at the entrance to the Hub.

It was the night after a full moon, a *Bomber's Moon*, his father used to call it, when Uberatu's car pulled up by the barn in the field at the back of Leofwin's Hundred. By the light of a torch, he unlocked the door and led three men into the room. He drew a curtain across the window, started the generator and switched on the light. An owl swooped through the chill air, its cry echoing through the forest, and the four men started to plan the night's activity.

Uberatu and Sven Ardnussam, who had the torch, walked through the forest to the Hub. Ardnussam was a large Norwegian who Uberatu borrowed occasionally from Raegenhere's staff at Dracasfeld. Despite his size, this son of Woden was nervous of the forest, so the light from the torch kept wandering. "Keep the light shining in front," Uberatu commanded, nudging the Norwegian's arm. They entered the wooden tunnel at the foot of the Hub. The torch picked out the shining door, with its strange inscriptions and heavy chain.

"They have the door welded," the Norwegian said.

"I can see that you troll, and speak English . . . I've told you not to grunt. Let's get the bolt cutters from the tree."

They went to the oak, where the tools were stored.

"All we need now is for Dracula to show up," Uberatu said, putting his black-bearded face close to Ardnussam's when they arrived at the oak tree, which looked massive in the moonlight. They crept around to the camouflaged cover.

"Look at weed," Ardnussam said, shining the torch on the tall lime-green foliage in front of the cover.

"Triffid." Uberatu was in things-of-the-night mode, ignoring what was there.

"Pliers." He pushed the large plant aside, holding its thick stem away so he could get to the wing nuts to undo them. Ardnussam shone the torch and Uberatu went inside the tree and got the bolt cutters. He pushed his way past the plant again. There was a mild prickling sensation in his hands that he felt on the way back to the Hub, but he thought nothing of it.

"Hey troll, hold the chain."

Ardnussam picked up the loop of chain with one hand, while he tried to keep the torch in his other hand focussed on the chain. In the wavering light, Uberatu looked at the inscriptions on the shining surface of the door at the end of the wood encased tunnel.

"Keep the light still," Uberatu shouted, and seeing Ardnussam's finger, he put the cutters near it and snapped them shut. He sniggered as Ardnussam pulled his hand away with a cry of surprise. "Hold the light steady or I might get your finger by accident." Uberatu grasped the chain in the jaws of the bolt cutters and tried to cut through it. There wasn't even a mark on the chain. He shifted the cutters to the hasp of the padlock but was unable to grip it because of its shape. The wavering torch beam played on Uberatu's hands.

"Look," Ardnussam said.

"Look at what, troll?"

"Hands of you, look." Uberatu saw his hands in the torchlight and he felt a surge of panic. Bright red blotches covered both his hands, and the burning sensation was getting worse.

"Oh, crap. It's that bloody weed." In his panic, Uberatu knocked the torch from Ardnussam's hand and the bulb went out. At the same time, the Moon disappeared behind rapidly moving clouds and twenty yards away in the blackness of the night Matt Roberts gave a good impression of a hunting dog-fox homing in on its prey with a snarling sound. In the tunnel at the entrance to the Hub, chaos and fear took over, followed by Uberatu and Ardnussam crashing through the undergrowth. Dearden's infrared video camera recorded all the panic, sound effects included.

20

Before Uberatu's encounter with the Hogweed, almost too many years to count back into the past, there was an exploratory trip to an 'E' Galaxy, type nine planet. The Travellers found what they were seeking. The topography was gentle and familiar, and they gave the planet the name of their home and they added the character that in their language and writing meant *The Second One*. They recognised similarities in the types of organic growth on the planet.

They shipped one of the great crystals to The Second One and around it built node *NJA 4902385* thus providing a permanent connection into the space-time transfer grid. Used over the millennia, *NJA 4902385* was part of a transfer chain leading to the outer universe. If the shift were not urgent, the Travellers would stay for a while, luxuriating in the pleasant surroundings before moving on.

Many years after the first transfer to *NJA 4902385* had passed into the Great Annals, the node was included in an exploratory transfer sequence across the grid. The target was a newly discovered galaxy that instruments indicated was home to many solar systems.

Initially, when the science of the Super Quantum was in its infancy, there were problems because small quantities of the original crystals were unpredictable. On average one in ten thousand space-timeshifts resulted in a crystal in one of the nodes locking. The molecular structure, normally fluid and manoeuvrable, would become unbalanced and freeze. *NJA 4902385* turned out to be one of the unpredictable crystals.

The group of pioneers were soon aware that the shift across the grid had gone wrong. As they had proceeded from node to node along the plotted course, they knew the process had taken far too long. Normally, with each of the crystals successively warping the grid, a shift would complete within a short space of time, typically in five heartbeats. The instrument showed that twenty-seven heartbeats had passed. The leader, Lan-Si-Nu warned the others who were looking at him for reassurance.

"There is an unstable crystal in the chain. All is not as it should be. We should be at our destination by now." Their course was pre-programmed so they had no option but to proceed and see where they ended up, and afterwards try to correct matters. Although young, Lan-Si-Nu was the veteran of many shifts across the grid, and those less experienced admired him. He over-rode his personal fears and kept his crew calm.

"I don't know which the faulty node is, or where we will end up," Lan-Si-Nu said to the others blurred in the haze of the protective cocoon. Then the control room, which switched from node to node, de-activated, so they needed to go to the portal at the top of the node to find out its identity, engraved into the upper door leading to the outside world. They realised they were fortunate because the frozen crystal in the chain was situated on the world with the privileged name of The Second One.

A faulty crystal could normally be re-calibrated, but the power source for the machinery on The Second One had become faulty too and was operating at a fraction of the required level, making recalibration impossible.

A small number of crews were lost in this way and, unless they could reset the crystalline structure, those crews were truly lost. A particular pulse rate of electron bombardment would restore it to normal activity and afterwards the space-timeshifts could proceed once more with confidence.

Unfortunately, for Lan-Si-Nu and his crew, the equipment to restore the function of the crystal had also turned out to be faulty, but they reasoned that, if marooned they were, the paradise world of The Second One was the best place for the marooning.

Hope was all but lost for a return home. The power system to *NJA 4902385* had been weak when they arrived, now it was failing. There was enough power to provide ambient temperature and background light and to give them a small surplus, but it was insufficient to accomplish any useful heavy-duty mechanical work, let alone to operate a trans-galactic dimensional shift. Electrical storms sometimes spiked the power level, but that only created a local cyclic timeshift. At those times, they would try to communicate with home, so far without success.

Compared to the inhabitants of The Second One, the Travellers were long-lived. Their lives extended to many tens of the life spans of the ones called *Earths* who inhabited the planet. The eight pioneers survived and made forays into the wider world, but gradually, one by one over the passage of time they aged and died, which sometimes made the survivors forget they were on a paradise world.

At night, the three survivors would exit the door on top of the hill and descend into the forest to forage for food. After the cold season, the plants with blue bell-like flowers were their favourite. They would cook these and savour the white ball-like part that grew below ground. Lan-Si-Nu and his two remaining crewmembers were not carnivores. In this way, and in their shunning of violence, they were unlike the inhabitants of The Second One, who could be so gentle and then, with what they falsely thought good reasons, could be so savage to their own kind and to other creatures inhabiting the planet.

When the Travellers first saw one of the Earths, they

thought they were disgusting, but after the passage of time, they became used to their ugliness. The Earths were different proportionally to the dimensional travellers, shorter by about a third, stouter and there was an assortment of skin colours ranging from light to dark, and they stank.

Another Earth named Jem Dearden came to live nearby. Like two others in the past, he became curious about the node and started investigating. He displayed courage and did not seem crooked in his motives. He could be the one to start the Earths on the Path. Lan-Si-Nu observed him closely. Jem Dearden and a small group of Earths became busy around the node and they dug their way through the soil to the lower door as others had done twice before, and they entered the node.

Fen-nu spoke to Lan-Si-Nu and Thal-Nar in their room hidden inside the depths of the hill at the rear of the space of the exhibits. "Shall we say it to them?" he asked. "Shall we give them the words of greeting and welcome?" Lan-Si-Nu was uncertain. He had to be sure the group were not dangerous, and that they would use the powerful new knowledge wisely.

If they turned out to be harmless, the Jem Dearden Earth and the others of his group could be of great assistance, but the contact would have to be with caution, and at the right time.

21

Wynter was panning the camcorder around the room. He focussed on Dearden and the others who were standing in front of the pointing figure to show the comparative size of the alien.

"My guess is that this one's a model, possibly life size, put here for the benefit of whoever passes through the Hub. You can tell the skin's not organic," Julia said.

"Looks like something you'd see in Madame Tussauds." Wynter moved up to the exhibit, taking some footage. "I wonder what the comments by the displays say."

"Hopefully we'll find out sometime. Do you see where this guy's pointing?" Dearden asked. Wynter focussed the camcorder onto the alien and followed its pointing arm to the plaque high on the wall.

"Does it remind you of anything, Jules? Look at the overall shape."

"I think it's a constellation."

"That's my thought, and I think it's where they came from." Julia pondered the interstellar implications. With every day that passed, there were new and remarkable discoveries.

They climbed the stairs to the next level and were in awe of what they saw. Doughty commented that he thought every feature of the room looked ergonomic. This room was sleek, with every engineered surface curved and blended into its neighbour. It was a similar size to the entrance room, and circular in shape. There were eight chairs. A central one at the front was large and ornate, similar to the chair on which the pointing figure sat in the room of the exhibits. In front of the central seat was a panel with keys marked individually with letters from the script they had seen elsewhere in the building.

Wynter went to the panel and touched it. It pivoted easily in multiple directions and Wynter pushed it into position in front of the seat. He tried raising and lowering it. Raised on a plinth behind the central seat, there were three others, and behind those, still higher, were four more seats. All of them were facing three large, faintly illuminated rectangular screens built into the wall.

Matt Roberts sat in the central chair and pulled the panel into position. "What do you think all this is?" he asked no one in particular.

"It resembles a flight deck," Doughty said. "But there are no physical controls, just buttons." He looked around the room. "Controls aside, have you noticed the doors set into the walls? Maybe they're cupboards for storage." He got up to investigate.

"Matt, forget it. The function of this place is a priority." Dearden wanted to get to grips with the timeshift.

"OK, guys, up to the next level?" Wynter said. He walked to the stairs and stood on the second step to video the layout of the room. Then he carried on up.

"The stairs have got deep spaced treads compared to the standard for building." Doughty measured the depth of a tread with a tape measure he had in his pocket. "Eleven-inch risers. Did you notice that the seats in the control room area are taller than we would use but about the same width as ours?"

"So they were tall and slender," Roberts said.

"They must have been, we use seven to eight-inch risers and with these being eleven-inch they might have been a third taller than the average man."

Dearden mentally calculated, "That would mean they were seven and a half foot tall." He tried to picture it standing.

"That sort of height would tie in with the height of the

rooms and doors," Julia said, as she followed the others up the stairs to the third level. There was a mass of equipment in the centre of the room, and there was a humming noise, deep and intense, but only just audible. "That noise is electrical if I'm not mistaken."

Dearden cocked his head on one side to hear the sound better. "Sounds like the noise you hear from a sub-station. That crystal at the centre must be the lower part of the crystal I saw when I was in the upper room." Dearden went over to it. Julia joined him and walked around the crystal, examining the apparatus attached to it. The crystal had eight facets. She touched it, and where she did there was inner movement. The lowest part of the crystal, where the facets met at a point, rested in a transparent socket, and its top disappeared into the ceiling. Halfway up the height of the crystal there was a disc Julia assumed was electronic because of the coils wrapped around it. Joined to the edge of the disc, four immensely thick leads curved upwards to where they joined the outer wall.

Doughty went to a bank of screens around the perimeter of the room. He watched movement on the centre one. "This screen looks active." A series of waveform patterns were moving across the screen, changing in height and pitch.

Wynter focussed on the screens for a few seconds, trying to understand the information, and then headed to the stairway. "Next level up now guys?" He went on up without waiting for an answer.

They came to a door half way up the spiral stairway. Wynter unlatched it and continued to the top. Dearden recognised the room as the one where he and Tomahawk went out of the door into the altered world. "This is where we were the other day," he said. "And there's the proof." Dearden pointed to the muddy footprints from his Wellington boots. He had been close to the wall, looking out, and Tomahawk's paw prints were there too.

"I thought you said the wall was transparent." Julia looked at the outer wall and the ceiling.

"They were transparent when the Hub was active."

"And you walked through that door into Anglo-Saxon England?"

"Too right I did."

"So there's been enough power in the thunderstorm to unlock the doors and partially activate the place, but not enough power to force a timeshift," Matt Roberts suggested.

"Looks like it, and the storm's passed over now, so I think we've missed the show this time."

"Missed the show he says . . . do I want this place to get active when I'm in it?" Wynter rolled his eyes expressively.

Julia left them in conversation and went down the stairs to the level below.

"I'd like to get inside their minds," she heard Doughty say from the level above.

She gazed around the room she had descended to. There were cupboards lining the wall, below them, were workbench type structures. As she bent down to look under one of the benches, she leant on a cupboard door. It was tall, a floor to ceiling door, the only one with a monogram on it. She heard the slightest sound on the inside of the door, a click, and a brief whirring noise. She was jumpy anyway, so the door surprised her and she moved quickly as it started opening. She called out in surprise. There was an answering shout from upstairs and the sound of running. Dearden came down the stairs two at a time, leading the way with his Beretta and saw Julia lifting something out of the cupboard from a shelf that was chest high. She put the object on one of the benches as Dearden and the others fanned out, Roberts with the Bowie, Wynter and Doughty sweeping the area with their pistols.

"What happened?" Dearden asked, Beretta out front, ready.

"False alarm, but thanks . . . I found this." Julia pointed to the object from the cupboard. It was a book with a richly decorated cover, and it felt distinctly cold to the touch.

Dearden tucked the Beretta into his belt.

The book looked inviting and Julia opened it.

None of them realised at the time how significant the moment was. On the first page, there was an illustration of the crystal and the equipment surrounding it. There was page after page of the script they had seen on the information under the exhibits. More than that, as they were to find out in due time, the book was their entry into alien thinking.

22

Uberatu was in a cold sweat with the pain in his hands and the thought of seeing the doctor. Thoughts of amputation crossed his mind. He tried to cancel the unwanted thoughts, but they kept returning unbidden, and his father's voice in his head told him to seek revenge. He shuffled down the road and into the surgery, trying to think past the pain.

"What time's your appointment?" the receptionist asked.

"I couldn't pick the damn phone up to make a damn appointment. He rested his hands on the windowsill near her, and she gagged at the sight.

He would teach her a lesson for gagging at him.

"I'm sorry Mr.—"

"Uberatu, Theodore Uberatu." She fumbled through the records and found his slender file.

"Please wait here." His attitude scared her. Her high heels clicked down a long passage, and she knocked on a door at the end. There was mumbled conversation. Platitudes. A minute later, she came back and went into her room, protected behind the glass partition.

"The doctor will see you at the end of surgery."

"What time?"

"About six-thirty."

"Can't it be sooner?"

"Sorry, Mr Uberatu, he's very busy tonight." Uberatu looked at his watch. It was five forty-five.

He sat on one of the benches and tapped his foot to upbeat music coming loudly through the speakers to help people forget their illnesses. He looked at his digital watch, five fifty-three. The others in the waiting room avoided his eyes and wished the hell he would go away. Two of them walked out.

"It'll have to be after six-thirty," Uberatu said loudly, parodying the receptionist in a singsong voice. She looked up, startled, and he waved his meat-red hands at her.

"Giant hogweed," the doctor said, after a quick look at Uberatu's hands. The way Uberatu had treated Suki Saunders, his receptionist, was bad. He rather liked her and wanted to take her out.

"Giant what?" Uberatu asked.

"Hogweed . . . you've touched hogweed."

"What do I do about that?"

"Keep out of the Sun."

"What the hell are you talking about?"

"Well, it's simple. When that round yellow thing's in the sky you have to stay inside." The doctor wrote out a prescription. "You're in danger of phytophotodermatitis if you expose your skin to sunlight. The pustules on the plant cause the problem. Initially, the skin goes red and itches. Does it itch, mmm . . . yes? It looks as though it does, I don't envy you one little bit. It'll burn like hell after a couple of days and blisters will form with smelly pus in them. The scars might last years, black or purple ones. You will be quite putrid to other people, and they will avoid you like the plague. Did you get anything in your eyes from the plant?

"Why?"

"If you did you might go blind. There are linear derivatives of furocoumarin in the leaves you've touched."

"What do I do now?"

"Don't touch it again. Here's a prescription for a topical steroid ointment. It will help reduce the discomfort. You must use sun lotion whenever the Sun's out from now on because the area contacted by the pustules will be sensitive to light and

U.V." The doctor handed him the prescription. "Mr Uberatu, I'm referring you on to a specialist. Is there anything else you want to talk about?"

There wasn't.

Uberatu walked out without a word and slammed the door shut. The doctor wrote out a referral to Doctor Baldock the psychiatrist because he detected an unpredictable undercurrent in Theodore Uberatu that he thought could be dangerous.

Back at home, Uberatu bandaged his hands after rubbing in some of the medication from the chemist. While he was doing so, he vowed he would repay Dearden in full measure for the cheap trick of the Hogweed.

23

Matt Roberts went to the hollow oak and saw the Hogweed had been disturbed. He was wearing heavy-duty gloves for protection, and he moved the weed to one side to could see if anything else was disturbed. The wing nuts he left tightened in the six o'clock position were all over the place, so he reported to Dearden that the opposition had been back. Templestone's guard duty notched up a couple of gears, and he was sitting behind a barricade of sandbags in the darkness of the tunnel with his Smith and Wesson ready.

Julia had the book she found open on a table in the top room of the Hub. The others were in the room below checking the rest of the cupboards. The one Julia opened accidentally had been the only one to contain information, all the rest contained what they assumed were spare parts. They were stacked and labelled, components in all manner of shapes and sizes. Each one identified with the characters whose shapes they were becoming familiar with, but whose meaning was unknown.

The book seemed to be a form of plastic. Julia bent one of the pages, trying to form a crease but it had an inbuilt structural memory, and it returned to its original state. She opened it past what appeared to be an index. There were photographs of constellations and deep space objects taken from the perspective of Earth. She recognised the constellations of Orion and the Pleiades, Canis Major and others that were familiar to her. She studied the images, and as she turned the pages, she was conscious of subtle differences in the shapes of constellations with which she was familiar.

There was an image of Ursa Major. Julia could see a difference to the Ursa Major with which she was familiar. The stars in the image were tighter together than the position she remembered in the night sky. The implications crowded in on her. When the images were photographed, captured in whatever way they were, the universe was younger, and the spread of the cosmos not as advanced as at present.

Julia turned to another page and saw a diagram of the equipment on the fourth and fifth floor, which included the great crystal, with each part labelled in the alien text. There was a sectional diagram of the building itself on the next page. Referring to the diagram, counting from the forest floor to the highest room there were five levels, and then the surprise, she counted five levels below ground.

Julia called to Dearden, "It's all here, Jem, all the information we need is here. Come and look."

Dearden and then Doughty came up to her from the control room, and she thumbed through the pages to show them the contents.

"It's a workshop manual." Julia turned past the exploded diagram of the apparatus built around the crystal. "And there's astronomical information too." She flicked through the pages of photographs and walked away.

"Do you know what the implications are with this?" she shouted back as she went to the stairs and disappeared to the lower levels.

"Hey, Jules, don't keep us in the dark," Doughty shouted.

"Just look at the photographs Mitch," she called up the stairs. "See if you can spot the difference."

Julia came back with some Portaircon bags and inert gas canisters for charging them. She touched the cover of the volume gently. "My guess is that this could be one of the most valuable artefacts that have ever been found." She put the book inside one of the bags, sealed it and charged it with the argon to stop any degradation.

A courier delivered a package, For Attn. Professor J. Linden-Barthorpe. She opened it. It was from Doctor Lukas Brovnik at Warwick University. Bill Templestone saw the physics department logo on the envelope and was curious.

Julia laid the package on the bench. "Doc Brovnik owed me a favour, so I took a blank sheet of the material I found tucked into the book and stayed while he started the analysis. He narrowed it down to being a type of plastic, and when he couldn't cut it and discovered its inbuilt memory he wanted to know where it came from."

"He would. You didn't tell him, did you?" Dearden asked.

"Of course not, hey trust me, will you?"

"OK, just checking."

"Fine, but give me some space, and listen. Brovnik was annoyed when I wouldn't tell him where the sample came from. I told him I was pissed off with his attitude and got as far as the door with the sample. Threatening to walk out quietened him down, and he agreed to start the tests. He tried concentrated acids and strong alkalis, all of them vicious chemicals, but not one of them had an effect on the material. He heated it with a blowtorch, and it made no difference. It took laser cutting to make an impression on it. After the initial tests, Brovnik concluded that the material is definitely a type of plastic, and it is unique."

"So what's the outcome?" Templestone asked.

Julia glanced at the report, "Brovnik says he was unable to break the sample into its individual chemical components, but he is ninety percent sure it contains tungsten in combination with other elements, maybe even converted biomolecules. There are still unknowns, but it means we can take the manual out and study it. It will be impossible to damage it."

24

The constellation of Ursa Major was in the centre of a photograph Julia printed off from the Newton StarMap website. It was next to an opened page of the alien manual, which also showed an image of Ursa Major.

"Can you see any difference between these images?" she asked the others grouped around the table in the great hall. She had spent close to an hour comparing the distances between the stars on both images with a rule and dividers, before calling Dearden and the others over.

"There is a difference. Do you know why?"

Templestone was familiar with the Ursa Major constellation, specifically, the part called the Plough. There had been a time he used it to navigate out of trouble when he was on a mission with SHaFT. He had drawn an imaginary line through Dubhe and Merak, two of the brighter stars, the ones furthest away from the handle of the plough. The line led to Polaris, which gave him the direction of true north. From that, he was able to travel in a south-westerly direction to safety.

It occurred to Templestone, as his eyes flicked from one image to the other, that there was a subtle difference between the two images. "In the book, Polaris isn't in line with Dubhe and Merak, and the shape of the Plough itself is slightly different to the Newton StarMap image."

He looked up as Julia came and stood by him.

"It is different, but *why?*" Julia waited a few seconds. "Compare the two photos and describe what you see."

"The stars of the Plough constellation are closer together in the image in the manual," Matt Roberts said. "Could be that the Newton StarMap is produced photographically. The artist's impression in the alien manual has errors in it."

"It isn't an artist's impression. It's a photograph of the heavens taken from Earth. The definition is superb even under high magnification. What the modern photograph tells us, when we compare it to the image in the manual, is that there has been a cosmic shift in the galaxy. A great deal of time separates these two images. The modern photograph shows that the stars have moved further apart."

They tried to come to terms with the timescale of events suggested by the two images lying side by side, and then Doughty went off on a different tack.

"Jules, what do you make of the writing? Have you come across anything like this before?"

"I haven't. Ancient writing is not my speciality. I know a man in London, Professor Trent Jackson, who could help us with it. I met him when we were working on a cave system in France. In language circles, his intellect is legendary. "

"Could your Professor Jackson make sense out of writing no-one has ever seen before?" Wynter asked.

"If anyone can, it'll be him. In that cave system, we found some unique fragments of writing, and Trent's knowledge of proto-languages enabled him to do the decoding. That prompted him to set up his research institute, GOELD, the Guild of Extinct Language Decoding. I think we should show him the manual."

"If you're taking that to Professor Jackson we need to have a copy in case you lose it. I'll do it now," Doughty said.

"There's something I've been trying to get straight in my head." Templestone had people's attention. "It was when you were first telling me about the crystal, Jem."

"I remember the conversation."

"Well, one of my hobbies a few years ago was watches. I bought them at auction, repaired them and sold them on. I liked the interplay of levers and cogs, but then, occasionally a quartz digital watch came on the scene. As time went by, more of them came on the market, and then people realised they could trust a ten pound digital watch to give accurate time as much as a thousand pound mechanical one."

"Get to the point, Bill."

"Shut it, Mitch, just listen, this is important. After a while, I started tinkering about with digital watches. I took them apart and analysed them. Although the levers and cogs in the mechanical watches were fascinating, the digital timepieces were more so."

"How come? Nothing goes on that you can see in a digital watch."

"Well done Matt, you've got it." Templestone sat back in his seat, folded his arms, and looked at the others as if the case was closed.

"Well go on." Roberts didn't get the point.

"Think it through, what are those movements based on?"

"Quartz crystals," Julia ventured. She started to follow Templestone's train of thought.

"Come on then, Priest, don't hold back," Dearden said.

"OK, but remember, this is only an assumption. Quartz is activated to work in a digital watch by an outside influence . . . electricity from its battery." Templestone looked around the room to gauge reaction. Julia took the idea forward.

"So you're suggesting that the crystal in the Hub could respond to an outside influence, but instead of marking the forward flow of time like the crystal in a digital watch, the crystal in the Hub alters time in some way."

"Exactly, and Jem's apparent journey back in time proves the theory. I am convinced Jem walked out of the Hub into the Anglo-Saxon timeframe, and don't forget, Jem is not the only person to have done it. Max Dearden said he'd seen the Saxon as well." Templestone had the attention of the others.

"I rest my case, but there is something else I'm going to suggest. The electronics going on at the Hub are complex, way beyond anything we can understand. We need someone on board who is more than just OK with electronics."

"The more who get involved, the less secure this whole place will be," Dearden said.

"I know that, but it's doubtful we'll be able to move forward without specialist help."

"Have you got someone in mind?"

"Do you know Electronic Services, in Coventry?"

"I've heard of them."

"Well, they took on a young chap a while back named Harry Stanway. He's the son of Des Stanway, an old friend of mine. Harry is a natural with electronics. He seems to be in touch with what's going on at a molecular level. I'm told he can make a complex electronic circuit up without even thinking about it."

"That might be so, but can we trust him to keep his mouth shut?" Dearden was cagey about who they brought on board.

"There's no worry on that score, and there's something else that could be relevant. I was chatting with him a while back, and one of the things he told me was that he's made a study of the subject of time."

"I trust your judgment Priest. Get in touch with this Harry Stanway of yours. Let's have him on board, sooner the better."

25

Templestone gave Harry Stanway a brief summary, mindful not to give too much away over the phone, other than saying there was a project he would be interested in that had to do with electronics and archaeology. He said he would be over in two days after he wrapped up a project that he was working on currently.

Julia rang Trent Jackson in London. She skimmed over events giving him enough information to hook him.

"What you are saying sounds intriguing but there's a contract we're working on and we're behind schedule with it. Can you come down and see me?"

They arranged to meet at GOELD, and then Julia called Doctor Tim Parker, head of radiocarbon dating at UCL, and arranged to meet with him after seeing Jackson.

Two days later, when Dearden and Julia were speeding down to London Euston on the Virgin Pendolino, Harry's Honda CX500 pulled up outside the studio. He was tall, with a shock of red hair matching his motorcycle and an almost permanent smile that won him both friends and enemies.

In the great hall, Bill Templestone prepared Harry by telling him that what they were going to reveal to him would be a chance to get his hands on some ground-breaking research.

"As long as you tell no-one about it, not even your grand-daddy," Wynter added, getting up close to Harry.

"I can't tell him, he's dead," Harry fired back. The smile didn't leave his face.

"Well, Harry my man, let's make sure of this. There sure

are some crazy events going on in the forest here, and if you decide to spill the Heinz 57 to any of your buddies, let me tell you I will personally take your Honda apart bolt by bolt and *squeeeeze* it to where the Sun don't shine. You get my drift?" Harry nodded and carried on smiling.

They gave him details, each adding information as it came to mind. Harry doodled on a notepad while they talked. He asked questions, and from the answers, he made sketches and did calculations.

He was quiet for a few seconds before he spoke.

"So this book you think is a manual is in London at present? We might make more progress if it was here."

"We've got a copy." Templestone went to the sideboard and unlocked the secure draw where Dearden kept his pistol. He took the folder out and put it on the table in front of Harry.

"Is the Devenish book here as well?" Harry asked. Templestone brought it over and gave him some cotton gloves to wear when he was handling the book. Harry started looking through it as Frieda Heskin brought in refreshments. Her husband Gil followed her in. He put more logs on the fire. He was sullen and said nothing as he tidied up around the large fireplace. When he left the room, Roberts looked up and cocked his head to one side, silently asking Doughty about the man's attitude. The response was a movement of uncertainty with his hands. Doughty had taken a dislike to Gil Heskin. Everything about him created suspicion.

"I don't know if we can trust him," Doughty said, in Harry's ear. "Be careful what you say when he's around."

Harry cut through the innuendo. "Forget him, it's counterproductive. You said Julia Linden-Barthorpe has done some tests. I want to run my own tests to see if our findings agree. Hang on a minute." He went out to the Honda, rummaged about in one of the panniers, and came back holding a box.

"This is a Proberstat extra-deep-search static meter. It measures charge differential." He took an extension arm out of the box and connected it to the meter. "You say that Julia found a considerable charge that was holding. With this baby, we should be able to see what potential the apparatus in the forest is storing. It measures up to 500 Kilovolts and it'll tell us when the stored potential is likely to discharge."

"What about the timeshift? Any thoughts on it?"

"One thing at a time Lee, I'm not into guessing. Let's run the tests first so I can do some analysis. Then we need the results from the language guy in London to see if we've got an understanding of the manual. What I will say is that there are some interesting fringe theories about the displacement of time. When can we take a look at the Hub?"

* * *

Harry's test with the Proberstat concluded that the residual high positive potential of the structure that Julia picked up was still present. He thought it was weird. Under normal circumstances, the high positive charge should have equalised by discharging to earth.

"The whole building has the properties of a capacitor. It's waiting for the right circumstances to discharge and equalise the potential." He was working through the logic as he spoke. "There must be all sorts of safety measures built in to prevent a surge in the wrong direction, otherwise we'd all get fried when we get near the building."

Harry spent time on each level, looking and analysing. He came to the level housing the lower part of the great crystal with the electronic apparatus surrounding it. Doughty went straight over to the spiral stairway and carried on climbing. Harry lingered, taking notes about the metallic disc with the massive flying leads attached to it.

He walked around the crystal and touched its facets. They were cold and smooth, and they coruscated slightly as he touched them. He took out his sketchpad and drew the arrangement of the crystalline structure, measuring each of the facets, and then he measured the collar wrapped with coils surrounding the crystal. Wrapping a tape measure around one of the flying leads, he divided the result by pi and noted the diameter.

Harry mentally calculated the amperage the flying leads would be capable of handling. He contemplated their huge diameter and shape and compared the arrangement to the flying buttresses strengthening the towers of a medieval cathedral, a different type of powerhouse.

Later, when all was quiet, Harry remained in the House of the West Wind with Matt Roberts for protection in case the opposition showed up. When it had become dark outside and quiet inside, a very tall, slender figure stood in the shadows and silently watched Harry working.

26

Dearden and Julia boarded a standing room only tube on the Northern Line from Euston. It was a six-minute journey to their destination, Tottenham Court Road.

A short walk from the station took them through an arched entrance into Beauchamp Mews, near the British museum. Trent Jackson's business at number seven Was a double-fronted Georgian building with a heavily glossed purple door. A brass plaque on the wall bore the initials GOELD, and below it, in small letters, *The Guild of Extinct Language Decoding.*

They entered a brightly lit entrance hall, long and wide, with mirrors, Art Nouveau prints and plush carpeting. The receptionist showed them to a room at the side. Dearden put the rucksack with the manual on a side table and sat opposite a large aquarium. It had a desert scene complete with sculpted Pyramids and a Sphinx. An Egyptian Uromastyx lizard stared at the newcomers.

A few minutes later, a tall slightly built man wearing a bow tie came into the room. He wore a Harris Tweed jacket with matching trousers, and brown brogues.

"Jules, my dear, it has been far too long."

"Trent, good to see you."

"You must be Jem Dearden," he extended his hand. "So what's this object you've found?" Julia vented the Portaircon bag and unzipped it. She put the manual on a table by the window and Jackson went up close.

"No need to worry about handling it. I've had tests done that show it's impossible to damage."

"Then why are you using the Portaircon bag?"

"Force of habit. I guess it's been ingrained over the years."

"Mmmm? Oh yes, best to be safe. Bring the book into the lab, will you?" He motioned them to follow. They entered a softly lit room that had separate work areas each with a spotlight. There were two technicians working on computers with large screens covered with unintelligible text. Jackson headed to a door at the back, punched a code into a numerical pad, and entered the room beyond. He handed Julia and Dearden a disposable coverall each, "We're going into a clean-room, so you need to put these on." He got into one himself.

When they were suited up Jackson went to another door. They felt a release of positive pressure as they went into a room that was pleasantly warm. Jackson shut the door behind them and indicated two chairs. He sat the other side of the large desk and pulled his chair in close.

"OK Jules, let me see." She placed the manual in front of him. Jackson tensed up as he looked at the calligraphy on the cover of the manual. He ran his fingers over the symbols. Julia opened the manual to the photograph of Ursa Major with the out-of-line Polaris and took the Newton StarMap website photograph out of her rucksack. She slid it in front of Jackson.

"Compare Ursa Major on the StarMap photograph to the one in the manual."

"That's Charles' Wain," Jackson said, recognising the constellation. He compared the layout on the StarMap with that in the manual, looking rapidly from one to the other. He opened a drawer in his desk and pulled out a magnifier with a lens for each eye. He slipped it onto his head and leant forward to look at the photograph in the manual. After a few seconds, he let out a low whistle.

"The definition of this image is extraordinary. There's no graininess in this photograph, and I'm at twenty times magnification."

"Did you notice anything apart from the definition?"

"You mean the layout of the constellation? Oh yes, I did. There are two possibilities as I see it. Either this photo is a fake, or it is incredibly old. I mean old as in cosmic time judging by the spread of the constellation in the StarMap image." Jackson looked up at Dearden. "Before we go any further with this, Jules mentioned your concern about keeping this item confidential."

"If anything about the function of the building where we found the manual leaks out into the wrong hands the damage could be unimaginable." Jackson looked at him, waiting for more. Dearden drummed his fingers on the desk and chose his words carefully. "The Hub causes a displacement in the dimension of time. Those with an ulterior motive could even manipulate historical events and cause a catastrophic paradox. That has to be avoided at all costs."

Jackson lifted an eyebrow and a smile crossed his features. "If you kill your own grandfather the universe will implode, you mean."

"I kid you not Trent, you may smile, but it's happening, the timeshift is real."

"Alright, real or not, let me reassure you that everything we discuss here will be kept strictly under wraps. You have my word on it."

Jackson started to turn the pages over carefully. Dearden and Julia looked on from their side of the desk.

"Mmmm. You have found something interesting haven't you, displacement of time or not." He crossed the room to a map on the wall and tapped a text frame in a region near the Persian Gulf.

"This is an example of one of the world's proto-languages showing its place of origin. It is an example of some of the earliest known written information. It is Mesopotamian, from the fourth millennium B.C. The development of an administration in that area we call the 'Cradle of Civilisation' stimulated the invention of the form of writing shown here." He tapped the example again for emphasis. "You might recognise it as cuneiform. The Sumerians were responsible for writing cuneiform as a form of communication, and for spreading it northwards along the Euphrates."

Jackson seemed to be distracted. "I must run this text through the archives," he said, taking the manual to a scanner. He copied some pages, saying nothing for a few minutes, then, "Have you had the artefact dated?"

"Not yet." Julia replaced the manual in the Portaircon bag and recharged it from a small cylinder of argon she took from her rucksack. "We need provenance, but we had to start somewhere and that was the language. We're off to UCL right now for radiocarbon dating. Tim Parker knows it's urgent. He owes me a favour."

"I know Tim well. I am sure he will do his best to get it tested quickly. Say hello for me, won't you?"

Julia and Dearden stood and followed Jackson out of the clean room and removed the coveralls. Julia caught one of the technicians leering at her, expecting more. She went up to him as Jackson was leading Dearden out the door. She whispered a threat in the technician's ear. He quickly turned back to his screen. His fingers went to the wrong keys.

Julia saw the fumbling and went out of the lab with a smile of satisfaction on her face. She had told the technician she would meet him out of work and break his jaw. She caught up with Dearden and Jackson in the hall. As they passed the door to the reception room, the Uromastyx was still staring.

"I'll ring you in a day or so," Jackson said. "Once I've had a good look at the text and delved into the archives I'll know more." He lifted his hand in farewell.

"This is incredibly interesting," they heard him say as they walked off down the pavement.

They took the short walk to the cluster of streets occupied by the UCL, the University College of London. The entrance to Tim Parker's laboratory was nestled at the end of a row of neat buildings in Bedford Way. Julia rang a bell outside and a voice came through a speaker on the wall.

"Step to the centre of the door so I can see you."

A camera showed the occupant of the room the other side of the door who they were.

"Hi Jules, come in." The voice said. The door unlatched and opened electronically.

Tim and Julia greeted each other with catch-up talk while she vented the Portaircon bag. She put the manual on a table near an array of reaction vessels, ovens and other equipment. Dearden gave Parker some background details about the site in the forest; enough to get across that the project was unique and urgent. When Parker felt the volume's pages he was immediately interested.

"What's this material?"

"That's only one of the questions we need answering, look at these." Julia opened the manual and showed Parker the photographs of Ursa Major. The implications puzzled him when she told him the photograph in the manual was genuine and the Newton StarMap website image was less than a month old.

"How *can* it be genuine?" he spoke in an undertone. He picked up the difference in the images as his eyes flicked from one to the other, and looked up for an explanation.

"We'll answer questions when we see you again. Please get us the results, Tim. It's a *very* complicated situation." She flashed him a smile, and it worked.

"OK, for old time's sake I'll do the dating, and I owe you, but I'll warn you, it's a lengthy procedure."

"Do your best please, Tim, the research we're involved with is unique and it's urgent."

"As it's you, I'll do my best."

"How's your security? If we're leaving this with you, it's got to be more than good." Dearden said.

"It's like Fort Knox. You went through some of it when you came in. Sometimes we test priceless artefacts here, similar to yours if it turns out to be ancient and unique. Our insurance covers against fire, theft, loss, and a whole gamut of other things, and it's pricey. Step back and take a look at the door."

He took a fob like a remote car key from his pocket and pressed a button. A steel shutter slid down from the ceiling. It snapped into position on the floor and deadbolts thumped into place from the side, sealing the entrance to the laboratory. There was a similar arrangement on a door at the back of the laboratory leading to the main part of the UCL complex. He demonstrated that too and then pressed another button and the shutters slid back into the ceiling.

"Satisfied?" Parker asked.

They wrapped up the meeting, and when they left him, Doctor Parker looked at the two photographs of Ursa Major. He was frowning, and his goodbye was a distant faraway wave as he attempted to come to grips with what he was looking at.

27

Harry was in the workshop looking at the notes he had written. He recognised the relationship of some of the electronic components to each other, particularly the metal collar wrapped with coils. It resembled a magnetron. He reserved judgement about its function until he could understand why there was a crystal at its centre rather than a metallic target. He had gathered samples of components stored in cupboards in the room where Julia found the manual. It included a small version of the crystal at the heart of the Hub.

Harry and Templestone examined the objects and matched them to illustrations of components in the photocopy of the manual. As they were leafing through it, they came to a circuit diagram of the electronic apparatus surrounding the crystal.

"Let's make a scaled-down version of the Hub," Templestone said. "It looks as though we've got most of the components. What we don't have, we can make. Doing that might help us learn how the Hub works."

* * *

The machine tools Mitch Doughty installed in the workshop next to the stained glass studio proved invaluable, and Templestone brought a newly machined item over to Harry. The shape was complex, and Harry admired Templestone's skill as he fitted it into place. Templestone then sat and watched Harry working.

"Harry, I'm puzzled."

"You and me both."

"No seriously, how come you can make a circuit up when all you've got is alien information?"

"As far as we are aware, the laws of physics are common throughout the universe. The script is alien but I can understand the relationships of the components. What I do have to learn is the purpose of the circuits themselves. Some of them are a completely new concept to me so I'm learning their function as we go."

Harry was winding the coils onto the metal disc they had made, counting the turns and insulating each coil with quick drying impregnation resin as it was finished.

"This metal disc I'm winding with the coils is the anode. With this magnetron, the crystal is the cathode." Harry took some pieces of pre-etched circuit board and the components he needed from his toolbox. He switched on a soldering iron and waited while it warmed up. Templestone heard how Harry worked but had never seen him in action. It was impressive.

"Now we'll connect the flying leads from the Magnetron to the drive circuits." Harry chose some heavy gauge cable, which he measured and cut to length.

* * *

It was late when Julia and Dearden returned from London, but the workshop windows were still ablaze with light. They could hear the sounds of hammering and sawing. Dearden pushed the door open.

The team were around some electronic gear built onto a metal frame on castors in the centre of the workshop.

"Harry, what's going on?" Dearden saw the familiar, smaller shape of a crystal at the centre of the components.

"It's a scaled-down version of the equipment in the Hub."

"I can see that . . . but why have you made it?"

Templestone looked up as he finished sawing a protruding piece off a metal framework. He picked up a file to smooth the sharp edges. "The best way to see how anything works is to strip it down and analyse it. We couldn't do that with the Hub, but we've back-engineered it, and learnt as we built this."

"When will you test it?" Julia asked.

"Soon, but we've got to be sure this baby will go through its paces safely when we switch it on. Processes are going on here that we know very little about." The sound of hammering came from outside. Dearden looked in the direction of the noise.

"That's Matt trying to get the old generator working." Harry had seen Dearden's glance. "This apparatus is going to draw a lot of amps, so we need to provide more power than we can get from the mains."

"When will we get the results from Trent Jackson and Tim Parker?" Doughty asked Julia.

"It could take a couple of weeks."

Harry straightened up from his soldering. "While you've been away, we've started to get a measure of understanding of some of the script. We've been identifying components in labelled diagrams and the parts lists."

"Parts lists?"

"Yeah, the guys who made the equipment in the Hub would have to work with parts lists, the same as we would."

Dearden looked at his watch. It was nearly midnight. "I've had it, tell me more tomorrow."

All but Harry Stanway called it a night.

* * *

"Didn't you get any sleep?" Dearden asked Harry next morning.

"I got enough."

"You'll wear yourself out at this rate."

"I won't while this project is on the boil. The challenge is like having a few shots of number five espresso."

Julia stepped through the door of the workshop with

Doughty. "Can you bring us up to date with progress?" she ventured.

"How much do you want to know?"

"Whatever you think we can take."

Harry swivelled his chair round, indicated seats, and explained.

"Last night I told you that the electronics around the crystal are based on the principle of a Magnetron. In the type of magnetron used in a microwave oven, a rotating electron stream flows from the anode, that's this outer ring with the coils, into a central metallic target called the hot cathode. This is where what they've done gets interesting. The arrangement in the Hub is very different to the science we're familiar with because the hot cathode target isn't metallic, it's the crystal." He touched the crystal and it responded with inner movement. "The electron stream causes the crystal to pulsate."

"So Bill was onto something when he was talking about the principle of a crystal in a quartz watch," Julia said.

"He was very close."

"What do you think happens when the crystal in the Hub pulsates?"

"It creates a force field that reacts with something out there." Harry pointed upwards.

"Remember, Nathaniel Devenish claims to have seen illuminated lines ascending into the sky from the Hub. Max Dearden saw them, and you did Jem."

"They were definitely there, in my peripheral vision."

Harry leant back in his chair. "When the crystal reacts with something out there, it bends the fabric of space-time."

Wynter came in partway through the explanation. "So that lump of rock's no ordinary pebble, is that what you're sayin'?"

"It is definitely *not* an ordinary pebble. I think this type of pebble is totally alien to our world, and I want to get it analysed." Harry reached under the workbench and held up another of the crystals. He gazed into its depths.

"Peter Bright over in Leicester will analyse it for us," Julia said. "He specialises in minerals and gemstones."

"Can we get this crystal to him ASAP, Jules? It'll help us understand what's going on at the Hub."

"I'll give him a call and set it up."

"Oh, by the way, Bill and I have given our equipment a name. We're calling it the *Super Magnetron.*"

*   *   *

Peter Bright gazed at the crystal when Dearden laid it on the glass counter. There was all manner of crystals and fossils shining in strong light below the counter top. Bright picked up Dearden's crystal, tested its weight and examined it.

"It's almost certainly a form of quartz. That's the generic name for silicon dioxide. This crystal looks like a form of rutile quartz, but you can hardly see the inclusions because it's so dark." He flipped down a magnifying glass hinged to his glasses and held the crystal close. "There's a depth to its interior I find difficult to describe." He turned it over. "It's as if the rutile element's moving, but that must be a trick of the light." He looked up. "It's big isn't it?" He took a test kit from under the counter and blobbed various liquids onto the crystal, in turn, to see what the reactions were. He wiped them off between applications.

"Where did you find it?" Bright asked the inevitable question after a period of dabbing the liquids in silence.

"It's been in the family for years," Dearden was vague.

"Do you know exactly where they found it?"

"It was somewhere in the forest, and it's a big place."

Bright pulled out two drawers containing samples from under the counter. Under a strong light he compared some of

211

them to the Leofwin's Hundred crystal.

"Your crystal is totally new to me . . . this sample set represents every known type of quartz and your crystal isn't here. It's most odd." He tested it for hardness and it was off the scale. Then he asked Dearden if he would let him try to cut a bit off and crush it to do a chemical analysis.

"Do it, that's what we came for."

Bright wrapped the crystal in thick felt then clamped it in a vise. He took a glass cutter and tried scoring a line around the facets of the crystal four centimetres away from the stub end. There was movement within the crystal. No scoreline appeared, but what he noticed when he applied pressure with the glass cutter, was movement in the dark regions of the crystal. It reminded him of volcanic magma, with its cool and hot areas vying for position.

"What the hell's going on in there?" Bright pushed his glasses back onto his nose. "This is a tungsten carbide wheel, and it's damn hard." He looked closely at the glass cutter and rotated the wheel with his thumb. "It's not even marking the surface, and look, the inclusions are still moving." He picked up a geologist's hammer and tapped the end he tried to score. He tapped harder and the movement within the crystal was more violent.

"It should shear." Bright hit the end harder. There was a burst of blue light with a simultaneous bang and whine like a ricocheting bullet. The shard of crystal made Bright duck as it hissed by his ear and embedded itself in the wall.

"Boy, that was some reaction." His voice was unsteady.

"Certainly livelier than fossil hunting," Dearden said, comparing the smoking remnant stuck in the wall to the ammonites below the counter.

*   *   *

"What did Bright say?" Harry asked, when they came into the workshop.

"Not much we didn't know before," Julia said. "It's definitely quartz, but it isn't one Peter recognised, and he's an expert with rocks and minerals."

"We learnt that we shouldn't subject the crystals to impact." Dearden described what happened. "Before he blew it up he told us the crystal is a form of rutile quartz, but instead of being locked the inclusions move randomly when pressure's applied."

"The more pressure's applied, the more violent the internal reaction is, up to the point where if the crystals are subjected to shock they explode," Julia added.

Outside there was the grinding sound of a starter motor. "Matt's struggling to get the generator started," Templestone said. It was a familiar sound to Dearden from when he was a child.

The sound of Roberts blowing on something came from outside through the open door. "He's flooded it," Templestone said, "He's blowing the glow-plug off."

A couple of minutes went by and then the sound of the starter motor came again, followed by the roar of the large diesel engine firing up, erratically at first.

Wynter went out into the car park where Matt Roberts was standing by the generator.

"Sounds like my old Dragster," Wynter shouted, looking at the dark smoke rising into the air. The others came out as Roberts fine-tuned the tick-over and the engine settled to a steady roar. The exhaust turned to a healthier colour.

"I never thought I'd hear the old Lycoming running again," Dearden shouted, above the noise.

"It'll be alright when the crap's cleared out of the cylinders. There's thirty-three point one kVA of raw power here for when you need it, Harry," Roberts shouted. He switched the generator off, and the revs died down.

"How close are you to running the Super Magnetron?" Dearden asked Harry, who was connecting the output of a step-up transformer to an isolator switch that had a long insulated handle.

"Not long now. Using the generator should give us more than enough amperage. There are a number of checks before we can do the first run, but we're getting close, I'll keep you posted." Harry was studying the screen of an oscilloscope. It was showing an imperfect waveform he needed to improve.

Templestone came over and sat by Harry. "Something's been puzzling me, how come there's no visible power supply for the device in the Hub?"

"I wondered who'd be the first to spot that." Harry put the screwdriver down. "Tell you what, Bill, do some research and see what ideas you come up with."

"You've got it worked out then?"

"Yeah, and I'll soon be tackling the problem of why it isn't working, but here's a clue for you . . . Nikola Tesla."

28

Harry was preparing for a test run at 9:00 a.m. Barrier tape surrounded the Super Magnetron, and four tower computers were set up behind an earthed shield to record data from the trial. The atmosphere was upbeat but nervous. It was 8:50.

"Almost time," Harry said.

"Are you confident it'll work? Dearden asked.

"This is an exact replica of the device in the Hub. I would be surprised if it doesn't work."

"Two minutes to nine Harry," Doughty called. Wynter had a camcorder on a small table in front of the crystal set to rotate one revolution in twenty seconds.

Templestone grasped the isolator switch handle.

"Are you ready?" Harry asked.

They were, apart from Wynter.

"You sure no crap's goin' to happen?" he edged to the door.

"No crap, something remarkable," Harry read the countdown to the start of the test from a stopwatch, "8 . . . 7 . . . 6." He pressed a remote button on his workbench and the Lycoming roared into life. "3 . . . 2 . . . 1 . . . ZERO."

* * *

In the barn on the westerly edge of the forest, three men were sitting around a wood-burning stove. In a stone built lean-to outside the barn, a small generator was supplying enough power for two lights, a kettle, a phone and a laptop.

The phone rang and Theo picked it up. The mole's voice was agitated, the message brief. He told Uberatu that Stanway was about to switch on the machine he had been building.

Uberatu hung up and immediately dialled Raegenhere.

"Raegenhere," it was always the same, no pleasantries. Uberatu outlined what the mole had said.

"Then do something about it. If the machine does the timeshift like you said it would, I want it, and Uberatu . . ." There was a threatening pause. "If you mess this one up you might end up in a ditch," Uberatu remembered the time when Raegenhere had put his arm around his shoulders and spoke in the same voice, cold as ice, and it scared him.

* * *

Dearden and the others were standing in a semicircle well away from the rig. As the last three seconds ticked by, there was a low octave electrical hum and the noise of cooling fans cutting in from the transformers ramping the voltage up.

"ZERO."

Templestone pulled the lever downwards, closing the circuit, and current surged through the flying leads into the Super Magnetron. Purple and scarlet striations glowed deep inside the crystal, moving more rapidly as the seconds passed, and the smell of ionised air filled the workshop.

Doughty kept his eyes on the clock . . . "Plus ten," he called out. Templestone was still grasping the handle of the switch.

"Plus twenty."

Harry counted down, "4 . . . 3 . . . 2 . . . 1 . . . OFF." Templestone switched off on Harry's call. The activity in the crystal ceased, and it became benign again.

Harry pressed the remote shut off for the generator. It cycled down and stopped. "OK folks, let's debrief."

"How d'you debrief a non-event?" Wynter was sceptical.

"It definitely wasn't a non-event." Julia described the violent movement she had seen deep within the crystal.

Doughty agreed, "It had internal energy, there was definitely something going on."

"Did anyone see something peculiar about eight seconds into the run?" Julia asked.

"There might have been a shimmering effect around the machine," Templestone suggested.

"That's what I saw. Objects were losing their substance, like a mirage," Julia added as she went to the crystal. It felt cold to the touch.

"The camcorder'll tell us," Wynter said. He stopped the rotation with the remote handset. Harry brought the camcorder over and connected it to his laptop. He started playing the recording.

They saw the countdown to the test, heard Harry's emphatic zero. As it rotated, the camera picked Harry up as he pressed the remote starter to the generator. Then Templestone was in the frame levering the heavy-duty switch. The machine in the workshop appeared, and then the images became less substantial. Twelve seconds in and the recording could be said to be faulty if the viewers hadn't known better.

The image of the inside of the workshop faded, and in the background, there was the suggestion of a forest and a church on a hill. A fortified wall came into view with a stone arch set into it, and then they saw a bearded man looking in their direction. The Sun reflected brilliantly off something attached to his belt. Wynter zoomed in.

"It's the sword, Jem," Julia cried out. "It's Aelfrythsgiefu."

"And that's Leofwin who's wearing it," Dearden said.

* * *

Uberatu was listening to the events in the workshop through a speaker connected to his surveillance gear. He heard the countdown, and the excitement about a sword with a foreign name and someone called Leofwin. Fengel was suspicious and asked Uberatu what was going on.

"Dearden and his team have just tested their machine," Uberatu said.

"What they were saying was weird," Beggs was uncertain.

"Come on Theo, what were they were talking about?" Fengel asked. His English was fluent, but he hadn't entirely lost his north German accent.

"You wouldn't understand what's going on, but the other day they found some golden objects in a pot. I heard them talking as they were taking stuff out of it."

"A woman just mentioned a sword, and the chap said it was Leofwin wearing it," Beggs said. Uberatu thought he might have told them too much about the gold.

"They're probably high on drugs. Up the nose and in the arm stuff."

"We could use some of that," Beggs commented.

Fengel looked at him cynically. "You speak for yourself, Beggsy. I am not into that. I want to look after my brain." He had an idea. "Theo, why don't we get the gold they found in the pot?"

"There's something far more valuable in their workshop. I want to catch them unawares when they are having one of their team talks, or snorting crack."

Fengel raised an eyebrow. "What exactly is in the workshop?"

"A machine they've been building, it's sophisticated." He would say no more about it.

29

The positive results from the tests of his Super Magnetron raised Harry's confidence that he was well on the way to understanding the operation of the device in the Hub.

While Harry was conducting the tests, it occurred to Wynter that they should try a CCTV camera to see if they could observe the temporal shifts live. It worked, and the CCTV camera, along with the table it stood on close to the Super Magnetron, disappeared from view during each timeshift. Curiously, the screen displaying the CCTV image displayed the view of the ancient world from the structure within Leofwin's Hundred, not from the workshop. There was always full control of the camera with the handset during a timeshift, and the table with the camera on it reappeared again when Harry forced a return to the present.

During one of the timeshifts, workers were digging in a clearing in the forest, laying the foundations for the manor house. A few days later, Wynter called the others over. The large television they were using as a monitor was displaying masons and labourers beginning to construct the house itself from a great pile of stones lying nearby. Harry was trying to fine-tune the timeshifts to be consistent. On another test, some years had passed and the house and the perimeter wall were showing signs of weathering.

Present in all the shifts were the people in the community living around the manor house going about their everyday tasks. Wynter even began to recognise some of the individuals. Templestone said that the process reminded him of a *Camera Obscura* he had once seen in a museum of Victorian life. He recalled how, in an attic, an arrangement of mirrors and lenses focussed on the street scene below, projected the images onto a white painted table for the viewers to look at.

Over the series of test runs, 1063 developed as the median year. There were no complete failures, and one shift was a great success, homing in on exactly the right scene like the re-run of a motion picture. Harry had programmed the Super Magnetron to timeshift to 1063. Against a backdrop of an ancient building site, a stonemason and his assistant were winching a keystone with its chiselled date, 1063, into position in the archway set in the boundary wall.

Wynter pointed to the screen, "Y'know, Harry, what intrigues me with this gizmo you've built is how the scene we're looking at is from the Hub in the forest, not from here in the workshop."

"There has to be a harmonic resonance between the Hub and our Super Magnetron. The Hub is much larger and I think it influences the smaller machine. Information exchanges between them. It's the only explanation that fits." Wynter seemed content with the theory, but a curious thought occurred to him when he saw two young boys kicking a roughly shaped ball to each other.

"How's it possible we can see what's happening back there all the time, Harry my man? Sometimes the scene don't change from the olden days even when your Super Magnetron's switched off."

"I've found I can keep the channel open with a passive bombardment of electrons to the crystal. Apart from that, Lee, things are happening here that don't fit in with laws of physics as we understand them at present."

At the end of the first week of test runs, Templestone took another phone call. A woman announced she had Tim Parker at UCL on the line. Templestone called Dearden over and

Parker got straight to the point.

"You've got monumental goings-on in your forest . . . I must speak to Jules, is she there?"

"I'll get her, so it's positive news?"

"You'll be surprised." Parker didn't elaborate. Dearden called Julia and she came to the phone.

"Jules, I have to see you."

"Why?" she asked.

"I can't tell you over the phone, but it's likely to put your ideas about archaeology through a fiery hoop. Will you still be at Dearden Hall tomorrow?"

"I'm here for as long as this business takes."

"Good, make sure you are. This is big. Can you pick me up from Hampton in Arden station at 11:50 tomorrow?"

* * *

In the barn beyond the forest, Uberatu heard the arrangement.

"Who the hell is this Tim Parker?" he asked.

"How the hell do you expect us to know?" Fengel was sick of Uberatu's domineering attitude.

With the way activity was escalating at Dearden Hall, Uberatu thought they were ready to use the machine again. The pain in his hogweed hands was excruciating and both Fengel and Beggs noticed his lips moving in a conversation with himself. They looked at each other and wondered what he was devising, and how deep he was sinking into realms of fantasy.

* * *

Julia was in the waiting room at the station and was scanning the information from the paper, *Forced Magnetron Theory*, that Harry Stanway had given her to read. Under any other circumstances, she would have found the information fascinating, but it was difficult to concentrate on it because of anticipating the news Parker was bringing from London. The public address system announced the arrival of the connection from Coventry, and she went onto the platform as it approached.

She spotted Parker with the Portaircon bag under his arm amongst the dozen or so passengers that arrived, He saw her and waved, then walked briskly down the platform. He started talking when he was still a few feet away.

"This is incredible, Jules," he stabbed a finger at the bag under his arm. "This book raises fundamental questions about intelligence within the universe."

"I've had suspicions about that, what makes *you* say so?" They reached Julia's Jeep and got in.

"Well, we know a lot about the *Cradle of Civilisation*, the human race originating in the fertile crescent of Mesopotamia. The earliest provable records give the mankind species an age of about six and a half thousand years, I'm sure you're aware of that."

"I'm with you on that. So what have you found?"

"Some disturbing information, I'll show you when we get to Jem's place."

Julia and Doc Parker breezed into the great hall where the others were waiting for their arrival. They knew the news was going to be important. The introductions were brief. Parker vented the Portaircon bag and laid the manual and some papers on the table.

"What I must say at the outset is how confident I am in the result of the tests I've done on the manual. At first, I didn't believe the figures were possible, so I ran four tests using different methods. One of them doesn't rely on the standard model of radioactive decay, but all four methods did give similar results."

"So how old is it?" Julia asked.

"Two point four eight million years, and it's indisputable."

"It can't be that old!" Parker's statement put her in a state of denial. There was general murmuring, which Parker interrupted.

"I assure you, it is that old. The material itself and the inert conditions it was stored in have enabled it to survive. I'm not surprised you're questioning it, Jules. I did at first, hence the series of tests to determine its age, rather than just one."

"If you're correct the findings will force us to re-think our whole body of knowledge about the ancient world. Let me see the results."

He fanned the sheaf of papers out. Julia bent over them and he explained the procedures to her for each dating method he had used.

"Tim, with all due respect, if your results are correct, they indicate there was intervention on the Earth way back in the past before the human race appeared."

"Yes, and because of that the textbooks will have to be rewritten."

Dearden was quick to speak. "They will not be rewritten. Seriously, Tim, you will say nothing about it outside this group of people. What's going on in the forest is to be kept under wraps."

Parker's excitement cooled. He raked all the papers back together on the table. As he stood, his chair grated on the stone slabs of the floor. He was angry as he faced Dearden.

"I have put hours of work into dating this damn book. One of the reasons I have done that, free of charge I might add, is to get this knowledge into the public domain. People have a right to knowledge and you're trying to censor it. Jem, I'm not one bit satisfied with you or the way your bloody setup operates." Julia went to Parker and put her hand on his arm. He shook it off.

"Tim . . . Tim, calm down. I felt like you, really, I did. I have been through all this myself. I wanted to publish too, but now I agree with Jem. What I can tell you is that an alien intervention in the Earth's past would not sit well with the current understanding of the history of humanity. Apart from that, the human race, in general, is not ready for access to the temporal dimension. There would be chaos. Most of us can't handle things right in our own timeframe, let alone in another one as well."

Matt Roberts came up to Parker. "Tim, I don't think you realise exactly what the thing in the forest can do. I think you're in need of some clarification, what do you reckon, Jem?"

Dearden nodded. "Harry, let's show Tim what your rig can do, then we'll show him the Hub."

Half an hour later Harry had finished checking safety-critical features of the Super Magnetron that were subject to high amperage. They arranged chairs in front of the large screen Dearden had installed on the wall of the workshop. Wynter switched on the CCTV camera and Harry ran the countdown. The generator fired up, and the test began.

Ten minutes into the run, Parker gasped and stood up as he saw a young boy and girl in Anglo-Saxon clothing driving a herd of cattle out through the gate with the dated keystone above it. He sat down quickly and was quiet as he saw the building that was clearly Dearden Hall, in the ancient form of an Anglo-Saxon great hall, without the building additions of later years.

During the test, Matt Roberts went into the car park to check the generator. He came back in and told the others that there were thunderheads over the forest, directly above where the Hub lay. Harry went out to look.

"It's creating a local atmospheric disturbance, we should switch off now. I don't know what'll happen if we leave the test running."

On Harry's signal, Templestone inserted the insulated lever into the isolator switch and opened the circuit. The scene they were looking at on the screen morphed from the Anglo-Saxon timeframe until it was displaying the inside of the present-day workshop. Harry pressed the shut off for the generator, and all went silent.

"Bloody hell," Parker exclaimed. There were knowing smiles from the others in the workshop.

"Other than *bloody hell*, what do you make of what you've seen?" Dearden asked.

"I guess the evidence is conclusive."

"I thought you might change your mind. Welcome to the club," Roberts said.

30

They were sitting around the table in the great hall. Harry was giving Dearden feedback on progress.

"We have a wormhole into the past. It cannot have been the intention of the makers of the Hub to have people going between 1063 and 2008. It would be a pointless use of such sophisticated equipment. I think there's a calibration problem, I'm working on that at present."

"Tim, you were getting in touch with Trent Jackson. Has he made any progress on the language front?"

"He's examined information from the codex underneath the illustrations in the manual. He says the region of early Celtic Urnfield culture in Western Middle Europe displays links to the language in the manual. He is convinced that there was a crossing of cultures somewhere in the distant past and that the written language in the manual may even be the origin of written language on the Earth."

Julia reasoned on this to the others as an archaeologist. "From what's been revealed so far, we know that the Hub pre-dates the Celtic age by an enormous amount of time. The interface between the Celts and the Leofwin's Hundred Aliens must have been minimal because none of the alien expertise passed into Celtic culture."

There was silence as they considered Julia's words. Then Templestone spoke up.

"Harry and I have managed to familiarise ourselves with some of the words and how they relate to components in the parts lists, but it's impossible to know how the words sounded."

"Anything to add, Lee?" Dearden thought Wynter had something on his mind.

"Only that we've no idea what else we might find in the Hub. The manual shows more levels below ground. There are bound to be more surprises down there, my man."

"That might be so," Parker said. "We need to be cautious. We could open the entire planet up to influences that could get out of control."

"Don't be so stupid," Harry's smile had gone. "It's obvious that whoever built the place left us the process to use. If there was a danger to the planet they would've made it impossible to get inside the building, or they wouldn't have built it in the first place."

Dearden agreed, "There's been no attempt to disguise the Hub, other than by putting it in a dense forest. I'm sure we were meant to use it."

The soft glow of large candles in holders on the floor lit the great hall, and the reflection of the flames from the burning logs in the fireplace was dancing on the walls. Dearden thought the progress the team had made warranted a celebration, so he sent Frieda Heskin to the wine cellar for a particularly good vintage Merlot he had inherited. She came up with five bottles of the Clos du Val 1985. Saying nothing, she avoided Dearden's gaze when she placed them on the large table. Dearden wondered what the silence was about, the Heskins had been offhand recently, but this evening of relaxation wasn't the time to challenge them. He uncorked a bottle, poured a little of the Merlot into a glass and handed it to Julia. She swilled it round in the glass and smelled the bouquet.

"That's good, Jem, top it up." It was a generous measure. He filled the other glasses and handed them round, then put more logs on the fire. He remained standing, leaning against the warm stonework of the fireplace, the place he enjoyed by habit. He looked at the room and his friends. He saw the warmth and felt the friendship, heard the pleasant conversation. By contrast, through the window that reached to the floor, his gaze drifted to the band of the Milky Way piercing the darkness outside. He shivered as he felt the wilderness of the forest and, enshrouded within it, the alien nature of the House of the West Wind.

* * *

Uberatu was in the barn with Fengel and Beggs. The laser microphone, aimed at the window of the great hall, had picked up the vibrations of the conversation and digitised them to allow Uberatu to hear what the group within were saying.

"Yes, now we've got them," Uberatu yelled, punching the air with his clenched fist.

Uberatu's outburst startled Beggs, and he dropped the hand of cards he had been shielding from Fengel. They came into full view. It had been a winner and would have taken some cash from the pile mounting up in front of Fengel. Uberatu and Fengel laughed at Beggs' nervousness and in response, Beggs kicked the portable table. It collapsed onto the floor, and he stormed outside, slamming the door in a fit of pique.

Uberatu left him to cool down for a few minutes, and then he followed him out the door and called softly into the forest night, "Beggs . . . come on Beggsy, there's work to be done before the Moon sets again." There was no response, "Beggsy," he called again, louder. "Let's sort the toys out. Come on back, but mind the fox crap outside the door."

Beggs was a bad loser and when he trailed back into the barn he saw Fengel shuffling the pack, ready to deal again with his recently full wallet by him on the table. There was a solitary two pence piece at the side of Beggs position.

"I thought I would be fair and give you a bit of a head start. Do you want another game?" Beggs felt anger welling up inside but managed to hold himself from taking a poke at Fengel's mouth. Uberatu saw the situation stacking up and intervened.

"Let's get serious, forget the cards, we're ready for the real game." He fumbled for a key in his pocket and winced with the pain from his hogweed hands. He unlocked a steel cupboard bolted to the wall. He took out a Luger P.08 Parabellum and a Kalashnikov AK47 that he gave to Fengel. He passed Beggs a hunting crossbow made of composite material, and some bolts.

31

Something had been bugging Harry about the effect the crystal had upon time. The thought half materialised on quiet occasions and vanished as quickly as it came. One of his conversations with Templestone caused the thought to return. Harry held onto it, and almost immediately, a solution occurred to him. He raced upstairs to his laptop.

He waited for it to boot up, tapping his foot impatiently, and then factored information into a program he had written. It was a mathematical model, and he entered one of the elements of an equation that he had forgotten to factor in previously. The result began to spill across the screen.

He shouted in triumph. The developing figures proved travel across the temporal dimension was possible by warping the fabric of space-time. An adjacent column of figures described the geographical transfer of objects by warping their co-ordinates.

A few seconds later, Dearden startled Harry when he burst into his room with a pistol in his hand. His eyes flashed quickly around the room. He had heard Harry's shout.

"No need for the gun, Jem, sorry, but I've cracked a problem that's been bugging me about the Hub for days. I realised—"

"OK Harry, it's late. As long as you're alright tell us tomorrow." Dearden pocketed the pistol. "Oh, and Harry," Dearden paused on the threshold. "Tell us in a way we can understand."

"I will Jem, that's no problem."

When they met next morning, the consensus was that they

wanted to be told the essentials, nothing over-complicated. Harry asked if they had heard of a theory known as an Einstein-Rosen Bridge. "The theory is that a wormhole in the fabric of space-time is a link to other places in the universe. There's conjecture that wormholes are links to other universes."

"Harry, my man, this one universe is enough for me," Wynter said.

"There may be surprises to come, Lee. When I was looking through the manual, I came across a diagram of a three-dimensional grid. It has been bugging me for days, and last night it all came together. I think the aliens may have given us a gateway to dimensional shift, both temporal and physical."

"As an introduction to that, think of width, height and depth, call them x, y, and z. Any object's position in space can be plotted with those rectangular coordinates measured from a point of origin, like this pen for example." He held a ballpoint pen up. "If we use that lamp over there as the point of origin the position of the pen could be described in terms of x, y, *and* z in relation to it. Six feet away from it, four feet to the left and two feet higher, in relation to the centre of the Earth, that is."

"Where's that taking us?" Roberts asked.

"I am getting to that. X, y, and z could describe the position of the Earth, or any other heavenly body's position in the universe, from a point of origin."

"Are there any clues about where the alien's origin is?" Templestone asked. He was pouring coffee from a cafetière. He handed the coffees around.

"I've no idea where the origin is at this stage, but we might be able to work it back from data in the manual."

"When we get Trent Jackson's translation results they might tell us about the origin," Julia said. "The Aliens have been pretty free with their information so far, and I can't imagine they'd neglect to explain their origin.

"The guy pointing at the plaque on the wall in the room of the exhibits may be pointing to the origin," Doughty suggested.

"He may well be," Harry said. "I discovered something else as well. According to my mathematical model, the Hub is capable of enabling travel in *either* the temporal or the physical dimensions, separately, or combined, although it doesn't do that at the moment and neither does my third scale model."

"Do you know why they don't?" Julia asked.

"Both machines need calibrating."

Harry opened the copy of the manual to a page marked with a post-it. There was a diagram of a geometric three-dimensional grid with a sphere at the centre. The grid lines nearest the sphere were warping down to its surface.

"Tell me what you see where the lines are touching the sphere," Harry said.

"The lines are intersecting on the British Isles, the shape's slightly different, but it's definitely the British Isles."

"Yeah, it is. And the warping of space-time is the only way a timeshift could happen, which is what this illustration in the manual shows occurring. The problem is that the original power supply to the hub is faulty. The way the Hub operates now is when an electrical storm causes the crystal to warp the grid towards it."

"What is the grid then, do you know?" Julia asked.

"I would hazard a guess the grid is part of a force field that binds the fabric of space-time together."

"So the lines we see in our peripheral vision projecting from the Hub when it's active are part of the grid," Dearden suggested, looking at the illustration.

"I do believe they are." Harry turned the pages of the manual to another he had marked with a post-it. "Look at this."

He slid the folder over to where Dearden was sitting. It portrayed a three-dimensional grid within which they could see the solar system.

"The manual is telling us that the race who built the device used its technology to tap into those lines of force, and use them as a transport system."

"And now we've found the technology they left for us we can go riding the lines," Templestone said.

"I think they've left this information to start us on the journey." Harry pulled the manual back and turned to another place he had marked. There were pages of tables laid out in three columns side by side with a fourth, narrower column to the right. He put a rule under one of the lines. "Do you recognise the layout of this lettering; we saw it in the room of the exhibits?" They bunched round to look. "I think they represent the coordinates for three-dimensional positioning. I bet a pound to a penny these tables represent the places the builders of the Hub have travelled to."

"A space traveller's almanac," Wynter said.

"I reckon so. The manual was put in the Hub to help whoever the finders were to start journeying themselves." Harry shut the photocopied manual. "That's the explanation in layman's terms. Now I'm going to learn how to calibrate the temporal dimension. Do you know what? I don't know where the hell to start."

"I'll give you a hand," Templestone said.

There were illustrations of waveforms in the manual. Each successive illustration had less malformation, leading to a perfect shape. Harry termed it the *alpha* waveform. He had a suspicion the waveform on his oscilloscope was showing that the Super Magnetron was out of harmony with the resonance of its crystal. He was sure that when he achieved the alpha waveform with both the Super Magnetron and the Hub, the calibration of the machines to the grid would be complete.

He also deduced he would need two calibration procedures, one temporal and the other spatial. Because the Hub was already operating in the temporal continuum, albeit to a particular time in Anglo-Saxon England, he decided to work on the temporal continuum first.

32

Harry was startled awake by Dearden's noisy entry into the workshop. The photocopy of the manual was open at a page showing the lines of the grid. They were intersecting on the surface of the third planet out from a sun.

"Been here all night, Harry?"

"All night and then some, but I've made progress." He yawned.

Dearden turned the page and saw a distant jewel-like planet in full colour in the blackness of space.

"That's the Earth isn't it?"

Harry glanced down. "Yes, it is," he stood up and stretched.

Dearden turned another page and studied the image. He could see the general shape of the British Isles on the left-hand page, and on the right, there was an aerial picture of a vast swathe of forest. In the foreground, there was a hill, clear of trees, with the Hub on the top.

"The Hub is active in this photograph." Harry pointed to the grid, distorted and pulled down to the Earth. Vague blue lines touched the Hub, one descending vertically to its centre, four others at ninety degrees to each other, curving down from the heavens in graceful arcs and touching the building. "I think that process will have tremendous consequences for us."

"You bet it will," Dearden thought of his conversation with Leofwin.

"I wonder if they're still adding to the exhibits in the museum room," Harry spoke through a stifled yawn. "What's the time?"

"Quarter past seven. You need some rest."

"I know. It's catching up with me now. The trouble is that I might be out of things for twenty-four hours if I stop, and I don't really want to be out of things. This is so exciting, Jem."

The autumn day was clinging on to high summer. The steel shutters covering the workshop windows were open and the Sun was shining too brightly through the window. Harry looked to see which shutter to close and saw a movement at the bottom of the window, the top of someone's head moving stealthily by. When he shouted, the others reacted. Dearden turned instinctively a split second before the door burst open revealing Otto Fengel with his AK 47 raised, and behind him, Antony Beggs with a crossbow.

They marched into the workshop, Fengel waved the AK and yelled at those inside to back up against the wall. On impulse, Harry pressed the red starter button under his workbench and the electro-generator outside roared into life. The distraction was all Dearden needed. The room burst into action.

Dearden rushed Fengel and knocked the AK 47 aside. At the same time, Doughty launched forward and hit Beggs in the throat with the heel of his hand. Dearden kicked Fengel in the groin, flooring him, and the AK went flying. Wynter snatched it in mid-air and Julia, at Beggs' side in an instant, forced his arm against the joint and wrestled the crossbow from his grip. Roberts unsheathed Mavis the Bowie and ran to the door, bolting it before pulling the steel shutters closed. Templestone switched on the lights and sat back down with his arms folded and watched the action with a smile on his face.

To Harry Stanway and Doc Parker, observing the action, the whole thing appeared to be a superbly choreographed manoeuvre. It was fluid, incisive and immediate, the threat taken out and the two attackers on the floor moaning.

"I know whose side I want to be on in a tight spot," Harry

said to Parker, looking at the two on the floor.

Beggs' mouth was bleeding and his hands were over his head ready to ward off an attack from Julia, who stood over him with one hand grasping his hair, and the other ready for action. Fengel was writhing on the floor, clutching his groin.

"Like old times eh? I think we'll need this." Templestone reached under the bench into a plastic bin and chucked some rope to Julia.

"Looks like our project's got a whole lot more serious," she said, tying the overweight man's wrists extra tight. She went to the other man. "What are you two after?" she asked, while she was securing him. His face had a hard edge; he said nothing, just moaned.

"You heard the lady, she wants answers, give them." Dearden recognised the overweight one as Antony Beggs, whose driving licence he took in the forest. He took a stab at the other man's name.

"Otto Fengel isn't it? Why are you skulking around on my land armed to the teeth?"

"How do you know my name?"

"Let's see." Dearden went to a cupboard and unlocked it.

Fengel followed him with his eyes. Dearden reached into the cupboard, took something out, and walked up to Fengel. He showed him the mobile phone they found in the earthenware pot. Fengel's name and number were on the display.

"How did you get my phone?" Fengel panicked. "Beggsy, how did he get my phone?" A few days ago, Fengel was convinced he felt the weight of the phone go from his pocket, and an unsettled feeling remained in his mind that he had never owned the phone in the first place. It was weird. He couldn't understand it. It disturbed him for hours afterwards.

Dearden moved closer to Fengel, "How come we found

your phone buried in the forest?"

"I have no idea—"

"We have to do what Uberatu tells us," Beggs interjected.

"From now on you're going to do what I tell you. Anyway, Beggs, you and I have some unfinished business." Dearden went back to the cupboard and took out Beggs' driving licence.

"Yours, I believe, let's pick up where we left off in the thunderstorm. I want answers." He held the licence up for Beggs to see.

"Don't you tell him anything, Beggsy." Beggs looked at Fengel scornfully, remembering how he and Uberatu had belittled him the previous night in the barn, and how Fengel cheated him at cards.

"Fengel's well in with Uberatu. He's an arse-licker," Beggs smirked triumphantly.

"Beggs, I will swing for you." Fengel kicked out with his feet, trying to stand up to get to Dearden, Beggs and his mobile phone.

Dearden pocketed the mobile. "This man Uberatu you mentioned, tell me about him."

"Uberatu and Raegenhere are in each other's pockets but Raegenhere's the boss."

"What do Raegenhere and Uberatu want?"

"We have no idea," Fengel interrupted before Beggs could answer.

In the barn, Uberatu was listening to the events in the workshop. The laser microphone was registering the vibrations of the conversation on the glass of one of the windows, converting it digitally into speech. He heard every word over the sound of the generator by attenuating the frequency. His plan was unravelling, so he decided to head back to Leamington out of harm's way.

Dearden and his colleagues were not the pushover Uberatu thought they would be, and his two warriors, Otto Fengel and Antony Beggs would have to think their own way out of trouble.

* * *

In the workshop, the interrogation of the two raiders was getting nowhere. Matt Roberts had been quiet for a while, and then he spoke up.

"I know how we can move this on."

"Is it related to Hogweed?" Julia asked.

"It's more original than Hogweed. We're going to test Harry's machine again, correct?" Dearden saw Roberts indicating the captives with a sideward nod of his head, and could see where Roberts' idea was going. He crossed to where the men were sitting on the floor and undid their bindings. Doughty covered them with the AK. Beggs fidgeted nervously, sensing the threat notching up.

"What you gonna do?"

"You'll soon find out. Get on the other side of that barrier," Dearden indicated the direction with his Beretta.

"Why?" Beggs walked forward. Fengel followed, slowly.

"We've been asking why you and the others have been skulking around on my land. You have come here armed to the teeth. I'm getting sick of you, and since you haven't answered, this will help loosen your tongues."

"What do you intend to do?" Fengel was defiant.

"We're going to see what you make of the year 1063."

"Jem, a word," Julia took hold of Dearden's sleeve. She pulled him roughly out of earshot of the others and whispered. "You don't intend putting them through a timeshift do you?"

"That's what's happening. There is too much at stake with the Hub to ignore the opposition. If they get hold of it, the consequences could be disastrous. The timeshift will be there and back Jules. We must find out what Raegenhere and Uberatu intend to do. We'll switch the thing on for a few seconds and then reverse the cycle. It'll soften them up to do some talking."

"That's totally irresponsible." Sometimes there was an impetuous side to Dearden she couldn't trust. Now he was pushing the boundaries too far.

Dearden broke off the conversation and went to where Doughty was covering Fengel and Beggs with the AK to make sure they stayed behind the screen.

"Ready, Harry? We'll switch on for ten seconds, and then re-start the cycle to bring them back."

"Don't do it Jem," Julia shouted. They ignored her. "Bill, you're not going to put up with this are you?" Templestone, usually the voice of reason, took no notice.

"Full power coming up for the first time folks," Harry called out. "There will be more noise this time, so be prepared."

"Here, catch this." Dearden threw Fengel a two-way radio Harry had modified. "Give us a running commentary."

"Running commentary of what?" Beggs asked.

"Your trip."

"Trip where, what's going to happen? Stop him Fengel."

"I can't stop him, Beggsy, he's gone mad; all of them have gone mad. Hey you, the woman over there," Fengel was imperious. "Are you going to stand by and let them do this?"

"I can't stop them," Julia was shaking her head with frustration. She went to the door and looked behind her. Dearden and the others were concentrating on the countdown. She went out of the workshop and slammed the door behind her.

Doughty still had the AK trained on Fengel and Beggs as Harry started the count from ten to zero. Wynter thought of the CCTV camera and darted behind the screen with it, startling Beggs. He switched it on and nimble as a cat was quickly back to the safe area by the outside wall. The count reached zero and Templestone closed the contact breaker switch. The revs on the generator stepped up to compensate for the surge of current drawn by the Super Magnetron. Harry looked at his watch. It was 2:45 p.m.

33

A young boy was leading a herd of goats across a field toward the shelter of the grounds surrounding a manor house. He had brought the animals into the village through a recently built archway of locally hewn stone. He was a gentle lad who, from an early age, had shown a love for creatures.

While he was still young his father, Earl Leofwin of Mercia had indulged him, allowing him the freedom to get to know how to handle animals, to lead them and to learn patience. If Ingwulf understood how to lead and care for animals with gentleness, it would prepare his mind for when it was his turn to lead and care for the folk in his dominion.

An autumn haze was gracing the morning with the promise of a good day to come. It was a surprise when dark thunderclouds formed. Within minutes, a storm threatened a small area of the forest. As a warm wind arose, leaves scattered, and the air became sultry.

"Wulfie," his mother's voice carried across the green as she called to him from the door of the manor house. The two sticks he used to drive the goats went up into the air in recognition of the urgency of his mother's call. A jagged shaft of lightning flashed over the forest and as the thunder rolled across the landscape, the lad broke into a run.

"Leofwin," Ingwulf's mother cried out in alarm. What was occurring over the forest was unusual. The wind picked up, swirling leaves around the compound and causing trees to move restlessly. The storm was imminent and she ran to get to her son. Leofwin, who had heard her cry, ran out of the manor where he was leading a meeting of the Witenagemot. The Ealdormen of the supreme council heard Aelfryth's call and with the weather getting wild they drew business to a close.

Aelfryth could handle most emergencies, so Leofwin knew there was something badly wrong when he had heard the urgency in her call.

"What is it Aelfryth, is there trouble?" he asked when he came close. He would never respond harshly to Aelfryth. When he first saw the woman, who had become his countess, her dark Celtic looks, her brown eyes and her dark hair had entranced him. He knew she was to be his life's companion.

He loved her for her inner fire, for her being different to the Saxon women who were part of the ruling elite of the English shires. Countess Aelfryth of Mercia she had become, but to him, she would always be Guennean, the tempestuous woman from Llangrannog, in the dark hills of Ceredigion.

* * *

The dogs were noisy, their hackles raised in response to the highly charged atmosphere. Birdsong, usually a constant background to life in the forest had become silent. Ingwulf came to grasp his father's hand, having penned the goats with the help of Ienur.

"The birds have grown quiet, something strange is afoot," Leofwin whispered to his son and to Aelfryth.

"They are frightened. See how they fly," Aelfryth saw the birds in a great flock, leaving the forest under the gathering cloud. She heard the horses in the stables. They were restless and skittish, barging against the sides of their stalls. Leofwin looked suspiciously at the forest where the trees were higher. Part of the western sky above the higher place looked as if the Day of Judgement had arrived.

"The House of the West Wind," he muttered under his breath, and then louder, "It's alive again . . . get into the house Wulfie. Aelfryth, get Blythe, make sure she stays with you.

Where is Ienur? Ienur, come here damn you." The houscarl came running. "Go, fetch me a sword, and make sure it's Aelfrythsgiefu. Bring whoever's guarding the great hall, and Ienur, be quick."

A minute later Ienur came back with the sword, Aelfrythsgiefu, and four armed men. Leofwin briefly explained what was happening, and led them out through the gate at an easy running pace toward the darkening sky over the House of the West Wind.

As they came to the large oak tree there was a lightning strike nearby followed by a blue afterglow that remained in the sky and vaguely lit the forest where the House of the West Wind lay. The lightning caused the armed men to slow down, but Leofwin encouraged them onward and they resumed the battle pace as if closing on an enemy. They leapt across the stepping-stones in Shadow Brook, and as they ran along the bank Leofwin drew Aelfrythsgiefu, and the other men readied their weapons.

The trees thinned out when they neared the House of the West Wind, and they had a better view of the sky through the tree canopy. They could vaguely see lines of blue light rising into the sky until they became lost to view, so high up were they. The men slowed their pace. Other than Leofwin, they baulked at the sight. One said it was the works of sorcery. Leofwin rallied them onward. He remembered the man with the wolf who came from the House of the West Wind. When he had touched the man's arm, he knew he was solid flesh and bone.

They reached the base of the hill as the lines into the sky were fading. Emerging from an open door in the building on the hilltop were two men, dressed in the oddest clothing. They were arguing with each other in a foreign-sounding tongue.

The two men scrambled down the hill. One of them, the

fatter one, was supporting the other, who was unsteady on his feet. The taller of the strangers spoke. The language reminded Leofwin again of the man with the wolf. He recognised words similar in intonation to his own language.

* * *

Wynter and Doc Parker raced over to the screen hanging on the wall to follow the progress of the timeshift. Julia was back in the workshop, and with Dearden and Doughty, she was following the mission duration clock. Templestone was standing by the switch with Matt Roberts, waiting for Harry's signal to cut the power supply. Parker looked at the machine and could see the active crystal, with bright purple and crimson striations darting back and forth against an impenetrable black background. Fengel and Beggs were no longer standing there.

"... 2 ... 1 ... *off*," Harry shouted.

Templestone pushed the long lever of the switch upwards to open the circuit to the Super Magnetron ... and pushed again.

"Damn ... the bloody thing's stuck," he shouted. Everyone turned to look at him. He was struggling with the handle. "I can't switch it off."

"Stand aside," Roberts shoved Templestone out of the way. He grabbed the lever, used his bulk to force the switch. He heaved, pitting his strength against the metal, and then lurched forward, almost losing his balance as the handle on the switch snapped, leaving the electrons coursing into the Super Magnetron and the switch stuck in the on position.

"Roberts, you fool, now what do we do?" Julia shouted.

* * *

Fengel and Beggs feared the worst after their capture by Dearden. With the weaponry in the others' hands, there was no way of escape. Fengel tried to put on a brave face but it was difficult at the wrong end of a Kalashnikov. At the point of the gun, Dearden made them stand close to the machine, behind the shield separating it from the rest of the room.

The first thing Fengel and Beggs noticed was a humming noise that they felt resonating deep inside. Everything became a blur, and after a second or two things became clear and they could see a change in their surroundings.

"Fengel, what have they done?" Beggs called, but Fengel was no help. He was struggling to maintain his own self-control.

"We are in the building in the forest," he managed to say. Fengel tried to maintain an air of authority, and his German accent became stronger. "I don't know how that can be, and look, the forest is different. Look, Beggs, over there." His hand was unsteady as he pointed. "See the building over there? It's the Dearden place. How have they moved us here, Beggs?"

Beggs saw the house through the canopy of foliage, and then caught sight of men approaching at a run, and the glint of weapons reflecting the sunlight. Fengel was in a state of denial, trying to take in the enormity of the changes. Coldness descended as his consciousness started to slip, and he grasped hold of Beggs' arm. "Air, I need fresh air, help me, Beggs," he called. He staggered toward the doorway, in the wall that had become transparent. Beggs thought of leaving him to suffocate but relented and supported him to the door. He turned the catch and pulled. The door opened and let in a draught of air. Fengel felt the breeze wash over his face.

"They have transported us somewhere," Fengel muttered. Beggs took no notice. He was looking at the men at the foot of the hill. "Those idiots are in fancy dress," he said.

"They might be, but those weapons look lethal. We'd better see what they want."

* * *

Roberts dropped the broken handle at the same time Harry rushed to the switch. The broken handle was locking the cover in place and the mechanism was jammed so the cover would have to be smashed to get inside and disconnect it. Roberts raced out to the generator and fumbled for the cut-off, pulled it, and the Lycoming started slowing down. He raced back into the workshop and looked at the others who were trying to work out what to do.

"What's the damage?" Dearden asked. His voice was clipped and urgent.

"The switch is broken, I'll have to—"

"Dammit, how long was the machine powered up?"

"Eighteen seconds," Harry said. "I was relying on an immediate re-run to reverse the timeshift and get them back, but we need to smash the switch and get inside to disconnect it, and then fit a replacement."

"How long to change the switch?"

"An hour, but we'll have to find a replacement first."

"Get to it Harry, quick as you can."

"How do you propose we get them back now, Jem? Presumably, you had an emergency procedure in mind in case things went wrong." Julia's sarcasm bit into Dearden and left him without a reply. She looked at the screen and saw some men binding Fengel and Beggs with ropes. Wynter was toggling the CCTV handset, trying to keep the receding group in view, as they walked through the forest.

"We'll have to organise shifts so there's someone by the monitor at all times," Templestone said, trying to establish order in the situation that had spiralled out of control.

* * *

When Fengel and Beggs reached the bottom of the hill, the

men surrounded them with their weapons uncomfortably close. Fengel picked up familiar sounds in some of the words used by the tallest of the men who, judging by the quality of his weapons and clothing, was the leader. The language had a resonance with his native German, but it was less guttural. Fengel tried responding in German, he thought there was a chance they would understand. The leader looked suspiciously at him, and gave a signal for his men to seize them, and tie their wrists. They were led captive through the forest, pushed from behind by the fierce individuals with spears.

When they were a short distance away from the entrance to the manor house, one of the armed men blew a horn. Guards opened the oaken gates, and the prisoners were marched through the archway into the manor house grounds.

Fengel and Beggs felt under scrutiny by the people going about their tasks in the hamlet. All of them were dressed in old-fashioned clothing. They passed a variety of small buildings arranged around a clearing. The majority had no window spaces, and they had roofs of thatch. They were rudimentary structures of wood, built over a pit, so that the people who were curious, and emerged to look at them, had to step up to the outside.

Dogs and chickens were wandering about freely and a man, sitting on a workhorse outside a low building, was carving a wooden plough, with the shavings gathered around his feet. He looked up as they passed by and then carried on working with his drawshave. A long stone building of two stories, a simplified version of the house Fengel recognised as that owned by Dearden, was at the back of the compound.

"Uberatu's sold us down the river," Beggs whispered to Fengel as they neared the entrance to the manor house. They had gathered a small audience of children who were following warily, and the adults they passed were curious. Most of the villagers had light coloured hair, and skin lightly bronzed by the Sun, and they looked upon Beggs as a curiosity with his dark hair and swarthy looks. They reached the manor house, and the guards forced them through the open door.

Wynter had the zoom of the CCTV camera almost on maximum and the group in the workshop saw the manor house door closing behind the prisoners.

* * *

Fengel looked around the room. It was gloomy but spacious. A cream coloured light filtered through windows filled with rectangles of a light-coloured opaque material. In the centre of the room, logs were burning on some stone slabs. Smoke drifted up past massive roof timbers and curled out of the room through a hole in the roof.

Their escort took them past wooden stalls projecting from the walls toward a raised dais on which there was a large table. Seated around it were the richly clad individuals of the Witenagemot. They stood as Leofwin stepped onto the dais and sat on the large seat at the head of the table. He indicated for the others to sit, and began conversing, sometimes gesturing in the direction of the captives.

Those on the dais were a motley collection of individuals. Fengel looked at the weapons they carried. Their swords and daggers appeared to indicate their status. Some of the weapons had handles of wood, and some appeared to be bone. Fengel noticed that the leader's was different. It was inlaid with stones that glinted in the flickering light of the fire, and the pommel and guard looked as if it was made of gold.

A meal was in front of each man at the table. Fengel nudged Beggs and whispered, "Those plates and dishes, they're gold, see how they shine." His voice grew louder as he gloated, and the men on the dais caught him looking at the tableware.

Leofwin stood abruptly. Taking hold of a lantern with an ox-horn window, he stepped down from the dais and spoke to two of the guards. They took hold of the captives by the arms and marched them to a door at the side of the room. There were stone steps leading downwards, lit by one of the guards holding a rushlight. At the bottom of the steps, there was a cell with an oak-planked door. Fengel and Beggs protested as the guards pushed them inside the cell that smelt of earth and urine. The door slammed shut, enveloping them in blackness, and they heard the guards slotting a heavy wooden beam, that had been leaning against the wall, into iron brackets outside. The crude lock sounded final.

"Look at what Uberatu's got us into now," Beggs said.

"I am unable to look, I can see only blackness."

After a short while, they sat on the floor of compacted earth. They could hear a hum of conversation upstairs. After a while courage returned, and they began to talk about their predicament. They realised the people upstairs must be curious about them, and would come back to question them. The odds would be against overpowering the guards, but Fengel suggested that if they loosened their bonds, they would be ready to take any opportunity for freedom that came along.

In the darkness, they turned back-to-back. As Fengel struggled with Beggs' knotted ropes, he tried to work out what had happened to them.

"When we were in the room on the top of the hill did you notice anything unusual about the forest?"

"It was huge."

"It was much bigger than before we went into the room."

"The Dearden place has changed as well. The outbuildings and the house are different."

"Everything has changed Beggsy, beyond all recognition."

"How could it?" Beggs felt panic in his stomach. Fengel was clawing at the end of Beggs' rope, picturing what he was doing in the dark. He threaded the end back through the knot, slipped the rope off and put it in his pocket.

"Your turn, Beggsy, get my rope undone, and then we'll tie each other back up with slip knots." Beggs started to manipulate Fengel's bonds, and the concentration of working on the knot helped the panic subside. "Beggsy, a few nights ago in the barn, Uberatu said how his father had been working on going back to where there was gold for the taking."

"There's gold for the taking on that table up there."

"Yes, and then he said the safest way to get the gold back was to bury it in some hidden place in case anyone was around when they came back to modern times. Do you remember how Uberatu shut his mouth when I asked him what he meant when he told us about coming back to modern times? What is it you English say, he became *clammed up?*"

"He clammed up because he was pissed out of his brain."

"Uberatu is sometimes out of his brain even without the whisky, but there was another clue. When he was sleeping, he was muttering. I thought it was meaningless drivel like you English often speak, but something he said makes sense now."

"It'd help if something about our predicament made sense."

"Think, Beggsy, remember what Uberatu was saying."

"I know he was cursing, telling someone to get off him."

"Get off me you bleedin' Saxon, he was saying, I think what has happened to us has something to do with what Uberatu was talking about."

"What has happened to us?"

"Do I have to simplify everything for you? *'Gold for the taking, Get off me you bleedin' Saxon'.* Add up what he was saying, Beggs. All the signs are telling me we've gone back in time."

"That isn't possible."

"You say that, but everything around here is too real for any other explanation. I think the machine in Dearden's workshop and the building in the forest has something to do with time travel." Unseen in the darkness, Fengel nodded towards the conversation up the stone steps in the great hall. "The men up there are too real to be in fancy dress, *and* there is the language. I am German, and I can understand some of it. Some of it sounds like old German."

Beggs laughed.

"You can laugh, Beggs, you fool, but I'm telling you, we are in Dearden's house, and we have been transferred to a period of time different to our own."

As the hours dragged by a greater chill descended on them than caused by the cold of the dungeon. Throughout their ordeal, there was a constant drone of conversation from the great hall. At least they were free of the ropes. If an opportunity came, they could make a dash for freedom.

They had fitful snatches of sleep. It seemed to Fengel that no sooner did he start drifting off into oblivion than Beggs would move or start talking, so he gave up on sleep and waited for events to take their course.

In the great hall, the light faded into evening. Ienur lit beeswax candles in brackets on the walls and the building eventually grew silent. The logs settled and the flames of the fire dwindled to a ruddy glow. The night drew on and people slept between the wooden stalls. Outside in the moonlight, the noises of the forest grew more insistent and a hunting owl flew through the darkness and swooped silently onto its prey.

Eventually, the first hint of dawn arrived, and with it, a cacophony of birdsong began in the ancient forest. A crowing cockerel caused a dog to bark and a man called out, silencing it. The scent of resinous wood-smoke from newly lit fires permeated the air, drifting like incense over the compound. The aroma of baking bread filled the air with the promise of hunger satisfied.

Within the manor house, people were stirring and going about their early business, and Leofwin and Aelfryth came down from their private quarters. Servants brought food and drink from the kitchen and Leofwin and Aelfryth sat with their children at the long table.

As he ate and drank beor, Leofwin watched Ienur raking the ash from around the remnants of the glowing logs from the previous night's fire. With kindling added, the fire soon gave out its heat and light again. He thought about the two men imprisoned in the cell downstairs.

An hour later, the men of the Witenagemot came from their lodgings and took their places at the table. Discussion commenced as servants poured beor into drinking horns and brought food to the table. Along with the affairs of state, the Ealdormen talked about the two prisoners and the House of the West Wind.

Fengel and Beggs heard footsteps the other side of the door. The iron brackets holding the header beam rang like a tuning fork when someone removed the oak beam. The door opened and morning light streamed in. Leaning back-to-back, Fengel and Beggs scrambled to their feet and two guards manhandled them up the stone steps, where they stood, squinting against the daylight, in front of the dais.

34

Julia was angry with Dearden. Sometimes he was too impetuous. The others were no better. They all went along with Matt Roberts' scheme, which ended in catastrophe. Because of that, it also dawned on Julia that Harry had a hard edge behind his easy-going exterior.

"Seriously, do you think we'll get those two back?" She asked him.

"I wouldn't have started the trial if we couldn't get them back." Harry was standing in front of the smashed switch with a hammer. The die-cast cover was lying in pieces on the floor. He started to disconnect the cables. "The complication is that Fengel and Beggs have been taken away from the Hub and for the return trip to work they have to get back to it. I'm sure I can get them back to our time, but it may take a while to make sure the Hub's working as it should be."

"Not too long I hope. Those two are unpredictable, and I'm not certain we will get them back."

"Come on, Jules, think it through. It wouldn't be reasonable for the builders of the Hub to send voyagers off into oblivion. The original travellers *had* to be able to get back home."

"That's true. But let's hope you get the science right to bring those two back before they create a kill-your-ancestor paradox."

It took longer than expected to find a replacement switch capable of handling the amperage needed to energise the Super Magnetron, and Harry finished installing the new switch as dusk was falling. All that remained was to connect it up.

Dearden pulled up a chair and sat astride it. Along with

Doughty and the others, he was watching the CCTV display for signs of the prisoners. As darkness descended on the Anglo-Saxon community, the animal skins covering the door and window apertures brightened as fires within illuminated them.

Wynter aimed the remote control of the CCTV at the Super Magnetron and pressed one of the buttons. "How is this happening, Harry?" he asked, as the camera panned across the scene slightly.

"I don't know for sure. I've got some ideas about it, but things are happening here that fly in the face of current understanding. We've got a lot to learn," Harry said. The scene of the Anglo-Saxon village captivated him.

"Ha, got a lot to learn? That's an understatement," Julia was ready to let fly. "You men created a monumental precedent sending those two on a timeshift, particularly you Roberts. It was another of your hair-brained shit schemes."

Roberts was ready to respond and Templestone tried to defuse the tension.

"We'll have to put boundaries in place about how much we can get involved with another age," he said.

"It's too late to think of bloody boundaries don't you think? We are now *thoroughly* involved." Julia stormed out the door, slamming it shut. Slamming was becoming a trait.

Harry was pensive and deep in thought. "She's right you know Matt."

"Right, right? What do you know about what's right, you're still wet behind the ears—"

"Cool it," Dearden cut in from across the room. "Jules can give her opinion. We'll learn from what's happened and set some ground rules. Matt, lay off Harry." Roberts lifted a hand in acknowledgement. He never tangled with Dearden.

Harry's mind was elsewhere. He didn't respond to Roberts'

outburst, but he added the voice of reason. "We mustn't interfere with events and cause a paradox."

"What sort of paradox do you mean?" Wynter asked.

Harry answered, "Think about this Lee. If one of us went back to a previous timeframe and killed one of our own ancestors, it would create an impossible situation. There is conjecture that an event of that sort could destroy this time continuum."

"Thanks for the advice, Harry; I'll bear that in mind."

Julia came into the room as Harry mentioned paradox.

"Let's hope destruction due to a paradox isn't about to happen courtesy of those two idiots you sent back to 1063," she went and sat alone. After a few minutes sitting quiet, she told Dearden she had received an email from Trent Jackson. He said that in the next few hours he would send her a report about his translation of the manual.

It took those few hours for Julia to cool down, and then she received the email from Jackson. She had lightened up by the time she came into the workshop.

"Come and listen to this, it's fascinating." She had their attention. "Trent has explained how he managed to decode the language. There's a lot in the report, so this is just an outline of what he says.

"The language is sophisticated and capable of expressing complex concepts and emotions and also mathematical principles in a logical form that we can understand." Julia was uncomfortable with what she was about to reveal next. It brought back memories of her Wiltshire dig. Trent tells us the next details in strictest confidence. This is what he's told us.

"A few years ago, an amateur archaeologist found a twelfth-century treasure hoard near Brighton. He unearthed gold ornaments and jewellery near one of the old pilgrim routes leading to Saint-Jacques de Compostelle. There was a stone tablet with script on it buried under the hoard, and the archaeologist who took over the excavation asked Trent do some on-site translation. The tablet, which he termed *Brighton 1*, was totally out of context. The material was high tech but buried *under* the medieval hoard. Trent proved by tests that the soil hadn't been disturbed since the burial of the hoard. He kept the nature of it quiet and feigned that he couldn't translate it. He took the tablet away, saying he was going to work on it. He still has it in a safe.

"Here's the really interesting bit. The tablet had writing on it in both an unknown script and script in some of Earth's proto-languages. Trent made the same assumption Champollion did when he deciphered the Rosetta Stone, that the languages were a copy of the same information in different scripts. He understands the proto-languages, and from them, he translated the unknown one. He says there was a reference to travelling over immense distances expressed in higher mathematics. *Brighton 1* was unique, and he hushed up the find because of its ambiguous nature compared to the accepted framework of archaeology.

"Then Jem and I turned up with the manual. As soon as Trent saw the script, he thought he recognised it. He didn't want to say anything until he checked his archives and the stone tablet in his safe to see if there were any links to our manual, which he calls *Brighton 2*. He checked it out, and he says the language is the same. I'll read his summary.

We are making good progress with the translation and have found Brighton 2 to be a manual for the operation of the machine you call 'the Hub', which is part of a space-time transport system. The Hub has an alphanumerical name code, which corresponds in English to NJA-4902385 and the inference by its numerical value is that there are many more of such links throughout the universe. Brighton 2 also contains a record of some of the journeys and destinations visited by the race who built the Hub.

"Trent closes the email by saying that he wants to get involved further when he has time. He concludes with the opening paragraph of *Brighton 2*. It's a message to whoever finds and understands it." Julia looked around the room, excited by what she was about to reveal.

This instruction manual and the mechanism NJA-4902385 is for the inhabitants of Earth, for when they are able to understand it, and are ready to use it. The same thing has happened to many other races, throughout this universe, and others.

Julia folded the piece of paper. "Gentlemen, that last phrase is rather ambiguous but we've been handed the baton. Now we've got to learn how to run with it."

* * *

"What's our next move?" Templestone asked Dearden.

"We must increase our security. Uberatu's always one jump ahead of us. He knew the Super Magnetron was ready to use, and he sent Fengel and Beggs to get it. First thing tomorrow, we'll do a bug sweep. When Jules told me she was going to give us some news from Trent Jackson, I placed half a dozen electronic scramblers left over from the Poland mission around the place. If anyone's prying, all they'll get is white noise."

"What was the Poland mission?" Harry innocently asked. Tim Parker was curious, too.

Doughty deflected the conversation.

"Harry, how close are you to switching back on, the last thing we want is those two running amok back there."

"As soon as I've tested the new switch I'll set up the return. I hope Fengel and Beggs are savvy enough to realise they have to get back to the Hub for when it's reactivated." Harry turned back to the oscilloscopes patched into the circuitry. He was still attempting to source the fault preventing him from achieving the alpha waveform shown in the manual. He started the generator, planning to work through the calibration again after installing the new switch into the system.

While he was working, Harry accidentally banged his head on one of the cupboard doors he left open. He reeled from the shock and rubbed the spot. It was tender and would show a bruise by morning.

Something about spatial co-ordinates had been bugging him for a while, and after he hit his head, the issue became clear. It had to do with accurately plotting the target coordinates of a geographical shift. If he were to transfer a person from one place to another, he would want guarantees. How could he guarantee the person sent through the spatial dimension would not end up on a railway line with a train thundering down it, or maybe even buried under the foundations of a building? He pondered, made some notes and drew diagrams. He reasoned on geostationary satellites, and then phoned his older brother Oscar, in the experimental division of Ranstad Nanotech. He told his brother he would email a circuit diagram and his reasoning on three-dimensional positioning. "Co-Orditrax would be a good name for the instrument, it will be very precise, and quite unique," he said.

Templestone had something on his mind. "Harry, you remember I was talking about the power supply to the Hub?"

"And I suggested you go away and research it?"

"Yeah. There isn't a power cable connected to the Hub."

"How did you do the research?"

"I used a pipe and cable locator. There is no trace of cables anywhere around the Hub."

Harry swivelled his chair around and pushed it away from his workbench. "This is what I think happens. There *is* residual lighting inside the building, and there *is* a controlled atmosphere. Instruments in the Hub are on standby, they partially activate when there is a surge of power from an electrical storm. My guess is that at some time in the past there was an event that caused a failure of the power supply, but an electrical storm partially restores it and creates the activity of the Hub."

"Which must be what happened when Jem went back in time and met Leofwin."

"Exactly. But I also think the malfunction has locked the Hub into a temporal loop between 1063 and 2008."

"So what *should* be providing the operating power?"

"Remember I mentioned Nikola Tesla. Have you heard of a Tesla Generator?"

"I came across that when I was doing the research."

"Then you probably also read about Tesla working out that the Sun has a colossal positive electrical potential in the region of 200 billion volts. The Earth's ionosphere captures some of the charged particles from the Sun. The expanse between the ionosphere and the Earth stores the electrical potential. Tesla's experiments proved it was possible to tap into that stored potential as an energy source. The alien race did that way back in galactic time."

Dearden was listening in. "But then the generating system developed a fault," he suggested. Harry nodded.

"Do you think you can put it right?" Julia asked.

"Once I've located the fault I should be able to repair it, then the Hub will be back to its full potential."

"I sure hope the Hub don't run away with us when you've repaired it Harry, my man," Wynter said, as he felt a chill of uncertainty. He wished he were anywhere else but near the forest and the Hub, but he was damned if he was going to give up and run.

35

Fengel glanced at Beggs as a bell started ringing rapidly outside in the manor grounds. Leofwin, who was standing on the dais looking at them, grabbed a spear from a receptacle at the side of the hall and ran to the door leading outside. The other men of the Witenagemot grabbed their weapons and followed Leofwin at a run.

The rider at the head of an armed column was approaching through the gate into the estate. He carried a staff with a banner depicting an eagle. Riders armed with spears and wearing chain mail followed him. At the centre of the group, a tall, finely dressed man accompanied two richly clad women.

Fengel saw his chance. "Get up to that table, quick. Get the gold plates and knives." They leapt onto the dais, on their way shedding the ropes and scattering food off the plates. Beggs spotted a leather bag at the side of the room. He grabbed it and bundled the tableware into it. Fengel reached for the leader's sword where it lay on the table and strapped the belt around his waist. Beggs slung the leather bag on his shoulder and grabbed a crossbow and a bundle of bolts lying by the back wall. Fengel ran to a coffer in a corner of the dais. Lifting the lid, he saw gold coins inside. He ran his hand through them.

"We need to go," Beggs shouted, "Forget that." Fengel grabbed some of the coins, stuffed them into his pockets and slammed the lid shut.

"We'll come back for the chest another time," Fengel said. He ran to a large horn filled window in the back wall of the hall, dragged a chair up to it, and heaved himself against it. It shattered, and he lowered himself down the other side. Beggs threw the leather bag with the gold through to Fengel and scrambled after it.

They headed for a large pile of logs stacked against the fortified wall and scrambled up it. Despite his bulk, Beggs heaved himself quickly over the wall. Picking up the crossbow from where he threw it, he ran along a narrow path through a bramble thicket, tearing his jeans on the way as he ran to the safety of the forest.

Fengel noted the lie of the Sun, panting between strides. "We need to keep the Sun in the same position," he called back quietly. He dodged around the thickly growing trees, and on through dense undergrowth.

"I can't . . . see . . . the bloody Sun," Beggs gasped. The distance between them increased as he trailed behind Fengel. "Need to stop, Fengel. Wait for me." He bent over with his hands on his knees, wheezing. "Must rest, Fengel." Fengel stopped and turned to look at Beggs who was overweight and had a purple cast to his face. Fengel looked for the Sun. It was still in the same position on his right, so he knew they were following a roughly straight course.

"A minute or two, Beggsy, then if you're not ready I'm off, and I have the gold," Fengel was triumphant. Beggs lay on the ground, with sweat rolling down his face.

"You bastard, Fengel. You would clear off and leave me here." Fengel was sitting on the ground, looking at an exquisite knife made of wrought gold. After a few minutes, Beggs sat up, reinvigorated by the rest and thoughts of the contents of the bag. Fengel put the knife away.

"Come on Beggsy, we must get away before they find we've got their riches." Beggs forced himself to his feet. They progressed down a narrow path winding through forest and undergrowth. After a while, they came to a deeply rutted lane.

Fengel cautiously looked up and down the lane to see if

anyone was about. "Let's go to the left. I am bound to have the direction correct. Unlike you, I am good at that sort of thing. We can double back through the forest toward the big house. They'll never suspect we would go back to where they imprisoned us."

They trudged up the lane, taking a parallel course a few yards into the forest to make sure they were out of sight to anyone who might approach. After a while, they heard the sound of running water, and rounding a thicket of hawthorn, they came to a stone bridge where the lane crossed a stream.

"They forced us over a stream when they first caught us. If we follow it against the flow we should pick up the track leading to the building in the forest," ventured Beggs.

"I think you're right, Beggsy." Fengel changed the leather bag to his other shoulder and flexed the one that felt chafed and bruised, and then he followed the bank of the stream where the trees grew close to the water.

It was still dark the morning after Fengel and Beggs' timeshift when there was a knock on the door of the workshop. Roberts had taken a turn overnight viewing the ancient manor house through the CCTV. He unlocked the door and opened it cautiously. His Bowie was unsheathed. It was Wynter. Roberts let him in and told him it had been an uneventful night in the Anglo-Saxon village. Wynter secured the door after Roberts left, and sat in front of the screen. He saw a darkened scene of small buildings dotted about the clearing surrounding the great hall. Lanterns were moving about, as people went about their early morning tasks. As the minutes went by, Wynter noticed the roof of the great hall as the ancient dawn picked out its detail. Coming faintly through the loudspeakers his ears picked up the tones of a blackbird, soon joined by a multitude of birdsong at the start of the dawn chorus.

He went to the door, unlocked it and looked out.

"Well, I'll be damned." He saw the dawn over the present day manor house rising in tandem with the one on the CCTV screen. He checked the Glock in his belt and then opened the steel shutters. The sound of the present-day dawn chorus blended with that through the speakers and the timelessness of the experience enthralled him. The Glock was way out of place.

"Damn." He glanced down at the gun, cursing having to carry it, then re-locked the door and settled down to watch the screen.

Some time later Dearden came into the workshop followed by Doughty. Wynter was quieter than usual, and Doughty asked if he was all right.

"Sure I am. I'm watching a sunrise that happened a thousand years ago and man, it's weird." After a while, a number of people on horseback appeared out of the forest from the direction of Heanton. The man in the lead held a banner, which displayed an eagle.

As soon as he saw the riders coming down the forest track, one of the guards patrolling the wall surrounding the manor house ran to a stone structure and vigorously hit a bell hanging from a beam in its roof. The sound of the rapid ringing in the distant compound came faintly through the loudspeakers.

The riders reached the gate in the wall, which guards opened to allow them to ride into the protected compound. A number of men ran from the manor house and then halted, waiting for the riders to reach them.

A movement caught Templestone's attention, "Look to the right, at the back . . . there." He touched the screen. "They're almost out of shot at the back. Zoom in, Lee." The scene shook a little as Wynter zoomed in, and then the image was lost. He panned the camera and picked the area up again.

"It's Fengel and Beggs," Wynter said, as he went to maximum zoom. The two men were scrambling onto a pile of logs by the defensive wall by the manor house and then they climbed over the wall. Wynter stood quickly, "Oh shit, they're on the run."

* * *

Leofwin welcomed the visitors, his brother, Earl Leofric of Mercia and his wife, Countess Godgyfu, and Leofwin's ward, Lady Rowan of Maldon. As they walked toward the manor house, Leofwin told his brother about the progress the Witenagemot made the previous day about the succession. He said feelings were running high that interference from Normandy was creating a threat to the Saxon nobility. King Edward was vacillating. The Earls wanted action to secure the Saxon lineage, and they wanted it to come quickly.

As they went through the door into the great hall, Leofric nudged Leofwin's arm and pointed. Leofwin stared in disbelief at the ransacked table. The remains of the meal prepared for them was scattered over the table, and there were pools of spilt beor. The household dogs were lapping it where it lay in puddles on the floor. Leofwin glanced up and saw the smashed window and the ropes that previously held the prisoners, scattered on the floor. He let out a roar of anger. The golden utensils, heirlooms from his ancestors laid out with luxurious food in honour of the Witenagemot, were no longer on the table.

"Those two sons of dogs have taken the valuables and my sword, Aelfrythsgiefu." Leofwin was beside himself with anger, matched formidably by that of Leofric. "Ienur, Ienur dammit, where are you? Rouse the guard. Cenhelm, get the horses prepared, quickly now, and Sigward," Leofwin shouted. 'Loose the mastiffs. Get them ready for the chase."

Ienur ran with the horse and handed Leofwin the bridle.

"This doesn't need us both, Leofric. You and your men stay here, guard the village." Leofric lifted his arm in acknowledgement as Leofwin swung into the saddle. Ienur held the bridle steady, his own horse standing by was restless, and the guard was forming up with the clashing of steel and harness.

Four mastiffs, each with a handler, were young dogs in training for the chase. They were yelping with anticipation. Another, standing quietly at Leofwin's side was an older dog, the leader of the pack. It was larger and more muscular than the others were, and it went by the name of Garr. He was both Leofwin's housedog, and a hunter. His handler slipped the leash off the studded collar. The horses were restless as Garr moved around them. With the noise from the other dogs, the horses nervously stamped the ground.

"Garr, by me now." The dog fell in close to the side of Leofwin's horse as he spurred it on through the gateway followed by the men at arms. They went at a fast canter around the outside of the wall to the place where the escaped prisoners had scaled it. The two hadn't attempted to hide their tracks into the forest, and Ienur pointed to a scrap of blue cloth caught on a bramble.

Leofwin dismounted and examined the escape route, holding Garr's collar. Ienur offered the cloth up to the muzzle of the dog. He sniffed it and whined, then made off into the forest leading the other four who were yelping with the thrill of the chase. Leofwin felt the excitement of the dogs. He mounted up and spurred Brannling after them.

Fengel and Beggs were on higher ground overlooking the compound. They could see a group of men and their leader, the man who had ordered them into the dungeon, and whose sword Fengel was now wearing. He was leading the armed men on horseback around the outside of the wall surrounding the manor house. Four large dogs were in front, while a fifth, a great mastiff with a studded collar, was leading them toward the escape route.

"They are on to us, Beggsy." Fengel saw the men on horseback ride into the forest. A faint breeze was blowing the scent of the two men away from the dogs so they were able to catch their breath for a brief spell.

"This is no good, Fengel. With those dogs on our tail, they're going to find us."

"Where's your spirit, Beggsy, remember if we get this gold home we'll be made for life." Fengel tested the weight of the leather bag. "It must be worth thousands of pounds."

Beggs heard the faintest of noises. "It's the dogs Fengel, they're coming this way."

"Come on then Beggs, you fat man, be quick. Let's head for the stream." They kept to the higher ground, and then worked their way into a valley where they could spy on those hunting them. The noise of the chase was growing louder and they heard the distant voices of men shouting.

They made off in the direction of the stream. At the foot of the slope, they heard the drumming of hooves approaching rapidly. A mounted man in chain mail, battle-axe held high, was bearing down on them, shouting fiercely as he came.

Fengel grabbed the crossbow off Beggs, turned and knelt. "Give me an arrow, *quickly.*" Facing the oncoming rider, he placed a bolt into the track of the already taut crossbow. He lifted it to his shoulder and loosed.

* * *

"There's some action at the back." Roberts pointed to the screen. Wynter panned the CCTV camera away from the escapees and focussed on a horseman who had come into view, galloping toward Fengel and Beggs with a battle-axe raised high.

"I don't like the look of that," Doc Parker said. The others jostled for position to get a better view. They vaguely heard the drumming of hooves, saw Fengel kneel, and then the rider toppled from his horse, which galloped on wildly.

"Zoom in closer," Harry's fists clenched.

"I'm doing my best, Harry, my man. I'll get the sonofabitch," Wynter panned around then zoomed in on the fallen man. They could see blood pooling on the ground from his throat, where there was a projectile embedded.

Harry swore as a whiteout hit the CCTV screen. He reacted quickly. Grabbing the handset off Wynter, he aimed it at the Super Magnetron and triggered the on/off button. The monitor screen went blank, and after he switched on again the scene of the forest filled the screen. Fengel and Beggs had disappeared. He shook his head as he gave the handset back to Wynter.

"Find them, Lee," Templestone said. He was standing at Wynter's side, uptight and impatient.

"I'm doing my best Priest, don't bug me."

The screen blurred as Wynter panned around the scene.

"There they are, to the left, heading for the stream," Roberts pointed and Wynter panned to the left, bringing them centre screen as Fengel leapt into the stream. Beggs stumbled as he jumped in and the water came up to his thighs. He recovered and lifted the crossbow and bag of bolts clear of the water. They became lost to view in the gloom of the trees where the stream gushed from the inner reaches of the forest through a gulley.

"Now what's goin' on?" Wynter exclaimed as he saw Fengel, with Beggs trailing behind, walking along the top of the gulley above the fast-flowing stream. A lone mastiff had the men's scent in its nostrils, and it was gaining on them. It was a heavy-jowled creature, and those watching the screen heard its barking, deep and distant. Fengel turned and froze when he saw the dog. He reached inside his jacket and pulled out something small and black. Those in the workshop heard a distant report and heard the dog yelp. It rolled into the gully and disappeared into the torrent below.

"How the hell did we miss the gun?" Dearden, looking over Matt Roberts shoulder exclaimed. He saw the unmistakable shape of a Luger Parabellum.

"It's because you didn't even think of looking for it," Julia was scornful. "The gun raises the stakes, paradoxes . . . remember?"

"What do you suggest?" Harry asked Dearden.

"We don't have a choice. The way they're going they'll create a situation that can never be put right. Sorry, people, there's no other way out of this, we've got to go back ourselves and put a stop all this chaos."

36

They gave themselves a three-hour slot to plan the Leofwin's Hundred mission. The planning was intense and Dearden was adamant he would go.

"I'm the cause of this situation, I'm going."

"If you're going, so am I," Doughty said, "You need someone to cover your back."

"And I'll tell you right now that this is an archaeologist's dream. If you think I'm missing out on a journey into the past you've got another think coming. Count me in." When Julia insisted, nothing got in the way. Harry stood quickly and went to a drawer at the back of the workshop. He took out two handsets, larger than the remote for the CCTV, and made for a far bigger hand.

"Listen up guys, this is important." He held up one of the handsets and checked the time on one of the three Caruthers Chrono clocks, governed by a transmission system from the NPL's cesium fountain atomic clock.

"It's now 10:05 on October thirtieth, 2008. I'll show you how to program the handset. You'll have this with you to get you back into the Hub on the homeward journey. We'll program the handset to take you to 11 o'clock on October thirtieth, 1063. You tap in the target time first, and then the date." Harry had stuck function labels on the buttons. He passed the handset to Dearden. It was cold to the touch and felt metallic.

"The builders of the Hub programmed it to respond to *find* and *go-to* commands using spatial or temporal coordinates, or both of them together. You punch in the coordinates of your target place or time, and then press *go*. The Hub then slews everything inside it to the target time and location."

"How do we unlock the door to get back into the Hub?" Doughty asked.

"When you're standing outside, press this green button and the door unlocks."

"So we can set our arrival before the time Fengel killed the horseman to stop it happening," Julia suggested.

"I've thought long and hard about that. It would be great to do it, but we don't know enough about altering life or death events by using the Hub. No paradoxes, remember?"

"Mmm . . . not good, but you're right. But when we learn more about the implications—"

"That may be a different thing," Harry said. "Right now, we'll only intervene in events we see shaping up," They watched as he set the target time and date. "All you need do is press this red button to enter the data when the Hub is activated, and away you go."

* * *

Dearden handed Doughty an emergency field kit he brought from the storeroom below the great hall, and to Templestone he gave an over and under shotgun from the armoury. Templestone broke the weapon and checked the breech. He inserted two cartridges, kept the gun open, and hung it over his arm. "Looks as though I'll be holding the fort until you get Fengel and Beggs back."

"You'll be good with that, Bill."

"Maybe, but don't get lost back there. I don't want it to be a permanent job."

"Jem . . ." Harry beckoned him over and gave him a pair of modified Motorola two-way radios. "When you're ten minutes into the timeshift we'll test the comms. We will make contact during the first day, but don't use the comms unless there's an emergency. You need to preserve the batteries."

"If there's anything significant we'll report back."

"Do that. I've set up round the clock shifts to stand by for incoming calls. I have also put a sensor into the circuitry so that when we transmit to you, your unit switches on. It automatically switches off after the call. You can switch Fengel's unit on with an incoming call but he'll have to switch it off manually afterwards. I didn't have time to do the full mods."

There was an awkward silence before Dearden spoke again. "You've become a big part of the team, Harry. I've really appreciated your help with this project, you know?"

"I wish I was going with you, it's the start of a new era."

"You'll get your chance, but when we're not so pushed."

Dearden cast a critical eye over the group, his two friends going with him and the backup team staying at base. Harry was standing by the controls of the Super Magnetron.

"Are you ready for this?" Dearden asked Doughty and Julia. Doughty hitched the emergency field kit onto his shoulder, and they nodded they were ready.

"Then let's go." The three took their positions behind the shield with a thirty-second countdown.

Wynter checked the screen. "CCTV is live. Recording equipment is good and rolling."

"The Lycoming generator is fully fuelled and ready when you are Harry," Matt Roberts said.

Templestone was standing by the switch. He inserted the lever into its socket and grasped it ready to switch on.

Harry pushed the remote start of the electro-generator at twenty seconds to go. The roar of the Lycoming punched the air, ready to send heavy amperage into the Super Magnetron.

"15 seconds," Harry read from the mission countdown Chrono, "10 . . . 9 . . . 8 . . ."

Dearden pressed the go-to button on the count of zero. On a microscopic level, a bombardment of electrons from the magnetron hit the surface of the crystal and distorted its surfaces. The internal reaction produced a harmonic with the great crystal in the Hub. The lines of force of the cosmic grid in the neighbourhood of the Earth curved down to the crystal, and the timeframe began to peel back through the years.

The three faded from the view of the team in the workshop. Harry Stanway noted with satisfaction that the Caruthers Chrono clock on the wall, rigged for mission duration, was running satisfactorily. He had programmed it to start with a press of the go-to button on the handset.

The *Mission Target Year* Chrono bore no resemblance to the other two, which were passive. The target LCD display was a blur that, if viewed in extreme time lapse showed time traversing down . . . down . . . down through the years.

In the workshop, the CCTV screen showed static interference for a few seconds and then those watching saw the scene steadily morph into the brightly lit colours of an autumn morning. Wynter panned the camera, analysing the ancient scene. Overhead, thunderheads darkened a local section of sky.

Matt Roberts darted to the window. Jagged lightning ripped through the swirling black clouds over Leofwin's Hundred, and the sound of thunder rolled across the landscape.

37

After Dearden pressed the go-to button on the handset the surroundings blurred and all went quiet for a few seconds, and he felt cushioned. The process was over in less than ten seconds and the cushioning faded.

Julia looked at the forest through the transparent wall. It was huge, as if it had no boundary. "The harmonic worked, we've been transferred to the Hub. Are we in 1063?"

"We should be if Harry's calibrated the machine correctly," Dearden said.

"Then let's hope he's got his maths right." Doughty was holding the AK 47 at the ready. He scanned the room. The CCTV camera was there, on the table in front of the great crystal, its red indicator light flashed every few seconds showing it was active.

Julia headed to the window and looked out. "There's Dearden Hall before the additions,"

Doughty could see a church and the roofs of some buildings through a gap in the trees. "And that must be Hampton in Arden, up on the hill."

"*Heanton in the Arden* in Anglo-Saxon times," Julia said.

"Ready?" Dearden asked, as he picked up the combat rucksack he had with him and moved to the door. He opened it and led the three over the threshold into the altered dimension.

A group of armed men were approaching the base of the hill. The tall blond haired man Dearden met before was leading them, with a bone-handled sword ready for use. Other men were fanning out, some on foot, others mounted, all of them with weapons at the ready.

Leofwin had seen the disturbance in the sky and had broken off the search for the escaped prisoners. The events in the forest had puzzled him. There had been an event twice in two days. This time, when he saw the disturbance in the sky, he knew what it was, and made straight to the House of the West Wind. Since the man named Dearden came down the hill with the wolf, Leofwin was confident he was dealing with something rational. He could not understand what was going on, but the place intrigued him and he had no fear.

On the way into the forest, they came across the warrior who had challenged the two on the run. Leofwin stopped and checked the man but he was dead. He had been a faithful servant and Leofwin vowed to avenge his death on the criminals. They moved on quickly, guided by the sound of Shadow Brook, and the clouds, dark and disturbed over the part of the forest where the House of the West Wind lay.

When they came to the foot of the hill, the Anglo-Saxons saw the door in the building was open and three individuals standing there. Leofwin recognised the one at the front as Dearden, who led the way down the hill and held out his hand as he reached level ground. Leofwin responded uncertainly because the shaking of hands was a sign of entering into a contract, and he had no business deal going on with Dearden.

Julia's Anglo-Saxon was academic but she spoke to the gathered men, introducing herself, and then she pointed to Doughty and Dearden and introduced them by name. The tall Anglo-Saxon man, clearly the leader, by his air of authority and rich clothing, was surprised at first when Julia spoke in his own language. To the man's ear, the woman's accent sounded smooth and attractive, foreign, but he understood her and introduced himself.

"This is Earl Leofwin," Julia said to Dearden and Doughty. The Ealdorman scrutinised the three people, trying to detect their motives. He put his hand forward to Dearden. They shook.

"Leofwin, we meet again." Julia translated for Dearden.

"Tell him I'm glad he's stopped sneezing," Leofwin said. There was laughter, and then the conversation became serious.

"We came a long distance to capture the two criminals who arrived here. We need your help," Julia said.

"We will help you. They killed one of my men and stole valuables from my house. We must search for them before their scent grows cold. Come, we will make preparations."

Doughty looked at his wristwatch. The guard walking by his side looked at it warily. Doughty held his arm up for the man to see the watch. At zero plus ten minutes, Doughty pulled the Motorola from his pocket and switched it on. The men surrounding them readied their weapons when Doughty keyed the on/off switch and the handset lit up.

Julia explained, "This is a radio. We use it to talk to people where we live. We can talk to them when they're a long distance away." Doughty tried communicating with Harry. All he could hear was static, and with no contact, it hit him just how isolated they were.

As he approached the entrance of the manor house with its Anglo-Saxon owner, Dearden recognised the pattern of the grain on the newly worked timber of the entrance door. One of his first jobs at Dearden Hall when he inherited it was to strip off the paint successive owners had applied to the door. It was hard work sanding it with a power tool, but the effort revealed the figuring of the grain. He had brushed protective oil onto the surface. The oil took a long while to soak in, but when it had done, the oak became a rich, golden colour.

The armed men escorted Dearden, Doughty and Julia into the interior of the great hall. It smelt of the wood burning in the middle of the room. The flickering light of the fire picked out some of the detail of the hall. There were antlers and boars' heads, on the walls, and mighty timber trusses high up in the dimness of the roof. There were candles spread about, and a faint smell of beeswax from them hung in the air, mixing with the resinous smell from the burning logs.

From somewhere higher up in the building, they could hear the sound of women's laughter, and light-hearted chatter. Dearden saw Leofwin's face ease into a smile at the sound of the laughter. There was a likeable quality about the Anglo-Saxon and Dearden sensed that the earl had a gentle side to his nature.

Leofwin spoke to Julia, introducing some of the men seated at the high table. It was an illustrious group of people. The first was a tall individual, full of self-assurance, with ginger hair cascading to his shoulders.

"This is Earl Leofric of Mercia, Leofwin's brother," Julia said. Judging by the scarred state of the chain mail Leofric was removing, he led from the front. The sword at his side was resplendent with gold and semi-precious stones. Standing by Leofric was Ranulf de Briquessart, introduced as an Anglo-Saxon sympathiser from the Frankish land across the sea.

In front of Leofric on the high table was an ornate helmet with a nose guard and gold embellishments. Dearden found it difficult to come to terms with the fact that the individual just a few feet from him was the man involved with an event that had become legendary, the naked ride of his wife Godiva through the streets of Coventry. Others introduced were all noblemen. They gathered around Julia and questioned her about the House of the West Wind, why they came from it and why they were wearing strange apparel. They were suspicious at first but seemed satisfied that she and her colleagues had come to capture the two criminals.

Leofwin's seriousness returned and he became agitated. He spoke to the Witenagemot and afterwards to Julia. Dearden picked up the words *man* and *goldhwæt*. "What was that about, Jules?" he asked. "I picked up the word *gold*."

"You heard Leofwin say *goldhwæt*. It has the meaning of greed attached to it, *greed for gold*. They stole Leofwin's gold tableware, and his sword, Aelfrythsgiefu." Dearden saw her eyes rise fractionally when Jules said the name, "And he wants to avenge the murder we saw. The man was in charge of Leofwin's farms hereabouts, he was well-liked around here."

Leofwin heard Julia mention the name of his sword, and it re-focussed him. He walked to the door and spoke to his houscarl, Ienur, who was waiting outside.

"See to it our guests have what they need, but stay with them at all times. I don't know if I can trust them." Leofwin signalled for some waiting men at arms to follow.

"It looks as though he's not going to let us help him capture Fengel and Beggs," Julia whispered, as Ienur came over to them, and two guards positioned themselves on the inside of the door.

The women in one of the rooms at the top of the stairs were curious. Over the past few days, there had been unusual activity, beginning first of all with the capture of the two men who came from the House of the West Wind, and after that, their escape.

Now another group of strangers came from the forest. One of them, a woman, was speaking Anglo-Saxon, but with a foreign accent. And then the sounds of preparation could be heard, the warlike clash of weapons, men gathering in the courtyard outside. Horses, restless stamping the ground, ready for the freedom of the ride. Curiosity ruled. The women had to go down to the great hall to see what was going on . . .

* * *

A serving man opened the door in the sidewall and four women came through. They were dressed in long, brightly coloured robes. Three of them stayed by the door. The other, who had long, lustrous black hair, came to Ienur and spoke to him while scrutinising the three strangers from the forest. She turned to the women by the stairs and called them over.

"This woman has a Celtic accent," Julia said in an undertone, as the woman with the dark hair walked around them with an easy confidence as if appraising them. She stopped in front of Julia and told her she was Countess Aelfryth, wife of Leofwin, and introduced the tallest of the other three as Countess Godgyfu, wife of Earl Leofric. One of the other women she said was her ward, the Lady Rowan of Maldon, and the last, Esma, Rowan's companion.

Rowan's physical beauty attracted Dearden. He sensed something else difficult to define in the background. A familiarity, as if they had known each other before. The strangest thing was that he knew Rowan felt the same.

Dearden had to force himself to look away from her light blue eyes to focus on Ienur, who was guarding them with a drawn sword. They were incongruous, the weapon and Rowan, and Dearden's focus began to drift. He pulled his mind back on track, and his patience frayed.

"Jules, tell this man it's urgent we get after Fengel and Beggs. This waiting's no good."

She translated, and Ienur replied briefly.

"Ienur's been told to make sure we stay here until Leofwin gets back. I'll speak to Aelfryth. I think she's got influence around here. I might get us some freedom." The conversation became tense after Julia spoke to the dark-haired woman.

"I told her we have powerful weapons with us. At first, she told me she didn't like my manner. Then I said how dangerous the two criminals are, and she agreed to let us go out to Leofwin, as long as we're guarded."

Aelfryth spoke to Ienur and he called over the two guards over from their post by the outer door, and Aelfryth indicated for Dearden and the others to follow.

Leofwin was on the village green, preparing his men for the chase, some were mounted, others were on foot, and there were dogs, noisy and straining on the leash. Leofwin frowned when he saw Aelfryth and the three visitors approaching, but Julia intervened, saying they came to help, and they had powerful weapons with them for protecting the village from the two outlaws.

"We have powerful weapons. Look at our dogs. They are young and eager. The scent of the men is in their nostrils."

"Those two men who escaped killed one of the young dogs that you were training."

"How do you know that?"

"We saw it happen."

Leofwin shrugged his shoulders. "Look at my fighting men and their weapons," Leofwin spoke with pride in his voice. "Tell your friends they can come if they wish. You are not coming, you are good at speaking our tongue, but you do not have the strength for fighting. You are a woman."

"What did you say?"

Dearden caught the anger in Julia's voice; saw the glint in her eyes. He knew how close anger sometimes was to the surface with Jules, how it could boil over.

"What's happening?" he asked, ready to step between her and Leofwin. She didn't answer, but her anger was seething. She looked around for something she could use to make an impression. There was a pile of roof tiles, with weeds around them. "You wait there," she bristled, pointing at Leofwin.

Leofwin drew upright in his saddle. Even his wife, Aelfryth, whose temper was sometimes dark and Celtic, never spoke to him like that. She could not match the fury he saw in the eyes of the woman in front of him. She was even wearing trousers, which was disturbing because it showed her shape, and it was attractive. He was curious and wondered what she was doing as she went to the pile of earthenware tiles left over from covering the manor house roof. She counted six out in front of Leofwin, and then took off her shoes and socks.

"I'll show you how strong I am. Look and learn. Mitch, hold these tiles." Doughty handed the AK 47 to Dearden. He grasped the tiles and adopted a semi-crouch. He had done this before, in another of her demonstrations.

"Here she goes again," Dearden said.

"Yeah, this is it." There was amusement in Doughty's eyes as Julia quietly stood in the style of Tameshiwari, a spirit test. She concentrated on the tiles, and drew herself back and round, feeling her inner strength coiled and held, ready for release. Her energy peaked and she snapped out in a perfectly executed roundhouse kick, shouting as the power lashed out, and her foot finished six inches beyond the tiles, which had shattered. At first, there was silence, and then cries of surprise from those gathered around.

Julia went to the front of Leofwin, mounted on his horse, and bowed to him as she would an opponent, then stood with her hands on her hips.

"What do you think now? Still think I'm weak?"

Humour replaced the puzzled look on Leofwin's face. "This is Julia," he shouted, and then quietly, "It will be good to have you with us, Jules," he used the shortened name he heard Dearden using. One of the men in the watching group came up and clapped Julia hard on the back, thinking she could take it. Another man, a muscular labourer, bent down to look at her foot, which was hard and calloused. He looked up from his position on the ground, and a smile creased his tawny features.

"Julia is strong and she comes with us," Leofwin shouted.

"What do you think he'd say if we demonstrated the A.K?" Doughty murmured to Dearden.

"We'll keep that for when it's needed."

Julia went to the side of Leofwin's horse and indicated for him to lean down. She spoke so only he could hear.

"Earl Leofwin, believe us when we say we can help you. Take it seriously when we tell you those two men can do you *great* harm."

Leofwin sat back upright and lifted his hand in acknowledgement, and then told Cenhelm to bring three more horses from the stables. They headed for the place where Fengel murdered the thegn. Earl Leofwin had Garr with him, but as good as the mastiff was in the chase, he was unable to get the scent of the two men on the run. They had vanished into the vastness of the forest.

During the evening, back in the great hall, they discussed the situation and as the hours went by, formal talk eased into friendly conversation. Dearden, Doughty and Julia became more familiar with the men of the Witenagemot, and Leofwin's family. They found his brother Leofric's personality distant and aloof, but Leofwin himself was friendly and communicative.

Godgyfu and Aelfryth were interested in where the three wayfarers had come from. Aelfryth wanted to know what their homeland was like and she asked many questions. Julia tried to explain where they travelled from in a way Aelfryth could understand.

Rowan enjoyed their company. The visitors were so different to her fellow Anglo-Saxons, somehow more challenging. In particular, she was attracted to the man called

Jem Dearden. She sat by his side and tried to talk to him. They were comfortable on the cushions placed on a stone sill by a tall window. Dearden called Julia away from the main group. She sat for a while with Jem and Rowan. After she left them, Dearden and Rowan taught each other words in their own languages by pointing at objects and naming what they saw. They laughed at their efforts of communication and became close during the hours of evening.

During those hours, the feeling came again to Dearden that he was *reacquainting* himself with Rowan of Maldon. As well as being beautiful, he had understood through Julia's translation that Rowan comprehended much of what he was saying although they came from such different cultures.

He recalled the chapter called *The Golden Maid of Maldon*, in George M. Gresham's *Warwickshire Legends*, which told of how the beautiful woman had disappeared into the forest one day. Dearden dismissed the legend as fanciful at the time. Now he realised the legend was probably about the woman at his side, and he wondered what would happen to her. Time had altered for him; its restrictions unfettered. He reached for Rowan's hand and kissed it. She didn't withdraw. Instead, she looked into Leofwin's Great Hall, saw no one was looking, and then drew close to Dearden and kissed him on the lips.

As if coming as an echo from the past, he thought of Jackie Mason. He still loved her, that would never change, but he seemed to hear her say that it wouldn't matter. *It will be all right Jem, look to the future . . . Let this happen. You will be all right.*

All too soon, tiredness began to overtake them. Rowan went away through a side door, out of the great hall and Dearden watched her go up some stone steps leading to an upper level of the manor house.

* * *

Esma lit the way up the dark stairs, shielding the candle flame with her hand. The room shared by her and Rowan was along the passage at the head of the stairs. Its window overlooked the green outside. In public, there was a necessary formality about their relationship. Out of the public gaze, they resumed the friendship that existed since they were ten-year-old children. They grew up together after their fathers died in the defeat of the Vikings during the Second Battle of Maldon.

Esma set the candle on a table in the centre of the room and lit two more from it, which she placed next to their cots.

"The one named Jem Dearden likes you," Esma said, turning to face Rowan. "He is handsome, and pays attention to what you say."

"I like him too. I hope he pays me attention because he wants to be with me all of the time. I think that is so. Jules had to help us understand one another's language, but I want him to love me, Esma. I want him to love me so much."

Esma changed the subject.

"Did you notice he does not smell of horses?

"I asked him about that. He said that most people where he comes from do not ride horses, and he told me that what he does smell of is Old Spice."

"If they do not ride horses how do they go about their business?"

"He told me how they do it. There is a word he used," Rowan's brow puckered as she tried to recall the word Jem told her. Esma waited for Rowan to tell her about the method of transport, and saw her friend's strong refined features, the long eyelashes and her slightly dark eyebrows, which curled down slightly at the ends toward her cheekbones.

"Kahz; that is what Jem said they ride in. Things called a kahz," Rowan said, as she settled in her cot and blew out the candle. Her mind was full of the images of the evening with the three people who had come through the House of the West Wind. She shivered at the thought. As far back as she could remember the rule was to keep away from the ancient building in the forest. Yet, as soon as she saw Jem Dearden, who came through that building, she felt a strong attachment to him, and she felt safe with him. Rowan thought how contradictory life is sometimes, and overly complicated too.

She was restless at first, but eventually she fell asleep and dreamed of riding with Jem Dearden in a fantastic vehicle called a kahz, which smelt of sage and rosemary, and all manner of old spice tucked within its crevices.

Straw mattresses were placed in three of the stalls at the side of the great hall for Dearden, Doughty and Julia. They were welcome after the day that tested the imagination. Dearden found it impossible to sleep. His thoughts dwelt on the remarkable evening with Rowan. Her near presence made him restless, and the vision of the Golden Maid of Maldon became part of him.

* * *

Harry was working on the transceiver base unit he had adapted to communicate with Dearden. He had added filters to counter the electromagnetic interference from the Hub and was upgrading components in the amplification circuit. Harry was convinced there should be communication, even if it was the slightest hint of modulation. Despite his upgrades, there was only white noise coming from the speakers.

The phone rang. It was Trent Jackson, asking if he could speak to Tim Parker.

Jackson told Parker the analysis of the language was nearly complete and he asked him if he could get back to London to help with some unexpected research. It had to do with some separate information he found tucked into the manual. Jackson said it was urgent, so within half an hour, Templestone had run Parker to Hampton in Arden station.

When Templestone came back, he and Roberts went into the forest with a camera to do some exploratory work inside the alien building. They entered the ground floor level.

"It's brighter in here," Templestone remarked as soon as he was inside. Roberts tried to recall what it had been like before.

"I think you're right. Let's look upstairs." They went to the control room. The lighting, previously a background glow, was definitely brighter. There was activity on the screens in front of the bank of seats.

"Harry's work's causing the Hub to activate, we need to get him here," Templestone said.

Harry had pushed Trent Jackson for a translation of the symbols on the function keys in the Control Room and he had received an email with the results. Coincidentally, within ten minutes, Roberts called, saying there was a difference in the lighting in the Hub, that the screens in the control room were active. Harry and Wynter rushed to the Hub on Harry's CX500. They rushed up to the Control Room. Harry took a quick glance at the activity on the screens. He referred to Jackson's email and, within minutes, had stuck squares of masking tape onto the keys, and wrote on them a translation of their function.

He was sitting on the large central chair. Templestone, Roberts and Wynter sat on the seats behind. Harry switched on the bank of computers and pressed the key controlling the charging circuitry. There was the heavy clunk of a relay cutting in. He had experimented with overclocking, but the boot-up speed of the alien computers left overclocking in the shade. Ambient light in the room became brighter, and a low-pitched hum coursed through the fabric of the building.

"Power supply's on stream." Harry indicated the display on the screens up front.

"So Tesla was right when he said power can be tapped out of the air and don't cost nothin. Man, ain't that cool."

"Don't jump the gun, Lee, but when the stability of this rig's one hundred percent, we'll really see what the beast can do."

38

Dearden savoured the freshness of the early morning. He looked skywards and took a deep breath. The sound of hammering from scaffolding surrounding the hall caught his attention. With the sunlight still below the tops of the trees to the east, it threw the trees into profile and cast long shadows on the ground.

There were two guards standing by the door into the Hall. Both held a spear and had a sheathed sword with a bone handle hanging diagonally across the chest from the shoulder. They were trying to look unconcerned but Dearden detected their interest in what he was doing. Nearby a man was washing in a tub of water on a bench. Dearden went up to him and practised one of the phrases he learnt from Rowan the previous evening. He recalled the tones of her voice.

"Mæġ Íċ?" *Can I*, he asked.

"Þé cunnan," *you can*, the man said, as he dried himself on a piece of old cloth. Dearden stripped to the waist and plunged his hands and arms into the water. There were remnants of a film of ice the other man had broken on the surface, and the chill of the water took away his breath. He splashed water over his head, and it refreshed him after his night on the straw mattress. He heard footsteps and turned to see Rowan and Esma coming toward him. Rowan held out some dry cloth to him and smiled.

"Íċ þancie þé," *I thank you*, he said.

"For you, I like to do, Jem Dearden," she tried some of her newly learnt words. He reached for the cloth and his hand touched hers, staying for a second longer than was needed. Dearden shivered in the chill of the morning and put on his shirt and jacket. He walked with Rowan and Esma toward the great hall. The memories of the previous night came flooding back as Rowan linked her arm through his. She was a fraction shorter than he was, and Dearden thought she looked in her mid-twenties. She had strong features and startlingly light blue eyes he found enchanting. When she spoke, Dearden understood a few of the Anglo-Saxon words preserved through the years into modern English, and he could guess at some of the others. Most seemed to have vague Germanic overtones.

They reached the door of the manor house and Rowan stood in front of him, preventing him from going into the building. Her hair moved in the breeze, and the Sun gave it golden highlights.

"Please, tell more to me about where you are from," Rowan asked in her own language. Dearden couldn't understand her.

"Wait, let's see if Jules is about," he put his hand on her arm, touched his ear and shrugged, indicating he needed help with the language. They went into the great hall and saw Julia standing by the fire in the centre of the room talking to Doughty. She looked up and Rowan asked the question. Julia translated and Rowan stood back and regarded them. Before Dearden could answer, her curiosity got the better of her.

"Do you all wear funny clothes where you come from?" She laughed and Dearden thought how delightful was her laugh, although he didn't understand what she said.

"Jules, this is going to be complex. What did she say?"

Dearden tried to frame an answer Rowan would understand. "We come from a different place in time, and our clothes are different to yours. See how Jules is dressed? She can run easier than you can because your clothes are too heavy."

"I would like to wear clothes like Jules."

"I'll see if I can order some for you," Dearden said, and he laughed. Then he summarised the world they came from as simply as he could, which was difficult. Julia translated as Dearden spoke. "We come from the future. Our world is different to yours in many ways."

"What do you mean when you say, from the future?" Rowan asked. Dearden took a leaf out of Lee Wynter's way of figuring the timeshift out.

"Imagine being able to talk to your grandmother when she was a young woman. If you were standing there talking to her, you would have come to her from her future. We have come from your future and we've travelled nearly a thousand years." Dearden paused to see if she understood what he was saying.

"That is indeed strange," she answered, and after looking around to see if any of her own people were close enough to hear, she looked at Dearden. All trace of her smile had gone. She drew closer to him while speaking quietly to Julia.

"Rowan is saying she ought to call the guard and have you thrown into the dungeons for practising wizardry, but as it's you, she trusts your explanation. She says she can see the truth in your eyes and she doesn't want to have to visit you in the dungeon and see you come to harm."

"Thank her for that, Jules. Tell her we came here to help, not to cause harm, and when we came through the House of the West Wind it was not by a trick of wizardry."

Rowan frowned, and her eyebrows tilted down slightly in the middle delightfully. She said, "No one goes near that building. It is not to be trusted, and yet you say you came through it. I have heard that only certain people go in and out of the House of the West Wind. They are different ones, not as we are, but taller and they are a green colour. I have never seen them, and we have never found out who those people are."

Dearden was struggling to find a reply, so with words ancient and modern, and by signs, he tried to converse. Julia translated when the conversation faltered.

"There is nothing about the House of the West Wind to be afraid of," Dearden said. "Whoever goes into the building needs to know how to use it. It's like taming a wild horse before you can ride it."

* * *

"I'm knackered Fengel," Beggs complained.

"But we've only been going an hour. You must lose some weight, look at your shape."

Just then, a small voice surprised Fengel, it was coming from his jacket pocket. "I know you're there Fengel, we're closing in." Fengel dived his hand into his pocket and pulled the Motorola out. The status display was showing the word, *Dearden*. There was a button marked transmit, he pressed it fiercely.

"Is that you Dearden? Get off our tail or you're a dead man. We'll be hiding behind a tree with a crossbow and that will be it, kaput, a bolt through the throat like the other man who crossed us."

Dearden disregarded the threat. "I'll tell you this once Fengel, so listen up and take note. I have had enough of you and Beggs, so has Leofwin. Give yourselves up now, or I won't answer for the consequences." Dearden put the handset away and shrugged.

He was standing next to Doughty and Julia on the greensward in front of the entrance to the manor, and Leofwin had six of his armed men ready for the chase. Sigward, in charge of Garr, held the piece of blue cloth caught on a bramble during the escape. As soon as the mastiff had the scent, he strained on the leash, eager to be off. The group mounted up, Sigward let Garr off the leash, and the horses followed the mastiff at a steady pace.

Garr followed the trail to the place where the thegn, Radulf was murdered. Blood still stained the ground and the dog lingered at the spot for a second or two. Sigward offered the blue cloth up to the dog's snout. He whined and was off again, leading the chase toward Shadow Brook. A light breeze was blowing from the opposite bank. Garr leapt into the water and swam over. The horses followed, with the fast moving water swilling around their hocks.

The mastiff scrambled onto the opposite bank and sniffed around briefly, then picked up the scent and was off, sniffing the ground deliberately. The horses followed, mud spraying from their hooves as they scrambled up the sharply sloping bank on the other side. They continued along a narrow pathway through the trees. Saplings and underbrush whipped past them until they came to a track leading off to left and right. Leofwin told Julia it was the lane between the villages of Berculs-Well and Myrig-Denu.

They eventually came to a steep track leading off through the forest to the left. Without hesitation, the mastiff led the way up the lane. Leofwin called back that the lane went past Bercul's Heall and on toward Coufaentree. At the top of the rising lane they came to a large building on the left that had smaller dwellings for workers close by. Smoke was rising from a hole in the roof.

Bercul, the owner, had respect for Leofwin whose influence spread far, and whose company people sought because of the generosity of his administration. The Ealdorman sometimes rode out, accompanied by Garr, and Ienur to see how the families who farmed his lands fared. Bercul always offered a refreshment and conversation when the Earl passed by.

At the sound of the approaching riders and the deep, excited barking of Garr, Bercul broke off ploughing in a field adjacent to the lane. The oxen came patiently to rest and he walked briskly over the field, accompanied by another man with a

293

spear. Negotiating a stile, they came into the lane. Both were wearing a Seax for protection.

The party dismounted and Bercul came over with a word of greeting for the Earl. Leofwin explained that they were hunting for two criminals who had robbed and murdered their way around Heanton. Bercul told Leofwin that the two men came by and caused trouble earlier that day. He described Fengel and Beggs who had made menacing demands in a language difficult to understand, and when Bercul refused their demands, they used a weapon that made a loud cracking noise and chipped some stone out of the wall of his house. He pointed out the impact mark from a bullet.

Bercul related how he and his men fought with the attackers, but the taller of them had wounded one of his Thralls, giving him a deep gash across his thigh from a long distance. After that, the raiders ran into the forest in the direction of Coufaentree.

Bercul wanted them to come into his house, a large stone-built place. The wounded man was lying on a course blanket with a dirty cloth covering his wound. Doughty indicated he wanted to look at it and gently eased the cloth away. He cleaned it, using iodine as an antiseptic, and bound the gash with a sterile dressing. The wounded man moaned as Doughty worked, but was grateful because, after the initial stinging, the injury felt easier. Julia talked to the injured man briefly. She reassured him that there was nothing to fear and that the wound would heal quickly if he kept it clean. The Thrall was a superstitious man. He had thought that the weapon was an instrument of the devil and that the wound came complete with a curse.

Leofwin was impatient to move on while the scent was fresh, so Sigward held the piece of cloth to the mastiff's muzzle to ready him once more for the chase. He whined, and Sigward released him from the leash and mounted up. The group of riders followed along a narrow uphill lane in the direction of Coufaentree. Before long, the lane entered the deep forest, and the light dimmed as the foliage met overhead.

After a while, the forest began to thin out and small, cultivated fields lay to each side of the track. There was a stone bridge over a clear river, and the track carried on toward the town of Coufaentree, built on a hill up ahead.

The mastiff continued the chase over the bridge, leaving the forest behind. The track widened into a granite-cobbled lane. There was a variety of buildings each side, some of wattle and daub with timber frames, and some of stone, and there were all manner of goods displayed outside for sale. The thoroughfare was busy, and the party of riders, particularly the three strangely dressed ones, attracted the attention of people they passed.

The walls and high towers of a fortified building made of red sandstone dominated the top of the hill. Its wide entrance gate was set within a massive barbican with a circular tower on each side where a number of men were guarding the fortress from the battlements.

"Coventry Castle," Julia said. They slowed the horses to a walk and rode on up the hill toward what Leofwin called the Brad Geat. As they drew near, the scale of the ramparts became apparent.

The exterior rounded walls of the gatehouse towers loomed high above them joined by a wide rounded arch. They could see a spacious bailey through the open gates and the wall of the buildings on the far side picked out in sunlight. As they reached the entrance, the gatekeeper and men armed with a variety of weapons came from a door in the right-hand tower on the far side of the gates. The gatekeeper spoke to Leofwin in urgent tones. Julia heard the conversation.

"He told Leofwin they've had trouble from two men," she said. "They forced their way into the Abbey of Saint Mary and assaulted the abbot, that's where we're going now."

Leofwin wheeled his horse around and spurred it downhill through a cobbled lane where the steel of his horse's shoes struck sparks off the cobbles. Half way down the hill they could see the long abbey and its outbuildings surrounded by grassland.

When they reached the bottom of the hill Dearden could see the river where it widened after passing around the city, and sunlight caught its surface at a millrace. A great water wheel was turning slowly and he could hear the distant rumbling of gearing in the mill-house. A horse was in the shafts of a four-wheeled cart half loaded with bulging sacks. A man came out of the mill with another sack on his shoulder.

Beyond the watermill, the river fed an extensive lake and a small boat was plying its surface under a single sail, heading for a landing stage near a building on the western shore. Sheep and cattle grazed in fields bordering the lake, which Leofwin said was Babba Lacu. Beyond the lake and the pastures lay the wild, dark forest.

They arrived at the three-storey entrance tower of Saint Mary's Abbey. There was a wooden balcony on the second storey. Standing on it was a man in the black habit of a Benedictine monk. He had seen the riders approaching. He descended the stairs and alerted some young lay monks to stable the horses.

"We heard you were on your way sir," the black-robed monk said to Leofwin, "Follow me if you will, Abbot Ceolfrith is in his apartment."

"How does the Abbot fare?" Leofwin asked as they climbed the stairs to the top storey.

"He is unwell after his injury. We were attacked by two men who showed signs of madness."

Julia reassured the monk, "We are hunting them, and they will pay dearly for the hurt they have caused." The faint sound of plainchant echoed through the building, and Julia stopped talking to listen. Reaching the top of the stairs, the monk knocked on a door and a voice responded from within.

The room was light and airy. There was a window fitted with horn set in lead in each of four gables, and the light penetrating the room bathed everything with a subdued cream colour. It was a plainly furnished room, with a desk, and a chair with a high back between the desk and the window. A sheet of parchment with neat script and illuminated capitals had a stone on each corner to stop it curling. Arranged on the desk were containers of coloured inks, and quills.

An elderly man was lying on a cot against the far wall. He tried to rise as the visitors came to him. Leofwin gestured for him to remain where he was and introduced him as the Abbot, Ceolfrith. His head was swathed in dirty bandages and blood was seeping through the cloth.

The Abbot described how two men had broken into the nave, and threatened him, shouting *gold . . . gold*. He said that the shouting was their undoing. His fellow monks, working in the gardens nearby, heard the noise, and frightened off the intruders with spades and mattocks and their fists.

"How did you get hurt?" Julia asked.

"One of them had a crossbow and the other had a small black weapon which made a loud noise. I remember nothing after that until I woke. My head was stinging and one of the brothers was binding it." He touched the bandage and winced.

"We'd better have a look at the wound," Doughty said. He unwound the dressing. "Good job Fengel's a bad shot." The bullet had caught Ceolfrith's skull a glancing blow.

"Would you and your men be able to fight off the men if they come back?" Dearden asked the abbot.

"Fight them off, my son? We have a simple life here. They are welcome to our candlesticks and crosses if that is what they want. But our faith in the promise of the coming Kingdom of the Christ they cannot take."

"Jules, will you tell Ceolfrith how we admire his principles, but Fengel and Beggs will be back. We may be able to prevent them harming more innocent people if we lay a trap for them. There's no guarantee it'll work, but here's what I suggest . . ."

39

Fengel and Beggs fled downhill from the town after their failed attempt to raid the abbey. They came to a large lake and walked through the shallows to throw any dogs off their scent. When they reached the far side of the lake, they felt it was safe to lie low and spend the night there. Fengel directed process of building a rough shelter a few yards inside the forest boundary.

They heard the sounds of the chase until dusk, and after an uncomfortable night, they awoke cold and miserable. Fengel began running on the spot, throwing his arms around to get warmth into his limbs. He felt he wanted revenge on someone, anyone, because of this desperate situation, and he swore at Beggs when he said that he would kill for bacon and eggs. Then the voice from Fengel's pocket spoke again.

"I know you're there, Fengel." He stopped exercising, startled by the voice. "This is your early-morning call." Fengel grabbed the two-way out of his pocket. Dearden's voice was making him jittery. He looked around to see if anyone was there, but there were only the all-encroaching trees. On the opposite side of the lake, the buildings of Coufaentree crowded the top of the hill. The massive walls of the castle keep looked threatening. He took the Luger from his pocket and felt reassured by its feel.

"Dearden's still on our tail," Beggs said. "I don't like it; he's too clever for his own good."

Another voice came from the speaker.

"You'll have to like it, Beggs. We're on your tail and closing in." Fengel moved quickly away from the lake back to their shelter hidden by trees. Beggs followed him.

"Come on, answer up," Dearden's voice said. Fengel

whispered to Beggs to keep his mouth shut and pressed the transmit button.

"Dearden, where are you?" he shouted.

"Like I said, we're closing in, Fengel. If I were you I'd give myself up, right now."

"Why? There are riches here for the taking." Fengel wanted to open up his options. He thought he might get Dearden onside using the lure of gold.

"No more questions, Fengel. We're after you two more than we've ever been after anyone before. You've got two choices. The first, give yourselves up and have a fair trial back in our own time. Second choice, stay on your killing spree and face Anglo-Saxon justice, which is lethal, and there's no plea for mercy."

Beggs dived his hand over and squeezed Fengel's thumb on the transmit button.

"Piss off Dearden, we'll take our chances here." Fengel pulled the two-way from Beggs and shoved him aside.

"Your choice," Dearden said. "Oh, by the way, this is a warning, keep away from all the gold in the abbey."

The radio went dead, and the trap was set.

* * *

Fengel suggested they move on, and they eventually came to a place where the forest was dense and gave good cover up to the water's edge. Sometime after mid-day, judging by the height of the Sun, they scraped a pit in the ground for a fire and found some dry twigs. Using Beggs' glasses to magnify the sunlight onto a small wad of dried grass, Fengel gently blew on it after it smoked and then glowed, and then it caught fire. He placed more dried grass on the flame, then small twigs, which began to crackle and burn. With the addition of some thicker branches, they soon had a useful fire burning which they kept low and hot in the pit. Beggs came back from the forest with a rabbit he shot with the crossbow, and they slow-roasted it over the fire on a sapling.

"Do you think the old chap in the church is alright?" Beggs asked, as he chewed on a hind leg. "He wasn't moving much after you shot him."

"I don't care about his condition. He got in the way, so I shot him."

"You need to sort your head out, Fengel."

"Me? You think I need to sort *my* head out." Fengel went quiet.

"How about the gold in the abbey?" Beggs said, through another mouthful of rabbit.

"We will find a way to get it, don't you worry."

As the day progressed, the risks involved in another raid on the abbey lessened in Fengel's mind as his desire for the wealth in the building grew greater.

Fengel suddenly stood. "We need to make a move." He hoisted the bag with the haul of gold onto his shoulder and kicked earth over the fire. Without another word, he started walking, keeping to the edge of the lake with Beggs following a few yards behind. The Sun began to sink low and red on the horizon and Fengel told Beggs it would be about an hour until darkness came to protect them. "We'll keep some distance between us and Dearden, and then we'll head back to the abbey." Fengel's plan was to be near the town after dark, and then they could shelter close to the buildings in the narrow streets until the coast looked clear to raid the abbey again. Fengel felt the shape of the Luger in his pocket and it gave him confidence that the coming night's work would be successful.

They came to the rotten pilings of an old landing stage jutting into the lake and settled down to wait. Water gently lapping around the remains of the woodwork broke the silence.

They hid in the trees nearby waiting for night to fall, and saw the glow of the Milky Way intensify. When it was finally dark, by the light of the stars and the rising moon, they continued to follow the water's edge of Babba Lacu, toward the town.

Fengel tried to gauge where the contours of the town lay by the faint glimmer of rushlights and candles on the hill. As they progressed, they saw the glow of a fire flickering distantly through the trees to the right of their path, which had dwindled to little more than a hint of a trail. They began to make their way through the trees toward the warmth of the firelight. Inwardly they both longed for company and warmth, but they were cautious with their approach. The distance was deceiving and it took almost an hour before they reached the source of the glow.

From the shelter of trees at the edge of a clearing, they saw a large group of men, women and children sitting around a fire, engaged in lively conversation. It looked as though the encampment was permanent because there was a large wooden hut at the far side of the clearing.

Fengel looked at Beggs, whose face had a reddish glow in the light from the fire.

"They must be up to no good out here in the forest," Fengel whispered. Beggs thought of the pot calling the kettle black, but he listened to what Fengel had to say.

"If we could get them on our side it would help us against Dearden and the others. With a group this size, we could ransack the Abbey easily, and get rid of Dearden." They crouched down low, looking at what was going on.

"Let's scare the hell out of them," Beggs whispered after an idea occurred to him. "We'll soon have them eating out of our hands."

"How will we do that?"

"First, we need some camouflage."

* * *

On their approach to the firelight, they had passed by a badger sett. They went back to it, put the leather bag with the gold into the hole and covered it with leaves to hide it. Fengel put some gold coins in his pocket to bargain with and rubbed his shoulders. The strap had dug in unmercifully and bruised them, but he had been loath to let Beggs carry it. Fengel made careful note of the position of the bag in relation to the hut for retrieval later, and then they wove leaf-laden twigs together for camouflage.

By the look of their unkempt appearance, the group around the fire were outlaws. There was a cross section of humanity, some even wearing once-fine clothing. Fengel counted seventy-two of them, and he thought he understood a few words from the hubbub of talk in the clearing. There were similarities to Niedersächsisch, the language of his forebears from Westphalia in the flat regions of Northern Germany. Fengel took the crossbow off Beggs. He wound the cranequin and latched the string ready for action.

Many of the group were sitting and standing around a fire in a pit. They were watching two young boys turning a deer on a spit. As fat from the animal dribbled onto the flames the fire flared, and the aroma of venison wafted into the night air.

An undefinable background noise crept in on them from the forest. The faintest of rustling sounds at first, and the vague tramping of footsteps coming on the breeze grew in intensity. The leader stood with his hand grasping his sword, listening. He drew his cloak around him and was a little fearful of what was approaching from the darkness. The flames of the fire guttered as the wind blew, and a chill colder than the frosty autumn air descended on the camp. Children ran whimpering to their mothers, and the mothers drew close to their husbands.

Suddenly, two figures came running from the forest. Green

men, they were, hoary and bedecked from head to foot with leaves and twigs growing from their bodies. There was a fearful cry from an old woman who had heard of the Wodwose, and after she screamed the name, others in the group repeated it. Not knowing what to do, or where to run for safety, primeval fear took over and they panicked.

Apart from a brave few, and the elderly who were unable to run, the group spread like startled rabbits from before the Wodwose. The man who was the leader of the group, Hosvir Big Arm, a descendant of the Vikings, stood his ground. Regalia hung around his neck on a chain, and an expensive looking brooch fastened a cloak draped around his shoulders. Fengel focussed on him for a show of power.

The crossbow bolt hit the left of the man's forehead. He spun round with the force of the projectile and dropped to the ground. The woman with him screamed and fell to his side. She clutched his head, sobbing hysterically, and pulled him close to comfort him. She clutched at the bolt, trying to pull it out but it was stuck fast and she was unable to move it, so she started moaning, fearful of the blood and his awful stillness.

Fengel pushed her out of the way and she spat at him. She leapt at him with her hands outstretched, her nails tearing at his face, ripping ugly scratches across his cheek. He punched her face viciously and bent down to the man he had killed. Shouting a harsh cry of victory, he raised the crossbow aloft, and then with exaggerated movements he pulled the dead man's sword from its scabbard. Placing the tip on a log near the fire, he gave the blade a hard downward jab with his foot and it snapped in two. Fengel undid the clasp of the dead man's cloak, snatched up the garment and draped it over his shoulders. He fastened the clasp, strutted around the fire with his arms folded in front, and took the place of the leader.

It was cold away from the fire and the need for warmth was

stronger than the outlaw's fear of the Wodwose. After all, the Wodwose got rid of the leader who was overbearing and self-important, so the people began drifting back to the warmth of the fire, but they kept on the far side of the flames from the one who had killed Hosvir Big Arm.

Fengel pressed home his advantage. In a voice rising above the crying children and the subdued frightened conversation from the perimeter of the clearing, he called out in Niedersächsisch that he was their new leader. He pulled six gold coins out of his pocket. They glinted in the firelight as he threw them into the centre of the clearing. The group dived into action, some into a patch of mud, fighting and tearing at each other to get to the coins. Others fought as fiercely to get to the fire.

Fengel had created pandemonium with the gold and he was confident he had the group eating out of his hand. They were living in mud and falling leaves and most were cowering on the outer fringe of warmth from the fire. But the bluff of the Green Man had worked. In the action, most of the leaves and twigs of the disguise had fallen off, so Fengel pulled off the rest and Beggs followed suit.

Fengel was wary as he walked amongst the outlaws. He fingered the Luger in his pocket as he touched the shoulder of forty-three of the strongest looking men. Most of them flinched as he did so. He indicated they should form a separate group away from the fire, and explained his scheme to raid Saint Mary's Abbey in a voice he made sound harsh. Showing them a few more of the gold coins, he told them they would be rich if they were successful in their raid on the abbey. They understood, by words and elaborate gestures, that they were to gather what weapons they possessed and take the forest track to Coufaentree. The promise of a reward in gold cut through any misunderstanding and they stealthily worked their way through the dark forest with a man at the front lighting the way with a rushlight.

The cry of a wolf echoed far away in the distance, answered by a nearer call. It brought home to Fengel how wild and alien the land was. He looked at Beggs, who was shivering. His face looked pale in the light of the Moon that appeared from behind a mass of dark cloud.

While they were picking their way through the trees, Fengel suggested a diversion would force attention away from the abbey and prevent the castle guard foiling the raid.

"A fire's always a good bet," Beggs said. "I saw some wooden hovels against the castle wall. They've got thatched roofs. If we torch one of them it'll be a good diversion."

"You surprise me. Maybe you're not as stupid as you look." Beggs' face took on a harsh aspect as Fengel's words sank in. He forced his feelings to calmness and consoled himself with the thought that his time would come at some point. As they walked, they talked the plan through and decided that Beggs would take eight men and head for the castle. They would hide in the shadow of its walls and break into one of the thatched buildings. Once inside they would set a fire, and when it was well alight, they would disappear into the night to a vantage point. When flames came through the roof Beggs would get his group to raise the alarm. After that, Beggs and his men would wait for the fire to be at its height, by which time Fengel, with the larger group, would have joined them and they would attack the Abbey. The townsfolk would be in a state of panic and occupied with tackling the blaze.

"Most places like the Saint Mary's Abbey have holy relics as well as objects of gold. There could be a remnant of the true cross, or a body part of an apostle or a saint. It would be in a small casket in a prominent place. Anything like that could be worth a fortune so keep your eyes open for it."

They came to the western side of Coufaentree and Beggs cut away from the main group with his eight men. They stole silently through the streets by ones and twos so as not to arouse suspicion, and arranged to meet at the thatched buildings by the castle wall.

Fengel, with his thirty-five men, reached the bank of Cheylesmore Brook nearest the town. Whispering in Niedersächsisch and by gestures, Fengel told his men to lie low and stay quiet. The glow of the fire from Beggs' diversion would be the clue for him to lead his men into the town to link up with Beggs for the assault on the abbey.

* * *

A messenger on Earl Leofwin's business was returning through the forest from the town of Tamoworthig. He was on his way to the Castle of Coufaentree, and being a local man, he decided to leave the old Roman road called Watling and head down a track that would take him through the forest. It would save him considerable time.

His horse was plodding its way along the track with little need for the reins. The messenger was surprised when, way up ahead, he saw the faint glow of a fire in the forest. Activity in the forest at night was unusual so he was curious about what was going on. After tethering his horse, he crept toward the flickering flames of the fire and saw a large group of men, women and some children, sitting on the ground. There were two figures covered in leaves and twigs standing in the centre of the group and a body on the ground. One of the things covered in leaves put a sword on the ground with its tip on a log and stamped on it. The sword shattered.

The messenger had an urge to run because of the unholy goings-on, but curiosity overcame his fear and he stayed put. He saw some twigs fall off one of the figures and realised they were men in disguise. The taller one was speaking to the people, who looked frightened. The man's accent sounded foreign, and some of his words were difficult to understand. The messenger crept closer to hear what was going on, and what he heard spurred him into action.

He retraced the way to his horse and commenced a wild ride down a moonlit forest lane to Coufaentree Castle where Leofwin's banner was flying above the barbican.

The guards recognised the messenger as he approached the rushlit area near the gate. They opened to him and he rode through at an urgent pace. He was breathless when he burst into the keep unannounced. Going straight to Leofwin without formality, he told him what he had heard, that a large raiding party was assembling near the village of Cheylesmore, from where they would move on Saint Mary's Abbey.

Leofwin reacted immediately and sent men to protect the abbey and pass the word to Dearden and the others to make haste back to the castle, where he was preparing for action. He called Ienur to get the horses ready and mobilised men at arms from the garrison. Extra rushlights illuminated the perimeter of the bailey, and when Dearden and the others ran into the barbican from the abbey, Leofwin was waiting for them. They saw the preparations for battle. Sparks were flying from a grindstone, which a man was rotating with a handle. The armourer withdrew a seax from the stone and tested its edge with his thumb.

"You don't have many men here," Julia said to Leofwin, as she tried to catch her breath after the run from the abbey.

"Not as many as I would like. I sent two hundred to join the King's army because the Welsh are rising again." He grabbed the bridle of his horse, Brannling, who was wild-eyed and restless with the sparks from the armourer's grindstone.

* * *

Leofwin and Dearden, with Doughty and Julia behind, rode out of the broad gate at the head of a column of men at arms. They came to Cheylesmore and rode past its manor, along a forest track, eventually coming to Cheylesmore Brook, which was wide as it neared its confluence with the Scir Burnan. Leofwin stopped two hundred yards or so away from a shallow ford and directed his men to a defensive position on the furthest bank from the town.

Leofwin instructed the men to spread out and wait silently. After a short while, one of his outlying guards came to him, saying he had overheard men approaching stealthily, conversing in low tones about a raid in Coufaentree. He had followed the raiders and saw them take cover behind trees close to the ford, where they were waiting, facing the direction to the town. Leofwin nodded his thanks and signalled for his men to keep to the shelter of the trees and move to the ford, where they would begin the attack.

Fengel was startled when the voice spoke again from the two-way radio in his pocket. It was Dearden, repeating the message to give himself up. Fengel was startled, but one of his men with good ears had heard muttering from over the river. He pointed out the direction to Fengel who instructed one of his men with a crossbow to aim a bolt in the direction of the voice. It smacked into a tree trunk near Dearden.

Leofwin commanded his archers to respond. A flight of arrows hissed into the darkness the other side of the river. Projectiles sped through the air in both directions with increasing ferocity and cries came from Fengel's position as longbow shafts found their mark. As the Moon appeared from behind fast-moving clouds and illuminated the scene, Leofwin gave the order to stop the action.

Dearden heard Fengel's impassioned voice. He could see

Julia faintly in the moonlight, and whispered, "Did you catch what he said?"

"Some of it. He's trying to spur them on with the promise of gold coins, and he told them he's going to use his thunder weapon to kill you and Leofwin."

"Even if he does use his gun we can't respond with our weapons unless we've got a clear shot."

"Maybe, but first chance I get I'll take him out with this." Doughty patted the stock of the AK47.

"I haven't heard Beggs recently, I wonder what they're cooking up," Julia said, as she glanced at Leofwin, who was directing the action from the front. A crossbow bolt had penetrated his shield, but he stayed in the open waiting for the rebels to make the next move. Julia went to him and pulled him out of the moonlight into the shelter of a tree.

She asked, "Did you hear Fengel rallying his men to cross the river?"

"I did. He told them he is going to use thunder weapon. Jules, you have those weapons. You must use them to stop him."

"You'll have to use your weapons until we see Fengel clearly." Leofwin couldn't understand Julia's reasoning, but there was no time to explain. There was sudden shouting on the far side of Cheylesmore Brook as Fengel's men charged up to the river on the attack.

"That's what we're waiting for," Julia said to Leofwin, as a few bolts tore into the cover around them. One of the bolts struck a man who collapsed close to Leofwin and lay still. Fengel's men on the other side of the river were yelling as they ran. The moonlight picked them out as they leapt into the river and began wading across. Some were waving swords and billhooks, and others with crossbows covered the advance from the shelter of the trees.

Leofwin raised his arm. "Steady, aim, loose." Arrows hissed to the other side, near to the trees and into the river. One of the men near the bank screamed and collapsed into the water as an arrow penetrated his chest, and he floated downstream. Another yelled as a shaft penetrated his shoulder, the force of it propelled him backwards and one of his comrades grabbed him and hauled him back to the bank. The others in midstream floundered and scattered back into the forest.

"Hold," Leofwin called.

Fengel's men re-grouped on the opposite bank and they surrounded the tall figure of Fengel, who had emerged from the water. Doughty raised the AK, his finger ready on the trigger, but he was unable to get a clear bead on Fengel.

"We meet again, Dearden," Fengel shouted from the middle of the group. "Don't think you've got away with this. We will be waiting for you, somewhere in the forest. You are dead, Dearden. All of you will be dead." His Luger reflected the moonlight as he raised it to fire.

"Down," Julia yelled as Fengel fired two shots in their direction. He was off-target and the bullets smacked through the undergrowth at their side.

Leofwin grabbed a bow off the nearest of his men and loosed a shaft at Fengel. It grazed his right arm and sailed harmlessly on into the forest.

"And you, Anglo-Saxon, you're dead as well . . . doot," he shouted in Niedersächsisch, before turning and running off into the forest with his men.

"Follow, now," Dearden shouted. He ran forward, leaping into the ice-cold river with Leofwin and the rest following, horses and men, churning the water close behind him.

They made their way along a lane through the forest leading to Coufaentree on the northern side of the river. Two men, sent ahead to scout the terrain, reported that Fengel and his group had disappeared into the night. There was no sign of them and they could be waiting in ambush.

There was a commotion at the back of the group. Leofwin called a halt and slipped out of the saddle. He handed the reins to a man at his side and went to see what was happening. One of the men who had the best eyes of all those around him had seen the faintest red glow in the sky in the direction of Coufaentree. It was dull at first but rapidly grew brighter.

"That's the reason Beggs wasn't in the skirmish," said Dearden. He had heard the word *brond* and remembered from talking to Rowan in the great hall that it was the word for fire.

"And it looks as though the fire's taken hold," Julia could see the glow in the sky through the intertwining branches overhead. The intensifying fire was reflecting off the base of a bank of low cloud. The riders dismounted and joined those on foot, leading the horses under low-lying branches. Dearden was uneasy with the slow pace of the men held back by the weight of armour.

"Jules, tell Leofwin we're going on ahead to make sure Ceolfrith is OK at the abbey." As they broke into a steady run Leofwin and his men tried to keep up, but the weight of their chain mail held them back.

Many of the buildings nestling up to the outer wall of the castle were wooden, and the roofs were of thatch. The inhabitants of Coufaentree dreaded fire, which, when it raced wild was an all-consuming enemy. When they heard the alarm bell ringing from the barbican, men, women and children, all who were able, rushed to give assistance. The fire had taken hold, and was about its urgent work.

Beggs was wearing a long cloak to disguise himself and he walked with his men surrounding him. He moved out of the way as the guards who Leofwin sent to protect the abbey came running to help with the fire. Trained for emergencies, they shouted instructions as they arrived at the scene. Beggs darted away from the milling townsfolk and signalled his men to follow him; they ran through the swirling smoke and sparks downhill to the abbey. They punched and kicked their way past the startled monks who had been standing at the entrance looking at flames leaping skywards on the other side of the castle. Overwhelmed by the savagery of the attack, the monks, most of them of a gentle nature, cowered near the wall as Beggs and his gang ran into the building lit by rushlights in brackets on the floor.

They came across Ceolfrith, who stood in their way, and tried to reason with them but they pushed him aside. They searched all the rooms on the ground floor and dealt brutally with two monks who tried to stop them getting to a large oak coffer in a side room deep inside the abbey. Ceolfrith went and stood in front of the coffer. He spoke firmly, saying that the contents of the coffer were for the people dependent on St Mary's through the coming winter. As he protested, one of Beggs men laughed close to his face and stabbed him in the shoulder. Ceolfrith cried out loudly and fell to the floor, but with an effort of will, he managed to drag himself away into the chancel.

Beggs dumped what gold they could find into two hessian sacks he had found in the stables and grabbing a battle-axe from one of his men, he smashed the crude locks on the coffer. He lifted the lid on a hoard of gold and silver coins. The monks looked on fearfully as the raiders plundered their livelihood, then one of the novices, a huge ugly fellow with two missing front teeth rushed in. He heard the noise in the abbey when he was in the latrine. He burst through the door and floored five of the men before Beggs clubbed him on the head. Minutes later the rampaging group ran from the Abbey and disappeared

313

into the night with their plunder.

With the aid of a crib-sheet transliterated by Fengel, Beggs told his men in Niedersächsisch that they were going to head for Heanton in the Arden. He said there would be a reward for their part in the raid when they got there, and he showed them a gold coin. They set off with a local man in the lead who knew the forest pathways well. The only word he understood in Beggs' instructions was Heanton, but he understood the gold coin very well. Beggs followed at the rear, with his crossbow ready for use.

They passed by the fire, which was burning fiercely. A crowd was milling about, shouting and screaming in the hot embers and someone had organised a line of people who passed buckets of water hand to hand from a well near the castle gate. They were trying to soak the thatch of buildings nearest to the fire. As he ran un-noticed wrapped in his cloak, Beggs coughed as he inhaled a lungful of smoke. He squinted at the flames and gloated on the success of his diversion.

Dearden, Doughty and Julia ran out of the forest and joined a well-used track leading into the town, where it became a lane called Cheylesmore. It was a narrow lane, and it rose up the contour of the hill to the castle at the top. Cheylesmore had a prosperous air about it and had houses and workplaces built of stone on each side. Many of the doors were open and people were emerging with buckets, running uphill toward the castle and the burning buildings. The glow from the fire was reflecting off the buildings and the faces of the people. Sparks and smoke were drifting on a breeze that was fanning the flames.

They came to the top of Cheylesmore Lane and into a scene of chaos. They ran past people who were shouting urgently, past the mayhem and the crackling of burning wood and thatch. Following the outer defensive wall of the castle, they ran by some stables, and some long, low buildings, all well ablaze.

Some of the buildings nearest the blaze on the other side of the lane were scorched and smouldering. A rough ladder was leaning on a building to access a thatched roof. A man at the top of the ladder was throwing bucket after bucket of water drawn from a nearby well over the thatch, and throwing the buckets down for re-filling. Everyone seemed to be shouting at once, adding to the chaos. Horses released from the stables were galloping about wildly, nostrils flared with fear. A man grabbed the reins of one, trying to restrain it as it ran by him, but he fell and it trampled him under its hooves.

Dearden and the others stopped briefly, but it was apparent nothing more could be done to help, so they ran on over the brow of the hill, past the barbican and onward to St Mary's Abbey. Julia was breathless when they reached the porch. "I don't like this one bit, there should be guards here," she said, between breaths. They ran into the building, past the great stone pillars supporting the roof high above. There was something on the floor of the chancel, near the altar. Dearden could make out two shapes in the shadows cast by the flickering rushlights. As they drew near them, they could see Ceolfrith, with a novice supporting his head and holding a rag to his shoulder. The young man looked up warily as Dearden and the other two drew close.

"Don't worry, we are friends," Julia reassured the novice, and the young man moved out of the way as Doughty knelt and checked the abbot's pulse. It was weak and his breathing was shallow. Doughty exposed the wound.

"There's some good first aid for this sort of injury. Help me get him up." Ceolfrith winced as they lifted him into a sitting position. Doughty got a metal flask out of his rucksack.

Undoing the cap, he tipped a small amount of liquid through the abbot's lips. He spluttered and opened his eyes.

"What's in the flask?" Dearden asked.

"Some of your Glenmorangie from back home," Doughty said, as he wiped the top and took a nip himself. The abbot breathed deeply and his complexion began to improve. Doughty cleaned up his shoulder and applied antiseptic and a field dressing. Ceolfrith grimaced and held his hand out for the flask. He took another deep swig, coughed, and told Julia what happened during the robbery.

40

The stench of the fire was in the air when they met soon after dawn in the feasting hall of Coufaentree Castle.

"We didn't bargain for the fire," Julia said.

"I didn't think they were clued up enough for that," Dearden responded.

"Don't blame yourself. No-one could have anticipated the fire, and there should have been guards at the abbey."

"I'm not blaming myself, it's happened. It's a pity Ceolfrith was hurt in the process. The bonus is that now Fengel and Beggs have the valuables from the abbey they'll be heading to the Hub to get back home. We can cut them off there."

"Maybe, but the hunt's still on until they're in my sights," said Doughty, as he tore some bread off a loaf and dipped it in a bowl of barley porridge. While they were eating, a local tradesman who heard about the robbery arrived with information that confirmed what Doughty said. At the height of the blaze, a group of swiftly riding horsemen passed him by going out of town. He was suspicious because everyone else was heading into the town to try to stop the fire. He said the group were riding toward the lane that went through the forest in the direction of Heanton.

Leofwin came in from seeing the horses were ready. He said there would be no mistakes now with the safety of the monks. He had sent eight men at arms to guard the abbey and warned them to stay at their posts through fire, hail or Kingdom come.

Fengel and his men hid in the undergrowth by Berculs Well after they heard the approach of horses. It was Beggs and his raiding party, and as soon as Fengel recognised who it was, he stepped out into the open. When Beggs drew near Fengel saw two hessian sacks slung across his saddle.

"Is that the haul from the abbey you have there? Let me see." He shifted the leather bag with the gold plates and knives off his shoulder and had his hand outstretched for the sacks.

"Wait." Beggs gripped the reins and held them taut as his horse moved restlessly. "You wait." He looked down at Fengel with newfound authority after the successful pillaging of the abbey. No more would Fengel get away with his arrogance.

"Listen." Beggs cupped his hand around his ear. He picked up the chink of harness in the distance, the beat of hooves and the barking of a dog. Fengel heard it too.

"Sounds like a large group. They are on our tail with that dog again, the big mastiff. I'll see to the dog first and then Dearden." The dog barked again, nearer now, deep and menacing. Fengel checked his Luger and topped the magazine up from a box in his pocket. "There's a bridge over the river further on. We will lie in wait for them there." They mounted up, some of the horses with two riders, and rode off in the direction of the bridge.

The river ran deep under Packhorse Bridge. Fengel could see five arches, with the river flowing through three of them. "We will ambush them there," Fengel said, making haste for the dry arches. Two of the men led the horses to a clearing in the forest where they tethered them while the rest crowded into the arches. Fengel eyed the lie of the land, and spoke to the men, saying he would reward them well once they put an end to Dearden and the others. To keep the group sweet, he gave a gold coin to each man. One coin was more than a man could earn in a year. He had a lot of coins in the sack, and his Luger was a guarantee of loyalty.

* * *

Leofwin was riding at the head of the column with Doughty, who had the AK ready for use. They reached a watering hole at the side of the track at Bercul's Well and dismounted. Horses had trampled the grass, and droppings littered the ground. Leofwin called for Hereward, a man standing quietly at the back of the group. He came forward, and after Leofwin gave him brief instructions to ride on and spy out what lay ahead, he rode off at a canter down the lane.

Hereward was familiar with the area and was well aware of the places where there could be an ambush. He dismounted when he was approaching Orm's Mill, and tethered his horse in the forest. He could hear the sound of water rushing through the millrace and the creaking of the great wheel. He watched for a short while to make sure there were no intruders. The movement of machinery inside the building and the grinding and clattering noise indicated the miller was at work. All seemed normal. Hereward went to the door and slipped inside. The chatter of gearwheels came from the floors above. There was dust in the air and flour trickling down a chute into a receptacle on ground level. Going up the stairs, he saw Orm feeding a sack of wheat into the hopper.

Hereward caught the miller's eye, and he came over when the sack was empty. After passing the time of day, Hereward asked Orm if he had heard a group of horsemen passing by. "They came this way earlier. They watered their horses and moved on quickly."

"Did they say where they were going?"

"No. They were a shifty lot, so I left them outside and carried on working, pretended they weren't there."

"You were right not to trust them. They have robbed and killed in these parts. Stay indoors if they come back. I'm going after them to see what their game is."

"Then have a care," Orm warned.

Hereward tethered his horse with the miller's pair in the stable at the back of the mill and moved on, following the trail of the outlaws on foot. When he got near to Packhorse Bridge, he could hear muffled conversation coming from the arches. Keeping to the trees, he moved round to get a better view and could see a large group of men engaged in lively conversation. Two were in front, the taller one waving his arms and issuing commands. Hereward moved to a place where he could see well. He noticed the smell of horses on the breeze. He couldn't see them, so he turned his head slowly from side to side, sniffing the air to locate them. They were somewhere on the other side of the river, and he needed to find a way over it to scatter them.

Suddenly, a hand grabbed him from behind and smothered his mouth. Another hand gripped the back of his neck. Hereward struggled for a second or two, and then grasped the thumb and bent it against the joint. He heard it crack and the attacker grunted and released his grip. Hereward whipped his knife out and jabbed back and upwards. An unkempt looking man sank to the ground. He dragged the body into the undergrowth then crept forward until he came to the river. He followed it and reached the remnants of a path that led to an ancient crossing point. There was a set of great stepping-stones, their rough-hewn tops showing above the surface of the water swirling around them. Hereward stepped over to the other side and made his way to where he could see Packhorse Bridge. He watched as a man came out from the shelter of one of the arches and went to the river to drink.

Fengel walked away from the group and indicated for Beggs to follow. When they were out of earshot of the other men Fengel spoke quietly. "We must keep some of the coins back to pay our way while we are here, but we would be best to bury the rest of the gold and dig it up when we return to our own time. Some of Dearden's people may be about when we get back, and we could have a fight on our hands when we arrive."

"OK, but we must bury it in a place we'll find easily, the landscape changes over the years."

"Good, Beggsy . . . good. You are thinking better now, and leaving your old stupid self behind. We could bury it where the old building is on the hill, which is obvious enough."

Fengel's arrogance hurt, but Beggs kept his anger down. "And after that, we can hide close to the building and wait for Dearden and the other scum to arrive."

"There's a problem with that, Beggs. Dearden may arrive with that Anglo-Saxon Chieftain and his gang. I think we should split up. One of us can ambush Dearden here at the bridge; the other can go and bury the gold."

"Who's going to do what?"

"Give me a coin. We will toss it up for the decision." Fengel held out his hand. A useful trick he learned was how to toss a coin so that the side he wanted would always show uppermost. It was like Braille, after the toss, he would feel the uppermost surface of the coin and know whether it was heads or tails. Beggs passed Fengel one of the gold coins from the sack. He made a pretence of looking at it, feeling the difference between heads and tails, and then he tossed it and caught it. "Heads," he shouted, after feeling the uppermost face of the coin.

Fengel withdrew his hand and revealed a king with large eyes and narrow shoulders gazing out of the gold. "Heads it is, my call. I will take the gold." He slung the sacks across a nearby horse's withers and lifted the strap of the leather bag over his head, testing its weight at his side. Beggs was suspicious of Fengel's motives, but thoughts of the Luger lying in the other man's pocket made him accept the situation without argument.

"You cut Dearden and his group off," Fengel said, as he picked up a crossbow and a bag of bolts and mounted the horse.

"I'll meet you at the hill after you have dealt with Dearden."
Fengel nudged his horse with his heels and rode off in the
direction of the House of the West Wind.

*   *   *

Hereward approached the horses cautiously. He untied
them two at a time and led them some distance through the
trees to a nearby lane he had seen. When they were together,
cropping grass at the side of the lane, he slapped one on the
rump, and then another. They cantered up the hill in the
direction of Heanton with the rest of the horses following.

Hereward circled back over the stepping-stones and ran at
a steady pace to Orm's mill. From there, he kicked his horse
into a gallop to Leofwin at Bercul's Well and reported the
situation at Packhorse Bridge.

When they reached Orm's Mill, they tied the horses to a rail
near the stable. Leofwin signalled his men to gather around
and instructed them to be silent as they approached Packhorse
Bridge. For the last few hundred yards, they kept to the forest,
guided by the sound of the river up ahead.

Dearden anticipated the action would be short if
Cheylesmore Brook had been anything to go by. Fengel's men
had shown themselves to be untrained and they lacked
discipline. It was mid-day. The Sun was behind them, an
advantage when the action began. Leofwin agreed when
Dearden whispered to him that it would be wise to start the
action soon. They fanned out to left and right. Leofwin, with
some of his men, took centre with Julia. Dearden took the right
flank with his group and Doughty approached the bridge on
the left with men armed with longbows.

They crept forward through the undergrowth.

Dearden stood in the open and shouted for Fengel and
Beggs to give themselves up. There was startled conversation

and hurried movement under the bridge.

Dearden waited for a response, and then Beggs shouted, "Get a load of this, Dearden. See how it feels." Then he spoke a command in Niedersächsisch from the crib-sheet left by Fengel. There was riotous laughter under the bridge with Beggs attempt at the words, and then some of the outlaws with crossbows took it in turns to dodge out of the protection of the arches to loose off a bolt in Dearden's direction. Taking advantage of the cover given by the steady stream of projectiles, some of Beggs' men raced into the open, yelling and swinging battle-axes over their heads. Others, armed with spears, billhooks and pitchforks, scrambled onto the bridge and charged along it.

Leofwin gave the command for the men with longbows, who had already nocked their shafts, to draw.

"No, hold . . . Jules, tell Leofwin to hold," Dearden shouted. Back at Orm's Mill, he talked to Doughty about using the AK. The idea could prevent loss of life all round if it had the anticipated result.

The bowmen stood back and Doughty lifted the AK. He loosed off some rounds in rapid-fire at the stonework of the bridge. The effect was instant. Beggs' men froze at the explosive force of the Kalashnikov. The bullets ricocheted off the bridge in the direction of the river, apart from one round, which whined off the parapet and hit one of the men in the thigh. He yelled out with pain and turned to run in the opposite direction, but he stumbled and fell, hugging the wound, and calling for help.

Then things quickened up, and most spread in disarray. They ran off the bridge, back into the shelter of the forest. They left their fallen colleague behind, but one of those who had run, a slightly built young man, stopped and turned. He walked along the bridge to the fallen man and helped him to his feet. He supported him, and they walked slowly away from the loud weapon.

"That takes some guts." Doughty admired the young man's pluck. Suddenly one of Leofwin's men lifted a longbow and nocked a shaft. At the same time, the young man on the bridge turned and saw what was happening. The bow was half-drawn when Julia saw what the man intended to do. She struck him on the arm holding the bow. He winced and yelled, dropped the bow and clutched his arm. He bent to retrieve the bow. Julia stepped on it and held it down. "That man is defenceless, leave him," she shouted. The bowman was one of the men who had seen Julia smashing roof tiles with her foot. He backed off.

The young man on the bridge lifted his free arm and held it up in a gesture of thanks. He continued his slow walk along the bridge with the injured man.

Fengel, on his way to the House of the West Wind, heard gunfire in the distance. His first thought was that Beggs was dead and the gold now belonged to him. He caressed the hessian sacks draped over his saddle, and hearing the running water he thought was Shadow Brook, he headed for it. He passed by a large oak tree, which he took to be the landmark leading to the Hub.

The path became less obvious as he led the horse toward the sound of running water. He eventually realised that he had gone further into the forest than he should have done and he felt disoriented amidst the maze of trees. He stopped the horse and gazed around trying to quell the sense of rising panic. He wished he had stayed with Beggs. Even though he enjoyed belittling him, Fengel realised he missed Beggs' company. He nudged the horse forward toward the sound of the stream.

The ground dipped away in front of him. He dismounted and tied the leather rein firmly around a branch and cautiously walked to the place where the ground fell away steeply into a picturesque dell. He looked back and saw the horse trying to reach some nearby grass, but the length of the reins restricted it. Thinking no more about this, Fengel made his way down the slope to a pool fed by a waterfall whose sound was magnified by the shape of the dell. Behind the waterfall, he could make out the dark shape of a cave which looked about twice his own height.

Fengel clambered over some large boulders and reached a rocky shelf at the edge of the pool. The water was motionless and deep away from where the waterfall gushed into the pool, and Fengel could see the bottom through the clear water. The cave attracted him. As he neared it, he could see it was dimly lit by the greenish light filtering through the waterfall.

There was a statue at the back of the cave. He was curious and ducked behind the curtain of water, walked a few paces, and entered the cave. The features of the statue were worn and indistinct, but the figure was very tall and thin and had large eyes. Fengel could see the vestiges of a pale green colouring on its hands and face. On its chest, there were circles of different colours. He was not usually a fanciful man, but he felt threatened and looked behind him. Because its colouring made it blend into the woodland, he failed to see a tall, slender figure with a green skin colouring gazing at him from the top of the slope. He turned his attention back to the cave.

Of the footprints embedded in the muddy floor, some were unusually large, but it did not occur to Fengel to question that. He was attracted to various objects of pottery that lay on the floor, and on a shelf hewn out of the rock at the side of the cave. There were containers with the remnants of food in them, which made him conclude that the cave must be a pagan shrine where people left offerings to appease the image at whose feet the objects lay. A very large earthenware container was on the shelf too, and a wooden plug meant to seal it lay at its side. He picked the wood up and his fingers stuck to it. They smelt strongly of resin.

Fengel looked into the container. Inside was something that had at one time been food, but now it was rancid and decomposed. He could see the skeleton of a small creature that had climbed into the container but was unable to get out. The stench turned his stomach and he gagged.

There was nothing in the cave worth taking, so Fengel scrambled up the steep slope. It was wet and slippery, and strewn with moss-covered rock. He lay out of breath at the top for some minutes, before making his way to the horse. The knot in the reins was different to how he left it. It had grown tight, and the horse was a few inches closer to the patch of grass. It gave another tug on the reins.

"Stop it," Fengel shouted, trying to pull the beast back to release the pressure on the knot. He grappled with the leather, and it hurt his nails as he tried to prise the tight loops apart. After five minutes, the knot was still tight. "You stupid bloody horse," his cry echoed plaintively into the forest. Fengel was not a horseman, so it didn't occur to him to undo the buckles holding the reins on the horse. Instead, he hoisted the leather bag and the sacks of valuables onto his shoulders, took hold of the crossbow, and set off away from the dell on foot to find the House of the West Wind.

He eventually found the large oak tree he was looking for and followed a track he vaguely recognised. He came to the stream, which was flowing slow and deep around large stones. He stepped across and followed the bank, and eventually he came to the foot of the hill with the building on its plateau. Fengel's shoulders were aching with the weight he was carrying, and he sank to the ground exhausted.

After resting, he looked up the hill and saw a dip in the

ground a few yards from the top, where there was a depression and less vegetation. He went to inspect the spot and kicked the ground with his foot. It seemed soft enough to be able to dig into it for burying the gold, and its position on the hill would be memorable, so he lugged the sacks up one at a time.

It occurred to Fengel that the leather bag and hessian sacks would rot during the intervening years until he and Beggs dug the hoard up back in their own time. A solution to keep the golden objects in pristine condition would be to use the large earthenware pot that was in the cave behind the waterfall.

He retraced the track for a while and then stopped and listened. The sound of the waterfall was distinct, so he headed toward it. When he drew near, he was surprised to see the horse with its head down munching the grass.

The branch he tied the reins onto had broken off, and was lying on the ground. The leather slipped easily off the fractured end. Now the horse was free Fengel thought he could use it to transport the container, so he stood at the top of the dell and selected the best route down. This time, he looped the reins over the remaining stub of the branch.

* * *

Back in the cave, he turned the container upside down and emptied out the evil-smelling residue. He tilted the mouth of the vessel into the waterfall to rinse it out and then held the circular piece of wood up to the neck. It would fit well. Once the gold was in the pot, he could knock the wood into the neck to seal it in, using a stone as a hammer.

A length of coarse rope lay on the floor of the cave. Fengel put it into the container and then lugged the vessel bit by bit up the slope to the waiting horse. He tried to keep the animal still while he looped the rope around the container a few times, then lifted it and secured it to the saddle.

He arrived at the base of the Hill and scrambled up the slope. He coaxed the horse up to the dip in the surface, untied the earthenware container and eased it to the ground. He led the horse down and slipped the reins over a high branch, then scrambled back up to begin burying the haul. There was a branch with a flat end nearby, and he used it to dig a hole.

It was exhausting work, and he was weak with the effort, but eventually the hole was deep enough for the treasures. He found a stone with a rounded end to knock the wooden plug into the pot to seal it. As he was leaning over the container with the first golden object in his hand, a harsh noise in the trees below startled him. He leapt upright, unaware that his mobile phone had slipped from the top pocket of his jacket into the container. Two wild boars crashed into the clearing, males, squealing and grunting, ripping with their tusks. After a short, vicious tussle, one ran off bleeding, with the other in pursuit.

Fengel carried on loading the objects into the container, working out what to do next. He would build a shelter and camp nearby until Beggs arrived. If need be they could live off the forest and wait for Dearden and his crew to show up.

Fengel had no use for Leofwin's sword. The Luger would be all the defence he needed from now on, and the sword would fetch a magnificent price back home. It was too long for the jar, so he placed it at the bottom of the hole and covered it with some earth to protect it from the weight of the container. Then he knocked the wooden plug home, rolled the hoard into the hole, and then backfilled it with soil.

Fengel had to commit the burial place to memory. A good reference point would be the door, so he stood on the freshly dug soil and eyed the door up, then lowered his gaze to the place where he was standing.

41

Julia called to the men under the bridge to give themselves up. There was some murmuring, and then Beggs sauntered out with his hands raised, followed by five others, including the young man supporting his wounded comrade. The young man spoke to Leofwin, at first haltingly, and then with more confidence.

"You showed us kindness. Sir, we live as we do because we have insufficient money for food, so we hunt for food in the forest, and have to avoid the men who own the land and the deer."

"I respect people who show courage and honesty. Tell me, what is your name?"

"Guy, sir. My name is Guy. I come from Warrewyk. Until last year I lived near some cliffs by a bend in the river." Julia translated.

"Tell Guy that Beggs and the other man, Fengel, are no good and that if he and his people follow them they will only suffer," Dearden said.

"We know what sort of men they are, but our life in the forest is hard," Guy pointed to Beggs. "That man, and the other, tricked us into believing they know wizardry. They have strange weapons and we thought they would help us, and we were frightened."

"Their help comes with pain, and their greed is never satisfied," Julia said.

"We have learned that, to our injury." Guy looked crestfallen and was at a loss for words. Leofwin prompted him, and he looked the earl straight in the eye. "Can we come with you? Your ways are different and appealing."

* * *

Aelfryth and Rowan heard the alarm bell announcing the return of Leofwin and his party. As they went out of the manor to welcome them back, Rowan was excited at the thought of seeing Jem again. Their first evening together was vivid in her mind, and she was looking forward to the evening to come. She held Jem's gaze and smiled. Leofwin broke the spell by dispersing the armed guards and directing Ienur to put Beggs into the cell. She walked side-by–side with Dearden into the great hall.

"The Witenagemot has gone to Tamoworthig to take part in more discussions on the succession. I will be joining them shortly," Leofwin said, as he removed his hauberk and stretched his arms to ease his muscles. "There is a man in the Kingdom of France they call Guillaume le Batard who is pushing himself into the court of Edward. He claims he's got a right to the throne, but we Anglo-Saxon lords want Harold Godwinson for the succession, it would keep the Saxon lineage secure." Dearden felt Rowan tense up as Leofwin mentioned Earl Harold.

Dearden nodded as Julia translated what Leofwin said. He already understood part of the conversation, but his concentration was on Rowan. She was vibrant, full of life, and her mannerisms were delightful. The flick of her eyebrows for emphasis as she spoke. The determined look on her strong features when she said, in a mixture of Anglo-Saxon and a few modern English words, that she would see him later in the evening. His gaze followed her as she crossed the great hall to the stone steps leading to the floor above. He pictured her in her room with Aelfryth and Esma. He was jealous of them because they shared her company, and he wanted to go to her.

In the quiet of the evening Dearden, Doughty, and Julia met with Leofwin in the great hall. There was no news about

Fengel's whereabouts from Leofwin's informants.

"Beggs is bound to have information about what he and Fengel plan to do. We'll leave him to stew for a while longer. Jem intends to interrogate him later on," Julia explained to Leofwin.

A chronicler sitting nearby took notes as they talked about the significant events of the day. Julia was interested in what he was doing and saw that he was using a bone stylus to write on a wax tablet. She took advantage of the situation about unanswered questions that had arisen during her study of the period. With Leofwin being close by she didn't intend a moment to be lost when she could get some first-hand answers.

In the cell down the stone steps at the side of the hall, chains manacled Beggs' hands to the wall. A beeswax candle provided a dim light that was too weak to penetrate the farther reaches of darkness. Dearden lifted the beam from the brackets outside the door and came in with some others. Beggs regarded them in the flickering light. His throat felt tight. There was a chill in the air, the combined heat from the candle and Beggs himself had caused condensation to trickle in rivulets down the sandstone wall, and they created damp patches on the earthen floor.

Dearden questioned Beggs about why Raegenhere and Uberatu were interested in the forest and the Hub. The cold and semi-darkness had done its work and Beggs had softened up. He told them about an organisation run by Raegenhere.

"He collects anything Anglo-Saxon. But it's more than collecting, it's an obsession and he gets most of it illegally." Julia quietly translated in the background for Leofwin.

"One time I heard that Raegenhere was responsible for the theft of the Sutton Hoo helmet and other gear that was on tour about three years ago. It was one night when Uberatu was on

331

a downer. I think it was when he found out you'd inherited that house of yours. We were in Uberatu's place at the back of your forest and he was pissed up."

"Uberatu's place at the back of my forest." Dearden looked at him sharply, "What are you on about?"

"The old barn at the end of the forest furthest away from your place," Beggs paused, "Hold on . . . you mean you don't know about his barn?"

"No, I don't, where is it exactly?"

"In a field off Northcote Lane. You can't see it from the road because the hedges are tall. Uberatu's put a sign on the gate that says *keep out, bull loose in field*, it keeps everyone out."

"It would. I'll have to give Uberatu a neighbourly visit. I might even pass the time of day on his jaw. Anyway, carry on, we're listening."

"Can you take these off?" Beggs indicated the shackles. Leofwin could see what Beggs wanted, so he released his wrists. Beggs rubbed them to relieve the soreness.

"It was the night when Uberatu was out of his brain with the drink, he does that sometimes. He started telling us about Raegenhere and the Sutton Hoo helmet. He said that when it's on display or goes on tour they use a replica, the real one stays in a basement under the British Museum. Anyway, the real Sutton Hoo Helmet was stolen from the basement, and it was Raegenhere who took it."

"I haven't heard about it being stolen," Julia said, breaking off from her translation to Leofwin.

"You won't have. Neither would I if Uberatu wasn't pissed up that night. The robbery was hushed up and Uberatu was delighted about the outcome. He kept talking about the embarrassment it would cause if news of the robbery leaked out. Museums rely on private collectors, and other museums all over the world loaning them items for display. Uberatu was saying how the British Museum would lose face. Other museums wouldn't trust them with loaned artefacts if word got out about the theft of the Sutton Hoo Helmet."

Julia carried on translating for Leofwin, keeping him up to date with the events Beggs was describing. The concept of a museum and even the need for one had been difficult for the Anglo-Saxon to understand.

Beggs continued. "Uberatu was in his old armchair knocking the drink back. He was on the hard stuff from the highlands and drinking it straight from the bottle. He was bragging about being part of the Sutton Hoo helmet theft. He told us the sort of lengths he and Raegenhere go to, to steal the objects they target.

"They needed someone working on the inside to help with the theft of the helmet, so Uberatu got a job at the Museum. There were other treasures in the basement that were part of the Sutton Hoo hoard too, gold buckles, brooches and bowls. All of it was taken by Raegenhere at the same time."

"How did they manage it, with the security in the museum?" Doughty asked.

"They went in as tradesmen. Uberatu is a scientist of sorts. He might be a bit weird but he's got a good brain, and he is cunning. He figured out how the security system was controlled and created a fault with it in the basement. Engineers from the security company came in and Raegenhere's men were hiding in the shadows in masks. They forced the engineers to strip at gunpoint and put on their clothes as a disguise.

"They walked in past the security guards cool as you like. No one was any the wiser, apart from one of the security guards who was in on it. He was getting a good payoff and went to the basement at gunpoint with Uberatu so it would look legit. Uberatu bragged that from the time they went in until they were on their way out, it only took thirty minutes."

"What's Raegenhere's role in all this?" Dearden asked.

"He provides finance for projects they work on."

"So they've got other things going on?"

"Yeah, and some of it's big. Raegenhere runs an advert on TV in Europe and the States when the price of gold is falling. He offers to buy gold from the public while it still has value. He buys it at a knockdown price from the suckers who send it to him. He melts it down and offloads the ingots back onto the market when the price of gold's rising, and he makes a killing."

"What are Raegenhere's intentions now?" Doughty asked.

"Well, I heard something else one night." Beggs broke off from his explanation and asked for a drink. Leofwin called up the steps and a servant brought down beor and drinking horns.

Beggs drank some and carried on. "I heard what Raegenhere said to Uberatu about an artefact he wants in his collection. When he gets to want something, he doesn't let it go. What's the word for that?"

"Obsessive," Dearden suggested.

"Yeah, he's obsessive. There's some big bank in the United States where this thing is that he wants. He said he would do anything to get it, and that while he was in the bank he would grab as much of the bullion nearby that he could transport. Then I heard him say he was getting stuff together to create a dirty bomb. He was going to use the dirty bomb to scare the shit out of the local population so they'd leave the area and there wouldn't be any opposition to his bank raid."

Dearden felt his pulse notch up a gear as Beggs' words sunk in. "Are you sure you heard right, that he was going to use a dirty bomb?"

"I'm dead sure he said that."

"Has he got the material yet?" Julia asked.

"He said he's getting it. At the time I heard the conversation he hadn't got it yet."

"Where's he getting it from?"

"He's located some radioactive stuff in Russia. The confusion with the breakup of the Soviet Union has made all sorts of things easy to get. He's had valuable religious icons from there as well."

"Where's the bank he's targeting?" Doughty asked.

"I don't know, he didn't say."

Doughty drew close. "You'll have to do better than that. If what you've told us is right, the situation is deadly serious, and we *will* get answers from you, one way or another."

Beggs didn't like how the conversation was going. He decided to tell them about a change in Raegenhere's behaviour he had noticed.

"Something's been going on over the past eighteen months. It might be a clue about where he'll hit a bank." Beggs became silent as he thought of the possible retribution from Raegenhere because of what he was going to reveal.

"Come on, don't hold back." Doughty tapped Beggs shin with his boot.

"OK, give me time, will you?" He shifted his leg and took a minute to marshal his thoughts— "Raegenhere's been over to New York a few times recently. I heard him telling Uberatu he's been cosying up with some contacts he's made."

"New York's a big place, be specific," Doughty warned.

"I can't. New York's all I heard him say."

"What bank's he targeting? Think back. Anything Raegenhere said may help." Dearden wouldn't let it go.

"Didn't you hear what I said? *I don't know.*"

Dearden nodded. He moved to the centre of the cell, pacing. "This is how I see it. We must assume that this information is correct, and Raegenhere is serious about an RDD. The bullion is a secondary issue. Loss of confidence in any large bank could create a problem for the financial markets, but that's nothing compared to the loss of life an RDD would cause." Dearden stopped pacing. "We have to get back to our own time to stop Raegenhere and his dirty bomb."

* * *

In the 1980s, the doomsday clock predicting nuclear Armageddon had taken a sudden leap from seven minutes to midnight to a scant three minutes to midnight. If it touched the midnight hour, nuclear war would be imminent. Acting on that scenario Sir Willoughby Pierpoint, as commander in chief of SHaFT, had formulated a rapid response strategy to deal with nuclear threats. He could see the growing tension with stockpiles of radiological weapons, coupled with the global increase of terrorism. Amongst other, wide-ranging strategies, SHaFT had perfected a method for dealing with an RDD incident. It had taken months of planning and intense training. None but the most senior government officials knew anything about the organisation, let alone its readiness for such an event. With any change of government, however, the outgoing premier always acquainted the man taking over about the existence of SHaFT.

Dearden could call on SHaFT's expertise but he needed more information, and quick. The way to get it was fear. "Do you know what a dirty bomb is?" Beggs shook his head.

"I'll explain. A dirty bomb, or an RDD, is a Radiation Dispersal Device. It is a weapon of mass disruption. If Raegenhere manages to use one in New York there would be an initial conventional explosion, which could kill or maim many people. That would only be the beginning because the explosion would disperse millions of radioactive particles. If there were a breeze, the particles would spread everywhere. An unknown number of people would die from radiation sickness.

336

"After the event, hundreds, if not thousands of people could develop all forms of cancer. Then there is the uncertainty. Imagine not knowing whether you would develop cancer because of the exposure. Can you feel the uncertainty, Beggs? Are you uncertain about what will happen to you, here in this dungeon?"

Doughty saw beads of perspiration on Beggs' forehead even though it was cold in the cell. He pressed the advantage home. "When's the attack going to be?"

"Thanksgiving Day."

"When is that, anyone know?" Dearden asked his colleagues.

"November the twenty-seventh, I'm giving a lecture to a group of American ex-pats in London on Thanksgiving Day," Julia said.

"You hope you will be," Doughty countered.

"What's today's date?" Dearden asked. He seemed distracted. He had his own watch with a date display but he didn't look at it.

Doughty glanced at his watch. "November the ninth, that's eighteen days away—time to mobilise SHaFT now?" Dearden nodded and then switched his attention back to Beggs.

"Where's Raegenhere's headquarters?"

"He's got a big place called Dracasfeld, in Wyverne Hardewicke. His collection's in a basement there. He's always shipping goods in and out in his Learjet." The tone of Beggs' voice changed. "He'll kill me if he finds out I've told you this."

Dearden ignored Beggs' fear. "Is Raegenhere having the components of the bomb shipped to Dracasfeld?"

"I don't know. I've told you all I know." Beggs slumped back against the wall. He suddenly stiffened. "I have remembered something else. I heard Raegenhere say the radioactive stuff would be coming in through Templehof."

Julia became attentive, "So from Berlin Templehof, the shipment could well be sent to the UK for Raegenhere to build the bomb at Dracasfeld and then fly it out to New York."

"I know Dracasfeld," Dearden said. "It's a big place with a high wall and large iron gates by a lodge. A helicopter flies in and out a few times a week. The flight path is over my place."

Beggs spoke again. "Dracasfeld is heavily guarded. Raegenhere doesn't take any chances."

"Neither do we," Julia parried, "Guys, we need to quit the chat and get back to 2008 to stop him."

"We do, but there's a problem with that," Dearden began searching through his pockets.

"What is the problem?" Julia asked.

"Fengel's still on the loose," Dearden was feeling in his pockets again.

"And?" Doughty felt uncomfortable.

"I've lost the handset to get us back through the Hub."

"What?" Julia rounded on him. "I hope you're sodding joking." Her stomach knotted.

"It must have been lost in the action at Cheylesmore Brook. I remember having it until then." Doughty went up to Dearden, close.

"So what the hell do we do now? We've got Fengel running wild with a Luger, raising a rebel force, that maniac Raegenhere toying with the atom in 2008 and you've lost the bloody way back. Well done, Jem, old chum." Doughty squared up to Dearden and Julia thought there was going to be violence.

"Cool it, both of you," she pushed between them.

Doughty backed off. He said, "Apart from finding the handset that you have so conveniently lost, the only other choice is to communicate with Harry using the Motorola. He might be able to energise the Hub at his end and get us back."

"We'd have the best chance of communicating with him if we're close to the Hub," Dearden added, trying to sound confident. "Harry told me he thinks the House of the West Wind acts as a relay for the carrier wave, so I suggest we go there and camp by it until the Motorola picks the signal up. He must be trying to communicate, that was the plan."

"It wouldn't be like him to give up, and while we're near the Hub, we can lie in wait for Fengel," Julia said. "But I hope to hell we're not marooned here."

Doughty nodded, "At least Jem would be with Rowan."

Dearden rounded on him. Anger twisted his normally passive features. "You leave Rowan out of this, you—" Julia put her hand on Dearden's arm and restrained him. She altered the anger flying around by what she said next.

"Listen. If we could leave Fengel here, it would reduce our problems by half. I'll ask Leofwin what he thinks about that, and stress how urgent it is for us to get back home. We could come back for Fengel." Dearden nodded and backed off. Leofwin heard Julia mention his name. He had been trying to follow the conversation that had developed an urgent tone.

"If we manage to get home can we guarantee a return to get Fengel?" Doughty asked.

"I damn well hope so," Dearden said.

Julia explained their dilemma to Leofwin.

"With what Fengel has done here, I will not guarantee his capture alive. I will speak to the Witenagemot. When will you go back through the House of the West Wind?"

"As soon as we can arrange it."

Leofwin re-attached the shackles to Beggs. They closed the door and slotted the beam in place, leaving him to his thoughts and the coming darkness. The candle burned low, and the flame finally died.

42

The school of hard knocks was the training ground for the young Raegenhere, known in his formative years as Reginald Arthur Heap. He was born in a high-rise tenement block towering over a sleazy part of Birmingham where crime was rife, and due to his upbringing, he fought for survival with a sharp edge to his personality. He learned to give out more punishment than he received, and early on in life he took to carrying a flick-knife. He had no friends, only acquaintances, and if one of them disagreed with him, or failed to pay up after the latest threat, Reg would threaten him with the knife and the culprit would submit.

Reg was a loner, and one day in a cold December, finding no inspiration in the streets of his home patch, he decided to roam further afield. He walked along the bank of the Grand Union Canal and ended up in the Jewellery Quarter.

The fifteen-year-old gazed in wonder into the lighted windows of the shops he passed. It was as if the glittering, golden displays on the other side of the glass were calling him. *Come, take me, I am yours*, they cajoled, *Reach out and hold me, feel my richness, take in my warmth and I will warm your heart forever.*

Young Reginald's heart didn't work in the normal way. A cold and merciless quality had developed over his short span of years. He was as hard as the stones in the jewellers' windows, and his mind was colder than the frosts of winter.

The heap of metal that was an excuse for a car, embarrassing to Reg whenever people he knew saw him in it, needed a new handbrake cable. It was a warm day, far too warm for his father to be working under the car.

"Hey, twerp, get us a beer out the fridge," were the words that tipped the scales. He was at the end of his tether being at his father's disposal. He despised the old man for the cruelty he dished out with his leather belt. Reg wandered disconsolately up the long flight of stairs to their flat to get the beer his father craved. He re-emerged a minute or so later holding a can of lager in glove-clad hands.

Reginald Arthur Heap knew exactly how hydraulic jacks worked and he was well aware of fingerprints.

The mobile incident unit and the ambulance arrived twenty minutes later. Albert Heap had died instantly and the only help they could give was to clear the mess away and cover the area with sand. Everyone assumed the accident was due to a faulty jack, and Reggie was a picture of innocence and grief.

The police and sympathetic neighbours looked on. They felt desperately sorry for the boy who sat with his head in his hands on the dusty kerb. As he sobbed, those with their comforting arms around his shoulders failed to realise he was sobbing with relief.

After the ambulance men gathered the bits together and took them away in a body bag, Reg told the neighbours he wanted to be on his own. Strange young man, they thought. His mother had left a few years ago and, although they felt sorry for him after the tragedy of his father, they were careful not to get too involved. Experience taught them to keep out of domestic incidents in case they crossed into the territory of one of the local thugs. Reg took the can of lager upstairs and as he drank, he toasted his future.

Boy, how he flourished with his newfound freedom! The world was at his fingertips and one night the Jewellery Quarter beckoned again. The operation he conceived was simple. It involved a window, a brick, a rucksack and a disused canal boat.

The brick went through the window and moving quickly he crammed what jewellery he could reach into the rucksack, and then he ran down to the canal where he knew an old canal boat lay. Years previously, vandals had holed the rusted hull. The vessel had sunk, and it rested in mud in three feet of water.

Reg shone his torch on the remains of the rusted decking at the bows and carefully stepped from the bank onto the part that looked solid. He lifted a trap and shone the torch inside. The water smelt foul, which would deter others from being too interested in what lay submerged. He put the laden rucksack into the water and it sank, exuding a stream of bubbles. Two minutes later Reg was on his way home down the towpath. Up on the hill in the Jewellery Quarter, all hell had broken loose. Sirens filled the night air, blue lights were flashing, and Reg felt proud of his accomplishment.

He thought about that evening every day, and after six months he went back to the canal boat with a hook that he had fashioned out of stiff wire fastened to a garden cane. On the walk along the towpath, he concealed the hook in his coat and waited until there was no one around. He stepped over the gap between the boat and the bank, lifted the trap in the floor, and hooked one of the straps of the rucksack. It was made of nylon, and although it stunk and was soaking wet it was still in good condition. He let it drain for a minute then put it in a black plastic sack, and made his way home to dry and clean all the pieces.

The baubles were shining as they lay on a towel on the coffee table, and gazing at their brilliance, Reg decided it would be safe to make discrete enquiries about selling his haul. He reasoned that not all that went on in the Jewellery Quarter could be legitimate, and he tuned in to the fact that there must be people up there who would move the goods on for a cut of the proceeds.

He went back and walked the streets that he imagined were paved with gold. He spent days watching and analysing, trying to seek out a business where illegal things might go on behind a window which outwardly looked legitimate. He homed in on a place in a small side street. There was a grimy window behind which sat a few choice items shining in the beam of a small spotlight. Above the window was a sign, *P.W. Smithson-Gubbenheim, (est. 1896), Dealers in fine gold antiques and bullion.*

For the next few days, Reg observed the comings and goings at Smithson-Gubbenheim. He sat a short distance from it on the steps of a disused workshop, strumming a guitar with an upturned hat in front of him, in which some of the people who passed by put coins. Occasionally visitors would turn up at Smithson-Gubbenheim's door, look around furtively and ring a bell before disappearing inside.

Back at home, Reg practised the patter he was going to use in front of a mirror. He looked through the pieces of jewellery and decided to take one of the rings inlaid with diamonds. He would say it was his grandmother's, and that she wanted it valued. He learned about hallmarks and worked out the information stamped on the inside of the ring. After a while, he knew everything about it, including its four-figure value.

Reg wondered if anyone was in the shop because it looked dark inside when he gazed through the window. He pressed the bell he had seen others use. After a few seconds, there was the sound of a latch releasing on the inside of the door, and a dim light came on. He went in as an elderly man with a hooked nose and a watchmaker's loupe attached to the top of his glasses appeared from a room at the back.

"Shalom, can I help you young sir?" the man asked in an accent with a lisp.

"You might be able too," the boy said, and launched into the story he had prepared. The man wanted to see the ring and he asked many questions. He tested the stones with a probe, which lit up yellow. Then he looked at the ring through his loupe and could see there were no flaws or inclusions in the diamonds. Michael Smithson-Gubbenheim had a good idea the ring had been in a jeweller's window at the top of the road. He had an unfailing memory for what was on display in the local windows, but *business is business, mensch*, and he had a customer in mind.

"If you find more like this, we might do business."

"There could be more, I'll have to check with granny."

The relationship began at that point, and it flourished over the next eleven profitable years. Over that time, Reg amassed a considerable amount of valuables for Michael Smithson-Gubbenheim from which he earned an excellent commission. There were trips abroad, visits to museums of national importance and backstreet dives where precious things changed hands in semi-darkness.

There were no questions asked about the acquisitions laid on black velvet after the trips. A smile and a wink sufficed if a project had gone well. Reg found the valuables and Michael shifted them for a handsome profit. Then one evening Smithson-Gubbenheim asked Reg to come to his apartment and he gave him some bad news.

"I've got cancer," the old man told him, "They've given me six months, my Yiddisher boy." The information floored Reg. He had become used to the arrangement with Michael and, as much as his malformed personality would allow, he was close to the elderly man. Later that evening Michael started to teach Reg the real tricks of the trade. He gave him the list of his customers who were prepared to buy any type of quality jewellery and the outfits who would buy valuables without traceability.

It was not a long illness. During the time they had left,

Smithson-Gubbenheim, who had no children, made Reg a partner in the business and treated him as the son he never had. The old man died, and at the reading of his will, Reg found he had inherited the business and Smithson-Gubbenheim's house in the country. In fact, Reg inherited everything, including multiple seven-figure money. Through the years following Michael's death Reginald Arthur Heap clawed his way sharply to the pinnacle of his trade.

During that time, Reginald developed a fixation for all things Anglo-Saxon. He began building a collection of precious artefacts from the bygone age. He had no emotional ties to his early life, and he wanted to be free of its clutter, so he changed his name to the Anglo-Saxon *Raegenhere*, and immersed himself in the ancient culture.

He luxuriated in his inherited mansion in Wyverne Hardewicke, situated in a wooded part of Warwickshire, and renamed it Dracasfeld, Dragons Field. Raegenhere's collection started with simple artefacts, brooches, coins and the like. He had the large basement below Dracasfeld to put them in, and he fitted it out with the latest security measures. In this hidden-away place grew his collection of precious metal, some of the pieces encrusted with gems and semi-precious stones. All of it with provable provenance but mostly with shady acquisition. The pièce de résistance was the Sutton Hoo helmet.

In the inner recesses of his mansion, he sometimes strutted around in a Saxon chain-mail hauberk. He would study himself in a full-length mirror, sword in hand, wearing a helm with a built-in face-guard with holes for the eyes. He would imagine himself as an Anglo-Saxon nobleman until he came to the eyes.

"Reggie, my darling, you've got my eyes," his mother used to say in her Brummagem accent, dressed in her filthy apron. How he hated his brown eyes, they should have been the Saxon light blue of the sky.

* * *

Investigations into Raegenhere's activities started one day when suspicious circumstances came to the notice of the authorities. Despite that, the activities grew ever more daring. There was no conclusive proof, ever, so never a prosecution. Some investigators managed to uncover tantalising bits of information and get on the trail, but heavy-duty threats warned them off. One investigator who had been over persistent and ignored the warnings got an answer with a silenced gunshot.

Raegenhere had advisers whose job it was to make sure he had no public identity. There was no doctor's record, no hospital or dentist's file, and the police, unable to finger him, scratched their heads as he breezed around and became richer and richer.

One morning he awoke with the germ of an idea. It was audacious and needed a lot of investment but he put it into action. In July 2007, a story appeared in Daily News America with the headline,

Ancient Artefacts Discovered Offshore.

The story revealed that,

Divers researching the wreck of the Republican Ironclad, Ramses, have found evidence of an early civilisation in the Hudson River near Governors Island. The research vessel, called the Vasco da Gama, that the divers are working from, is under the command of a British philanthropist who wishes to remain anonymous. The operation is likely to continue for at least another twelve months.

43

The dungeon door slammed shut and Beggs heard the heavy wooden beam drop into place in its iron brackets. Alone again, he watched the candle burning. The molten wax dripped down the side of the candle and pooled at the bottom. He despaired when the shadows pressed in on him. He wanted to arrest the burning, to slow time down.

Dearden walked to the green near the pool in the manor house grounds. He switched on the Motorola and tried communicating with Harry. Stressing the urgency, he asked him to program the Hub for a return and listened for a response, but all he heard was static.

Doughty and Julia were avoiding him. With Dearden, any difference was over in minutes. Doughty was not usually off with him, but he could understand how the stress of the situation affected Mitch. Jules sometimes, uncharacteristically, flew into a rage. Afterwards she would become silent for a while before coming round and then bringing everything into the open.

Dearden made his way to the Hub. The sense of isolation pressed in on him and the feel of his Beretta reassured him in case Fengel was about. He heard a movement along the track ahead and dodged behind a tree, as the sound of footsteps grew louder. More than one person was crushing the fallen leaves.

Dearden stepped out. He had the Beretta raised as Doughty appeared with Julia from where the track bent to the left. Doughty lifted the AK and then realised it was Dearden up front. His reaction was frosty. He lowered the weapon and Dearden pocketed the Beretta. They exchanged a few words and then Dearden carried on by himself to the Hub.

He switched on the Motorola when he reached the Hub and repeated how urgent it was to get them back to 2008. There was no response. With the light failing, and feeling the isolation, Dearden made his way back to the manor house.

Doughty and Julia said nothing to each other until they got near the great hall. Julia was sick with apprehension at the way things had become between them and Dearden. She stopped and faced-up to Doughty.

"It's no good, Mitch. We can't let Jem losing the handset get in the way. With all the action we've been through any of us could have lost the damn thing." He nodded his agreement.

They healed the rift over the next few hours and next day rode out looking for the handset. They retraced their steps leading up to the battle at Cheylesmore Brook, but it was a hopeless task, and their sense of isolation grew. Their attempts to communicate with Harry continued without success, and they were acutely aware of the remaining charge in the battery. Aware too of time slipping by toward Thanksgiving Day in 2008. Then their luck changed when they were at their lowest ebb.

They had returned to the Hub and tested the door to the upper room. It was still impossible to open it. Dearden tried the Motorola, repeating the call for help. He waited for a response. Initially, there was nothing but then they heard a faint reply that came and went in waves, with interspersed static.

"Jem, you . . . cutting out . . . faulty compon . . . tact supplier . . . we'll try . . . ain."

Dearden replied urgently into the comms but there was no further response. They were elated with the small success, and after they discussed the fragmented message, they concluded that Harry was locating upgraded components for the Motorola base unit. Although the reception was poor, Harry's words brought hope to the situation.

Dearden keyed the transmit button and described the situation. They waited by the hub for another two hours, testing the comms, but there was still only static, so they returned to the village. Nevertheless, the brief, broken words they received lifted their spirits. Return to 2008 could be within reach.

"What's the battery level?" Julia asked.

"Forty-nine percent. I'm hoping it holds out."

Dearden's inability to do anything immediately about the Raegenhere situation irritated him. He always carried his Beretta in case Fengel appeared, but the slower pace of life in the Anglo-Saxon village compensated for his ill temper. He could spend more time with Rowan with Fengel gone missing.

Dearden and Rowan sometimes walked in the nearer reaches of the forest in the early evenings before the stars shone. The nights were cold and there were sharp frosts at dawn, but the days were pleasant for the time of year and Dearden delighted in telling Rowan about the world he lived in, and what she heard fascinated her. He used his increasing knowledge of Anglo-Saxon to tell her about the great changes there had been in the ways people communicated and travelled. He told her about the world beyond the shores of England, and with her increasing command of modern English, she told him about her life in Maldon and Heanton in the Arden, but she would reveal nothing about her childhood, other than how good Leofwin and Aelfryth had been to her.

Late one afternoon they walked down a well-trodden path leading to Shadow Brook. The Sun had drifted low in the west and the Moon was rising in the afterglow of the day. They followed the water upstream and found a small clearing at a place where it widened out and deepened. They sat on the grassy bank and conversed quietly. They enjoyed the peaceful setting although it was cold.

"Your land of Arden is beautiful, Rowan."

"I know of no other, and it's made more beautiful because you are here," she said, smiling. The colours of the sunset were enriching her beauty. They kissed and vowed quietly in words of English ancient and modern that nothing would come between them for all the time they had together.

"Our land is full of beauty, but the forest can be a strange place at times," Rowan said, sitting up attentively as the baying of a dog-fox broke the spell.

"The House of the West Wind is unusual, but it is the forest that has brought us together, and we must count ourselves fortunate for that." Dearden paused, thinking of the forward flow of time and the changes it would bring.

"Rowan, many years from now there will be a storyteller, a writer who speaks about a moonlit place like this, and he threads his story with magical words. His name will be William Shakespeare." She laughed at the name.

"Is he a soldier?"

"No, but he wields mighty words with a pen and in my time people from all over the world come to a place not far from here to listen to his words."

"Is the world a large place?"

"Far larger than you may think."

"Do you know some of this Shakespeare's words?"

"This place and you remind me of some of them." He remembered some of the words of the Immortal Bard, a sonnet from his schooldays, and he spoke them to her.

Her eyes glistened at the sound the words made. "I don't understand them all, but I can hear the music the words make."

Sadness slipped into Rowan's eyes. "I want to hold on to these times we are sharing, but you will go back to your time because of the people causing trouble and I will be here without you. These times we have together will be a memory, like a jewel we are given as a keepsake." The uncertainties to do with the Hub crept into Dearden's mind. He held her close and tried to reassure her that nothing would stop him from returning, but he wished he could have spoken with more conviction.

Just then, to add to the uncertainty, the sound of someone walking through undergrowth came from some distance away. Rowan looked up, about to speak. Dearden placed his forefinger on her lips and indicated to keep quiet. He raised himself so he could see over the crest of the bank and looked in the direction of the sounds. Fengel, carrying a crossbow, passed by a gap between the trees, and then he was gone. Dearden ducked down and took the Beretta from his belt. He whispered in Rowan's ear.

"It's Fengel, I'm going after him." He raised himself up into a crouch and grasped Rowan's hand, indicating to keep low. They followed the noise as Fengel pushed his way through the undergrowth but the sounds faded into the distance and the noises of the forest took over. Dearden cursed himself for being too slow, but he couldn't have done much else without endangering Rowan, and that he was not prepared to do.

That episode and all of the complexities involved with the different times they were born into caused Dearden to realise he was putting Rowan in acute danger. His emotions had been ruling his actions. If their relationship continued the almost certain outcome would be children and with them the potential for a temporal paradox. He could not be fathering children who, even with the slightest chance, could be his own predecessors. Neither could he expect Rowan to go with him to his own time, to a way of life so alien to her own. He was so much in love with her, and he knew she felt the same about him. The dilemma he faced was how he could resolve the situation, compounded as it was by the nuclear threat to New York.

Dearden was generally self-sufficient and tough. That was his nature, but Rowan of Maldon was part of him and he was at the mercy of a situation that was twisting him apart inside. He cursed his strong sense of duty to see justice done with Raegenhere; and he cursed the fact that he knew of the danger to the citizens of New York, but he had to live with his sense of justice. Dearden worked out that the only way to deal with the situation would be to cool things off with Rowan. He would find a solution once he resolved the problems back home.

Rowan had scarcely left Jem's side in recent days. She linked her arm through his and leant against him as they walked.

"When you go back to your time how long will you be away?" she asked. She had sensed a cooling in his attitude to her, and that his departure must be imminent. She felt she had to challenge him about it. He tried to reassure her that he would return as soon as he could, but she would have none of it. She wanted him to stay, or at least to give her a definite time he would be coming back, two weeks, a month. It became impossible to reason with her.

Then she decided to avoid him, thinking the tactic would make him respond in the warm way he used to. There was one particular time when Dearden and Doughty had returned from the Hub. Ienur opened the outer door and showed them into the anti-room to the great hall. He knocked on the inner door and Leofwin called them in. He was with Aelfryth and their children around a large fire. Garr, at Leofwin's feet, stood and growled as the door opened. Leofwin commanded him to stay and motioned Dearden and the others to bring chairs from the edge of the room closer to the burning logs at the centre. The smoke was rising to the roof and curling through the hole above. Ienur threw more logs onto the fire and the flames created dancing shadows on the walls.

Some men of the Witenagemot were still present and Julia was in animated conversation with them. Although the others drew up chairs to the fire Rowan remained by herself, sitting on a bench by one of the tables, working on some embroidery. She glanced at Dearden and returned to her work, and Dearden felt sick to his stomach.

Leofwin spoke to Dearden and Doughty, struggling with the mix of Anglo-Saxon words and modern English that he had learned. "You people wanted the answer about the man Fengel from the Witenagemot . . . this is their decision. We will take care of Fengel, but we may not give him to you alive."

The decision brought relief. They could move on and deal with the emergency in 2008. The return to their own time was sealed, and Dearden, with a heavy heart, made a mental switch into battle mode. There were too many lives at stake in 2008 to do otherwise. If all went well, there would be a world of time to put things right with Rowan.

* * *

Leofwin wanted to talk privately with Jem and he called Julia over to help with translation.

"You're leaving soon Jem. I want you to come and walk with me. Just you and me. We will try to understand each other but Julia can follow in case we are stuck with the words. Mitch can come with her for protection." Leofwin got up and Garr followed close on his heels, he and Dearden walked through the gate toward the forest with Julia and Doughty carrying the

AK, following at a distance.

They came to Shadow Brook, walked along it for a while, and sat on the bank at the place where Dearden and Rowan had spent time together. Leofwin and Dearden managed to understand each other.

"Jem, do you have someone close to your heart?" Dearden was surprised with the frankness of the question. It took him a few moments to think out his reply and the words to use.

"A few years ago I was very close to a woman named Jackie Mason. She died, and I missed her a lot. Now it weighs less heavily. But why do you ask?"

"I think you have someone else now."

"Is it that obvious?"

"It is to me. I have known Rowan of Maldon since she was a child. As soon as you came here, she changed. I have seen you together. You are meant for one another."

"Don't you think I know that? It is very difficult and the problem lies in the different times Rowan and I live in. It is impossible for me to live here. The reasons are complex. I have many commitments where I come from. Apart from that, it wouldn't be right to take Rowan away from all she knows."

"You should not be speaking for her. That is her decision to make. She has no living family other than one person who she is not very close to. Her father brought her up after her mother died in childbirth. Now her father is dead. He was a great friend of mine. We stood side by side in battle and we swore to stand side by side through the rest of our lives. That's why Rowan is with Aelfryth and me."

"What is her background? She won't tell me."

"The Lady Rowan is high-born. Her only family is an uncle. He is Harold Godwinson the Earl of Wessex. We want him as king."

Dearden was silent for a minute, and then, "I must make my

situation clear to you. The men I told you about are creating a desperate situation in 2008. Doughty, Julia and I can stop them. I also love Rowan more than I thought I could love anyone. What would you do in that situation?"

"Does what's happening back in that place where you come from have to come before the feelings in your heart?"

"It does. Many people may die if we don't go back."

"Jem, you are a good man. Many would put their own desires before all else. Go back. Get the lawbreakers to face justice but then return. You and Rowan are meant to be together."

"I don't need you to tell me that."

Leofwin nodded and leant back, supporting himself on his elbow. "I've got another question. Tell me about the House of the West Wind. Help me understand what happens."

Dearden called Julia and Doughty over. He asked Julia to tell Leofwin to maintain secrecy about what they were going to tell him. Leofwin listened. He was puzzled at first, but he was able to comprehend the concepts of time that were involved after Julia's explanation. Afterwards, he accepted that the events that went on in the forest, passed in folk tales and songs from father to son, were controllable. He probed the three with questions, asked them to tell him about 2008, and his eyes grew wide with wonder.

Shortly after their discussion, Leofwin rode out to see a gold founder in Beorma-ing-ham. He talked to the artisan about a ring he wanted making and they discussed designs.

"There must be three figures on it," he said to Oeric, who was working on a sword hilt with inlaid garnets. "One of the figures must be a woman, and two must be men. Can you make a ring like that for this finger?"

"I can make the ring you want. I shall use lost wax because of the detail, and that is a lengthy process. It will be costly."

"Make it, whatever the cost. It will help me remember three very unusual friends."

When Leofwin returned from the gold founder, Julia asked him if she could walk into Heanton in the Arden. Time was running out to see the village in its ancient form. Leofwin agreed, and with Dearden and Doughty, Julia walked along a rutted uphill track. She sketched the layout of the village, and as they walked about, they attracted curious looks because of their clothing from those who saw them.

"A camcorder would've been the icing on the cake."

"It would. Bring one next time," Dearden had a swift return in mind.

They arrived back at Leofwin's manor house and Rowan came toward them. The others carried on and left Dearden and Rowan alone. Conversation was difficult. Dearden had thought the moment through and decided that when he knew they would be leaving he would break the news to Rowan in cheerful tones and reassure her about his return. When it came to it his tone was sombre, and it set the mood for what was to follow.

Rowan knew that in a time of war, men would feel compelled if they were highborn, or if they belonged to a feudal lord, they would be compelled to go and fight for one of the contending sides. Womenfolk would resign themselves to seeing through tears, the one they loved walk off with what weapons they could muster, possibly never to return.

Rowan reacted in the way her upbringing as a noblewoman conditioned her to behave. She showed restraint and listened to what Dearden said with unsmiling grace, but Rowan had an appalling temper hidden below the surface. The restraint disappeared, and she slapped Jem viciously on the cheek.

"Why did you allow this to start when you came here

unbidden?" was what he understood. He was unable to keep up with the angry words, and there was fire in her eyes. He would recall later how magnificent she was at that moment. She matched his own temperament and the fire was better out than held in.

"OK . . . hold it . . . hold it." He grasped her wrists to stop the rage.

"You must not go away," she sobbed. "You must not go away like some warrior on a hopeless mission . . . and not come back. I love you."

"And I love you, Rowan. I will come back." Rowan turned away. "Look at me," he said. "You mean everything to me, but if I don't do what is right and just I wouldn't be worthy of those close to me, especially you. I must make sure the terrible crime those men are planning doesn't happen."

"You're like all the others. You do what your head tells you and you don't listen to your heart." She pulled herself free from his grip and walked away, her shoulders sunk in despair, leaving Dearden doubting his judgment.

"I take it all isn't well," Julia said, as she walked up to him.

"Too damn right all is definitely not well, but let's get on with it. The sooner we get hold of Raegenhere and his thugs, the sooner I can put things right with Rowan."

As contact with Harry could occur at any time, they prepared to camp at the base of the Hub and wait. The days they had spent with the Anglo-Saxons of Leofwin's household had created affection between them, and they were all isolated in their thoughts. Rowan kept her distance, but Dearden sometimes caught her looking at him. When their eyes met, she turned away.

Dearden and Doughty checked their weapons and re-packed the rucksacks. They went to the dungeon and released

Beggs' shackles. They tied his wrists, and as they led him upstairs, he struggled to keep his eyes open in the strong light.

Dearden, Doughty, and Julia, with Beggs tied to her by a rope, walked away from Leofwin's manor house down the track into the Forest toward Old Jack and Shadow Brook, and inward through the forest to the Hub.

At the place where the forest became dense, they turned and saw Leofwin, Aelfryth, and Rowan standing outside the gates to the manor house. With a heavy heart and a curse for the men who were forcing them to go, Dearden saw Aelfryth put her arm around Rowan's shoulders to comfort her. Leofwin gave them a backwards glance as he walked back in through the gate, and he lifted his hand in a gesture of farewell.

44

It was a day and a half since Fengel heard gunfire coming from the direction of Packhorse Bridge and still Beggs hadn't shown up. He was either dead or captured. Fengel had found a secure place to hide where the forest was thick with undergrowth. It was near enough to the Hub to get to it quickly if he heard anyone approaching, so he gathered underbrush and saplings to make a shelter. His ability to improvise was one of the reasons Raegenhere and Uberatu hired him when he answered the advertisement they placed in their local newspaper. They were looking for an *'Ex-military individual for private security detail and protection of a CEO in the financial industry. Must be able to use initiative and work without supervision.'*

They interviewed a number of candidates. Three nightclub bouncers, a zoo manager who was an Aikido blue belt, an ex-bus driver and some others. When Otto Fengel walked into the Lodge at the entrance of Dracasfeld, they could not believe their luck. They wanted a mercenary with no family connections and they got just that with Fengel.

When he told them he had been on active duty as a Corporal in the French Foreign Legion they were immediately interested. Talking between themselves after his interview, they worked out why he failed to progress any higher than the rank of corporal. He had an arrogance problem. They guessed he was like that in the Legion. They brought him back into the room for further grilling. Fengel revealed that the Legion gave him a dishonourable discharge after he beat up his commandant.

Raegenhere sent him out of the room again. "Fengel must be a tough cookie if he beat his commandant up and escaped from the Legion. Do you think we can knock him into shape?"

"Money always works. Promise him big, reward him small. Let him think there's more to come so he's always hanging on for it."

"He has no family so he won't be missed if we need to waste him."

"That's true," Uberatu said, so they hired him.

Now he was trying to escape from 1063. The Legion was hard and he survived. This was hard in a different way. He was ravenously hungry and was on the hunt for something to roast on a spit over a fire outside his shelter. He heard a snuffling noise that sounded like food coming from the direction of a thicket. He checked how many rounds he had in the Luger. Four in the magazine, thirty-seven in the cardboard box, but he ought not to use the gun. It would give away his position.

Fengel placed a bolt in the crossbow and approached the thicket with caution. Although he was upwind of the thicket a rank stench came in his direction. Suddenly a huge boar burst out of the bushes. Its red-rimmed eyes, which seemed too small for its head, were targeting him. The beast charged. In a flash, he let fly with the bolt, which buried deep into the centre of the creature's skull. Its legs collapsed while it skidded to a quivering halt a couple of feet in front of him. He bent down to examine the kill.

While his attention was distracted, a man walked out of a thicket behind him holding a spear. He had a mop of red hair and a red beard that was matted and untidy.

"Hola, that was a good kill," he shouted from behind Fengel, who was startled and fell onto the creature's corpse to the amusement of the giant of a man. "And you were quick with the crossbow," the giant complemented him before changing his tone. "I was following that animal little man, it's mine." The man's attitude became serious.

Fengel understood most of the words the man said. Because of the man's size, he tried a friendly approach.

"Why are you creeping about in the forest and surprising an innocent hunter?" he asked.

"I am Earl Leofwin's Keeper of the Forest, I guard his deer and swine . . . and everything else," the man said, as he indicated the forest. "You are not an innocent hunter. All of the livestock here belongs to my lord the Earl."

"He can keep the boar." Fengel began to re-wind the cranequin at the same time as working out how to deal with the man. He decided to be conversational. "What's your name?"

"I'm called many things, some good some bad. I was christened John but mainly I am called Tom O'the Wood." As he spoke his name, the giant drew a large sword and hit the stock of Fengel's crossbow, knocking it to the ground.

"The weapon is better out of your hands," he said.

Fengel accepted Tom O'the Wood's chastisement. He gazed at the man. The giant's clothing and his unkempt appearance gave away his struggle for survival.

"How does Leofwin reward you for your work?"

"My reward is for me and mine to get food from the forest. We have a shelter in the village near the Earls homestead."

"You've got a hovel where your family sit in mud when rain comes through the roof."

The man stroked his beard. "We have sufficient for our needs."

"You don't. Look at you. Your clothes are ragged and grimy with mud. Your wife and your children's clothes are ragged and they go cold and hungry. Winter is here. It grows cold with frost at night."

The man looked up and sniffed as if testing the coming

winter air. His heavy brow furrowed. "You are right. My family sometimes goes cold, and their clothes are ragged."

Fengel pressed the advantage home.

"Have you heard of the riches in the Earl's manor house?"

"That I have, but the Earl is a good man and he keeps the valuables for the use of the village and the church, so have a care lest your greed catches you out."

"Leofwin has everything, you have nothing. If he were as good as you say you would not be walking around in rags. He keeps his workers poor. Look at you, creeping about through the mud, in rags."

Fengel's words hit home. Tom O'the Wood's anger welled up inside him.

Fengel saw the change. "I can help you," he said.

"How?"

"Come with me. Help me deal with some vicious men led by one named Dearden. He is plotting to kill me. In return, I will help you get riches beyond your dreams, and I've got a weapon more powerful than anything you've ever seen." He pulled the Luger out of his pocket and showed it to Tom O'the Wood who went to grasp it, but Fengel snatched it away before the giant could get it.

"Catch, my giant friend, there is more where this came from." Fengel flicked one of the gold coins from his pocket into the air. Tom lunged forward and caught the coin. He sat cross-legged, testing the gold with his teeth as he faced Fengel, whose foot was resting on the boar's warm haunches.

"Well?" Fengel asked.

"We'll see." Tom looked at the result of biting the coin and he smiled. He was holding more wealth in his hand than he had ever held before. He stood up. "Your talk of riches interests me. We will see to this man Dearden and we will get the gold, but in the meantime," he stuck his forefinger and thumb into his mouth and blew a piercing whistle. A few seconds later four men came into the clearing. Two had roughly hewn longbows at the ready.

"You see we come prepared when we work in the forest. Lads, this man whose name is Fengel is offering us riches," he turned to face Fengel, who showed surprise at hearing his name. "Yes, we have heard you are causing trouble in these parts. We will see if you can make us rich. I shall send for others to help us but remember this, little man. If you trick me I will kill you, and my friends here want some of your coins as well."

Fengel got more coins out and handed them round. He had the Luger in his other hand.

Tom spoke to the bowmen, gesticulating rapidly. They nodded and walked off into the forest. Soon there was the sound of galloping horses as the bowman rode off to outlying villages with the message from Tom O'the Wood that there was to be a rising against Earl Leofwin. Tom O'the Wood put his arm around Fengel's shoulders and he escorted Fengel along a narrow woodland path to a camp the Woodsmen used.

News travelled fast about the rising and the reward of riches afterwards. With a man the size of Tom O'the Wood leading the rising, there was confidence in the outcome. Two hours after the messengers left, men started drifting into the woodsmen's camp carrying whatever weapons and sharp implements they could lay their hands on.

45

Dearden checked the battery level on the Motorola. There was forty-seven percent left. He pressed the transmit button.

"Harry, Dearden here . . . come in." Nothing came through the speaker other than static.

"He's supposed to have someone standing by in the Hub all the time. What the hell's he playing at?" Julia was getting short of patience, but as the words left her mouth, the Motorola hissed into life. They heard Harry's voice, faint and broken up.

"Jem is . . . you? Speak . . . I will try . . . augment the signal." They ignored the gaps and Dearden pressed transmit.

"It's critical that you get us back to 2008, *big* trouble is going to happen in the United States on Thanksgiving Day." He repeated the message, but it was impossible to say whether Harry heard it because there was no further response.

* * *

Roberts and Wynter woke Harry as they came into the Control room. He had worked well into the early hours. They chatted for a minute or so and then they carried on to the upper room. Harry turned back to the oscilloscope. The new components he installed seemed to be stable.

A while later Red Cloud and Possum Chaser came into the Hub for the first time. They went in through the entrance at ground level and climbed the stairs to the room with the exhibits on the second level. They had heard about this particular room from the others but were taken aback by what they saw when they reached the top of the stairs. They could see how large the area of the room was, that it went a long way back into the side of the hill. Rather than being circular like the room below, it was an elongated oval shape

Red Cloud was a superb reader of surroundings. He often saw signs others would miss, a skill sometimes bordering on the uncanny. On their way through the room, he nudged Possum Chaser. She gave him a sidelong glance and saw him flicking his eyes and moving his head slightly in the direction of the furthest wall. He had seen a slight movement in the shadows.

The sight reminded Red Cloud of the figures near the base of the tribal totem pole in the village on the reservation where he grew up. There were two figures near the back wall, humanoid in form, but not exactly human, because they were tall and thin, and they had odd features and green skin, which unnerved him.

The large eyes had an intense look, but there was no sign of anger or bitterness. Red knew the eyes were a window to the inner motives, and the beings were peaceful. He lifted his hand in his traditional sign of welcome and the strangers lifted their hands in response. Their hands had three fingers and a thumb. It was difficult to tell whether they were male or female. They looked emaciated. Whether they actually were emaciated or had light body mass he couldn't tell. An opening appeared in the wall at the back of the room and another of the beings joined the first two. The three of them were dressed in some sort of uniform that looked worn. On the chest were the faded remnants of badges that once must have been colourful emblazons.

The three went to an opening and walked through to a room beyond. The wall closed up behind them.

"Who were they?" Possum Chaser asked.

"More to the point, *what* were they?"

"Let's tell the others," Possum Chaser walked to the stairs quickly. Red held back, gazing at the place where the three figures had been, and then he followed her to the control room.

When they reached the top of the stairs, the scene in front of them was surreal. Harry was sitting by a bank of panels that looked like the controls of a vehicle. He was deep in concentration, hunched over the Motorola base unit.

He didn't hear the two people come up behind him, but their shadow fell across the screen of the oscilloscope close by and he turned to see Red Cloud and Possum Chaser standing there out of breath and looking nervous. Harry turned back to the oscilloscope, concentrating on attenuating the carrier wave on the comms unit. He almost had a perfect sinusoidal curve. When it was perfect, communication should be possible with Dearden.

Possum Chaser tapped him on the shoulder. "We have something to tell you."

"What?" Harry's curt response was unusual, and it cut them short. There was silence for a few seconds. Harry glanced over at the CCTV screen, shrugged his shoulders and resumed his task. "Sorry, I need to concentrate, this is important."

"Harry, who is in charge when Jem is not here?"

"Bill."

"Mmmm . . . Harry, there are others in the building."

"Yes. Lee and Matt are here, I think they're in the top room. I'm not sure where Bill is."

"But there are others, different ones—"

An incoming signal on the Motorola interrupted Red. Harry gestured for silence and made a careful adjustment with his screwdriver, just an eighth of a turn, but again there was static and the moment for Red to tell Harry what they had seen downstairs was lost.

46

Dearden was sitting against a tree with his back to the hill, with Doughty and Julia Linden-Barthorpe sitting nearby. They had tied Beggs to a tree. Doughty scanned the surroundings and breached a round in the Kalashnikov.

Julia stood suddenly. "We could try communicating with them through the CCTV. They should be monitoring it. If we get close to the Hub we can shout and hold up a message to attract their attention."

Dearden latched on to Julia's idea. "The wall of the hub will be transparent for Harry when he views it on the CCTV. If we write a message on the wall he'll see it."

"As long as he's still looking," Doughty pointed out.

Dearden shrugged the comment off. "Harry's reliable, there's no reason he won't be looking. There's some clay in the bank at Shadow Brook, I can use that to write with. Cover my back while I get it, will you?" He passed his Beretta to Julia, who stayed to guard Beggs.

They found the outcrop of clay and Doughty faced away from the fast-moving stream while Dearden leant over the bank and dug his hands into it. He rolled it into a cylindrical shape on the way back to the Hub and then wrote a message in reverse on the wall. Harry would see it the right way from inside the Hub. When Dearden had finished he stood back and spoke into the Motorola.

* * *

Harry gestured for Red and Possum Chaser to be quiet as a voice came through the speakers. It was broken up but recognisable. Harry pressed the transmit button, but before he could speak the broken-up voice came through again.

"Harry . . . you th . . . come in."

"Jem, keep speaking, I need to augment the signal." Harry moved the miniature potentiometer a quarter of a turn and glanced at the waveform on the oscilloscope. There was an improvement when Dearden's voice came through again, the message increased in volume and then faded. It had an overlay of background noise. Harry gave the potentiometer another eighth of a turn and Dearden's voice came through loud and clear. Harry glanced at the CCTV monitor and frowned as he realised the scene was the same as it had been a short while before.

"Damn, the screen's frozen." He leapt out of the oversize chair, startling Possum Chaser, who was standing close by. He rushed to the monitor and switched it off. After ten seconds he switched it back on, hoping the monitor would re-set itself. The forest scene flashed onto the screen, and Harry saw some words written in large reddish brown letters as if hanging in mid-air. He realised the words were on the outside wall of the Hub, which was transparent because the Hub was active.

HARRY GET US BACK NUKE BOMB NEW YORK

Harry could see Dearden with Julia at his side. They looked as though they had been living rough. Dearden had a beard, and Doughty, equally dishevelled, was at the bottom of the slope facing the forest with the AK47 to his shoulder ready to use.

"That message is urgent, and look at the state of them," Possum Chaser said, as she got closer to the monitor. Harry waved his hand for silence as Dearden's voice came through.

"You must get us back to 2008, there's big trouble coming up in the States on Thanksgiving Day, the handset to get us back is lost. You'll have to get us back manually." Dearden sounded tense.

"Jem, I hear you. Give us more detail."

"OK, make sure you get this right. You have to dial a phone number. Make a note of what I'm going to tell you, and destroy the note when you've made the call."

"Whatever you say, Jem, but why the secrecy?"

"Never mind that, I'll explain later." Dearden gave him the number.

"You'll hear an automated response. You'll be asked to leave a message. Say this, *Await call for go. Details on next instruction. Bogie is a man named Raegenhere. Incursion target to be 'Dracasfeld', Wyverne Hardewicke, Warwickshire. Added to that is a nuclear threat to New York November twenty-seventh, about which maintain silence until further contact. Dearden, ID code 3746TTP, SHaFT Cell 1. Call ends.* Harry, repeat the message back."

He did, and Dearden's voice came again.

"Harry, how close are you to having the co-ordinates to timeshift us back home?"

"Give me two or three hours and we'll have you back. I need to check the integrity of the power supply to the Hub. Let's do a time check. What do you have?"

"I have 1435 hours."

"Your time's still on the nail with ours. I'll set up the Hub for a 6 p.m. timeshift. That is 1800 hours. Jem, don't be late."

"Don't worry, we won't. Now listen, this is important, when we get back there's going to be some action. Just go with it and keep your head down. Tell Templestone, Roberts and Wynter to prepare themselves for action. Tell no-one else."

"How about Red Cloud and Possum Chaser? They're here with me."

"Tell them they have to keep shtum about what happens." Red and Possum Chaser nodded that they understood.

"They're good with that Jem, but I'm mystified."

"You stay mystified for now. Hey, Harry, it's good to hear your voice. Out."

"Likewise, Jem. Out."

Harry was puzzled as he went to the phone and made the call. He had seen Dearden and the others in action in the workshop. It had been lethal, and now Dearden was telling him to prepare for more action. The situation sounded toxic. Harry looked at his watch, 1514. The time left to 1800 made it critical to configure the return.

"Red, we need to get Templestone, Matt and Lee up here. See to it will you, and Red, be quick."

Red and Possum Chaser had heard Dearden say over the comms that the situation was urgent so telling the others what they had seen downstairs would have to wait.

* * *

Leofwin prided himself on having an effective spy network throughout the part of Mercia under his influence. Not that he enjoyed that method of peacekeeping but it was necessary because of the instability of the times and the lawlessness that sometimes surfaced. The forest was an ideal shelter for those outside the law. Most people were law-abiding but the odd few were intent on trouble.

The men in Leofwin's network kept a low profile. They ensured that society ran along within a loosely legal framework. Leofwin was not a harsh Ealdorman. He understood minor misdemeanours would always occur and he overlooked them, but he needed to know what was going on.

The man Tom O'the Wood sent out on horseback to raise men to his cause went by the name, Brunloc. He had ridden into the village of Keres Leah and he stopped at the alehouse where a green bush was on its pole outside the building, telling passers-by that ale was brewed and ready.

It was dark within, and a number of fowl were milling about pecking crumbs dropped by the customers. Brunloc found a number of the local men inside who had finished working the land for the day and were talking in a huddle by the glowing fire. He asked them how the crops had done and whether the village was prepared for winter.

The other side of a stall, away from the light of the fire, Osbryht, one of Leofwin's men was listening to the buzz of conversation. They were talking in low tones, which was suspicious. Normally when men drank, the talk was loud and unrestrained. To remain alert, Osbryht drank slowly, rather than have the ale fuddle his head. An elderly man bent with arthritis who had help from the village poor chest was saying the signs had been in the leaves that the coming months of winter would be harsh. He remarked that the crops had not ripened in the quantity needed to get the village through the winter cold that was upon them early this year.

Brunloc worked on dissension. He indicated for the men to draw close. In a quiet voice, he told them how they could end their struggles by rising against Earl Leofwin. One of their leaders of the rebellion, he said, was a man named Fengel, who had a powerful weapon that would make short work of Leofwin's forces. There was a forceful murmured agreement about joining the uprising and Brunloc told the men to meet in the Woodsmen's clearing near Myrig-Denu where Tom O'the Wood was waiting. There was a gap in the partition and Osbryht had his ear pressed tight to it. He heard the plotting, how the rebels would raid Leofwin's Great Hall and make off with the coffer that held the gold coinage. Tom O'the Wood's messenger had done his work and he made off to the next village, Cuna Dun, to seek more support for the rising. Leofwin's man waited for a short while to save arousing suspicion, and then he took his horse from the stable and rode off swiftly to report what he had heard.

Rowan, Leofwin and Aelfryth had returned to the Manor House after saying farewell to Dearden and the others. Rowan was distraught and went to her room where Esma consoled her as only a trusted friend could. Not long afterwards, they heard a horse galloping into the manor grounds. It had been hard-ridden and was wheezing and blowing. Esma darted to the window and saw a man dismount from the horse that was foaming at the mouth. Rowan signalled Esma to open the door and leave it ajar. She wanted to hear what was going on. She recognised Osbryht's voice, and he was talking urgently.

"My lord, I bring news of a rising, the man Fengel is behind it, aided by Tom O'the Wood." Rowan caught hold of Esma's sleeve and pulled. They crept downstairs and peered around the door into the great hall. They saw the Earl unable to contain his anger when he heard the news. They saw Osbryht step back a few paces when Leofwin vented his anger with curses and threats, lashing out at a chair whose legs broke with the onslaught.

The fury was over as quickly as it had risen and with his hand on his sword hilt Leofwin pressed for more details of the rising. Osbryht said he had heard the attack was imminent, and that on his way back to Heanton he had alerted men, who he knew were loyal to the Earl, to make haste to the manor house to give their support.

Leofwin gave instructions to set the alarm bell ringing. The men of the nearby villages would hear it and bring their families inside the protection of the fortified wall surrounding the manor house. As Leofwin began these preparations to repel the uprising, Rowan and Esma went into the great hall.

* * *

Dearden and the other three were sitting with their backs to the wall of the Hub waiting for the six o'clock deadline when, in the distance, coming on the breeze, Julia heard a bell ringing rapidly in the distance.

"Listen," she said. "Can you hear that?"

"Hear what?" Doughty listened, and then he heard it too as the breeze shifted, the sound of a bell ringing from the direction of the manor house.

"Oh hell." Dearden grabbed his rucksack. "It's the alarm bell at the manor. If it's Fengel with his Luger they'll need our help. You two carry on back, I'll get Beggs."

He untied Beggs from the tree and with the Beretta in one hand and Beggs' rope in the other, he pushed him forward into a run. "Move it or I'll leave you here for whatever drops by," he said. He glanced at his watch. It was 1450.

Rowan and Esma joined the clamour of preparation. Aelfryth was at Leofwin's side, and Garr was there, standing with his master. After the alarm began to ring a commotion arose outside and the harsh metallic sounds of military preparations came as the guard in the small garrison made ready to repel the assault. The great hall was a hive of organised activity as Rowan and Esma made their way to Leofwin.

"Get some belongings together. Dress in warm clothing in case we are overrun and have to flee for safety." Leofwin had the Castle of Coufaentree in mind. "I only hope we don't have to flee through the night if we are overrun."

Rowan motioned him out of earshot of the others. "I must stay here and wait for Jem. He might hear the alarm and return."

"Don't count on it. There is important work he has to do." He looked at her. She was pale and drawn. "Go and prepare.

Jem needs to find you alive if he does come back. Go daughter, and be quick about it." Rowan and Esma rushed upstairs to prepare for flight. Even the urgency of the situation didn't lift the veil of despondency that descended after Rowan had watched Jem walking off into the forest. "I will be back," he had said. She could still hear his voice speaking the words he had learned in her language, saying how much he loved her. She had said the same to him and the memory forced tears to her eyes. Rowan wiped them away and searched her room looking for warm clothing ready for escape. She gave a hwitel to Esma and chose one for herself. She put it around her shoulders and pinned it together at the front with her favourite brooch, and then she walked around the room touching items she had known since her childhood. She placed the ones she treasured most, and her mother's jewellery, into a leather bag.

"Esma, you must take some of your belongings too," she said. They had similar likes and dislikes. She thought back to how they were mistaken for sisters because they looked so alike. The time she had played dead and put oxblood on her clothes. The elderly cook shrieked and burst into tears. She was frightened half out of her wits when the other child jumped out at her from behind a door and the one covered in blood stood up. The result had been a severe scolding from Leofwin.

So many memories . . .

Men who were armed and dangerous would be about. It could be a perilous journey through the forest if they had to flee after sundown. Leofwin was right. If flee she must, maybe to the castle of Coufaentree where she would be safe, at least, as Leofwin said, she would be alive for when Jem came back.

Dearden and Beggs arrived at the gate to the manor. The guards recognised Dearden and opened the gates. Julia and Doughty were waiting for them. The gate slammed shut behind them and they ran to the great hall where Ienur and six guards were protecting the entrance. Ienur hammered on the door to the great hall with the pommel of his sword. There was a call from within to enter. Going past Ienur, Julia asked him to take care of Beggs and Dearden passed him the rope.

At the far end of the great hall, Leofwin stood in his hauberk and a helm with eagle embellishments in gold. He had another sword at his waist similar to Aelfrythsgiefu. Its bejewelled pommel glittered in the flickering light from the candles illuminating the hall and his new golden ring flashed on his right forefinger. He was standing in the middle of a group of men at arms who lowered their weapons when they saw it was Dearden and the others who had entered.

Leofwin raised his arm in welcome. He signalled them to come and join them. He was hoping Dearden and his friends would hear the alarm and return. Leofwin had told the houscarl whose task it was to strike the bell to hit it harder than usual so that its sound would carry further. Leofwin knew that with their understanding of Fengel and his weapon, Dearden and his friends would be valuable allies. He told Ienur, who had Beggs on the end of a rope, to take him down to the cell and place a guard in front of the door.

"What's happening?" Julia asked Leofwin.

"There is an uprising. All the signs tell us the coming months will be bleak and Otto Fengel is playing on the fears of the village people. He has told them that the contents of the coffer will help them when there is meagre food over the winter, and that his weapon will help them raid our treasury coffer." Leofwin put his hand on Julia's shoulder in a gesture of affection. "You have come back to help us, how long before you have to go back to the House of the West Wind?"

She glanced at her watch. "We can stay two hours."

"That should be enough." Leofwin went to the wall and

lifted a candle from its holder. He called Ienur and asked him to go and get a nail. He pointed out the thin rings around the candle spaced down its length. "The candle burns one ring to another in one hour," he dripped some molten wax onto the long table and stuck the candle into it. Ienur handed him the nail and he pushed it into the wax two divisions down. "When the nail drops you have to go." His countenance became serious and without another word, he went to join his men on the defensive wall.

The population of Heanton had hastened to the grounds of the manor house after hearing the alarm. The men of the village were always ready to take up arms because violence was never far away. They came inside the defences of Leofwin's Manor with their families, weapons and what armour they possessed. Word soon passed to others loyal to Leofwin, and they came from nearby villages, some on horseback others on foot.

Dearden and his colleagues mounted the steps to the walkway along the perimeter wall and met with Leofwin. He was looking at the forest from the protection of the embrasures, waiting for signs of movement amongst the trees. A handful of his men were operating the gate, others on the walkway had crossbows, and others possessed spears and swords for close combat. A few who had the skill to use them had longbows. Fires were alight on the ground a few feet away, and on them, cauldrons of water were boiling with wooden buckets on ropes close by, ready to tip over and scald attackers who attempted to scale the wall.

Leofwin turned to Dearden and called Doughty and Julia, from where they were keeping watch by the embrasures. "My friends, I think there is a way of making this action short and decisive. Tell me if you agree with my idea."

He outlined his plan and started to walk toward the steps, but stopped and came back to Dearden. He took him to one side and spoke quietly.

"Jem, we've had to deal with dangerous problems before, but this time it is different with the threat Fengel poses with his weapon. It may prove difficult, but if you need to go before the fighting ends, we will survive. There is something else." Leofwin's demeanour took a serious edge. "What is going to happen to Rowan? I will not have her hurt again. If necessary, I will use force against you to make sure she is not hurt."

"I am sure you would."

"I ask you again, what does Rowan want to do?"

"She wants to be part of my life, in my time, but if she were to do that there would be great changes she would have to get used to."

"Could you prepare her for that?"

"I would show her the changes a little at a time, but would it be right to take her from everything she's familiar with?"

"Jem, what does *she* want to do?" Leofwin was distracted as the sound of the bell rang from the church tower on the hill in Heanton. He scanned the distance. Where the trees thinned out slightly he saw a large number of men approaching over the fields from the direction of Bercul's Well. They looked disorganised as they climbed over the drystone walls and fanned out into the shelter of a thicker part of the forest.

Leofwin put on his helm, which glinted gold and silver in the sunlight. Julia thought him an imposing figure as he strode along the wall to get a better view of the approaching enemy. There was disciplined silence among his men. The horde was approaching through the trees and they halted for a few moments at a long bowshot from the fortified wall. Then they began to advance over the open ground, chanting in time to their slow pace, striking their shields with each footfall.

Leofwin assessed the rebels to be about one hundred and fifty strong. As the advance continued Julia pointed out Otto Fengel in the midst of the crowd, and Leofwin identified the large man at the front.

"That's Tom O'the Wood, even under the boar's head I recognise him because of his size. Tom is a good man but he's mistaken in his judgment. I want to persuade him to give up his ideas." Julia told Dearden and Doughty what Leofwin said, but as soon as the words were out of her mouth Tom O'the Wood broke into a run and his men started to yell as they followed him. At the head of the horde, Tom, with a large spear in his hand, uttered a hideous squeal like a wild boar.

"Ready with the plan?" Dearden said to Doughty. The ones attacking were fifty yards off when Mitch Doughty got a clear bead with the Kalashnikov on Tom O'the Wood's thigh. He fired, and the report startled birds from the trees bordering the forest.

Tom O'the Wood stopped the animal noise and fell to the ground. His voice changed to a falsetto whimper. The scene became like a frozen tableau. The rebels couldn't understand what had happened to the strong giant to cause him to lie on the ground moaning like a child. All they knew was that the people on the fortifications had injured him. A few that had been in the Packhorse Bridge skirmish recognised the sharp cracking noise associated with the injury, and it terrified them.

They scattered in the direction of the forest. Doughty tried to pick Fengel out in his sights, but the man was lost in the crowd. There was a cheer from Leofwin's men and they aimed whistles and catcalls at the running mob.

Leofwin looked first at the Kalashnikov and at Doughty. "You did well, my friend," he said.

"It would've been better if I'd finished Fengel."

"They are not organised and they are frightened, they will

not be back," Leofwin reasoned.

"You can rest assured Fengel will be back," Dearden said. He checked his watch. It was 1638 hours. Leofwin saw Dearden using the timepiece and detected the urgency.

"Are you going now?"

"Within the hour we will have to go. First, we will bring Tom O'the Wood in and see what he knows about Fengel. Cover us Jules. Mitch, let's go."

Doughty passed the AK to Julia and they followed Dearden down the steps from the wall and out through the gate. As they made their way over to Tom O'the Wood Julia swept the edge of the forest with the assault rifle, looking for movement.

The boar's head stared at them uselessly as Dearden and Doughty helped Tom O'the Wood stand. Tom saw Leofwin coming toward them, and he groaned as he faced the man against whom he rebelled. Leofwin lifted the boar's head off.

"Tom, you are a fool," he said. "I expected better of you. Now I must decide what to do with you." They assisted the man into the great hall where Doughty had the emergency field kit, and Julia told Tom O'the Wood that Doughty was going to attend to his wound. The wounded man lay on one of the straw mattresses at the side of the great hall, and Doughty slit the cloth of his garment to get to the wound.

While he was cleaning the wound, Dearden questioned Tom about Fengel's plans. Julia translated the man's gruff tones that he did not know what Fengel's plans were, but if he knew where he was hiding, he would kill him.

Leofwin stood at Dearden's side. "My friend, the candle burns low. One more thing needs to be done." Leofwin held onto Dearden's sleeve and pulled him to the stairs leading up to the private living quarters. "Sit here," he pointed to a seat with its back in the shape of a bull's head. "I passed the word to Rowan that you are here. She is going to come with you."

47

When Dearden came into the great hall before the action, Rowan heard his voice. She regretted her earlier outburst and wished she could retract the angry words. When she heard his voice, she had renewed hope and a thrill of anticipation. She was nervous as she waited for the outcome of events. She held back the urge to go down and see him but it was difficult to wait and do nothing. Esma sensed her distress, so she came over, sat close to Rowan, and clasped her hand to reassure her.

After a while, they heard a squeal like a boar, a familiar sound from the forest. Esma felt Rowan flinch at the feral noise, and then they heard the roar of an angry crowd. The noise of many feet rushing toward them. A loud cracking noise followed, which startled the birds. Suddenly there was dead quiet, disturbed by the cry of a man in pain. Rowan put her ear to the horn-inset window to hear what was going on. There was the sound of confusion, frightened voices, and then running.

Rowan opened the window and there he was, Jem with Mitch Doughty, and Julia following a few paces behind holding the weapon Doughty usually carried. They were in the clearing beyond the fortifications, heading for a man lying on the ground with blood dripping from a wound in his leg.

Rowan closed the window and sat back down. Her heart was thumping. After a short while, she heard footsteps coming up the steps and onto the landing. There was a knock on the door. She held her breath expecting it to be Jem and signalled for Esma to open the door.

Rowan was disappointed; it was Leofwin, but he encouraged Rowan to hurry downstairs, and then he left them.

She felt a surge of excitement as she finished putting her belongings and childhood mementoes into the leather bag. Esma, her face flushed with activity, was doing the same.

Rowan looked around the room, at its woven wall hangings depicting colourful hunting scenes in the forest. The furniture took her eye and she lingered on the threshold. She grasped Esma's hand and as they ran downstairs, she put the memories behind her. Jem was sitting at the side of the doorway. He stood quickly and she rushed to his arms, sobbing with joy and relief.

Aelfryth came to where they were standing. There were tears in her eyes as she held Rowan close. The years they had together made Aelfryth love her like a daughter. They had been close and she had taught Rowan the womanly things. Like in the days when Rowan was young Aelfryth took her by the hand, and this time, in her voice that had the lilt of the hills of Ceredigion she told Rowan to always support Jem. Aelfryth had grown fond of the man from the House of the West Wind.

"Be at his side and he will love you in return, Rowan," she said, looking at Leofwin with the look in her eyes she had when she was especially close to her husband.

Leofwin pulled Rowan to him. "Godspeed, my daughter," he said. "Go with Jem Dearden and be happy in your life. He will take good care of you, I trust him to do that. He says he will try to return and tell us how you are faring after your journey to his world." Leofwin's eyes were moist. He was a hardened warrior, but at that moment, he thought of his friend. A friend who was dying on the battlefield years before to whom Leofwin gave the promise to look after his daughter as he would his own child. Leofwin put Rowan's happiness before his own, and he let her go.

Dearden glanced at his watch. It was 1700. A movement on the candle caught his attention and the nail marking the time to leave dropped out and clattered onto the table.

"Time to go," he said.

Grasping Rowan's hand, Dearden walked swiftly to the door to join the others and they ran toward the gate. Rowan looked behind briefly.

"Is it all clear out there?" Julia called. The guard signalled it was as they gathered at the entrance. The great gates swung open, Julia tugged on Beggs' rope to speed him up and they were through. The gates slammed shut heavily behind them and the gatekeeper dropped the beam into its brackets.

Doughty had the emergency field kit slung on his back and the Kalashnikov at the ready. Dearden shoved the Beretta into the left side of his belt, butt forwards for quick access. Julia had Shotokan. It was all she needed and there had been plenty of proof she could handle it with consummate skill. All was silent as they neared the forest other than the sound of their running and a blackbird piping melodious notes. In the distance, another blackbird gave an answering call, which was timeless in the lowering light of the Anglo-Saxon day.

Fengel was hiding behind a large tree out of sight from the manor house. A few of his men had re-joined him and he told them to be silent. The manor and its grounds had quietened after the failed raid, but there was the occasional movement of lookouts keeping an eye on the forest from the fortified wall.

From his hidden position Fengel espied the gate opening. Six people ran out led by Dearden with a pistol in his belt. Beggs was at the end of a rope and Doughty came last armed with the Kalashnikov and a pistol. Fengel wound the cranequin of his crossbow for another shot. He liked the brutal feel of it.

He was on his guard because Dearden and his colleagues were dangerous. Fengel's ego still smarted over how Dearden and those at the manor overcame his attack. He had been in the French Foreign Legion with its regime full of machismo.

For Dearden to force him into this outlandish place against his will was the final insult. He consoled himself with the thought that revenge was close, and there were riches to dig up when he got back to his own time.

The light was fading fast. It was a waning moon without cloud cover. Dearden's team could only travel at the speed of the slowest, who was Beggs. As they hurried through the forest, Dearden planned strategy.

"Harry will be in touch soon after we get to the Hub. When the door unlocks we need to get into the building quickly. The light from the Moon will pick us out and make us an easy target. I'll cover the sides with the Beretta. Mitch, cover our rear with the AK. Jules, you get Rowan, Esma and Beggs inside the Hub. It's vital we get him back alive to help us nail Raegenhere and Uberatu."

Fengel stopped a short distance from the Hub in a hidden place close to the track Dearden would be following. He explained to the few men who remained with him that he would be leaving them when the House of the West Wind became alive. It was difficult for them to understand what he said, and they looked at him with fear in their eyes, but he had some gold coins left from the abbey and he passed some to each man. He won their hearts with the gold coins, but they looked on warily as he topped up the magazine of his Luger. They knew not to trust either him or his weapon. Fengel's plan called for patience and cool thinking. He breathed deeply a few times to cool his apprehension and then he felt he was ready.

Occasionally small events creep into the affairs of man and set larger events in motion, which happened when one of Fengel's men trod on a dry twig. They all froze. Fengel waited to see if any of the six he was tracking heard the noise. There was no sign they had.

Julia got close to Dearden and whispered, "Don't turn, someone's following. I heard a noise to the right,"

"I heard it too; we're nearly there now." Dearden's hand tensed on the Beretta. He glanced at his watch. "Harry'll be through in five minutes, I'll let Mitch know someone's about." He took the Motorola out and triggered the On/Off switch ready for Harry. The unit lit up and he heard the familiar static as he slipped to the rear to warn Doughty.

"I heard it," Doughty said, readying the AK one-handed in his right. He gripped the Colt M1911 in his left.

Julia tied Beggs' rope around her waist so both her hands were free. "One false move and I'll kick your balls into touch," she warned as they reached the base of the hill. Dearden checked the time. Thirty seconds to go.

In the gathering gloom, Fengel failed to see a gnarled root growing across the track where he was leading his men. The root looped out of the ground and then snaked back into the earth again. Fengel's foot caught in the loop.

"Shit," he hissed as he pitched forward. A man at his side caught him. One of Fengel's men with a longbow took Fengel's curse as the command to shoot a shaft. The arrow narrowly missed Doughty and hit a tree nearby. In a second Doughty had the AK up and the moonlight picked out the man in his sights. The others looked for cover. Doughty fired, but he missed, just as Fengel raised the crossbow to his shoulder.

* * *

Harry was sitting at the control panel in the Hub. He had spent the last few hours refining the calibration and he was tired. He thought it would be easy after the installation of upgraded components but it turned out to be a lengthy process that needed verification after each adjustment. With less than an hour to go, the distortion disappeared and the Lissajous curve on the oscilloscope was perfect. Harry was confident that when he called Dearden the transfer would go without a hitch.

Earlier in the day when Harry understood the gravity of the situation when he read Dearden's message, he realised just how desperate they were to get back. He was taking no chances with the power supply so he got Matt Roberts to tow the Lycoming through the forest to the Hub, and from the generator, a thick cable snaked up through the floors to where Harry connected it to the power supply.

Lee Wynter and Matt Roberts were standing near Harry. It was close to six o'clock. The room was quiet and the men were tense. With a minute to go Harry started the countdown and spoke into the microphone to prepare Dearden.

There was no reply.

At the thirty-second mark, Harry pressed the remote start button he rigged to the side of the control panel and the Lycoming roared into life on the forest floor.

At five seconds to zero Wynter slammed the isolator switch shut to connect the generator to the circuitry of the Hub. The system powered up as the cascade of electrons coursed through the flying leads. Screens on the wall in front of them flickered into life, and a series of alien symbols and graphics appeared on the screens. As Harry took control of the Hub, he spoke into the microphone.

"Up the hill, now!" Julia snapped into action and pushed Beggs up the hill. Halfway up the slope two spears narrowly missed her and buried their tips into the ground. She grasped Rowan and Esma by the hand and pulled, urging them to hurry. Dearden was following closely, sweeping the area with his Beretta while Doughty stayed as rear-guard to cover the others' retreat up the hill. The Moon highlighted the nearby tree trunks but the darkness in between was full of menace. Doughty crouched low, Colt in one hand and Kalashnikov in the other ready for Fengel and his men to appear out of the darkness, aware to wing not kill, unless it was Fengel in his sights.

At the top of the hill, Dearden turned to face the forest. He ordered Beggs to get to the ground as a man appeared from behind a tree and launched a spear, which sliced into the ground nearby. At that moment, the Motorola crackled into life and Harry's words came through sharp and clear.

"We're on Jem," Dearden placed himself between Rowan and the forest and didn't respond immediately.

Harry's voice came again, "Jem, come in, are you there?"

Dearden thumbed the transmit button, "Harry, do it, the timeshift, do it now."

Within seconds, the faint blue translucent lines became visible, radiating from the Hub. Storm clouds gathered over the hill, monotone shades of moonlit grey and black gathered and became angry thunderheads. A vivid burst of lightning split the air.

A violent wind arose and tore at the remnant of leaves on the trees and those lying on the ground, adding to the confusion. Through the storm wind, Doughty saw Fengel moving forward. He was lifting the crossbow to his shoulder. Doughty knew he could deal with Fengel. Being from his own timeframe there would be no temporal paradox so he raised his Colt and fired.

It was a difficult shot and the storm played havoc with his aim. He missed, and Fengel ran toward the hill crossbow raised with half a dozen men behind him. Doughty fired and missed again but it had been close enough to unnerve Fengel, and he and his men bolted back to the cover of the trees and their shrouding darkness.

Fengel surveyed the scene from behind a large tree and he saw feint blue lines from the building arcing high up into the darkness. Lightning pierced the air and a fierce wind blew leaves and debris about. His chance had come to get inside the Hub. He knelt. The howling wind was blowing his hair and clothing wildly as he slotted a bolt into the track of the crossbow.

Dearden threw the door open and Beggs scrambled in as Dearden stood aside and shouted for the others to get inside. Doughty, half way up the hill, raised his Colt again and loosed off two more rounds in quick succession to cover Julia who was pulling Rowan and Esma up the last few yards to the top. Fengel saw his opportunity. He came into the open and saw his target.

Rowan rushed to the door leading to safety and a new life with Jem. She saw him just behind. Not long now, they would soon be together. How she loved him! She pushed Esma through the door and turned to see if they had escaped the attackers, and Dearden shouted to get inside.

Fengel was near the base of the hill. In the moonlight, Dearden saw his face twisted and full of anger. The crossbow was at his shoulder loaded with a bolt for piercing chain mail.

He yelled above the sound of the wind, "Dearden, hey Dearden, here's a gift for your woman," and he fired. Rowan gasped as the bolt struck her in the back. As she fell, Esma screamed and sank to the ground clutching at her. There was an anguished cry from Dearden and he dropped to the ground at Rowan's side. The emotion took over and he couldn't think what to do, fight, shout in anger, hold her . . . try to get the vicious offending thing out of her back.

Mitch Doughty reacted with an instinct born from years of discipline and training. He switched the emotion off and ran down the hill leaping over and around the obstacles in his path toward Fengel who was re-winding the crossbow.

Fengel looked up. He would go for Dearden next. He put his confidence in the crossbow and forgot his Luger. He forgot it took thirty seconds to tension the crossbow. Three yards from Fengel Doughty stopped, and Fengel stopped his winding. He saw Doughty in the two handed stance of a marksman, and fear filled his eyes just before the gun was fired.

It was a double-tap, one to the head one to the heart, and Fengel still had an open-mouthed look of disbelief on his face as he dropped to the ground blood pumping from the wounds. He twitched and lay still. Doughty turned, and as he raced up the hill to get to the shelter of the Hub, a longbow shaft hissed through the air and pierced his calf.

He cried out in pain and fell to the ground. Dearden, through force of will in combat mode again, reacted instantly when he heard Doughty yell.

"Get the women out of sight," he shouted to Julia as he ran down the face of the hill. Strangely, and there is no accounting for people's actions under threat, Beggs, his hands tied, grabbed Rowan's garment and helped Julia drag her into the Hub. He held his hands out to Julia and she untied him.

Dearden scrambled to the door supporting Doughty who was moaning and dragging his injured leg. Beggs took over, supporting Doughty as Dearden slammed the door on the outside world. Dearden ran downstairs into the control room and punched the Go To button on the keyboard, then raced back up the stairs two at a time. The surroundings outside became blurred. Dearden hoped to hell Harry had programmed the timeshift correctly to 2008 and not to some other place in time.

48

The humming of the high-tension circuitry was fading as Harry, Wynter and Matt Roberts raced up the two flights of stairs from the control room. They saw a desperate scene. Julia and Beggs were next to two women, strangers in unusual clothing. One of them was lying on her side with an arrow-like object protruding from her back, gasping in agony with her blood pooling on the floor.

Julia spotted Harry and Wynter as they came to the top of the stairs.

"Where's Templestone?" She asked, without preamble.

"Standing guard in the workshop," Wynter said.

"Jem, throw me the Motorola." Julia caught it, switched it on, and adjusted it to the frequency assigned to the workshop. Templestone picked up.

"Priest, we're back at the Hub with two injured. Get Green and Mallett to the Hub to deal with battlefield injuries. This is serious, get them here quick."

"What's going on?"

"No questions, Priest, get them here now."

"Consider it done."

Julia turned to Beggs.

"See that Afro-Caribbean man there, that's Lee Wynter, stick close to him. Lee, take care of Beggs. Make sure he doesn't escape. Oh, and Beggs, thanks for the help, I'll remember it."

Jack Green and Bob Mallett were the surgeon and anaesthetist attached to SHaFT. They were always on call because SHaFT could go into action at any time. For that inconvenience, they got a handsome paycheque each month, and they lived with their wives and children in a large house at Hill Wootton that came with the job. It had a hangar housing a Eurocopter fitted out as an air ambulance. With Mallett at the controls, they were airborne and on their way from Hill Wootton within minutes of the call from Templestone.

Dearden was cradling Rowan in his arms, trying to comfort her and telling her to stay with him, to stay awake. His experience of battlefield injuries told him that if the medics arrived there might be a slim chance Rowan would survive, but they had to arrive quickly and time was running out. He had taken her from all she knew only to die in a place foreign to her. But why were the women he got close to destined to die before their time? Jackie Mason first, now Rowan.

"Why Mitch, why has this happened? I'm going back to get that bastard Fengel. Anger took over and Dearden checked his Beretta and stood up.

"It's done, Jem. Fengel's dead." Doughty was leaning with his back to the wall. He was pale and sweating. He patted the Colt, "Head and heart." Dearden felt the burden of guilt and heard the deathly silence in the room, punctuated by Esma's sobbing and Rowan gasping in pain. He held the bolt, torn between pulling it and leaving it where it was.

Wynter was examining the arrow sticking through Doughty's leg. Harry was with him, pale at the sight of the blood but ready to help. Doughty reached for the emergency field kit Matt Roberts was holding.

"Can't wait for the bloody medics," Doughty said through clenched teeth. "Got to help Rowan." He was grimacing with pain. "Pull this damn thing out . . . do it, Lee. Get it out so I can help her." Wynter nodded. He would need to break off the fletch and grip the arrow by the protruding barbed tip. Then he could pull the remaining shaft through Doughty's calf.

"Lidocaine, get it," Wynter commanded, holding out his hand to Roberts who quickly found the anaesthetic in the field kit. Wynter sprayed the area of the wound and called over to Jules. He threw the can over to use on Rowan.

"Spray it around the entry point of the bolt." She nodded.

"Knife," she held her hand out for Matt Roberts' Bowie and cut Rowan's gown open and sprayed the entry point of the projectile with the topical anaesthetic. The tension eased from Rowan's eyes.

Wynter held the arrow firmly near Doughty's calf to keep movement in the wound to a minimum. Grasping it with his other hand, he sharply bent the shaft. It snapped off cleanly.

"Petroleum Jelly," Wynter called out. Roberts found it and handed the pot over. Wynter rubbed some around the stub of the shaft to lubricate it. Holding the protruding end by the bodkin tip, he swiftly pulled the remaining shaft through the flesh. Doughty yelled out with the pain and Roberts, finding iodine in the kit, handed it to Wynter who liberally applied some to the wound with a lint pad and put on a field dressing. After a minute Doughty stood up. He was unsteady and his leg was throbbing unmercifully, but he fought through the pain and Wynter helped him to where Rowan was lying.

"Let me get to her." The others moved out of the way and Doughty looked at the wound. "It couldn't be much worse," he said, as he applied more Lidocaine. Rowan's complexion was grey and had a damp pallor to it. Her pulse was irregular and weak. Her eyes flickered open and then shut again. Green and Mallett were good but they would have to be quick.

"Jem, you've got to be prepared." He put his hand on Dearden's arm, "I think we're going to lose her."

Rowan moaned. Dearden was on his knees at her side and touched her brow, brushing some wisps of golden hair from her eyes. They opened, and he saw their bright blue. Her lips moved as she implored him to help, and he could do nothing.

"There is help on the way," Julia said to her, in Anglo-Saxon.

"Jules, tell her to hang on, tell her to stay with us, for God's sake tell her. Julia spoke the words and Doughty dripped Glenmorangie through her lips from his flask. Rowan coughed as the strong liquor did its work, and she revived. She smiled at Dearden. Then her eyes closed and her body went limp. Dearden gasped.

Templestone took the urgent call from Julia. He stood quickly, saying that something was badly wrong and he had to get the medical team to the Hub. He rushed to the secure line and rang the medics. Red Cloud and Possum Chaser heard what was going on. "OK let's go, they may need us," Red Cloud said, as he moved into action. Possum Chaser followed and picked up a heavy-duty torch on her way out into the night.

A while later a little out of breath they reached the Hub. As they arrived, they heard the harsh beat of rotors as the Eurocopter approached Dearden Hall. On the upper floor, Dearden looked through the still transparent window of the Hub. He could see the navigation lights as Bob Mallett circled the helicopter above the car park of the Hall where the floodlights were bright in the distance.

Red Cloud and Possum Chaser went in through the lower entrance of the Hub and rushed up the steps. They ran into the room with the exhibits and, in the back wall where they had seen the beings that other time, there was an open door, and beyond it, a brightly lit room.

They were there again, the strange ones, waiting near the door. Then they were coming toward Red and Possum Chaser. There were three of them, very tall and slender. Red and

Possum Chaser stopped in their headlong rush.

"There's something wrong upstairs," Possum Chaser called to them. The words had almost stuck in her throat and her heart was pounding.

"Yes, we know, we will come with you," the one in front spoke in a low, melodic voice. The three walked toward them with a sort of loping gait. They were big, real big, Red thought, as he backed off slightly. One of the oddest details about them was their skin colour. It was much like the old-fashioned paint colour called Eau de Nil.

They stopped in front of Red and Possum Chaser.

"Don't be afraid, we will help you," said the one in front in clear English with an accent Red was unable to place. "We must go to the Portal now." There was urgency in its voice.

"You go first," Red Cloud said, thinking that with their long legs they would put on a good turn of speed. They did. Going up through the control room the leader glanced at the flashing screens and spoke to the ones behind him. Possum Chaser thought it was a beautiful sound.

"They speak like music that reaches deep inside," she said to Red Cloud when they talked about it later.

They reached the top of the stairs and entered the topmost room that the beings had called the Portal. Surprisingly quickly for their size they crossed the room and stood behind the group surrounding Rowan. She was unconscious and breathing in short, shallow gasps. Those around her were so intent on trying to help that they failed to notice the ones who had entered the room.

"Jem," Red bent down and spoke softly, close to Dearden.

"What?" Dearden was trying to ease the bolt from Rowan's back.

"Jem, leave it," Doughty advised, "Wait till Green and Mallett get here, it may be barbed, they'll know what to do.

The chopper's arrived; they'll only be a few minutes now."

"I think they'll be too late," Julia whispered close to Doughty's ear. "She's fading, we must let her go."

"Jem." Dearden recognised Red Cloud's voice. He turned to lay into him and—

"Bloody hell . . ." Dearden stumbled as he tried to stand and get away from what was behind him. The others reacted in the same way and tried to scatter.

There were three of them standing there. They were like the pointing figure in the exhibition room.

"You are Harry Stanway," said the one with decorations emblazoned on its chest. The being's eyes focussed on Harry.

"Yes, I'm Harry Stanway, who are you?"

"We will tell you soon, but your friend needs help. She will die if we do not intervene." He took a piece of equipment out of a pocket in his tunic. It was about the size of a mobile phone but had what looked like a lens on it. He focused the object on the wound and pressed a button. A bright blue light with inner movement played on the wound and the deeply embedded bolt started to lift out from Rowan's back. The alien focussed the instrument on each of her temples in turn.

"Hey, my tall friend, what's happenin' there?" Wynter asked the one holding the instrument.

"Your friend's body is rejecting the projectile and healing from within. The trauma in her mind will be forgotten." The barbed bolt clattered to the floor and the wound started to close up before their eyes.

Harry's smile returned. Of late, with all the tension, his smile had gone. "Guys, I knew it. I knew they'd show up," he said to no one in particular. "I can't believe it, of all the people who've dreamed of this moment, and it's ours. Jem, Jules, first contact is ours." He saw Rowan moving.

There was the sound of a vehicle four floors below as the

medical team arrived in Julia's Grand Cherokee. Two of the three beings stood and went to the stairs and conversed. The one using the healing equipment, who seemed to be the leader, knelt and examined the wound that had diminished to a red mark on Rowan's skin. The two aliens descended the stairs and the leader stood to its full height. It towered two feet above Dearden who caught an acrid smell from it.

"She will be alright now," it bent down and picked up the crossbow bolt. "Let her rest. We will see you again." With that, it turned and walked swiftly to the stairs.

"Wait," Dearden called from where he was kneeling by Rowan. The receding figure stopped briefly and looked at him with its head slightly to one side, questioning. "Wait," Dearden said again. "Who are you, where are you from? Tell us . . . please."

"A time will come when we will tell you, Dearden. Until then you must wait." It spoke with a melodic tone Dearden recognised from the time he was ill and feverish in the forest. Lan-Si-Nu went swiftly down the stairs.

The appearance of the aliens had shaken Doughty but he forced the event to the back of his mind. He hobbled to the door, opened it and looked down into the clearing. Green and Mallet had the tailgate of Julia's Grand Cherokee open. They were lifting out two rucksacks of medical equipment.

"Up here," Doughty called. The medics scrambled up the hill toward the light inside the Hub. Doughty sank to the floor on the inside of the door and leant on the wall. Out of habit, he lifted the AK and checked the breech before laying it on the floor and then engaging the safety on the Colt. *Two rounds gone, not bad for a successful conclusion*, he thought.

Rowan was telling Julia and Esma how she had remembered light and warmth before she awoke. She looked around the room; saw the shining surfaces, lights illuminating the room without giving off the smoke of beeswax candles. She could see the Moon in its glory high above the forest through a huge colourless window. She turned to Dearden. They were together now, which was all that mattered, and there were so many questions . . .

* * *

Green and Mallett were nonplussed. They knew their compatriots well. They had been through tough times together. Whatever happened must have been dire to get a call for help with battlefield injuries. There was a woman on the floor. She seemed OK. Doughty had a leg wound, which wasn't bad enough to warrant the helicopter flight.

"Why did you call?" Jack Green asked Dearden.

"I'll tell you later. Believe me, we were desperate."

"What is this place?" Bob Mallett, the black haired, short and wiry anaesthetist-pilot asked. He looked around and saw the great crystal in the centre of the room.

"Welcome to the Hub," Dearden said, "And as our friend Harry Stanway here said a while back, welcome to the strangest place on Earth."

"Guys, the emergency's over other than Mitch's injury," Julia said. Jack Green looked around the group making a cursory assessment. Doughty looked pale and, like Julia and Dearden, dishevelled, as though he had been living rough.

"What happened to Mitch?" Green asked Julia.

"Lee took an arrow out of his leg, so he needs some attention, and over there is Rowan of Maldon, and Esma. To add more to your confusion, they're Anglo-Saxon."

Green looked doubtfully at Mallett, who gave him a sidelong glance.

"You get us into some unique situations, Captain Dearden," Mallett said. "This one takes first prize."

"I'm sure it does. Let's get back to the hall, then we'll tell you more. Prepare to have your imagination stretched." Dearden turned to Harry, "Did you make the call?"

"I did, but there wasn't much response from the other end."

"Did the phone beep afterwards?"

"It did."

"How did it sound?"

"Like the Greenwich time signal, it beeped six times, but it was five long and one short."

"That's OK, the organisation's aware there's an operation pending." Harry wondered what organisation Dearden was on about, but let it go. Dearden made a mental calculation of the time left to Thanksgiving Day. *Four days to go.*

Roberts tried to open the top-level door to outside but was unable to, and the wall had settled back to being opaque. He shook his head in disbelief as he looked at Rowan and Esma. Then led the way down the stairs through the internal levels of the Hub.

They came to the museum level and Possum Chaser pointed to the wall at the end furthest into the hill.

"That's where we first saw the three that came and helped," she said. "They were walking from somewhere behind that dome-shaped case." Dearden made a mental note of where she was pointing. He looked at Rowan and was thankful beyond measure for the intervention of the aliens. He wanted to spend time with them. More than anything, he wanted to ask if there was any way he could help them. Their giving attitude endeared them to him, and they looked, there was no other way to describe it . . . they looked as though *they* needed help.

As they walked down through the remaining levels, Dearden explained to Rowan and Esma, in his mix of Anglo-Saxon and modern English, about the method of transport they would be using to get to his home. Rowan remembered about the kahz. He said this one had a name, Grand Cherokee. It would make a roaring noise, but he reassured her the noise was normal. Esma was fascinated, excited and nervous. She said she was willing to try the transport, just once.

Dearden slung his coat around Rowan's shoulders to cover the cut in her clothing. He saw that the place where the bolt had penetrated wasn't even marked now. They walked through the wooden tunnel out into the clearing and Harry secured the door into the Hub with the armoured padlock.

Dearden looked into the night sky, and in his peripheral vision, he noticed the fading luminescence of the cosmic grid. With Julia driving the Jeep, he helped Rowan and Esma into the back. Doughty levered himself onto the front passenger seat and slammed the door shut. Julia revved the engine, and as it growled Rowan grasped at Dearden for reassurance. He looked at her profile in the moonlight and saw a smile playing on her lips and her features bright with anticipation. Their lives together had come back from the dark events into the light, and he knew now that everything would be OK.

49

As they jogged along the bank of Shadow Brook, Bob Mallett heard Harry saying in between breaths that the Hub was more reliable now for temporal shifts. Mallett nudged Green to move closer to Harry to hear what he said. It was something about needing other adjustments to restore the spatial shift component.

"That place has given me information overload," Green said, speaking close to Mallett's ear.

"Jem said those two women are Anglo-Saxon. He's got to be winding us up."

"That's not like Jem. Something serious was going on back there, and there's Doughty's wound which penetrated completely through the gastrocnemius. I want answers when we get to Jem's place."

"I think that chap up front's a Native American, they called him Red Cloud," Mallett said. His breath condensed in the frosty air. "This is really odd."

"It is, but with the chief up ahead we won't lose our way."

* * *

As Julia drove the Cherokee into the courtyard, Rowan, speaking Anglo-Saxon, asked her what the thing was that looked like a great insect. The helicopter's rotor blades were locked in position to stop them rotating. They were fluctuating in the breeze, which from Rowan's point of view made the machine look alive. Julia said, "It's a wagon that we use for travelling through the air like a bird or a dragonfly."

Rowan studied Julia's face, "I do not believe you," she said.

"It's true. Jem warned you that there would be many

changes. That is one of them. We can fly using machines like you see there." Julia stopped the vehicle and opened the door for Rowan and Esma to get out. They shivered against the cold and Esma held on to Rowan's arm for reassurance under the brilliant lights illuminating the car park.

"This is Leofwin's House but it has grown big since earlier today," she whispered as they neared the entrance porch.

"It has, but the wood of the door is older than when we left, see where the grain has opened. Leofwin only had the door made last year. I saw the men come back with their axes when they cut the tree down. Now the oak is old." Rowan touched the door and as Dearden and Doughty caught up, she opened it with the familiar iron catch. They went into the entrance hall where Frieda Heskin was waiting with Gil. He saw Doughty's injured leg and helped him to a settee in the great hall. Frieda looked at Rowan and Esma and questioned Dearden with the look in her eyes. He introduced them.

"Rowan will be taking care of the house now, but she's got a lot to learn so I'd appreciate your help with that. This is Esma; she'll be helping out around the place too." Dearden could tell by her expression that his words had unsettled Frieda.

"Don't worry. The changes won't affect you or Gil."

"If you're not showing us the door I'll be pleased to help." Frieda linked her arm through Rowan's, and taking Esma by the hand they went into the great hall. It was an outward display of amiability, but she wasn't comfortable with the fact that things were odder than usual around Dearden Hall.

When Mr Dearden went away, he sometimes came back looking knocked about. A while ago he came back with a wolf he named Tomahawk. Now he had come back with two women in old-fashioned clothing. This time Julia Linden-Barthorpe and Mr Doughty were in on it too and Mr Doughty was badly injured. It concerned Frieda that more was to come, and when it did come, what form would it take and would she be able to handle it?

* * *

Doughty was lying full length on one of the settees and Julia was next to him holding a glass of water. Templestone had drawn up a chair and was listening to Doughty's explanation about how he got the wound. Julia had told Templestone to expect two guests and he raised his hand in greeting and stood as they entered the room. Dearden introduced him to Rowan and Esma, telling them he was a very special old friend.

"Not too old, I hope." Templestone smiled, but Dearden looked preoccupied and Templestone knew him too well than to press for details about what happened when he was away. He would find out soon enough.

Rowan looked around the room and saw many changes. The dim lights on the wall had no flames. They did not flicker as candles should do, which was unusual, and the lights picked out the smallest detail where they were shining. At the end of the room, the massive fireplace with its blazing fire cast a welcoming glow onto the surroundings. Rowan had been used to the fire being on stone slabs in the centre of the room, with some of the smoke escaping through a hole in the roof, where slats of wood over the hole shielded the inside from rain. Now the smoke was disappearing up a hole in the wall, and stone slabs now covering the whole floor had the polished look of many years of use. The compressed earth floor of a few hours ago had disappeared, and there were some colourful woven tapestries scattered randomly over the stone slabbed floor.

"Who changed all building?" Rowan asked, in a mix of hers and Jem's language.

"Different people have made changes over the years,"

"Did you put the stones by the wall where the fire is burning?" Dearden struggled to find the words he needed to use. He called Julia over to help out and the conversation continued with her help.

"After Leofwin's time my ancestors, the de Arden family added the fireplace to the building. It was done many years ago. You see, the de Arden's owned this house after a man named Guillaume le Batard became king. They made a lot of changes to the house to make it bigger."

"If Guillaume le Batard became king what happened to my uncle, Harold Godwinson?"

"There was a great battle at Senlac. King Harold was killed." Dearden didn't add any more detail." Rowan was silent and he saw she was upset at the news of her uncle's death. "Rowan, I'm sorry to give you bad news." He held her close and thought how surreal it was to be giving Rowan news almost a thousand years old.

* * *

There was the sound of excited conversation as the group coming on foot from the Hub came into the great hall. They went to the fire, which was welcome because there was a heavy frost. Jack Green warmed his hands and then stitched Doughty's wound on both sides of his calf. Mallet asked why Dearden called the helicopter out for Doughty's injury, which was mild in battlefield terms. Dearden cut the questioning short.

"We're grateful for the turnout guys, but there's more going on here than we've got time to explain. There was a life or death issue, but it got resolved." Dearden went to the secure phone in a recess at the side of the great hall. He hesitated before lifting the phone and spoke again to the medics.

"You'll be in action again before long. I suggest you return to base and get some sleep." He lifted the phone and spoke to Sir Willoughby Pierpoint about the New York threat. The conversation was brief, and they agreed to meet the following morning at Pierpoint's cottage in Radway.

When Dearden rang off Pierpoint made a call to the United States, and then he phoned Arthur Doughty to bring him up to speed with the events that were gathering momentum.

Dearden took Templestone to one side.

"What's happened with the Heskins, the hard edge has gone?"

"Gil's brother in Rugby was seriously ill and they've been worried sick about him. Gil used to take him his medication and DVD's to watch, but his brother died two weeks back and things are settling down, but Gil still has his quiet times."

Dearden frowned. "Uberatu and Raegenhere have been getting information somehow because they've always been one jump ahead of us. I thought it might have been the Heskins, but if it's not them, who is it?"

Quiet descended on the old house and Dearden was thankful for a few hours without intense activity. He had prepared Rowan and Esma for the medics' departure in the helicopter, warning them there would be loud noise and fierce action when the machine took off. There had been awe, uncertainty and fear as the helicopter became airborne with the harsh clattering of rotors and a windstorm of debris.

The objects in the great hall enthralled Rowan. She went from one item to another, picking them up if they were small enough to handle and examine. She came to the television and touched the surface of the screen. It was black and shiny and seemed to have no purpose. Dearden explained that it was a way of giving information and entertainment to many people at the same time. He switched it on. Rowan backed away but then stood transfixed by the scene of wild horses racing across the plains of the Camargue.

She looked behind the television and asked Dearden where the horses were. He said they were in a memory that everyone could look at. She shook her head in disbelief, crossed the room to a cupboard with glazed doors, where she smoothed her hair as she saw her reflection in the mirror behind the shelves. Leofwin's dining table was nearby. It was shorter than it was a few hours ago. Previously it had ten legs now it had six. Rowan was surprised at how quickly the carpenter had done the work. She rubbed her hand on the smooth surface and sniffed her fingers. They smelt of beeswax, and there was the dark patch where Leofwin put the candle on the table when he ate a meal at night. Sometimes the wax burned away, and the remaining flame on the wick burnt the table.

Rowan spoke in Anglo-Saxon and Julia translated. "Jem, I know this table. I saw men cutting the boards and smoothing them. It was made from the same tree as the door into the house," She bent down to look at the patina on the table. "All this is very confusing. There were ten legs, and the table didn't shine like this earlier today." Esma came to the table and examined it. The differences to Leofwin's Great Hall mystified her too. Julia had warned that they would experience many changes, and she had seen her childhood friend near death. The unusually tall green person in the House of the West Wind had knelt by the Lady Rowan and touched her with the item with a light shining from it. Now Rowan was talking as if nothing had happened.

Frieda Heskin and Julia showed Rowan and Esma upstairs. The layout of the area above the great hall was much changed.

They came to a corner where the long landing turned to the left. It was where the door to Dearden's room lay. Rowan cautiously opened the door and went into the room. It was dark beyond the glow from the light further down the landing.

"We need candles, where are they?" she asked Julia, who translated, and Frieda smiled as if she had a trick up her sleeve. She felt for the light switch and turned it on. Esma clutched Rowan's arm, startled at the instant light on the wall over the bed when no one was there to light it. Dearden's desk was near the window, with the high-backed office chair by it. The curtains were drawn. Rowan took in the surroundings.

"This is Leofwin and Aelfryth's room, but now it is much smaller," Rowan said, looking at the layout.

"It is Jem's room," Julia said, as she went back out onto the landing. "We'll show you and Esma your room." Rowan lingered for a minute, remembering how things were. When she got to the light switch, she turned it off, then back on, and then off again, and smiled conspiratorially at Esma.

* * *

"Tell me about your new friends in the Hub," Templestone said to Dearden when he caught him on his own on the far side of the great hall.

"The three that helped us? I can't tell you much other than that they are alien. Where from I don't know, but they saved Rowan's life. She had a crossbow bolt in her back, Bill. She was dying, and the aliens pulled her back." Dearden straightened up. "Fengel did it but he's dead now. Mitch shot him. It's difficult to believe everything that has happened since we went through the Hub."

"What actually did happen?" Templestone asked. Dearden didn't respond straight away. Templestone took hold of his sleeve, pulled him round face to face. "Jem, you've been away over three weeks. What happened other than finding a lovely girl?"

"We went back to how it used to be around here . . ."

Dearden described the place as it used to be, and he told Templestone about the people of the ancient time who they grew to know as friends. He described the events at length and told him about Beggs' interrogation.

"Beggs spilt the beans that Raegenhere is out to cause big trouble. I mean *nuclear big*, that's why we're getting SHaFT involved. Right now, I need to get some logistical planning done and then get some rest. I'll tell you more later on." They went back to the others at the refectory table, which was some yards from where it was when the Witenagemot met around it.

"Matt, give me a hand to move this table."

"Where to?"

"Toward the fire about eight feet, and we'll turn it through ninety degrees to where it used to be years ago."

50

Raegenhere's idea developed over a number of months. Now it was ever-present in his fertile mind. The idea was conceived when he overheard a conversation from the next table in Hermes' restaurant, on one of his visits to the 47th Street jewellery area in Midtown Manhattan.

The next table had been talking about the local architecture and they mentioned an open top tour they had been on that passed through the financial centre. The tour guide said tunnels honeycombed Manhattan, which included a 1960's nuclear shelter converted to a wargames experience, and he spoke about some massive storm drains leading to the harbour.

Raegenhere thought nothing more of it until, when he was back home in the UK, a television program came on called *Metropolis Underground.* The previous week had been about underground London. This time it was about underground Manhattan. He was riveted to the detail when a map showing the subterranean workings stretching for miles around Manhattan came on screen. They passed close to many of the banks, which gave him the germ of the idea. After that, Raegenhere spent hours researching underground Manhattan. He found that in the early years of the twentieth century there had been an open competition to design a new building to house the Federal Reserve Bank of New York. Its address was to be number 33, Liberty Street, Manhattan. The company of architects named Scott and Bulwer won the competition and got the contract to build the Federal Reserve. The construction started with the vault of the bank lying on bedrock fifty feet below street level, and thirty feet above the level of the sea, which lay a few city-blocks away. Raegenhere's attention fixed on the part of the design brief for providing updated storm drains to take surface water away from Manhattan.

He found some growth statistics about the Federal Reserve Bank on the internet. By 1927, eleven percent of the world's gold reserves were in its vault. By 2008, the Federal Reserve was in possession of more gold than Fort Knox. Over six thousand metric tonnes of bullion belonging to many nations lay in the vault today. Raegenhere felt the gold-itch gnawing, telling him it was his for the taking if he could find a way into the vault.

Hunched over his laptop one night he came across a remarkable fact that brought his ideas together. The 1933 Twenty Dollar American Gold Double Eagle was stored in a vault of the Federal Reserve Bank. He read that no coin in the history of numismatics was as valuable as the 1933 gold Double Eagle. In a 2002 auction, it realised 7.59 million US Dollars. Raegenhere wanted the coin, and when he wanted something, he obsessed about it and was prepared to move heaven and earth to get it.

When he studied the plans of the area, it dawned on him just how close the vault of the Federal Reserve Bank was to the storm drains. It was a heaven-sent opportunity for anyone daring enough, and with sufficient resources, to mount a raid on the vault. He measured the distances on one of the 1920s scaled architectural plans that showed the foundations of the bank and the area of Manhattan surrounding it. The storm drain servicing the Liberty Street area passed within ten feet of the bank vault, and opened into the harbour near the Blazing Saddles bike hire at South Street Seaport.

Going in through the storm drain would involve difficulties and a lot of expense, but the reward and the challenge getting it would make up for the outlay. It would be impossible to familiarise himself with the internal security of the vault without having someone on the inside, so he got Wilbur Gant involved. Gant was a devious character with a convincing attitude, an up and coming swindler who was developing a stand-alone name for himself. Gant got a security job at the Federal Reserve twelve months before the start of the operation. Raegenhere paid him well to get information about vault inspection times, layout and entry policy.

Gant worked hard at the bank and promotion followed. He sometimes worked in the vault, supervising movement of bullion from one pallet to another. He discovered that the bullion representing the national wealth of Nigeria was stored near the place where Raegenhere and his team would break into the vault. If all went well, after he had taken his primary target, the 1933 Twenty Dollar American Gold Double Eagle, Raegenhere planned to try to bankrupt Nigeria.

Once, when Gant was in the vault after a downpour of rain, he heard the sound of water that had drained from the streets of Manhattan rumbling as it gushed through the storm drain, which lay on the other side of the furthest wall. Gant told Raegenhere that because of the background noise, disturbance made during the break-in would go un-noticed. Nevertheless, Raegenhere wanted an effective diversion to empty the area topside. He hit on the idea of a dirty bomb and a disguised phone call to a local radio station a few days before the detonation of the bomb. At first, he thought of this ploy as a hoax, but one night he came across some information that made him realise how easy it would be to go for the real thing. Raegenhere's mind worked that way. It had to do with power. He ignored the consequences because he had no conscience.

He took the 1987 Goiânia incident in Brazil as the model for his operation. After some research, he discovered that in 1987 thieves had stolen ninety-three grammes of cesium-137 chloride, a mere thimble-full, from a hospital. Four of them died quickly. Shortly, twenty more in close proximity to the material developed severe radiation sickness. Over two hundred people were highly contaminated. Nearly a thousand received a dose exceeding the acceptable yearly amount of radiation. Several city blocks had to be demolished in the decontamination process that followed . . . yes; a dirty bomb would empty Manhattan quickly. Raegenhere's self-esteem soared.

A friend of a friend said he could source the radioactive material in the old Soviet Union if the payment was in US dollars. The thirty pounds of conventional explosive, the detonator and the high precision timing gear, was easy to obtain, and he already had an ex-army bomb-disposal expert as a freelance gun for hire who would build the bomb.

Raegenhere needed a vessel to accomplish his plans, and it came to his notice that there was a vessel recently taken out of service that was heading for the breakers yard. It was the Vasco da Gama, an ageing ship built by Incat, in Hobart, Tasmania. It weighed in at three thousand tonnes, and in its prime, it could speed across the water at forty knots powered by four powerful Lips Waterjet engines.

Raegenhere bought the vessel for its scrap value. It had been in poor condition but after extensive refurbishment, it became a beautiful private yacht. The Vasco da Gama had the sleek look in the catamaran style typical of Incat, but there was a major difference. It was a research vessel. The central hull flared out at the centre to house a moon pool. An iris-type of arrangement could open or close it to the sea. In use, the iris would slide open, ballast tanks in the outer pontoons would be flooded, and the vessel would sink by three metres. This would give hidden access to the ocean from the moon pool.

There was an old Republican Ironclad warship, the Ramses,

lying on the bed of the Hudson River off Governors Island. It was a popular spot for amateur divers, and Raegenhere advertised diving trips on the wreck, accessed out of the moon pool. To give the presence of the Vasco da Gama credibility Raegenhere planted some ancient pottery on the ocean bed near Governor's Island and announced an exciting find to the newspapers. A typical headline was like the one in the New York Daily News,

Evidence Of An Ancient Civilisation Found Nearby . . .

The Vasco da Gama became a trusted local presence supposedly engaged in seabed research. Using that as a cover, Raegenhere's plan was that his team would work with laser cutting equipment in the storm drain. The lasers would cut through the wall of concrete like hot water through ice. When it came to the break-through, Raegenhere, on hand in the Vasco, would exit through the moon pool. He would swim to the storm drain and take charge of the entry into the vault.

The time came for action, and late one evening, the ship, low in the water with its ballast tanks full, drew close to the quayside and moored near the Blazing Saddles Bike Tours and Rentals in South Street Seaport. Within the hour Raegenhere, leading a team of divers, moved the tunnelling equipment in sealed containers underwater the short distance into the storm drain. Raegenhere counted off the yards with a mechanical road wheel, starting underwater at the sea wall. At the place where work was to commence, he sprayed a fluorescent mark on the tunnel wall and instructed his workmen not to go any further than eight and a half feet into the ten feet thick wall.

"When you reach that point stop and wait for when I come back for the breakthrough on Thanksgiving Day." He smiled at the poetry of the situation; how he would have his personal thanksgiving day when he pocketed the Double Eagle and transported bullion into the hold of the Vasco.

His men started a silenced generator and the laser cutting commenced. Feeling cock-a-hoop, Racgcnhere walked to the storm drain entrance and swam back to the Vasco. A chauffeuse drove him to his Learjet, and he left for the UK to be on hand for the delivery of the cesium from Eastern Europe.

* * *

Back at Dracasfeld, Raegenhere grew increasingly irritable waiting for the shipment to arrive from Chechnya. He had told the contact he wanted the consignment delivered by the 20th November. The Russians agreed on the date and agreed to fly the package, in a lead-lined box, to Flughafen Berlin Templehof by private charter. Raegenhere's Learjet would pick up the consignment and bring it to Wellesbourne Mountford. If the schedule had gone to plan he would have had enough time to get the device built and flown to the States, but the consignment was late. The dirty bomb was critical to create the panic needed to empty Manhattan by the twenty-seventh. It was the evening of the twenty-third and the shipment had not arrived. No one answered the supplier's telephone and Raegenhere's rage was murderous.

There were days of inaction, and then a telephone call startled him. The caller had a strong Russian accent,

"Sir, Templehof is not allowing any more inbound flights due to permanent closure on the thirtieth of November."

"What?"

"Sir, I think you heard me. Temp—"

"What do you mean, Templehof's closing?"

"Sir, I don't know how it can be. We were not told of this."

"Damn Templehof, and damn you to hell. Why didn't you

get the package sent to an airport that isn't about to close, you stupid half brained Cossack." Raegenhere's usually sallow complexion reddened and he flung a heavy glass ashtray across the room. Uberatu dodged, and it hit the far wall and shattered.

"You're getting it for a good price," said the uncertain Slavic voice.

"I don't care about the price. Look, forget Templehof and get the package sent straight to the States."

"To which airport sir?" The Russian loosened his tie and undid the top button of his shirt. The deal worried him from the start, now he doubted his judgement accepting it.

"Just find an airport near New York and get the package there quick. Forget the paperwork, just get the shipment arranged and call me back . . . today do you hear?" Raegenhere was about to ring off but he raised the receiver again. "Vladimir, don't let me down or you won't ride a horse again, do you get my drift?" He flung the phone down. Uberatu picked up the pieces of glass, although his hands were sore from the hogweed. Raegenhere didn't even thank him, so he threw the shards back onto the carpet.

Raegenhere couldn't delay any longer. He flipped the cover open on his notebook and flicked a switch on a box connected to the telephone that disguised his voice. He dialled a number in the States for Radio WNYC. Reading from the notes he had practised in front of a mirror, he told them that a dirty bomb would be detonated somewhere in New York. He said it would happen in the next few days, but gave no definite time because he wanted them to get worried. There was scurried movement and urgent muffled voices.

"Wait," a nervous voice said. "When—" Raegenhere put the phone down to stop them getting a trace. He looked at Uberatu, who smiled uneasily.

"And so it begins. Theo, switch the radio on." Uberatu went

to the radio and switched it on with difficulty. There was pain in his hogweed hands. Raegenhere had pre-set the waveband. Someone was announcing that the radio station had received a message, threatening New York City with a nuclear device.

Raegenhere knew how people's minds worked. As soon as the radio station broadcast his message, panic in New York would shift into overdrive. It worked like a dream. To add to the chaos, as soon as the broadcast went out media stations all over the States picked it up and spread the news. After a few hours, Wilbur Gant called Raegenhere to say the city was emptying fast. No one knew that the most audacious robbery in history had begun below ground.

Raegenhere was sipping brandy when the phone rang. He grabbed the receiver.

"What?" It was Vladimir with a choice of destination, Westchester or Teterboro.

"Make it Westchester; I have a man there already. When will it arrive?" Vladimir gave him the ETA of 0120 hours, Eastern Standard Time, on the twenty-seventh. It was cutting time to the bone but there were no choices. "You'll get the money by bank transfer when the package is picked up in the States, if it's on time." Raegenhere ended the call. The plan was coming together. God help anyone who got in the way.

Uberatu interrupted. "Are we off to the States, boss?" Uberatu liked the States and they had used Westchester before. Raegenhere paced the room. He was tight and pensive.

"Boss, I've got men waiting to get started at a workshop we've hired. We need a decision."

Raegenhere talked while he paced. "OK Theo, the flight's confirmed. Do not forget to pack the Hazmat suits. I don't intend getting fried handling the stuff if there's any leakage. Also, get onto Stet Burford over in Larchmont, tell him to get the decontamination unit set up at the workshop, and Theo, this is important. Speak to our man on the ground at Westchester. Here's the number," he tossed a piece of paper over. "Tell him to get a diversion going at the airport at 0100 hours Eastern Standard Time, something big that'll help the shipment from Russia fly in un-noticed."

Raegenhere stopped pacing and slumped into a chair, brooding about the coming action. The phone rang again,

"What?" A voice on the other end replied, speaking in hushed tones that Raegenhere could hardly hear.

"There's going to be a raid on your place tonight. Dearden's been planning something but it wasn't obvious until tonight."

"That sonofabitch doesn't leave off does he; what time will it happen?"

"I heard midnight."

"Is it really? So what. My security can handle anything Dearden throws at us."

Uberatu made the call to Raegenhere's man in Westchester and called the Learjet crew who were on standby, to prepare them for the destination.

Uberatu went back to the room where he stayed when he was at Dracasfeld. When he opened the door, Snarl, who was lying on a rug, lifted his head and stood, growling deep down. Uberatu approached the dog, whispering pleasantries. He tossed a biscuit and then attached a leash.

With Snarl on the passenger seat and the leash tethered to the door pull, Uberatu drove to a garage in the village. The mechanic, who he paid to do the occasional job on the side, looked up from his paper when Uberatu walked in.

"Look after the dog for a few days Ozzie, will you? We're off to the States."

"If I must, when you off?"

"Tonight." Uberatu handed Ozzie the leash, along with

some Schmackos and six large cans of cheap dog food. He walked out the door leaving the two together. After the door closed Ozzie eyed the dog up, remembering what happened last time. He touched the scars on his hand.

Snarl eyed up the Schmackos and fixed his gaze on the soft target holding them.

51

Pierpoint was aware of the urgency of the situation when he received Dearden's message from Harry Stanway. He had no details, other than it had something to do with a house called Dracasfeld and an RDD threat to New York. Dearden never called for a mission unless serious issues were involved, so Pierpoint prepared the unit commanders to be ready for action at short notice. He researched Dracasfeld on the internet and in his encyclopaedic databank but found that there was no useful reference to it.

The previous night, after Dearden rang and gave him more details about the RDD threat, Pierpoint had rung the US Secretary of Homeland Security. Milt Herschel in Washington DC had a secure line and using it Pierpoint told Herschel about the threat but didn't get as far as offering SHaFT's expertise before Herschel cut him off.

"I've already heard about it, it's all over the news, but we have another big problem that might get out of hand. We don't want a particular group to know we're onto them so keep this under your hat" Pierpoint wondered what was coming. "They're called *Bedayat Jadeeda, New Beginning.* They are a splinter group with a big grudge and we've heard that they have some cells on US soil preparing to attack our oil refineries. The problem is we don't know which ones. I don't like to say this Will, but we're spread real thin on the ground. There are over twenty-five refineries in Texas, let alone the rest of the US"

"You need some help with the other issue," Pierpoint stated.

"Are you offering?"

"I am."

"Thanks, Will. I can give you a few men this end to deal

with the Manhattan problem, but it won't be on a large scale."

"Prepare them and give me contact details, I'll make the arrangements," Pierpoint paused. "Milt, I take it you're giving us the green light."

"I am, gladly. There was a broadcast about the nuclear device on Radio WNYC, and the news is spreading like a California wildfire. There's chaos in Manhattan."

After Milt Herschel put the phone down he conferred with the commanders of the National Guard on a conference line and they mobilised reservists in New York State. Within six hours, a cordon was set up around New York City. The majority of the vehicles passing through it were fleeing out of town.

The news of the nuclear threat spread like a virus. In an attempt to mitigate panic, security down the Eastern Seaboard was tighter than it had ever been. It was impossible to keep the military activity under wraps. There were reports on social networks that the Government was hiding a terrorist threat to attack the capital. Conspiracy theorists fanned the flames and began blaming the Illuminati, Eisenburg, and their like.

One newspaper fielded a large black headline that filled the front page,

Armageddon May Be Around The Corner.

With theories and Chinese whispers rife, people were moving westwards in huge numbers. The Dow-Jones was down. The Dollar started sliding against Sterling the Euro and the Yen. Gold was in great demand and everything was coming up roses for Raegenhere who was offloading some of his bullion onto the market from his vault at Dracasfeld.

The United States government, doing what governments do, outwardly denied the seriousness of the situation. They advised people to return to their homes and jobs. Homeland

Security bluffed that such threats occurred on an almost daily basis.

The people didn't believe a word of it.

Radio WNYC received another message. A warning. This time the FBI was listening in.

To prove you must take our threat seriously, we will destroy the freighter, Petros, lying 1000 feet north-west of Governors' Island. It will occur at 11:30 a.m. today.

There was also a demand to deposit a billion dollars into an account in Switzerland. If money appeared in the account, the detonation of the dirty bomb wouldn't take place. Raegenhere knew the US Government wouldn't cave in to blackmail, but the demand added his sense of power to the threat.

The message to WNYC came ten minutes before the threatened event. Police launches at full throttle tried to clear the area. Of immediate concern was the threat to a ferry, the James C. Nesbitt, en route to Wall Street's Pier 11. It would be passing within fifty feet of the Petros at the critical time.

The James C. Nesbitt, one of the few ferries running during the emergency, had left the Marin Boulevard dock at Liberty Harbor, Jersey City. It was making good time and had executed its southerly turn to run down the centre of the channel to the north of Governors Island. When the captain received the urgent message about the Petros, he snatched a map of the area, made a quick decision, and announced a change of destination to the crew and passengers over the public address. The ferry listed violently as it altered course. Some of the women screamed and the men tried to stay tight-lipped.

Many of the passengers were on their way to join family and to make a quick escape from New York. A few diehards were on their way to work in the city despite the nuclear threat because they thought they were indispensable. The James C. Nesbitt's new course was to the west of Governors Island where they would then head for a pier at South Street Seaport which was one inconvenience too many for some of the passengers. A number of them organised themselves into a committee and were on their way to the bridge to challenge the captain about the change of direction and get compensation for the inconvenience.

The James C. Nesbitt had started to veer away from the Petros, and she drew parallel to the northern tip of Governors Island at the same time the committee entered the bridge. It was 11:30 a.m. There was a sudden and violent explosion and flames leapt skywards from the Petros, which was uncomfortably close to the ferry. Hot shrapnel blasting through the air struck people lined up along the rails of the ferry who were trying to work out what was going on.

There were screams from women and children. Men tried to be brave but some were unable to pull it off. Many of them had been working in the city on the fateful day in 2001 when terrorism struck at the heart of America. A large wave approached the James C. Nesbitt, and some knew about big waves from a recent tsunami that had struck the Philippines. The captain didn't have enough time to turn the vessel to face the wave bows on but was doing his best. The giant wave struck the ferry, lifting it sharply, and then it dropped.

Down on the car deck, chains secured all but five vehicles to the deck cleats. Ordinarily, the inefficient anchoring would have gone unnoticed, but not this time. The loose cars rolled forward and then careened backwards, colliding with other vehicles with the swell of the wave below the ferry. There was extensive damage, and petrol was seeping over the deck from a car with a ruptured fuel tank. A deck hand watched the moving cars in disbelief before rushing toward them, dropping the Lucky Strike he was smoking as he ran. It landed in the petrol, which exploded.

52

In Pierpoint's study in the cottage at Radway, Dearden reassured Pierpoint that the New York information was reliable, and briefly mentioned the timeshift. Pierpoint hesitated when he heard that, which was unusual because he was never usually at a loss for words. He redirected the conversation and told Dearden that US Homeland Security said they would be grateful for any help they could get with the RDD problem.

For two hours Dearden and Pierpoint planned logistics for the raid on Dracasfeld. If they stopped Raegenhere taking the nuclear device to the States, there would be no need for further SHaFT involvement. The authorities in the States would close the situation down.

Dearden left soon after the session. Uppermost in Pierpont's mind was his mention of a timeshift. Years ago Jem's father, Maxwell talked to Pierpoint about the strange goings on in the forest attached to his ancestral home. At the time, Pierpoint had accepted what Max said without criticism. He thought that what Max was saying was the product of an overwrought mind.

Max sometimes disappeared for days on end. Even his wife didn't know his precise whereabouts. All he said before he went was that he was going to do some archaeological research in the forest. Sometimes he went with a one-man tent. When Max showed up again he would talk to his close friends, which included Pierpoint, about what he experienced when he went through the building in the forest. Pierpoint thought it bizarre that Max sincerely believed he had been in the forest spying on an ancient village and some equally ancient Anglo-Saxons.

Pierpoint recalled Max's enthusiasm about what he thought were real events. He and Arthur Doughty had gone along with it to humour their friend. When they talked among themselves, they thought Maxwell was losing his mind. They looked into what they could do to help, and Pierpoint met with a consultant at Warwick Central Hospital, but not long afterwards Max died.

It came as a shock to Pierpoint that Jem Dearden, in almost the same words as his father, mentioned the building in the forest and the Anglo-Saxons. Pierpoint hid his reaction to this from Dearden because of the imminent threat to New York. He must ask questions later, but it made him think he should have taken Maxwell seriously all those years ago.

* * *

Doughty was sitting at the table. His injured leg was feeling easier with the painkillers. He was on the internet, researching Dracasfeld. He found scraps of information about the building under its previous name, Wyverne Hardewicke House. There were no details about its current use, but there was historic information showing floor plans. He printed the old plans off, but he needed access to planning applications to see if there were any recent alterations. He was unable to retrieve any information because of a rule forbidding access to details about Wyverne Hardewicke without the permission of the owner.

Doughty rang Harry, who was in the workshop, to say that he needed to get into the local planning authority's archives for details of planning applications relating to Wyverne Hardewicke House. When he came into the great hall, Harry winked at Doughty and told him to move over. Harry fingered the keyboard, and minutes later Doughty was searching through the archives. There were no major alterations to the outside. Doughty knew from Beggs' interrogation that Raegenhere had a secure vault below ground, which showed up on the plans as extensive cellars. There were no recorded structural changes to the interior, or alterations to door and window positions on plans submitted after Raegenhere, shown on the application as Reginald Arthur Heap, moved into Wyverne Hardewicke House and renamed it Dracasfeld.

By five in the afternoon of Monday, the 24th November, Doughty had printed off the floor plans and elevations of Dracasfeld. Dearden emailed the information to Pierpoint, who gave the go-ahead for the raid. In preparation, Dearden organised Matt Roberts to do surveillance to determine the security setup of the target ready for the raid in the early hours of Wednesday the 26th November.

Roberts was at Dracasfeld at midnight, hidden amongst an outcrop of rhododendron. He reported in a whisper over the comms that there were armed men walking about the place. Teams of two were patrolling a corridor running inside the front wall of the building. Roberts saw their blurred shapes passing by stained glass windows. He noted times and intervals and recognised the patrols by the height and shape of the blurred figures and the colour of their clothes. The timing was too regular for them to be professionals.

During that night, Tomahawk was restless. His snarling woke Dearden. He slid his dressing table drawer open, took out his Beretta and went to investigate. On the landing he peered through the window overlooking the courtyard and Tomahawk's enclosure. In the moonlight, Dearden could see the wolf standing at the edge of the run looking through the wire at a fox almost muzzle to muzzle, then something disturbed the fox, and it ran off toward the forest.

Another movement caught Dearden's eye. At the foot of

one of the outbuildings, sitting cross-legged, picked out in the light, which came and went with the clouds scudding across the Moon, was Red Cloud dressed in an eagle feather war bonnet. Possum Chaser was sitting by him, cross-legged with a war-drum between her knees. Through the double-glazing, Dearden could just hear the beat, insistent and primeval, and their voices in Lakota Sioux were harmonising with the beat of the drum.

Dearden pocketed the pistol and watched the scene. The singing stopped and occasionally the glow from Red Cloud's pipe picked out the tawny colour of his skin. Dearden felt tensed up, and made his way back to his room. Red Cloud and Possum Chaser were feeling it too. They expressed their feelings through their Great Plains culture, Red Cloud in his war bonnet, and the elemental sound of the war drum. The uncertainty, added to by the nearness of the forest and the alien building it contained, was palpable in this part of England.

When Dearden got into bed, the thoughts of coming action made him sleepless. All too quickly, the needs of the many, those who would be at the receiving end of the RDD in the States, were forcing him into action. They were catching up with the needs of the few, he and Rowan, who was in a room just down the corridor.

He wished he hadn't heard of SHaFT. He had to go to her. Damn Arthur Doughty and Nos Successio Procul Totus Sumptus—

Then it was morning, Tuesday the 25th November.

53

In the Warwickshire countryside, a plain stretches forth at the foot of Edge Hill. Half a mile from the foot of the hill is the area where, in 1642, the first major bloodletting of the English civil war took place. Some of the more superstitious inhabitants say that, on its anniversary, the fierce noise of battle comes after night has fallen and the mists are rising.

Nestling at the foot of Edgehill is the village of Radway, with its honey-coloured houses and drystone walls of Hornton Ironstone. A silvery haired man with an outwardly quiet disposition, which belies his inner strength lives there. He is tall, with a wiry but muscular frame, and although he is in semi-retirement, he is still very active.

Local people sometimes wave and stop to chat on their way past his cottage, which is large, and set back from the road behind a hedge with a large parking area. A mature garden extends from the front and around both sides to the back. Sometimes passers-by notice Willoughby Pierpoint's distinguished figure as he cultivates the garden.

Occasionally, more now than in years gone by, he rests on a bench under a large apple tree. Its leafy canopy gives luxuriant shade on summer days, and in wintertime, its thick trunk and branches quieten the force of the winds that blow across Kineton Plain.

Willoughby Pierpoint is a Knight of the Realm. He is forthright and has a strong sense of justice driven by experiences when he was younger when he saw unspeakable atrocities. Back then, as a high-ranking officer in the SAS, Will Pierpoint, with a small number of elite fighting comrades, headed up a mission to help a government in part of British

Commonwealth Africa. The bitter experience of going deep cover to gather information about insurgents dug deep into his soul. He had been powerless to intervene when, from the shelter of an outlying field of maize, he saw the massacre of a village, men, women, and children.

In the long hours of that night, after the knives stopped their brutal work, he vowed he would do something, anything, to prevent the exploitation of the weak and vulnerable. Less than a year later, he met up with one of his army colleagues, Arthur Doughty. The night of the massacre still cast an ominous shadow that gripped him at times. Over a few drinks, they had the germ of an idea of creating an elite force of specialists dedicated to enforcing justice. What they dreamed up was an under the radar unit they called SHaFT, the SHock and Force Team for justice.

With his connections to the mandarins of Whitehall, Willoughby Pierpoint persuaded those in the highest places to support the formation of the group. With the founding of SHaFT, Pierpoint was able to tackle injustices head-on and kick the hell out of them wherever they occurred. It was the SAS and more. They operated in the shadows and achieved results that became legendary. Rumours and conspiracy theories about the group grew. There was never any hard evidence about their existence, but so trusted in the halls of power did SHaFT become, that, when called on from the high levels to deal with injustice or threat, the group were free to operate without recourse to either military or government.

To outward appearances, its members were ordinary civilians. Some were ex-military, and for those who were not, training brought them to military standard, and better.

Sir Willoughby Pierpoint negotiated the short distance from his cottage to Kineton Base in one of the luxuries he allowed himself, a 1980 Bentley Mulsanne. Choosing the roads skirting the site of the battle of Edge Hill, he drove past the high-security fences beyond which the Ministry of Defence owned a great swathe of land, and he was in a hurry.

MoD Kineton housed the largest ammunition dump in Europe. Pierpoint passed by the start of the floodlit site to his left where the hedge bordering the high fence was low. He glanced at the huge grass covered semi-circular mounds, each the size of an aircraft hangar, with more volume below ground than above. Each mound contained a storage facility. There were forty of them. Written above the entrance to each one was a code, stating what class of ordinance lay inside.

At the entrance to the site, heavily armed guards recognised the Bentley but still stopped it, checking that the driver was who he should be. One of them examined the trunk, and another the engine compartment, whilst another checked under the car with a mirror.

The entrance to one of the semi-circular mounds was different to all the rest. Above the massive steel sliding doors of Dump 4 was the Latin phrase, *Nos Successio Procul Totus Sumptus*, and there was a shield above it with a bull in the centre flanked by a lion each side facing inwards, and scales above. It was the headquarters of SHaFT.

Pierpoint walked through the workshop facility past where a team of men were working on one of a recently acquired group of six Lockheed F 104G Starfighters. They appreciated his interest and answered his questions about their progress. Next to the aircraft, military vehicles were ready for use. Pierpoint went to his office and punched a security code into the keypad. The object he wanted was in his safe. It had been lying there since Max Dearden died. After he picked it up, he drove back to his cottage at speed. The past was niggling him and he had to clear it up with Jem.

* * *

Gil Heskin took the call. "It's Sir Willoughby Pierpoint sir, he wants to talk to you on the scrambled line. He says it's urgent." Dearden went to the secure phone and lifted the receiver. Pierpoint wanted to talk about what was going on in Leofwin's Hundred. Dearden told him that time was pressing because of the imminent mission to Dracasfeld, and he would explain after he returned.

"I need to know what the building in Leofwin's Hundred is about, Jem, and I need to know now."

"You've asked a bigger question than you think, but I'll bring some information over. I think you'll find it interesting."

Dearden arrived at the cottage.

"The New York problem has taken a serious turn," Pierpoint said, before Dearden could get a word out. On the way to his study, Pierpoint gave him the details about the James C. Nesbitt and Raegenhere's message shortly before the sinking. It was another notch etched into Dearden's mind like a groove in a gun butt. Deep inside, he vowed to remove Raegenhere in whatever way it took because of how he got between him and Rowan.

"Now New York's out of the way, let's get down to the reason I've asked you here, Leofwin's Hundred. What exactly is going on?"

"I've brought some information along. Just be open-minded when you look at it."

Pierpoint thumbed through the diaries and the copy of the manual found in the Hub, and Dearden explained what happened when they went through the Hub into Anglo-Saxon England. Pierpoint listened with a puzzled look on his face.

Dearden took his laptop out of its case and booted it up on Pierpoint's desk. He put a DVD into the drive. It self-booted and the images of an immense forest came on-screen. Some warriors in an ancient style of clothing, armed with swords drawn and spears levelled, met Jem, Mitch Doughty and Julia Linden-Barthorpe at the foot of a hill. Pierpoint heard the ancient language spoken by Julia to the leader of the warriors. They moved off together through the forest to the community of buildings with the larger one at the centre, which had similarities to Dearden Hall, although it was smaller.

Dearden ejected the disc. What he had seen confused Pierpoint. The moving images of the ancient people, the house similar to Dearden Hall with wooden scaffolding and stonework that looked new, set in a great swathe of forest challenged his reasoning.

Pierpoint recalled what Maxwell Dearden said about the forest, that it was huge. No one had believed him. Max had called the building in the forest the Hub, the same term Jem used. Pierpoint went to his desk and took the object he retrieved from Kineton Base out of a drawer. It was a Polaroid photograph, signed and dated by Maxwell Dearden. It showed a bearded man with a jewelled sword half out of its scabbard. Jem recognised Leofwin of Mercia and his sword, Aelfrythsgiefu. His father had taken the photograph through the transparent wall of the Hub.

Pierpoint noticed that the leader of the men in the old Polaroid photograph was the same as the man on the DVD who led the warriors who met Dearden and the others. What he had seen convinced Pierpoint to take what Jem Dearden was telling him very seriously.

Wednesday 26th November.

Dearden got some time alone with Rowan. He needed some rest and they lay in bed. He explained that the mission to stop Raegenhere and Uberatu would begin that night.

"Jem, Frieda said that you go away and sometimes come home injured. What do you do when you go away?" They were warm and had the curtains open. Jem turned on his side and looked at Rowan. He pulled her close and wondered how to explain about SHaFT, and what to keep secret. Rowan had asked many questions in the days she had been living in his time. Up to now she had skirted around questioning him about what he called *missions*. This time she ventured further.

"The night can hide bad thoughts that lie in wait for us. We need not secrets," she said. Dearden kissed her and thought how delightful was the scent of Dior. There was a certain naivety about Rowan, a childish innocence, and he wished he could stay with her. He would have to tell her about SHaFT so she could understand. He looked into her eyes.

"This mission will soon be over, Rowan, and then I'll tell you."

"Very well. I will be patient, but please have a care Jem, and come back quickly."

They dressed and went downstairs into the great hall. Soon after, unexpectedly, Harry came into the room. He apologised for intruding when he saw Dearden and Rowan together.

Dearden spoke quietly in Rowan's ear. "I shall be back. Remember, nothing will keep us apart, not even time itself with the House of the West Wind close by." She smiled as they pulled away.

"Harry, I depend on you to look after her," Dearden called as he went out the door to prepare for action.

54

Pierpoint rang Dearden, and the news wasn't good.

"The cesium won't be coming into Berlin Templehof. We've just learned that the airport's been closed, permanently."

"That's a complication we didn't want, Raegenhere will have to get the shipment re-routed."

"I'll get Kineton Base to contact Central Air Traffic Management. They'll have got re-scheduled flight information from the old Soviet Bloc, and it should give us a potential destination for the package."

"We'll still have to clean Dracasfeld out to make sure the stuff hasn't come in through the back door."

"No changes there, Jem. You're still heading up the Dracasfeld mission tonight. Rendezvous at my house in Radway at 2300 hours. Target ETA is midnight."

"What's the latest situation in the States?"

"Homeland Security has stepped up their airspace security to amber around New York. The Americans are jumpy. They're treating Raegenhere's threat as an attack on their sovereign territory."

"Then I take it the jet's ready to get us to the States in case we can't stop the bomb this end."

"It's on the tarmac, tanked-up and ready to roll."

* * *

Twenty-eight men of SHaFT assembled at Sir Willoughby Pierpoint's cottage. After a twenty-minute briefing, Dearden led the incursion team through the November darkness, down a private lane leading from the back of the cottage to Kineton Base. Six armed military police who Pierpoint had forewarned

J. J. Overton

about the mission emerged from the blockhouse. Dearden spoke, and the cops verified identities. Steel gates opened and heavy anti-attack barriers slid apart to let the team through. They headed to Dump 4 and passed through a personnel entrance in the steel hangar doors. The team walked through the open space to an administration area, where they assembled in the ops room.

The first of two drop-down screens displayed close-up photographs of Raegenhere and Uberatu. The other screen had an image of the floor plans of Dracasfeld and the layout of the grounds. Dearden began the briefing.

"This mission has been called at short notice because of an ongoing threat to the City of New York on Thanksgiving Day, which is tomorrow. The threat is nuclear and involves an RDD, a dirty bomb. These two men are the cause of the problem; they are both dangerous and unpredictable. This man, the leader of the operation, is Reginald Arthur Heap, also known as Raegenhere," his image increased to three times life-size. "It is important that we get him alive to answer questions. We are raiding Raegenhere's mansion, a place called Dracasfeld at Wyverne Hardewicke. We are looking for the hardware they'll use to build the nuclear device, and we also want evidence of Raegenhere's activities that have financed his terrorism. Gather any records you can find on hard-drive and paper." Theodore Uberatu's image came up large. "This is Raegenhere's accomplice. Treat him with kid gloves. I have personal experience that he is unbalanced, and he is mean with it too." The briefing went on for several more minutes, during which Dearden answered questions and finalised strategy.

The teams assembled near four transports, which outwardly looked civilian. Below the body shell, they had Kevlar protection and were one hundred percent military. Three of the vehicles each held a specialist team of eight, with Dearden leading Alpha, Doughty, leading Bravo, his wounded leg injected with a nerve-blocking agent, and Matt Roberts, leading team Charlie. The fourth vehicle, with the four-man Delta team, Mop-up, was for clearing loose ends after the mission.

The crews boarded the transports. Each man carried a Heckler & Koch G36K assault rifle equipped with a Universal Tactical Light. They had side arms, night vision, body armour, and a Geiger counter clipped to the belt. Two massive outer doors slid apart from the centre as the electric motors engaged. Silenced V8's rumbled and the column moved away from Dump 4, down the lanes of Kineton Base and past the security blockhouse at the main entrance.

Sir Willoughby Pierpoint remained in the command centre. With his small team of specialists using a bank of sophisticated equipment, he commanded SHaFT operations, wherever they took place.

55

The teams pulled up a quarter mile away from the perimeter wall of the Dracasfeld estate and settled in to wait. A few minutes later Roberts raised Dearden on the intercom. There was a lot more going on at the house than there was during the previous night's surveillance. He suggested the occupants were gearing up for action.

Midnight came and with it Thanksgiving Day. *We succeed at all costs.* The motto went through Dearden's mind. It had to come good tonight. He checked his watch.

"Are you ready?" the unit commanders acknowledged they were.

"On my mark . . . Go."

Dearden's driver gunned the engine. The vehicle got to the perimeter gates in seconds and sent them crashing right and left. The reinforced rails at the front of the vehicle sustained paint damage, nothing else.

Dearden's vehicle sped along a driveway and then over a lawn toward the front entrance. It skidded to a halt. There was a double door at the top of a short flight of stone steps. In seconds, the team had smashed the door open with an enforcer ram. In the background, Dearden heard the twin Pratt and Whitney Canada turbines of Green and Mallett's Eurocopter, on hand for medical emergencies.

A security patrol in the corridor near the front entrance didn't know what hit them. As the raiders smashed through the door shouting *guns, guns, down, get down,* the patrol was startled into submission. Dearden and Wynter secured them, and their squad of six spread out around the square entrance hall. A corridor led off left and right. They split up. Dearden with three of the team took the stairs leading to Raegenhere's private rooms, while Wynter and three men, advanced down the corridor to the banqueting-hall.

Doughty and team Bravo burst through an ornate window into a servant's passageway at the rear of the building. Doughty split from his unit with three men and headed down the passage toward the sound of gunfire. The other four of his team headed the opposite way, heading for the main fuse board. They warned the rest of SHaFT over the comms to assume night vision and threw the master breaker, plunging the house into darkness.

Doughty reached the entrance hall and saw the two men Dearden's team encountered secured on the floor. He heard a movement on the landing above and swung the Heckler and Koch up to the sound. His UTL picked out a guard creeping along the landing. There was a quick exchange of fire, and then the outnumbered guard dropped his weapon and raised his hands. Doughty motioned with his UTL and shouted for the hostile to join the prisoners below, where he was zip-tied.

Doughty and his three men came to a library with glass-fronted cases full of leather-bound books and Pre-Raphaelite paintings hanging on the walls. Three shots came from somewhere above. Doughty picked out a set of stairs in the corner of the library with his UTL. More shots came, and with his Heckler and Koch to his shoulder, he led the men up. Dearden was there with his team spread out in the darkness in a defensive formation. Doughty's UTL picked out two more of Raegenhere's men sitting in a corner with their wrists secured. One was holding his bloodied shoulder and Dearden was retrieving the man's pistol off the floor.

Matt Roberts' team crashed into Dracasfeld through a door in the corridor to the rear right of the building just as two guards rushed past to help their comrades. One of them loosed off some wild shots in Roberts' direction. One hissed by his ear and he responded with Mavis the Bowie, pinning the man to a beam by his sleeve. Roberts retrieved his Bowie, got the prisoners secured, and with his team of seven he ran down a passageway and found the stairs leading to the cellar. Two hostiles at the foot of the stairs heard the noise of gunfire, and when the lights went out, they took cover behind a stone pillar.

Through his night vision gear, Roberts' man saw a foot poking from behind the pillar and he shot it. There was a yell and the man fell forward clutching his foot. His comrade appeared into the light of a UTL with his hands raised. Roberts pushed the man over to his wounded colleague, told him to sit, and asked for the combination to unlock the vault door. Both hostiles were silent. Roberts, equally silent, removed Mavis the Bowie from its sheath and demonstrated its sharpness on his forefinger. He touched the knife on the ear of the man shot in the foot, who flinched when he realised Roberts was serious and blabbed the combination. Roberts fed it into the keypad and pulled the heavy door open.

Inside the vault, crouching in the darkness were two guards who heard what was happening through a two-way intercom. As the massive door was opening, they fired through the gap. Roberts' team broke to left and right and under covering fire, they advanced into the vault. More shots came from inside, and as one of Roberts' men threw in a stun grenade he cried out that he was shot in the stomach. The grenade exploded and Roberts and the others rushed in apart from one who dragged his colleague to safety and yelled *Man down in the vault*, into the comms. Team Delta responded and came in to evacuate the man, while Mallett and Green landed the in the Eurocopter to give emergency treatment and onward transport.

Roberts' team's UTL's penetrated smoke left by the grenade. They picked out two guards on the floor, one with his arm at a grotesque angle and the other, moaning with a wound in his thigh. Roberts shone his UTL around the vault. It was clear. He spoke to Dearden on the comms and asked him to get the lights on.

Wynter began to video the contents of the vault. "Man, this place must have the wealth of a nation in it," he said to Roberts. He walked around the room, focussing on works of art wrought in precious metals. Many of the pieces were in their own glass display case, labelled with history and place of origin. He passed Egyptian and Sumerian treasures, golden figures from the high Andes and exquisite pre-Columbian cast gold.

Farther on in the room there was a smelting furnace and a crucible with particles of gold glinting on its interior surface. Nearby were moulds for pouring molten gold into ingots. Pallets had ingots stacked on them in a criss-cross fashion, and there were containers holding jewellery ready for melting down, one each for gold, platinum and silver. Wynter moved toward the centre of the room where there was a larger showcase. The object in the case was dark, made out of hammered iron, with gold decoration. He read the inscription below it. *The Sutton Hoo Helmet.* Close by it there was an empty case. He read the inscription, then, "I'll be damned," he exclaimed. Wynter lost no time in calling Dearden on the comms. "Get down to the vault, Jem. You need to see this . . ."

* * *

"Over here." Wynter called Dearden to the empty exhibition case. Dearden read the label.

The 1933 Twenty-Dollar American Gold Double Eagle.
The World's Most Valuable Coin. Current Value,
Seven And A Half Million Dollars.

"This case is waiting for its exhibit," Dearden said.

"It seems so."

Dearden sat in a leather director's chair in front of the empty showcase, trying to get into Raegenhere's mind.

"The man has an obsession for well-known high-value artefacts. There's the Sutton Hoo Helmet." Dearden went and stood by it. "If the gold Double Eagle is in New York, its location will give us the precise target of the raid. It looks as though the nuclear threat's a diversion to help Raegenhere get his hands on a coin with a face value of just twenty bloody dollars."

The voice of Sir Willoughby Pierpoint cut into the team's headsets from Kineton Base. It was the first time he had communicated during the Dracasfeld mission, although he heard all of it.

"We are finding out where the Double Eagle is stored right now."

"OK, but there's no sign of the cesium yet," Dearden replied.

Doughty came into the vault with some of his team. He was limping. "There are Raegenhere's private rooms we've got to search yet. Another few minutes and we'll know if the cesium's here."

"OK Mitch, I hear you," Pierpoint said. Then he spoke to Dearden. "Jem, as soon as we locate the Double Eagle we'll organise the next stage of the operation. We're onto it with all our resources." Pierpoint went silent when he heard the sound of automatic fire over the comms.

"Seems as though you're busy."

"You could say that." Dearden headed to the action and finished the conversation with Pierpoint on the way. He caught up with the rest of his team on a higher landing. They had broken through a locked door into a large sitting room, which had a high ceiling and period furniture. He heard footsteps coming fast up the stairs behind him and whipped around with his Beretta. It was Wynter.

They went past the wrecked door. The room breathed opulence. A French Ormolu Clock sat on the mantel of a carved marble fire surround. Above it was a large mirror with a heavy gilded frame. Dearden caught the reflection of himself and his team fanning out through the room. Their image was incongruous amidst the antique surroundings, dressed in black combat suits and helmets with night vision gear hinged out of the way.

Slightly ajar in the panelling at the side of the sitting room was a disguised door. Wynter spotted it and snatched it open. Inside the small room a man who said he was the estate manager was hiding behind a curtain. Persuaded by the nearness of Wynter's Heckler and Koch, he led them to a door at the foot of a flight of stairs, which he said led to Raegenhere's sleeping quarters.

Two of Dearden's team went up the stairs. The first up kicked open a door at the top. He surveyed the room with his night vision gear and then led off into the room with his assault rifle to his shoulder, sweeping right and left as he went. His colleague found the light switch and warned to come off night vision. He flicked on the light.

"Clear of hostiles." Dearden heard the voice in his helmet, then, "Testing for rads." There was the slow clicking of a Geiger counter, and then, "Clear, no rads."

Dearden went up to the bedroom. It was a wide-open space with a four-poster bed opposite wide stone-mullioned windows. Clothes were scattered over the floor. It was out of character with the rest of the house, which was tidy to the point of obsession.

Wynter came into the room.

"Raegenhere's fled the nest," Dearden said.

"I used a bit of persuasion on the estate manager," Wynter said. 'He says Raegenhere and some hangers-on flew to the States from Wellesbourne a few hours back."

"Sir Will, did you get that?" Dearden asked into his mike.

"I did. We're onto Wellesbourne air traffic control to get his flight plan, and Jem, get this, the Double Eagle's in the vault of the Federal Reserve Bank of New York. It's Stateside for you, ASAP. The bank's on Liberty Street, Manhattan."

56

The four vehicles drove through into Dump 4 and the doors slid shut with a heavy metallic clang. A board hanging from the roof with the shield and motto of SHaFT, *Nos Successio Procul Totus Sumptus*, was swinging in the draught from the doors. Dearden looked at the words and then at Doughty, limping painfully by his side. He gave a wry smile in Doughty's direction.

"Not bad," Dearden said, looking at his watch. It was 0135, "But there's no rest for us."

"With Raegenhere in the States, I've got my doubts it'll go smoothly. Right now, I'm going for another shot in the leg," Doughty said. He limped off to the hospital bay.

Team Delta handed over the prisoners, the injured to the hospital bay under armed guard, and the uninjured to holding cells for interrogation. Dearden and Roberts turned down the corridor that led to Pierpoint's office leaving the other men to make their way to the crew-room for de-briefing.

"The job's only half done," Pierpoint indicated for Dearden and Roberts to sit.

"Don't I know it," Dearden said. He was rather short on respect.

"Yes, I'm sure you do, but listen up. We've got information from Wellesbourne airfield. Raegenhere and some of his accomplices took off at 2200 in a Learjet bound for Westchester White Plains. They're calling at Shannon and then Gander for refuelling."

Dearden grimaced. "Then we'll keep this de-brief short."

"Obviously." There was a knock on the door and Doughty

came in. His limp had gone after his shot of painkiller. Pierpoint asked him about the leg.

"I'll be fine for a few hours."

"You take care." Pierpoint took care of his men. "Mitch, what can you tell me about our man who was injured?"

"It's serious, but the medics say he'll be mission ready again after a few weeks convalescence."

"And the prisoners?"

"Some are cooperative. Five are injured, two hospitalised. The others banged up in the cells near Beggs."

"Antony Beggs is a strange man but he seems to have had a change of heart." Pierpoint had interrogated him earlier.

"He needs to be on the winning side, whichever it turns out to be. Time will show his true motives."

"Time always brings hidden things into the light of day, Mitch," Pierpoint said. He noticed Dearden checking the time, and the discussion turned to New York. The knowledge they had was sketchy. There would be loose ends in the States, so the mission would have to continue with intelligence gained as it progressed.

Dearden stood. "Time for the briefing."

They went through to the ops room.

Pierpoint and the other commanders were sitting at a long desk on a raised platform at the front of the room. On the desk in front of each of the four positions was a tag bearing their names, Pierpoint, Dearden, Doughty and Roberts. A fifth position, Arthur Doughty's, was empty.

Pierpoint stood and took up a position in front of two maps projected onto the wall. One was of the greater New York area, and the other was an enlarged map of Manhattan Island.

"Gentlemen, there has only been a partial success tonight. However, Raegenhere has had his wings clipped. He has stolen millions from the gullible who were short of cash over the past few years, and we have put a stop to that. When the next phase of the mission is complete by this time tomorrow night, you will have eliminated the suffering Raegenhere intends to cause stateside. Thank you for your efforts thus far tonight. Now, I'll hand you over to Captain Dearden."

Dearden came to the front centre.

"We've learned from flight control at Wellesbourne Mountford that Raegenhere filed a flight plan for Westchester White Plains airport near New York with his aide Theodore Uberatu and some others. He plans to refuel at Shannon and then at Gander.

"As we didn't find the cesium for the RDD at Dracasfeld, and with Raegenhere's hurried exit, we can assume the shipment's been routed directly to an airport near Manhattan." Dearden used a laser pointer. "This is where we're landing, Westchester White Plains, New York State. There is potential for contact with Raegenhere and his men anywhere between Westchester and the Federal Reserve Bank of New York, which he intends to raid. It is situated at 33 Liberty Street, which is here," Dearden pointed to the place on the map of Manhattan. "The Federal Reserve is a large building. You see a picture of it, with its floor plans, here." Lee Wynter pressed a key on his laptop, and an enlarged picture came up on the wall.

"Raegenhere's plan is to empty Manhattan by threatening it with a radioactive dispersal device. He telephoned a message to Radio WNYC about the attack and it didn't take long for people to start leaving New York City to head for safety." Dearden indicated for Wynter to key the remote to the large television on the wall. CNN, US was showing live footage of traffic leaving the New York area, making for the New Jersey Turnpike heading south, and the Taconic State Parkway going north. It was chaotic.

"Try News Twenty-four Lee." Wynter found the channel. The news feed at the bottom of the screen said that the population was continuing to leave New York City after a second threat came from the terrorists. They claimed to have placed a radiation bomb somewhere in Manhattan, set to detonate on Thanksgiving Day.

"The next phase of our mission is for us to fly to New York to find the RDD and prevent its detonation. We also intend to apprehend Raegenhere and Uberatu."

"Why can't law enforcement in the USA sort it out?" asked a voice from the back. Pierpoint answered.

"The US Government usually doesn't like outside agencies working inside their national boundaries, but they have another situation that is taking a lot of their resources. We have worked with The Secretary of Homeland Security previously, and when we offered our assistance with the RDD threat, he accepted. Homeland Security has assigned us a squad from their anti-terrorism unit, and the National Guard has set a cordon around Manhattan. This is a joint-op, but we'll be taking the lead because of our expertise in dealing with this type of threat."

"It's not going to be much of a Thanksgiving Day over there," another man said.

"It could be a Thanksgiving Day they'll prefer to forget if we don't succeed in this mission," Dearden added. He finished his coffee, which was bitter, black and hot.

Pierpoint stood up.

"We've been on to Gander flight control with a request to delay Raegenhere with whatever formalities they can devise to buy us more time. Their aircraft is a Learjet 60 XR. Its range determines that they have to make a refuelling stop at Gander. We're using the Special Missions Gulfstream G550 and we can make Westchester in one hop. We're tanked up and the engines are running," he checked his watch. "We'll be rolling at 0345 hours GMT. We have an ETA of 0435 hours Eastern Standard Time at Westchester White Plains. Captain Dearden will deal with any further questions on the flight. That's all gentlemen, best of luck."

Pierpoint left for the command centre, leaving Dearden to finish off the briefing.

"Listen up. Mitch Doughty, Matt Roberts and I will lead over in New York. We need thirteen men. It will be a full complement for the Gulfstream. As usual, your involvement is entirely voluntary, who's up for it?"

There was a unanimous show of hands.

* * *

Shortly before Dearden led the raid on Dracasfeld, Raegenhere's Bombardier Learjet climbed to cruising altitude, bound for a fuelling stop at Shannon, Ireland. The first thing Raegenhere did once airborne was to go to the pilot and tell him to forget the flight plan to Westchester.

"Sir, you are joking aren't you?" The pilot was suddenly very uncertain.

"I am not joking. I never joke," Raegenhere's attitude was vitriolic. "My man on the ground at Westchester says all hell's going to break out there soon. Get us to another airport near New York."

"Which one?"

"I don't know which bloody one. Land in a field for all I care. Just find a landing place, which is what I pay you to do. Oh, and by the way, once we have refuelled at Shannon, we'll be flying straight to the States. Cut Gander out."

"The fuel level will be critical if we don't stop at Gander."

"There's nothing like a bit of excitement to heighten the senses," Raegenhere scowled as he walked off to his cabin. He sat opposite Uberatu and Ardnussam. Uberatu was staring at his hands. He flexed them, trying to relieve the pain from the hogweed.

A short while later the pilot left the controls in the hands of the co-pilot. He came aft and told Raegenhere the new destination was Republic Airport, an hour away from the waterfront in Manhattan. A smile spread across Raegenhere's face. Manhattan was emptying exactly as he planned, triggered by the broadcast of his first message. With the second message, the exodus had moved into overdrive, and he hadn't even planted the bomb. He closed his eyes and was soon asleep, with the innocent sleep of a psychopath.

57

The transport drew to a halt near the Gulfstream Special missions G550, painted Midnight Blue. There were no outward markings other than a large italicised SFT in black on the tail fin, which made it virtually incognito. SHaFT ran the aircraft with a crew of two Pilots, a Flight Engineer and a Navigator, which left space for sixteen men and their kit and the two medics. Terry 'Tez' Macaulay the lead pilot came from the flight deck and called for the team's attention. He gave them the flight information in an accent vaguely Scottish.

"We'll be climbing to forty-five thousand feet and cruising at 500 knots. We have an ETA of 0435 Eastern Daylight Time into Westchester White Plains." He pointed above his head, "The in-flight display here will show our progress. We take off in two minutes. Relax and enjoy the flight."

The twin Rolls-Royce BR710 engines spooled to maximum and the Gulfstream was quickly airborne. It climbed at a steep angle to cruising altitude. Dearden always found take off in this aircraft exhilarating. On a signal from the flight deck, he released his seat belt and went to the forward bulkhead to carry on with the briefing.

He got the team's attention. "As soon as we land turn on your Co-Orditrax unit. When we are stationary check that the readout matches the GPS co-ordinates on the in-flight display on the bulkhead up front. Remember, Co-Orditrax is in the prototype stage. It *should* register your position in three dimensions anywhere on the surface of the globe, and Ranstad Nanotech wants your feedback on it. Next, when we land at Westchester a Major Dan Rockwell will meet us with onward transport to meet up with anti-terrorist police in Manhattan.

With any luck, he will have impounded Raegenhere and his aircraft. Rockwell will also give us documentation to cover our presence in the States. Any questions?"

"Any information about how Raegenhere intends to get into the bank?" Vin Rodick called out.

"Nothing definite. The operation will develop on the hoof after we land. We want *anything* to give us a clue about Raegenhere's whereabouts in Manhattan which will lead us to the bomb."

There were no more questions.

Dearden went to his seat and studied the satellite images of Manhattan. He tried to think the way Raegenhere would, to get into his mind. The problem with that was Raegenhere's unpredictability. It was impossible to work out where he would plant the bomb. Dearden had been on his feet almost twenty hours, and he was dog-tired.

* * *

Raegenhere's contact set a fire in a hangar at Westchester County Airport. When it was well under way, the pilot of a BAE Harrier GR.7, stolen from the collection of an oligarch in the former USSR, gained altitude. He had been flying in under the radar from the north. When he reached a pre-determined point on his flight plan, he radioed in with a false report about engine trouble. The pilot said he was on his way to an air display later in the day, and requested permission for an emergency landing due to an engine problem. Not long afterwards, an F-16 Fighting Falcon joined him on the starboard wing and escorted him into Westchester, the nearest airport for an emergency landing, and peeled off when the Harrier was on the ground.

With the current threat level at severe, the military had a heavy presence in the air. Raegenhere needed to exert some persuasion. A gun to the temple of the wife of the chief of air traffic control in their home at Westchester ensured the Harrier could slip in un-noticed. The pilot was told to taxi to a particular holding area and he followed the marshal to a dark place, away from the fire.

The canopy lifted and the pilot, Vasily Kalugin, looking extra-heavy in his flying suit, grabbed a rucksack and clambered down the ladder wheeled into position by an attendant. He asked where the men's room was, and said specific words the marshal was waiting for. The answer confirmed the plan was running smoothly and Kalugin made his way to the toilet.

He recognised the row of lockers from the description radioed to him en route. The picture of a pin-up stuck on the front indicated locker 23, the one he was to use. Feeling the comforting shape of the silenced pistol in his pocket, he ducked his head to see if the cubicles were empty and then went to the locker. He found the key on top of it.

At the back of the top shelf was a wad of fifty-dollar bills and he flicked through them to make sure the amount was about right. He put the rucksack on a hook in the locker and taking out a bag of clothes left for him, he went to a cubicle and stripped off his hazmat suit, and the rest of his flying gear.

Although there was a chill inside the washroom, he was sweating profusely from the layers of clothing he had been wearing. The suit he changed into fitted well, and the material was better than any he had owned previously. He slipped on a lightweight thermal golfing jacket with a logo on the breast pocket, and listened to make sure he was alone. Kalugin let himself out of the cubicle and was surprised to see a man using the urinal. He hadn't heard him come into the men's room.

The man went to one of the washbasins. He looked into the mirror and saw Kalugin staring at him. Kalugin was holding a flying helmet and a pressure suit, and a bulging black rubbish bag. Things didn't look right. Being on security detail, he asked the man behind him what was going on.

Kalugin said nothing. He crossed the room to locker 23, put everything inside, and locked the door. Then he placed the key back on top of the locker.

"I asked you what you're doing." The security man raised his voice and thought of the pistol at his belt. The pilot turned and smiled at his questioner. He held his hand out in a gesture of friendship. The security man felt the tension ease and offered his hand, but the Russian grabbed it and pulled, whipping the security man's arm up and back. Kalugin's other hand darted to the exposed neck and grabbed hold of the windpipe. When he squeezed, the security man's eyes widened in surprise and then bulged. He thrashed about, and his mouth opened as he gasped for air. His free hand grappled with the assailant's, trying to prise the fingers away, but he slid down to the floor as he lost consciousness. The Russian held on for another thirty seconds and then felt for a pulse. There was none. He dragged his victim from the washroom through a door at the side into the dark.

Kalugin had always wanted to live in America. He had completed his part of the deal, and with no more thought for the man lying dead at his feet, he disappeared into the night clutching the large bundle of dollars to start his American dream.

Another figure who had had waited patiently came from the shadows. It was he who had started the fire in a disused hangar containing flammable materials. It was soon burning fiercely. His next task was to take the cesium to Manhattan.

It took a while to cover the miles to the workshop in South Street. The courier arrived at the workshop door and delivered the radioactive package to those waiting, who were dressed in hazmat suits. He received a wad of banknotes, but he wasn't aware that he had also received a lethal dose of radiation from the container he handed over.

It was delicate work. There could be no mistakes with the cesium. Raegenhere's bomb maker was sweating in his hazmat suit. He finished the wiring and placed the bomb in its casing. Feeling drained, he went to the far side of the room and sank into a chair. Shortly after, five men left the building in a hurry. Three went in the direction of the harbour-side. The other two in protective gear drove off to the right into Beekman Street and on toward their destination. It was shortly before dawn and Manhattan resembled a ghost town. On board the Vasco da Gama in South Street Seaport, Raegenhere pulled on his diving suit.

*   *   *

Dearden awoke to the altered tone of the engines as the revs decreased. He forced his eyes to focus on the in-flight display. The flight was almost over and the lights of Westchester town were visible forward of the port wing. Dearden looked at his watch. ETA was as planned, two hours before dawn. The control tower had advised Tez Macaulay about the fire, and he could see it raging in the distance as he lined up for his final approach.

Out of the port window Dearden saw two Lockheed-Martin F-22A Raptors on a parallel flight path, and looking past Doughty, sitting on the starboard side, he could see two more of the F-22s. As the Gulfstream headed for the runway Dearden could see fire-fighting vehicles tackling the flames, which were leaping skywards from two of the hangars.

As the Gulfstream descended Dearden saw the pilot of the lead Raptor picked out in moonlight give a quick salute, and then the aircraft peeled off and engaged their afterburners.

Dearden looked at the chaos on the ground as Macaulay, himself an ex-fighter pilot, tooled the Gulfstream down to a smooth landing.

Dearden spoke into the microphone of the Situations Awareness System on his wrist.

"We are now on the ground in Westchester. Mission continues Stateside." Pierpoint and his team of analysts, monitoring the operation from Dump 4 in Kineton, heard Dearden's call. The SHaFT cell donned black combat gear and zeroed their Co-Orditrax units when the Gulfstream came to a halt.

A flight handler showed them to two Hummers, where four men in US Marine uniforms were waiting to take them to New York City Hall to team up with the squad of anti-terrorist police. As Matt Roberts and the others put their kit in the trunks and boarded the Hummers, the flight handler escorted Dearden and Doughty to a security building to collect documentation.

A man in US Army camouflage with a major's flash and a pistol in his hand rose to meet them. He could see the eyes of the two black masked men who came through the door.

"Are you Captain Dearden?" he asked, as a woman came in through another door.

"I am, and you must be Major Rockwell." Dearden had a description of Rockwell and he weighed up the stocky individual with a weathered complexion. He was above average height and had a livid scar that started in his hairline and ended below his right eye. Rockwell saw where Dearden was looking. "Afghanistan, a Taliban bullet." Dearden nodded and looked at the woman. She was auburn haired and of medium height and build.

"Who's this?" he asked.

"Kate Connaught, she's heads-up security at the Federal

Reserve Bank of New York. If there's anything you need to know about the internal layout of the bank she's your person, but before that have you got anything you should say to me?"

"Traitor's Gate," Dearden used the security phrase agreed by Pierpoint and Milt Herschel. He nodded hello to Kate Connaught.

"Your official documents." Rockwell handed Dearden a sheaf of papers, one for each man on the mission, all un-named, all marked 'Concerning the bearer of this document'. Dearden handed Doughty a copy, and briefly scanned one himself. It bore the White House seal and the signature of the President.

"I see you're prepared," Dearden said, indicating the weapon in the major's hand.

"We have to be, these are uncertain times." Rockwell stowed the gun in his drop-leg holster.

"Has a Learjet landed here recently?" Dearden asked.

"Nothing has landed other than you and a Harrier with engine trouble. It was heading for an air display tomorrow."

"Tell me about the Pilot."

"There's no information, apart from it being an emergency landing, and it appears that some of the rules were side-lined to allow it to land. We're looking into it."

"Where's the pilot now?"

"He's disappeared. I've got men looking for him."

"He may be our man and you've allowed him to slip through the net."

Rockwell said nothing, but Dearden saw him colour up and look evasive. He spoke to Dearden, trying to be efficient after overlooking the Harrier pilot. "You will shortly be taken to City Hall Park, where Lieutenant William O'Hanlon Junior and his men will meet you—"

A tall athletically built individual came through one of the doors and interrupted Rockwell. His face was smutty from flying ash. He was about Dearden's height and introduced himself as Mike Buchanan.

"I'm head of airport security here at Westchester White Plains. I heard you were coming, but just who the hell are you?" He could only see their eyes.

Dearden showed him his authority with the presidential signature. Buchanan looked at the document and then looked back at Dearden and Doughty.

"Why have you guys been brought in?" he avoided Dearden's direct gaze.

"Mister Buchanan, you've been told we would be arriving. Answer this question. Have your air traffic control diverted a Learjet?"

Before he could answer, a phone on the desk rang, and in an instant, Buchanan grabbed Kate Connaught, who screamed as he pulled her towards him and pointed a gun at her head, then the door slammed open and two gunmen burst in.

"Drop the gun Rockwell," Buchanan snarled. "Get over to the wall with your hands raised. Do it, all of you or the woman dies,"

"Mike, what are you doing?" Kate had trusted Buchanan. They dined out last night.

"What am I doing Kate? I'm playing for a different team. Oh, Kate . . . Kate, it was so good last night, but don't look worried. Just shut your mouth and raise your hands where I can see them." He pushed her over to the wall and indicated for Dearden and Doughty to follow by waving the gun. On their way over Dearden gave Doughty a slight nod of his head.

"You're probably wondering what this is all about," Buchanan said, as he indicated the two gunmen. He strode over to Dearden and punched him in the stomach. "That's one thing it's all about." He rubbed his knuckles and grinned. "Raegenhere wants you stopped right here." Dearden had seen what was coming and clenched his stomach muscles. Unarmed combat training made his muscle tone rock-hard, but he gasped and collapsed to the floor, moaning. Buchanan didn't get why his hand hurt so much. He raised his pistol in Kate's direction and hit her on the jaw with his other fist. She dropped to the floor.

"Hey, creep, pick on someone your own size," Doughty was provocative. The distraction worked. Buchanan turned on Doughty and gave him a left to the stomach. He responded like Dearden and feigned collapse.

Dearden staggered to his feet and moaned again for effect. "Damn you, Buchanan," he gasped, clutching his stomach with both hands . . . "what happens now?"

"What happens now is a Thanksgiving Day firework." Buchanan thought that he was dealing with a pair of pussies.

"You'll never get away with it," Doughty challenged.

"Never," Dearden emphasised, still staggering.

"Oh, but we will,"

"You're the weak link in the chain, Buchanan." Doughty was aiming to undermine Buchanan's ego. The ruse worked, he began bragging and spilt information.

"The canister's in the workshop being assembled right now. You're too late to stop it."

"Where's the workshop?" Dearden tried to sound casual.

"Wouldn't you like to know?" Buchanan realised he had said too much and went to Dearden with a closed fist.

Rockwell stepped in before Buchanan got to Dearden, "How did you get past my men?"

"Easy. You know the saying *can't see the wood for the trees?* You have too many men, Major. They're tripping over each other dealing with the fire, which we set, by the way. Us? A few men in the shadows. Raegenhere's informant told us you were coming, Dearden, you and your weak sonofabitch friend."

Doughty tensed. Dearden nudged him on the back of the arm. *Act at the earliest opportunity.* The front of the arm would have meant *no action yet.*

The phone rang again. Buchanan's glance at it was all it took. Dearden and Doughty launched themselves at the opposition. Doughty took one of the two gunmen who had come in last. It was controlled but lightning quick and the roundhouse kick with his injured leg broke the man's jaw while his colleague, momentarily confused, took Dearden's first and fourth finger one to each eye and went down clawing the floor, temporarily blinded.

Rockwell was slower. He was nearest Buchanan and hurled himself at him. A shot went into the ceiling, another into one of the walls, then Buchanan gave Rockwell a right, which broke his nose with a crisp snap.

Dearden glanced at Kate Connaught. She was out of harm's way so he leapt over the desk and punched Buchanan hard and fast. As they were going down to the floor Dearden wrestled the gun from his hand and gave him a knee to the groin. Buchanan cried out in pain, came to a sitting position and Dearden knocked him flat with a right to the jaw.

Doughty secured the other two with zip ties from his pocket and came over to Buchanan. He secured his hands behind his back, punched him in the stomach, twice, good and hard, and said, "That's poetry."

"Get that phone, Mitch," It hadn't stopped during the action. Dearden checked Kate, who was coming around. An ugly bruise was forming where Buchanan hit her. Rockwell was more serious. His nose was misshapen and would need hospital treatment.

"Your wife won't recognise you, Major," Doughty advised.

"Well thanks a bunch," Buchanan retorted nasally, dabbing his bleeding nose on his sleeve.

Doughty lifted the phone. "What?" He asked. There was a pause as a woman on the other end thought about how to reply.

"Just who the hell is that?" she asked.

"Just who the hell wants to know?" Doughty, hyped with adrenaline, shouted into the phone.

"I have the Secretary of Homeland Security here for Major Rockwell. Will you try to be civil with him?" The line went dead for a second or two. A man's voice came on.

"Dan, do you still have the place in lock-down with the fire you've got there?"

"You're not speaking to Major Rockwell, Mr Secretary," Doughty said. He covered the mouthpiece with his hand. "Secretary of Homeland Security," he spoke in a low voice to Rockwell. "He's asking if the airport's still in lock-down."

"Am I speaking to Major Rockwell?" shouted the Secretary after the phone had gone silent on him.

"I said it's not Dan Rockwell, are you deaf?" Doughty shouted, in no mood for games.

"I'll thank you not to piss me off, son. I need to speak to Major Rockwell, now."

"Major Rockwell is incapacitated at present; his nose has been splashed." Rockwell got out of the chair and held out his hand after wiping the blood on his trousers.

"Give me the phone, it'll take more than a damn broken nose to keep me down," he grabbed the handset off Doughty. "Rockwell here, Mr Secretary. The airfield is secured but there has been another incident."

"What other incident, and who the hell was that I was speaking to?"

"He's with the specialists helping with the Manhattan situation. There has been an attack at this airport, sir. The people planning the Manhattan raid sent in some operatives who penetrated our security. The situation is now in hand."

457

"I hope it is. So the bunch from the UK has arrived?"

"They sure have in full measure." Rockwell glanced at Buchanan and his two men at the side of the room. Milt Herschel spoke again.

"The fire and those illegals who came in . . . Major Rockwell, you say you now have that situation in hand?"

"We have sir."

"You better have, *Major* Rockwell. If it isn't, it's your ass that's on the line, not mine. Feel like being sergeant again?"

"You can rest assured sir that the situation is resolved. Now, if that's all, *sir*, I need you to get your ass out of my face so I can go check on my men." Rockwell slammed the phone down on its cradle.

Dearden questioned the gunman whose sight was in jeopardy about the location of the workshop where Raegenhere was getting the bomb assembled. The gunman didn't intend talking and Dearden intended him to. His voice took on a dangerous edge. "First, about me," He warned. "Sometimes I'm not nice to know, particularly when innocent people like those in New York are threatened. I get impatient. Therefore, I want answers. Your name, for openers."

Silence. The man looked at Dearden as best he could.

Dearden got close and pressed the man's eyes. "Your name."

"Mavisson."

"OK Mavisson, I'm not going to leave this room without answers. You have a choice. You are almost blind and I presume it hurts. Do you want a broken leg as well?" Mavisson shook his head and tried to shrink away from Dearden.

"Where has the package been taken to?"

"It's been taken to the workshop."

"Good. Where's the workshop?"

"In Manhattan."

"*Where* in Manhattan?"

"South Street, near the junction with Beekman. They've got a place behind a roller shutter where they're working on the bomb."

"Where is this roller shutter door exactly?"

The man was turning his face this way and that, trying to see out of his damaged eyes. He drew a sharp breath as a stab of pain gripped him.

"Beekman joins with South Street near Brooklyn Bridge. Turn left into South Street from Beekman and you'll see some scaffolding fifty yards or so down on the left. Before you get to the scaffolding, there is a disused shop with a wide roller shutter door. That's where they're building the bomb and where they've taken your men."

A chill went down Dearden's back. He crossed to the door and looked out. The Hummers had gone. Buchanan smirked. "See how good we are, Dearden? Always one jump ahead. Anaesthetic into the Hummers, and we moved your bunch to a quiet place. Harm us and they're dead."

"If you hurt my men I will personally break your neck," Dearden countered, "But for the time being try this for size." Dearden took out his Beretta. He breached a round and put a shot through the fleshy part of Buchanan's right thigh. Kate Connaught put her hand to her mouth, afraid of the summary justice as Buchanan roared with pain.

Dearden spoke quietly through Buchanan's noise. "You won't be one jump ahead for a while now, Buchanan. Remember this, you *don't* harm my men. You don't hit a woman, and you *don't* use a nuclear device on an innocent population. Do those things and you get bad results." Dearden went back to Mavisson who was cowering in a corner of the room. "What happens next depends on how helpful you are. Remember the eyes, Mavisson. Remember Buchanan's leg.

Tell me, where's Raegenhere putting the bomb?"

"I don't know, honest I don't." Dearden moved closer and raised his pistol. He fired a shot into the floor next to Mavisson. The man cried out, he was wincing with the pain from his eyes.

"Your kneecap will be a good trade off against all the men, women and children that will be harmed if that bomb isn't stopped. If I have to cripple you to get the information I will. Your answer, Mavisson."

"I am telling you the truth; you've got to believe me."

"It better had be the truth." Dearden put his pistol in his belt and spoke to Rockwell who no longer thought Dearden was a pussy. "We need a vehicle and your best driver to get us to South Street immediately." Dearden glanced at his watch. He had changed it to Eastern Daylight Time. By 0517, they were on their way to City Hall Park.

58

Harry Stanway desperately wanted to communicate with the alien race. Their intellect and technical expertise attracted him but they had gone to ground. He thought the Native Americans, with their uncanny perception and skill in tracking, could help find them. Harry asked them to help him, and they told him how they had seen the three aliens at the back of the museum room some days before they had helped Rowan.

"It was exactly here," Possum Chaser said to Harry as she tapped the wall at the back of the room. Harry rapped the wall so hard it hurt his knuckles, but there was still no hollow sound to indicate a doorway. Red Cloud took off a leather thong from around his neck and tapped the wall harder with a stone threaded onto it, but still, it didn't sound hollow.

"Do you think the aliens have gone back to their home?" Possum Chaser asked. Harry shook his head. He knew they hadn't gone away. He sensed at times when he was on his own in the Hub that he did have company. He had sometimes picked up movement from behind reflecting off the screens. The aliens were interested in what was going on but were letting him and the others learn by experience. Judging by their response when Rowan was wounded he thought they would intervene if he started doing anything life threatening.

Possum Chaser turned at the sound of a footfall behind them. It was Bill Templestone. Red Cloud noted Templestone's side arm butt forward in his belt. Bill was taking no chances when he walked through the forest.

* * *

Harry was in the control room, deep in concentration. His

fingers were manipulating the buttons on the central keyboard. He looked at the screens on the wall to see the result.

"I'm going to do a geographical shift this time," Harry said to those seated and standing around him. He told them earlier he was going to try something different. Julia and Templestone looked on with interest. Rowan and Esma, now in jeans and T-Shirts, looked puzzled.

"I'll explain. Come with me." Harry led them to the top level of the Hub and pointed out a small table on which were a sandwich and a half-eaten apple.

"I'm going to move the table and the things on it from here to Dearden Hall." He led the way back downstairs to the Control-Room and took his place in the central seat in front of the keyboard. They gathered around waiting for him to start. Julia looked at Harry sitting on one of the chairs made for beings far taller than he was. His feet were off the floor. He looked slightly ridiculous, Harry, with his powerful intellect looking like a twelve-year-old sitting in a chair for grown-ups. Julia remembered, as a child, sitting on a chair at Moat Field Cottage with her feet swinging because they couldn't reach the floor, and it felt the same now as she took her place next to Harry in one of the oversized chairs.

He was becoming familiar with the characters of the alien alphabet and his fingers moved over a series of buttons. He looked at the central screen to see the result. A shape appeared which he knew meant the geographical coordinates for the shift were locked-on. He pressed a larger button at the centre of the keyboard and there was a noise from above that reverberated through the building. Then the noise stopped and the shape on the screen changed.

"Let's see what's happened."

Harry ran up the stairs to the room the aliens called the portal. The others came after him. The table had disappeared.

"OK," he said, "Let's get to the great hall and see if it was successful."

Frieda Heskin could tell there was something important going on. Mr Dearden was away again, this time with Mr Doughty and some of the men with whom they associated. She was clearing away the ashes from the previous evening's fire in the great hall with her back to the room when she heard a peculiar noise behind her, a sort of high-pitched whine and then a thump.

A small table was in the middle of the room and she knew it hadn't been there before. There was a plate on it with a sandwich and an apple that had a few bites out of it. She felt frightened and her heart beat faster when the thought occurred that she couldn't trust her senses. She had to tell someone what had happened. Her husband Gil was out getting supplies so she went across the courtyard to the studio to get help from Lloyd Perkins who was with another man who had been set on to help with extra work in the studio.

Perkins tried to understand her. She was mumbling about something that had happened in the great hall, and she looked pale. Perkins told her to slow down and he and the other man, Karl went to look. They wondered what sort of prank Frieda was pulling. It was some sort of invitation to share one sandwich and an apple that were on a small table.

"It's not enough lunch for the three of us Mrs Heskin, but thanks for the offer."

"No . . . no, you don't understand, it's the table, it appeared out of thin air," she said, which was when Harry Stanway came into the hall.

"There it is." He went to the table and took a bite out of the sandwich. "Amazing. Teleportation works on a local scale."

"How did you do it?" Templestone asked.

"I found out how to hitch a ride. That machine is so clever."

"You hitched a ride?" Julia asked.

"I've linked the Hub into the Navstar GPS network."

"Which means?"

"The Hub was built for greater distances than the half mile I've just demonstrated. Once it works as the makers intended I'll be able to move an object to any place on Earth." *And beyond* was the thought he kept to himself.

"How accurate is it?" Julia asked.

"The specification is the same as the latest military grade survey device, plus or minus three millimetres, but it has self-corrected error positioning anywhere on the Earth's surface."

"Let me get this right," Templestone went to the table. "You punched in the coordinates of this position in the great hall, and the Hub moved the table to it, and frightened poor Frieda half to death in the process."

"That's about it. Sorry Frieda, I'd have warned you if I knew you'd be in the room when I sent it."

"Please warn me next time."

"What about height?" Julia butted in. "The table ended up with its legs on the floor, not halfway into it."

"Like I said, the positioning has a self-correcting feature. GPS calculates the z-axis, height, both by triangulation and by reference to fixed datum points on the Earth's surface. Before I set up the geographical shift, I went into the great hall and measured the global coordinates of the position I wanted the table moved to. After I programmed the Hub to those co-ordinates you saw what happened. The shift worked. Once it's fine-tuned the physics of the system will automatically seek and find the z-axis in a spatial transfer."

"How about sending the table back?" Templestone asked.

"We'll go and program the Hub to do that." Harry went over to the table and took a bite from the sandwich. "Mmm, it still tastes good, so the information's not corrupted."

Back in the control room, Harry programmed the machine with the global coordinates to return the table to the Hub. He punched the *go-to* key. The shapes on the screen became active. There was a noise above them and then the activity ceased.

Templestone looked at Harry, "Upstairs?"

"Yeah." Harry managed to go up two at a time.

The table was where it had been previously, and Possum Chaser was standing there munching the apple.

59

Corporal Rol Merrick, at the wheel of the Chevrolet Avalanche, pushed the V8 to ninety. During the frantic ride, Dearden thought of Rowan's words before he left, to take care of himself and to make sure he came back. If he did not come back soon she said she would come looking for him with Red Cloud and Possum Chaser. He smiled as he pictured them on the hunt.

Dearden leant over to Doughty and spoke quietly in his ear. "They were tipped-off from our end. Buchanan was waiting for us."

Doughty nodded. "Raegenhere and Uberatu knew we were going to raid Dracasfeld as well. Who's ratting on us?"

"No-one in SHaFT. The psychological tests would pick that sort of behaviour up. No one in SHaFT would put their life on the line *and* be a traitor at the same time."

"I agree. It has to be someone at Dearden Hall, and there's not many it can be."

* * *

Merrick skidded to a halt at the edge of Manhattan's City Hall Park shortly before quarter to six. At the edge of the park, a crew of nineteen of the New York Anti-Terrorism Division were waiting for SHaFT in a Bluebird All American Mobile Command Center. One of the officers, dressed like the others in camo and Kevlar body armour, said he was Lieutenant O'Hanlon.

As Dearden conferred with O'Hanlon and his squad a helicopter came overhead, descended, and hovered, its rotors clashing with the silence. O'Hanlon spoke into a comms set and the helicopter ascended. In the subdued light of dawn, Dearden could just make out the letters NYPD as it banked sharply and headed north. An eerie quiet descended onto the normally busy Manhattan.

With Merrick leading, they reached South Street on foot. The two Hummers were at the side of the road, unlocked. No one was inside and there was a vague smell of anaesthetic when Dearden opened the doors. He lifted one of the trunk lids and the team's kit was there, same with the second vehicle. Fifty paces more and they came to the roller shutter door Buchanan told them to look for. Two men stationed themselves one each side of the entrance, semi-auto pistols ready.

The pavement was uneven and a light was shining through a gap under the door. It was a small personnel entry door with a Yale lock let into the large roller shutter. Doughty looked at the hinges. They were well oiled. He took his Colt 1911 from his belt and breached a round. With his other hand, he selected a small probe from his side pocket and inserted it into the gap by the door catch. He glanced at the other men behind him to check they were ready and levered the catch. It responded and he pushed the door, which swung silently inward. Doughty grasped it as it opened and he stepped over the threshold, sweeping the room with his Colt. Dearden with a Geiger counter, and then the others, followed.

It was a large open room lit by low wattage bulbs with green enamelled shades. The room smelled damp. Black mould had spread two feet up the wall, which had plaster dropping off in patches. There was evidence that the front part of the building had once been a food store, and there were rat droppings scattered about. A faint light was showing under a door at the far side of the room. They crept up to it and listened.

There was conversation the other side the door. Doughty

looked at Dearden as he heard a voice he recognised. It was Dave Beecham, their bomb disposal specialist challenging someone in the room. The reply gave the position of one of the enemies.

Dearden pointed to his eye and then at the gap under the door. Doughty took a fibre-optic viewer from his rucksack and handed it over. Dearden poked the end of the tube under the door. He looked through the eyepiece and pointed out the direction of the hostile speaking to Beecham.

Matt Roberts' voice came from the room. Dearden was surprised anyone got the better of Roberts. Dearden manipulated the fibre optic again. He followed the sound of Roberts' voice and saw him amongst the team tied up near a wall to the right. He did a sweep of the room and counted seven captors with a variety of weapons, and they looked edgy. There was more conversation with Roberts playing one hostile off against another to weaken their resolve.

Another fifteen seconds of observation and the layout of the room and the position of each captor was clear. Dearden indicated which of the hostiles each of his men were to take, and with the fingers of his left hand, he counted down from five and kicked the door. When it burst open and hit the wall all hell broke loose.

Dearden took out the man by Matt Roberts with a shot to the shoulder. Doughty disabled another with a bullet to the leg and Beecham lashed out at a man near him. He brought his heel down on the man's head and put him out of action. A spray of machine gun fire from a kidnapper in the middle of the room narrowly missed one of O'Hanlon's men.

Three hostiles sitting at a table to the left stumbled from their seats as they clambered to defend themselves. Dearden ran at them followed by Doughty and two of O'Hanlon's squad. One of the men at the table, more prepared than the others, grabbed a pistol and fired at Dearden. The bullet creased his cheek and he felt blood trickling from the wound. Dearden swung a right to the shooter's jaw. He heard the bone snap and moved to the next target, a man who stunk of sweat who was struggling to get out of the tangle of chairs. One of O'Hanlon's squad had him in his sights and a shot rang out. They were going berserk, Dearden needed survivors to interrogate, and what was going on with O'Hanlon's men was not the way with SHaFT.

Another of the kidnappers got from behind the table and had O'Hanlon in his sights. Doughty fired before the man steadied his aim. The bullet went through the shooter's hand. As he dropped the gun, the shots ricocheted around the room. The captors saw they had no chance against the group in black who had stormed in from the street, and they raised their hands.

Doughty got the Geiger counter out of his rucksack and went to where the SHaFT team were on the floor tied by the wrists and ankles. The instrument registered a radiation level slightly above normal, but safe without long-term exposure. He swept the instrument back and forth around the room to locate the source.

"We're onto something." The signal increased when Doughty went to another door. "The package could be in here," he said, backing away. He looked at the readout. "We're safe enough unprotected if we keep away from that door." He went over to the scattered chairs, righted one and sat on it. His leg was throbbing again. He reached into the emergency field kit, pulled out a hypo and gave himself another shot of nerve blocking agent. He unwound the dressing and looked at the wound. It was still OK.

O'Hanlon's men secured the prisoners while Dearden went to release the SHaFT team, tied to each other with their backs to the wall. Most had recovered from the anaesthetic.

Roberts started explaining.

"It was the four marines waiting by the vehicles at the airport. We weren't quick enough to stop them before they lobbed anaesthetic into the vehicles. I woke up in the Hummer with a lousy head outside this place."

Dearden nodded. "Give me Mavis." He held out his hand and Roberts shifted to one side so Dearden could get to the Bowie. He cut Roberts' ropes first and then Green and Mallett's. Dearden felt for his men. They had their pride dented but procedures would be set in place to make sure a similar thing didn't occur again. There would be practice, surprise attack with anaesthetic gas back home on the MoD land at Kineton Base. Dearden took stock of the situation. Three of Raegenhere's men were dead. O'Hanlon's team had gone on a turkey-shoot. It was fortunate some of the opposition survived for questioning.

After they cut free the last of SHaFT, Dearden and Doughty got into NBC suits and went to the suspect door with a Geiger counter. The reading increased immediately they got into the room. It was a large room, maybe a warehouse for the shop at the front in its commercial days. Doughty swung the Geiger counter around from left to right and located the highest reading. It led to a workbench on the right. Half way along the bench, the count came to maximum.

"Looks as though this is where they assembled the weapon," Doughty said. He took a magnifying glass out of a pocket on the leg of his NBC suit and examined the surface of the bench. There was metal sheeting covering the surface. In one small area, a patch of dust was glowing.

"The bomb's been here."

"That's bad. It's anyone's guess where they've taken it."

Doughty stood away from the workbench and looked

around the room. There were some tall metal two-door cabinets at the side of the room furthest away from the radiation. One of the doors was open. The count was little over background level when he reached it. Inside there was what at first looked like bunched up rubber sheeting. He dragged it out and saw a familiar shape.

"Wetsuits. Why are wetsuits here?"

"For diving, presumably." Dearden dragged the rest of them out, four altogether. There were compressed air cylinders in another cabinet. The pressure gauges showed they were ready for use. Doughty wrenched another door open, more diving equipment, depth gauges, and dry-bags.

"There's something else here." He took out a bundle of paper held together with an elastic band. There was a brochure displaying a ship, saying it was available for charter. It was a sleek looking vessel with the name Vasco da Gama on the prow, and there were half a dozen tourist brochures. Doughty thumbed through them. One of the brochures was for the Blazing Saddles Bike and Rental Tours, situated at the Seaport across the road from the workshop. There was another brochure for the Wall Street Heliport. Yet another gave information about various piers along South Street Seaport with times of low and high tide, docking rules, and other things useful to a mariner.

Dearden took out a folded object from the bottom shelf of the cupboard; it was a Land Searcher map, the detailed type used for hiking. It showed historic monuments in Manhattan circled in red. Each one had a line connecting it to a text box containing a brief description at the side of the map. A roughly drawn highlighted circle made one of the text boxes stand out. The legend said Storm Drain, circa 1923. Dearden traced the route of the storm drain. It ran very close to Maiden Lane and the Federal Reserve Bank of New York, and led to the East

River at South Street Seaport where the outflow had been marked with a red highlighter. Dearden spun round and startled Doughty.

"That's it! They're entering the storm drain from the harbour. That's what the diving suits are for." Doughty saw where Dearden was pointing on the map. The evidence fitted.

"OK, well spotted old chum." He slapped Dearden on the back. "Let's see what else is here." Doughty spread the brochures out on a workbench well away from the cesium particles. One, The Financial District was thicker than the rest. Dearden opened it up. There were different sections designed to help tourists. In *Places to Eat Out*, two were highlighted red, the Cabana Seaport and Harbour Lights. The next section was *Parks and Gardens*, another, *Museums and Art Galleries*. Dearden flipped the pages, looking for highlighted items.

A map in the centre of the brochure folded out to show the whole area. Each place of interest had a letter by it, indexed in a list on the bottom right. One of the parks was marked with a letter J, highlighted with a bright red circle. A shape had been doodled by it. Dearden tried to make out what the doodle was. There was a word written on it, which was chillingly obvious.

"Bingo," he whispered, understanding the mushroom shape and the word, *BOOM*.

Dearden slid his finger urgently down the list, "J . . . the letter J, which park's that?" He came to J. "Thomas Paine Park. Mitch, grab a wetsuit, we'll scrub everything down, and then we're going diving."

"Hold on." Doughty said. "Each one of these brochures is part of their plan. What's the ship for, the Vasco da Gama?"

"Anyone's guess. The brochures imply they're using it in some way." A plan was forming in Dearden's mind as they went to the decontamination unit and scrubbed themselves and the diving suits down. Roberts tested them with a Geiger counter.

The reading was slightly high but was within acceptable safety limits.

* * *

In Dump 4 at Kineton Base, the crew in the control centre were in touch with things happening on the ground. They were building an ongoing picture of the Manhattan mission as events unfolded. The policy of mission control was non-intervention, unless there was information vital to the progress of a mission, or if lives were in danger.

Sir Willoughby Pierpoint spoke into the comms. All on the mission heard his voice in their headsets.

"This is Pierpoint, Kineton Base."

"Manhattan mission, Dearden,"

"Jem, you have evidence Raegenhere is using the Vasco da Gama. It was originally a research vessel. We have uncovered documentation that tells us Raegenhere bought the ship and restored it to its original spec. It will do in excess of forty knots." Pierpoint paused as if reading from notes, and then, "This is interesting, the Vasco da Gama has a moon pool for undersea access, how could that fit in, any idea? Pierpoint out."

Pierpoint looked at the map linked to the Co-Orditrax system. The operator zoomed onto South Street Seaport and changed to satellite view. Detail became visible on the screen as the zoom increased. By the side of each man, a number represented his identity. Dearden was number one. At the bottom of the screen, a table displayed the global position of each man on the mission in three dimensions. The co-ordinates were shifting constantly as the men moved about.

Dearden scanned the surroundings as he led the team across the East River Bikeway. There was a sign pointing to the four-masted Windjammer, Peking, lying at anchor in the harbour, and they could see the ship's masts high above the surrounding buildings. Moored alongside the tall ship with about fifty feet between them was the Vasco da Gama, its name painted in bold letters on the prow. Men were moving about on the main deck above the triple hulls.

"The ship from the photograph," Doughty looked at the sleek lines.

"It's one beautiful vessel." Dearden was working on a strategy now he had all the factors in mind. He leant close to Doughty. "Pierpoint told us the Vasco da Gama's got a moon pool. This is what we're going to do."

* * *

There was no better bomb disposal team than Dave Beecham and Chuck Catesby his backup. They got to Thomas Paine Park, and the four of O'Hanlon's men who went with them assembled a decontamination unit. Beecham and Catesby surveyed the surroundings and planned the search. The park had mature trees and beds of shrubbery. A road surrounded it, and buildings with shops were on the further side of the road from the park. Benches and waste bins were dotted about, adding a further complication to the scene. The additional manpower for the search would save precious time.

"We're looking for *anything* out of the ordinary," Beecham said. "Spread out around the outside of the square on the far side of the road. Go clockwise and work inward toward the centre of the park. Check waste bins, shop doorways and any alcoves you come across." Catesby gave them each a Geiger counter from his kit.

He switched his counter to demonstration mode and an almost joined together clicking came from the instrument.

"That's similar to what you would hear if you get close to the bomb. The radioactive material the terrorists are using will be contained in a chamber but there is contamination on the outside of the casing, which the counters would pick up. If you find *anything* suspicious, call us. Do not deal with it yourselves. OK, let's get to it."

60

The men of SHaFT could see the Windjammer, Peking, from the shelter of the Blazing Saddles building on South Street Seaport. The four master was alongside a pier where there was a wide gangplank up to its main deck. On the farther side of the Peking lay the Vasco da Gama, moored to a pier where there was no shelter for a stealthy approach. Dearden could see the vessel was low in the water, suggesting the moon pool was below water level and open to the sea. Three of the crew on the Vasco were on the lower stern deck. Dearden spoke quietly to the team over the comms, saying the tall ship would give them shelter, and they would use it as a base for boarding the Vasco.

A bell sounded on board the Vasco da Gama. The men who were working on the stern deck disappeared below.

"That's our cue, let's go." Dearden led the team at a run across the tarmac onto the jetty, up the gangplank and onto the Peking. An elderly woman was tidying the deck at the top of the gangplank with a broom, and she used it to bar the way onto the vessel.

"I'm sorry but the museum is shut until the emergency is over," her voice trailed off as she realised most of the men were in combat gear.

"I am also sorry ma'am. I'm with the NYPD Anti-Terrorism Division." O'Hanlon showed her his authority. "We need to board the Peking to help us apprehend the people responsible for the situation here in Manhattan. We believe they are using the ship moored by the next pier." She smiled and held the broom to one side. The NYPD officer bringing up the rear winked at her as he passed. She smiled again, this time at the handsome eyes, and wished she was forty years younger.

They went below decks where Dearden briefed the men to stay and await further instructions. He and Doughty climbed into the wetsuits from the bomb factory and went to the jetty on the opposite side to the Vasco.

They entered the water between the Peking's hull and the pier and swam downwards. The water darkened as they struck out below the keel of the windjammer and then swam the short distance to the Vasco. Coming to the starboard pontoon, they eased themselves under it and floated up toward the moon pool, which was brilliantly illuminated. They waited in the shadow below the surface. No one was about, so Dearden and Doughty swam slowly upwards.

On the deck surrounding the moon pool there were a number of capsules arranged ready for underwater transport. The streamlined capsules had a propeller with a guard, and controls for steerage. On each side was the logo, 'Deep Move 3000'.

They heard the sound of approaching footsteps on the steel decking the other side of one of the doors. Dearden got close to Doughty and spoke in a whisper.

"Storm drain, now." Doughty acknowledged with a nod of his head. They turned and kicked down under the keel of the Vasco toward the harbour-side.

The dark gaping exit of the storm drain soon came into view below the surface of the water. They swam into the drain and as the light penetrating the water from above diminished they switched on the lights attached to their headgear.

After a short distance the ground started to rise sharply. Doughty followed Dearden's cue and switched off his helmet light. A few more yards and they broke the surface of the water and waited for a minute for their vision to adjust to the light. Refracting from outside, the light picked out the surroundings in a cold green colour. The tunnel was semi-circular, about fifteen feet from the floor to its highest point, and the floor sloped to a gulley at the centre where water was rushing down the slope to empty into the ocean. Dearden and Doughty took their Situations Awareness comms sets from a dry bag, switched on and clipped them to their belts.

The floor of the tunnel levelled to a gentle slope, and at that point, well above the tide line, they removed their fins and cylinders and walked on ahead. After a while Dearden grabbed Doughty's arm and held him back. He picked up the faint sound of voices echoing from a distant part of the tunnel. They walked on, and as they were approaching a bend, reflected light from ahead gradually intensified. Rounding the bend, they could see the source of the light way up ahead. They walked cautiously into the darkness taking care there was no hidden drop. They had travelled about half the distance to the light and the activity ahead when Matt Roberts' voice came through Dearden's earpiece from the Peking.

"Things are happening on board the Vasco, they could be making ready to set sail."

"Understood," whispered Dearden. "We'll be active down here in ten minutes. On my call get over to the Vasco. Board through the moon pool and secure it."

* * *

With the bomb threat having worked so well, Raegenhere's confidence made him feel invincible. He had the dirty bomb timed to explode in Manhattan when they were under way on board the Vasco with the Double Eagle and the bullion in the hold.

Raegenhere was standing near to the laser cutter wearing protective glasses. The four men operating the cutter had been working in shifts. They had reached the point in the tunnelling process through to the vault where he had told them to stop and wait for his return, so he would be on hand for the breakthrough. They had passed the time until he arrived playing cards to the exchange of money, and then Raegenhere came back and the final stages of laser cutting had started. As they began to break through, light from the vault became visible, first like a spiders' web of brightness through the fractured reinforced concrete and brickwork, and then with a sharp brilliance that pierced the blackness of the drain. They attacked the wall with renewed energy.

Security in most departments of the Federal Reserve was as good as it could get. The entrances, one from Liberty Street and the other from Maiden Lane, were equipped with the most up to date electronic security measures. Motion sensors were in strategic places throughout the bank, particularly on the basement floor leading to the entrance to the bullion vault. These would alert the armed National Federal Reserve police force if there was any unauthorised entry, but it could only work if the police were on duty inside the bank.

Wilbur Gant, Raegenhere's contact in the bank, had telephoned the CEO at his house to say that no further personnel were in the building. He said he would remain there on security detail. The CEO mistook Gant's actions as courage beyond the call of duty. In reality, it guaranteed Gant a bunch of banknotes for his part in the action when the raid was over.

* * *

In Thomas Paine Park Beecham and Catesby had eliminated the bomb being located in any of the buildings. They reasoned that for maximum effect it had to detonate out in the open or in a place that would blow apart easily and allow maximum dispersal of the radioactive particles.

Catesby had seen a Johnston 4000 street sweeper arrive at

the far side of the park. The operator stopped the vehicle and walked away a few minutes back. Catesby stopped his search abruptly. It occurred to him that the street sweeper shouldn't have been there. Beecham wondered why Catesby had stopped and followed his gaze. Simultaneously, they broke into a run toward the street sweeper. Calling the other men over the comms, Beecham told them to get back to the command center.

Catesby switched on his Geiger counter and when they got near to the sweeper, the count was high. They backed off, and when the counter registered normal, Beecham whipped two NBC suits out of Catesby's rucksack. They got into them and raced back to the sweeper.

The device wasn't in the cab.

"Has to be in the Hopper," Beecham shouted. He looked the vehicle over. The welds joining the metal plates of the fabricated hopper had been ground away and Beecham realised it had been done to make the hopper blow apart easily when the explosive detonated. He climbed onto one of the mudguards and hoisted himself to the top of the vehicle. There was a large flap for emptying the rubbish from the hopper. The flap would normally open when the vehicle's hydraulic system lifted the hopper. Beecham saw that the linkages were dismantled, enabling the flap to be lifted by hand. He examined the area for booby traps. It was clear. He lifted the flap a fraction and then held it open with a wedge from his tool kit.

He called down to Catesby. "I'll sweep it for triggers."

"Take your time."

"Don't worry I will. Trouble is I don't know how much time we've got." Beecham probed the edges of the hatch once again. "It's clear—here goes." He lifted the flap slowly and rested it gently on the roof of the hopper. He took a Maglite from his pocket and looked inside the dark space.

"There's something bulky here, I'm going in." He switched on his Geiger counter and climbed through the hatch. The response from the counter was high. Beecham focussed his Maglite on the object and spoke urgently to Dearden on the comms.

In the darkness of the storm drain, Dearden quietly acknowledged Beecham's target acquisition call. He could see six men brightly outlined in the light way up ahead. One, who was large and muscular, was standing near Raegenhere who was in sharp profile looking at the results of the breakthrough. The other four, judging by the state of their clothing, were the ones who had done the work. Only Raegenhere and the big man appeared to be armed and their weapons were in holsters.

"Two to six," Dearden whispered in Doughty's ear. "What do you think of the chances?"

"Better than even, do you want Raegenhere?"

"I'll take Raegenhere and the two nearest him. You take the three nearest the hole into the vault."

Raegenhere was facing the hole cut into the wall. About fifteen feet behind him was the blackness of another tunnel that had its exit four feet above the floor of the storm drain. Water was cascading from it.

The lights from the interior of the vault illuminated the nearby area of the storm drain, picking out the pile of debris from the vault wall, and the four workmen. They looked fatigued. Dearden and Doughty moved silently forward.

* * *

In the ops room in Dump 4 at Kineton Base, Sir Willoughby Pierpoint, Art Doughty, and the rest were intent on the progress of the mission, listening to the ongoing observations of the SHaFT team as events unfolded. Pierpoint sensed the mission was reaching crisis point. He had something in mind and he needed information from Dearden. He spoke into the microphone.

"Kineton Base, Pierpoint. Come in, Jem."

"What?"

"Describe your surroundings."

"What the hell for? This is not the time."

"I need to know. Do it, Jem, now. Give me some dimensions, relative heights, widths, and angles."

"Relative to what?" asked Dearden.

"Relative to the centre line of the storm drain. Give me the layout, come on man hurry."

Dearden did as Pierpoint wanted. It took five minutes and some mental arithmetic, then the communication ended, leaving Dearden puzzled. He put the call from his mind. He had to speak to Roberts.

"Matt, are you at the Vasco?"

At Kineton Base, they heard Dearden's whispered question to Roberts. Pierpoint looked at the readout from the Co-Orditrax and flicked his eyes up to the satellite map. He told the operator to zoom to one hundred feet above street level, and then to fifty feet. There were two dots visible, numbered 1 and 2, Dearden and Doughty in the storm drain slightly to the right of the Federal Reserve Bank. Pierpoint noted the coordinates and then the ops room heard Roberts answer Dearden's question about his location over the speakers.

"We're in the sea, starboard of the Vasco. Waiting for your call." Pierpoint could hear water. He pictured Roberts and his team in the sea ready to board the Vasco.

"Go for the moon pool now," Dearden said. He touched the back of Doughty's right elbow. In the deep shadow, away from the lights, he raised his left hand. Doughty could see it silhouetted against the work lights. Dearden counted the seconds off, thumb, then one finger at a time, 5 . . . 4 . . . 3 . . .

Roberts and his team acted on Dearden's command. After deep breaths to oxygenate their lungs, they slipped under the water, feeling their way through the twilight under the starboard pontoon of the research vessel. They swam to the centre hull and drifted up into the moon pool. Their sidearms, made of carbon fibre and ceramic, were in their hands as they released their breath steadily on the way up.

Two of Raegenhere's men were standing on a gantry thirty feet above the moon pool. The fourteen men of SHaFT surfaced as one.

Des Upton and Vin Rodick were First Strike. There were two silenced shots. The bullets found their mark in the fleshy part of the thigh of each of the targets. One crumpled to the floor of the gantry. The other lost his balance and, with a cry, he toppled off the gantry into the water. Des Upton swam over and dragged the man to the steps onto the decking. He hauled the man up and the rest of the team spread out around the moon pool.

Four companionways led away into the vessel, one each to port, starboard, the bows and the stern. The team split up. Roberts with half of them went in the direction of the bridge, near the bows. They hugged the wall and came to a room labelled 'Communications'.

Roberts put his ear to the door. Music was coming from inside. Roberts, dressed in lightweight black combat clothing with kit hung about him, cut a threatening figure with a bandanna for his long black hair. He eased the door open and stood directly behind the occupant of the room who was tapping his foot to a beat on the radio.

He touched Mavis the Bowie on the crease of the man's ear and put his hand firmly over his mouth. A stifled squeal came from between Roberts' fingers as the comms engineer leapt involuntarily and sank back in his chair. His ear began to bleed.

"Stay quiet and you won't get hurt anymore," Roberts whispered into the other ear. The man nodded. Roberts zip-tied his wrists, gagged him, and marched him out of the room. There was a key on the inside of the door. Roberts removed it and signalling to his two men in the corridor to move on with the prisoner, he locked the door and pocketed the key.

On the bridge, the Captain of the Vasco caught a reflection behind him in one of the windows. He held out his hand to receive the coffee he asked for but instead of giving him a coffee a man dressed all over in black gave him a fist to the chin, and he fell unconscious to the floor.

The men in black looked sinister, and they took the bridge crew by total surprise. The Vasco's crew had been making ready for sea with a promise of a reward after the voyage and they were unprepared for the sudden reversal of fortune. They were at gunpoint having their wrists tied.

The Small Unit Situations Awareness coms hissed into life and Wynter confirmed the engine room was secure. Then the rattle of gunfire came from below. Roberts and his team raced from the bridge down a companionway toward the action. They came to a closed door that led to the ship's lounge where the shooting was raging. They halted and listened, analysing what was going on. Des Upton and Vin Rodick were inside with Peter Moore. Roberts glanced up as Wynter and his unit joined him from below.

There was a lull in the gunfire. Roberts spoke into the comms. There was no response from Upton or Roddick, and then there was violent movement inside and more shooting. A tense few seconds and then, "OK Matt, clear to enter."

"We have a man down," Rodick said, as Roberts entered the room. It was a scene of mayhem. Wrecked furniture littered the room and shattered glass from a large mirror behind the bar crunched underfoot. Pete Moore turned around as the others walked into the room. He was leaning against the bulkhead, his left arm hanging limply by his side, and his face had an ashen look.

"Sorry, Matt, I've been hit." On the bridge, Green and Mallett heard what the injured man said and they headed to the scene of battle.

The last of the assault teams with Lol Penrose in the lead entered the lounge.

"Upper decks are secure," he said to Roberts.

"OK . . . Jem, SHaFT is in and the ship is ours," Roberts said into the comms. He looked around and saw five men huddled in the corner at the far end of the room. Vin Rodick was covering them with his pistol. He threw a bunch of plastic ties to one of men of the captured group.

"Secure them," he told the prisoner. The man secured his comrades and then Rodick zip tied him.

"OK, get them off the ship and onto the hard," Roberts said. "Lee, get O'Hanlon's squad to pick up the prisoners for de-brief. Lol, continue making the ship ready for sea." Lol Penrose was a Cornishman and a born sailor. By looking at a running sea, Penrose could assess the vagaries of its moods and currents and plot a safe course. He made his way to the bridge.

In two areas of Manhattan, Thomas Paine Park and the storm drain fifty feet below Liberty Street, the situation was tense. In Thomas Paine Park, five minutes had gone by since Beecham had entered the hopper of the Johnston street-sweeper. Although the weather was cold, he was sweating. Catesby was with him, they were kneeling in front of the bomb that was at the rear of the hopper.

Beecham zipped his tool kit open and Catesby was holding a flashlight. The tussle with the bomb maker's mind was on. It was a large device, and unpredictable. An *extra-large sum of money*, in bomb disposal terms. In Beecham's estimation, there were about thirty pounds of RDX-C4 explosive packed around the canister of cesium-137 chloride. The bomb maker had intended maximum dispersal of the radioactive particles. A moment of doubt crossed Beecham's mind. The time constraint was a pressure he could have done without but his force of will made him focus. That is what made him the best in his field. He took a small screwdriver out of his toolkit.

"Where's Rastus?" Catesby asked putting his hand over Beecham's, to prevent him going any further.

"Coming out now, but the little sod will have to scrub down after this one." Beecham reached into the toolkit and brought out a stuffed toy cat, he sat it by the bomb.

Beecham carefully removed a steel cover. Below it was a digital timer, which appeared to double as a trigger. It was reading 49 minutes and 20 . . . 19 . . . 18 . . . 17 seconds, counting the time down to destruction. He could see a mechanical booby trap, so there were multiple levels of protection, the signature of an expert. Beecham could see numerous decoy wires built into the circuit. He could usually get into the mind of a bomb-maker and disarm a device using logic, but this was different. It was outside the box illogical.

"We need to either disarm this or dispose of it, and quick," Catesby said, looking at the readout.

"I know. The problem is I can't get into his mind. Raegenhere has picked a good man to build this. He's triplicated the circuitry. If I cut the wrong wire or work on the wrong circuit, I'll trigger the bomb. I don't have enough time to test the circuitry."

"Zero's in forty-five minutes."

"I know, and there's limited choices."

"There's one big choice. The sea."

"You're right Let's go."

They scrambled out of the Hopper and ran to the cab. Catesby grasped the bottom of the plastic dash and pulled. It broke away exposing the wiring harness. He selected two wires at the back of the ignition switch, pulled them away and touched them together. With a shower of sparks, the Cummins diesel rumbled into life.

Beecham triggered the comms and spoke to Roberts.

"We've located the bomb, but there's a problem. The security is triplicated and there's a countdown running. There's no time to get into the circuitry. We have a plan b that involves you."

"Shoot," said Roberts.

"Jem asked you to get the ship ready for sea. Is it?"

"Lol Penrose has the water-jets idling."

* * *

Dearden used his fingers to count to action, 3 . . . 2 . . . 1. There was gunfire and shouting as they rushed forward. Shock and Force, all the noise they could muster to create confusion. Raegenhere and his five men were startled immobile. Dearden shot Ardnussam in the shoulder and one of the workers in the thigh. Doughty, coming in from the left, took two workmen down with shots to the leg. He shouted at another of the workers still standing to get on the floor. The man dropped into the water coursing through the middle of the drain. Doughty dragged him out to save him drowning.

Raegenhere was wide-eyed, like a rabbit in the glare of headlights. Dearden stood between him and the tunnel coming in at right angles. He shoved his Beretta hard into the base of Raegenhere's skull.

"This is as far as it goes."

Raegenhere turned, his features livid, his fists clenching and unclenching. He recovered his composure and then smiled. "So you think you're going to stop my project do you?" Dearden, standing close to him, looked into eyes that were cold and without compassion.

A noise came from behind. Dearden's muscles tensed at the metallic CH-CHAK of a semi-auto slide, and then a voice he recognised came from a few feet behind him, the voice of the man who had followed him in Rugby.

"Put the gun down now, Dearden. Do it slowly. You too Doughty . . . yes, you can face me if you wish. You can look at the face of the man who's going to kill you."

Dearden turned to face Theodore Uberatu, picked out in the light from the bullion vault against the blackness of the tunnel behind him. He was standing on the lip of the smaller tunnel four feet above the floor of the storm drain. He leapt down brandishing a Sig Sauer.

"Did you think I wasn't here?" Uberatu asked. "Surprising how useful it can be obeying the call of nature. I was pissing in the tunnel." He clenched his free hand, still bandaged from the hogweed.

"You'll do more than piss when I get hold of you, Uberatu. We've got unfinished business."

Raegenhere backed away. Pulled a pistol from his belt. He pointed it at Doughty. "Better men than you have crossed my path. They're dead now." He pointed to the ground. "Kneel."

Ardnussam reached for the gun he dropped when Dearden shot him. He groaned with the pain in his shoulder.

"Can you cope with three cannons aimed at your head, Dearden?" Raegenhere asked. "Tie them up Ardnussam, make it tight," Ardnussam complained he was in too much pain to do any tying up.

"I pay you to do as I say. Bite through the pain and do it!" Dearden was still standing, and Ardnussam hit him on the head with the pistol. The blow was weak due to the Swede's wound but it still stung and Dearden felt the side of his head start to swell. Doughty stepped forward to help Dearden but Raegenhere was quicker. He shoved his pistol against Doughty's ribs. "Get over by the vault and kneel."

They slowly complied, looking for something . . . anything to win an advantage. Raegenhere moved closer. Uberatu came to his side, standing with his back to the side-tunnel.

"I want to finish them. Can I do it?"

"No, you damn well can't," Raegenhere said.

Doughty was psychologically astute, cool under pressure. He exploited Raegenhere's rising anger.

"Go on Reg, let him do it."

"My name is not Reg; it's Rae-gen-here."

"Raegenhere. Strange name, what does it mean?" Doughty asked.

"It means what I want it to mean, but Raegen's Force is good enough for you." Calm entered the psychopath's voice. The change was so quick it was uncanny.

Get him to talk about himself, Doughty thought. *Get the focus away from us. Buy time.*

"You've been quite a force with what you've achieved. You've made millions out of gold, haven't you?"

"And will continue to do so."

"There's a rumour going around that the Sutton Hoo Helmet in the British Museum is not the original." *Butter the vain bastard up,* Doughty thought, *Play on his vanity.*

"You've run some clever operations Raegenhere."

"The rumour's correct. The original is at Dracasfeld and the beautiful object lying a few yards from where we are now, the 1933 Gold Double Eagle will join it. Men have killed to acquire that coin, and there is bullion for the taking in the vault. Look, can you see it glittering? Manhattan will be a small sacrifice to pay."

"The way you cleared the area certainly was original," Dearden said, as he struggled to stand up.

"That was my pièce de résistance. Getting the cesium chloride had its problems but none I couldn't overcome."

Doughty stood too, grimacing with the pain from the arrow wound. They were making progress. Dearden was aware Pierpoint would be hearing everything, recording it, compiling the evidence. Raegenhere had allowed them to stand, but then he stiffened. "Wait, what are you doing?" His eyes looked empty. "You are in my way. Get back on the ground." His face distorted with hatred again.

Dearden wasn't fazed.

"We can get you out of this situation, Raegenhere. Stop the detonation of the RDD. There is no need for it because you have cleared the area with the threat of the bomb alone. You can get the bullion now. Look at it through there. Walk through and get it, leave it at that."

"No!" Raegenhere's self-control disintegrated. A moth fluttered out of the vault and headed to the work light. Raegenhere's hand flew out and grabbed it. He crushed it and threw the remains in Dearden's face. "Say goodbye to your friend, Dearden. It's time for the long sleep."

Dearden didn't intend giving Raegenhere the satisfaction of seeing any fear, but at that time, deep in his mind, for split seconds, events from his life started to re-play like a motion picture, scene by scene. The time with his father and the walk into the forest on his strong shoulders. His mother, he hoped she wouldn't take his loss too heavily, and Rowan . . . how he loved Rowan, she had brought meaning to his life again, and dear old Templestone. He would be one of the few who would get to know what had really happened. That was the way with SHaFT . . . it had to be that way.

The comms set had been relaying the action to Dump 4 at Kineton. Sir Willoughby Pierpoint suddenly stood.

"We've got everything we need to take them down. Let's get our lads out of there."

He rushed to the command centre and went out the door at the back into his private office. There were few rooms in the country more secure from the outside world. He dialled a mobile number and only waited a second.

"Linden-Barthorpe."

"Jules, it's Willoughby Pierpoint. Are you and Harry ready at the Hub?"

"On your call."

"Do it now, there's not a second to lose."

61

Dave Beecham gunned the engine of the street sweeper. With Catesby on the running board, hanging on to the cab by the open door the vehicle sped toward South Street Seaport where the Vasco da Gama lay with its engines idling.

Soon after he received the instructions from Dave Beecham, Matt Roberts, on the bridge, heard the deep sound of the Cummins diesel faint in the distance then rapidly getting louder. On his way toward the Vasco, Beecham outlined his plan to Roberts over the coms.

Roberts ran down the gangplank as the street sweeper took a left turn onto the jetty on two wheels and stopped with its front end a few feet away from the edge of the jetty. Catesby leapt off the running board and ran to the back of the hopper. The rear door was wedged open enough for him to get inside.

"Keep your distance, radiation," Catesby shouted. Beecham raced to the back of the sweeper. Catesby stepped onto Beecham's locked hands and climbed into the hopper. He looked at the digital readout, 39:14 . . . 13 . . . 12 . . . 10 . . .

"Have you got the launch ready?" Beecham shouted as Catesby passed him the bomb.

"It's attached to the starboard rear davits," Roberts called back as he led the way up the gangplank a few yards ahead.

"They running free?"

"Checked out and ready"

"Then let's get this piece of crap stowed down in the centre hull bilge, and Matt, get a decontam unit set up for Chuck and me well clear of the centre bilge."

"It's done," Roberts shouted. "And the stopwatch is set to the countdown you gave us." When he reached the bridge

Roberts gave orders to cast off to his skeleton crew of six, while the rest of the SHaFT team left with Raegenhere's crew to hand to the authorities.

The crew slipped the moorings and the Vasco began to move astern. When there was sufficient clearance, Penrose turned the vessel using the bow and stern thrusters and made way toward the channel on the easterly side of Governors Island. The normally busy waterway was devoid of traffic, and as soon as the Vasco reached open water, Penrose gunned the throttles. The vessel picked up speed and rose onto her pontoons.

In the centre hull bilge, Beecham had wedged the nuclear device against a bulkhead near the bows. He and Catesby negotiated their way through to the outer pontoons and wrapped RDX-C4 around the base of the seacocks. Catesby pressed the detonators home and set the timers to trigger the RDX five minutes before the bomb.

They came out of the bilges, scrubbed down in the decontamination unit, and got into clothes Roberts left for them. As they raced through the lower decks, they propped bulkhead doors open with the fire extinguishers nearby. Beecham raised Lol Penrose and asked what distance they had made from the harbour.

"We're through the channel between Sandy Hook and Breezy Point Tip. Our heading is south-easterly, ten nautical miles out of South Street Seaport and we're at forty knots."

Beecham calculated. "Matt, prepare the launch for a quick exit." He glanced at the stopwatch, 23:15 . . . 14 . . . 13 . . . 12; it would be tight. Roberts gave the order for two of his crew to go aft and swing the launch out over the side of the ship in preparation for lowering.

Still below decks with some minutes to spare, Beecham and Catesby returned to the outer bilges to place extra charges.

Near the bows of the starboard pontoon, Beecham placed a lump of the RDX across one of the welded seams of the hull plates and Catesby inserted a timer detonator into it set to explode at the same time as the other charges. Quickly over to the port pontoon, where they placed more charges. Another glance at the stopwatch, 18:43 . . . 42 . . . 41 . . . 40. Beecham raised Roberts.

"We're almost out of time. Stand by to abandon ship. Chuck and I will be topside for decontamination in two minutes. Stop all engines, open the moon pool sea-doors and flood the buoyancy tanks." On their way to the bridge, they could sense the ship's forward way slowing, and then it began to rock gently from side to side.

Beecham and Catesby dried off and dressed while Matt Roberts counted off the crew ready for evacuation. "Give us an update," he said to Beecham as they went aft with the crew. Beecham looked at his stopwatch.

"We have eight minutes to get clear of the vessel and then our charges will blow. Five minutes after that the RDD will detonate."

"Get the launch lowered," Roberts called as they approached the stern. Two men by the davits swung the launch out and the winches started lowering it. A rope ladder was hanging off the deck rails and as soon as the launch reached the water, the men started to descend the ladder, which was swaying with the rolling of the waves.

The first man on the launch got to the tower housing the controls and pressed the starter button. After a few moments, the marine diesels fired up and the last man scrambled aboard with three minutes to detonation. The engines picked up to full throttle and the launch sped away from the Vasco.

Beecham's charges exploded dead on time. The Vasco's hull tore open below the waterline, and as the men on the speeding launch watched, the ship began to go down by the bows.

"Good work," Matt Roberts said, above the groaning sounds from the stressed hull of the sinking vessel as tons of water cascaded in and forced air out. The surface of the water around the vessel thrashed as the sea claimed the hull. After less than two minutes, the Vasco tilted at a crazy angle, its stern high in the air as it slipped into the depths.

The shoreline of Sandy Hook appeared to the left of the launch and Breezy Point Tip could be seen low on the horizon to the right. As they headed between the two outcrops of land, all but the man at the controls were looking at the place where the Vasco da Gama had disappeared.

Beecham was concentrating on his stopwatch, waiting for the RDD to detonate. The wreck would need to be marked as dangerous on nautical maps and its position would be marked with a *keep out*, and a *radiation hazard* buoy.

The last seconds ticked away.

4 . . . 3 . . . 2 . . . 1 . . . zero . . . In the distance, the surface of the water lifted into a huge dome as the high explosive ripped through the stricken vessel. There was the sound of a muted explosion, and they felt its concussion through the keel of the launch.

Two seconds later Sir Willoughby Pierpoint, who heard the detonation over the comms, congratulated Roberts for a job well done, and the launch sped on toward South Street Seaport.

* * *

In the storm drain, all seemed lost. Uberatu had tied their hands, and Dearden was trying to blow the remains of the moth from his face. The time for talking had gone and then, in his earpiece, Dearden heard the voice of Sir Willoughby Pierpoint.

"Jem, say something, say anything to stall them for a minute or two." It only took a second for Dearden's brain to click into gear.

"The Double Eagle's a fake," he called out.

"Bullshit. It isn't a fake."

Dearden saw Raegenhere's frown.

"Someone did the same with the Double Eagle as you did with the Sutton-Hoo mask. They stole the coin and left a fake."

"No . . . it's authentic!"

Pierpoint's voice came through the earpiece.

"Jem, Mitch, get ready,"

In the dark tunnel opposite where Dearden and Doughty were kneeling a light appeared. It was iridescent, a bluish light, faint at first but growing brighter. Dearden and Doughty looked at it, and all the others turned to look. A puzzled look crossed Raegenhere's face and Uberatu's mouth dropped open. The superstitious Ardnussam scrambled towards the bank vault, and the four workmen went after him over the debris, trying to get away from the tunnel in the face of the inexplicable.

Dearden and Doughty had to take advantage of the diversion, tied though their hands might be. They struggled to their feet, leaning on one another for support. The blue light was becoming brilliant, banishing the blackness of the storm drain and they could hear a noise like a storm wind, which was gathering in intensity.

Dearden could see two rushing black shapes, one of them half the height of the other, silhouetted against the brilliant light. Ardnussam cried out, leapt over the debris into the bullion vault, and hid behind the wall and there was sudden movement as the rest of the group ran about in blind panic.

Dearden sniffed the air. "Recognise that?"

"Ionised air, high tension current . . . Jem, look." The two shapes were running towards them in the smaller tunnel, their shadows were growing black and huge on the wall of the storm drain. The shapes solidified. One carried a powerful light and a jewelled sword that shone brilliantly as it caught the blue light in the background. The figures reached the edge of the tunnel. The shorter one, Tomahawk Shahn of Offchurch, raised his head and howled as if to the wild sky, and the sound reached deep into the core of Dearden's being. And Julia was there, with the sword, Aelfrythsgiefu in her hand.

Tomahawk's teeth were vicious in a savage growl as he leapt onto Uberatu. He was unable to withstand the wolf's attack. He went to the floor, splashing into the gulley at the centre of the storm drain with Tomahawk's fangs close to his face. Raegenhere fired some gunshots at Julia that fell wide, and still running, she leapt from the ledge with a perfectly executed Shotokan flying kick that thrashed Raegenhere to the floor. Aelfrythsgiefu flashed in her outstretched hand and stopped short of his throat.

Raegenhere could say nothing. His distorted dream was over. Not prepared to live with losing everything he had built up, he raised the pistol to his temple and pulled the trigger. He pulled repeatedly. Click . . . click . . . click . . . on the empty chamber.

62

Sir Willoughby Pierpoint spoke directly to the President during a crisis meeting with the Chief of the Defence Staff and the Secretary of Homeland Security. He had been able to confirm the elimination of the threat to Manhattan and the Federal Reserve Bank of New York. He reported that the contents of its bullion vault remained intact. Work was set in motion to repair the wall of the vault and rebuild it to three times its original thickness.

The President's spokeswoman reported the updated status of the New York situation at a specially convened press conference broadcast nationwide on television. Reuters picked it up and it went worldwide. The message for Manhattan was that the threat had been contained. People could go home.

In a live statement on television the President confirmed the end of the emergency in the New York area with no loss of life, other than the unfortunate ones on the James C. Nesbitt, and those who died in the panic to leave Manhattan. He gave an altogether fabricated explanation of how the government had dealt with the emergency. He also spoke of the terrorist threat to the oil refineries that had ended with the death of the entire group calling themselves the Bedayat Jadeeda. Left unsaid was anything about the intervention of SHaFT.

Late that evening, when no one else was in his office, the President made a phone call to the UK using a scrambled line.

"Sir Willoughby, thanks are due from a grateful nation that will never get to hear what you and SHaFT have done for it. Tell me, why do you and your men do it?"

"Because we seek justice in an unjust world, Mr President."

"Mmm. Tell me Will, do you ever fail in your missions?"

"'Nos Successio Procul Totus Sumptus', Mr President, *'We Succeed At All Costs.'"*

"Yes, Sir Willoughby, I believe you do. You have helped us out of a hole. Your fee and expenses will be paid into your account in Switzerland within the next 48 hours."

* * *

One morning in December, not long after their return from Manhattan, Dearden fulfilled an arrangement he had made with the registrar at Cheylesmore Manor in Coventry. In the company of just a few people closest to them Rowan and Jem were married, using Jem's ancient family name, the Norman-French de Arden. It was a simple affair with no publicity and Rowan's wedding ring was the one that Red Cloud found in the forest before Jem's journey back to Anglo-Saxon times. It had on it three figures, a woman and two men. Neither Jem nor Rowan would ever know it, but it was the ring Leofwin commissioned a gold founder in Beorm-ing-ham to make to commemorate his three very unusual friends.

Dearden was chatting to Templestone outside the stables, home to four newly purchased thoroughbred Arabian horses, two mares and two stallions. Dearden looked up at the sound of hoof-beats rapidly approaching. Two young women dressed in jeans and jackets against the cold rode into the courtyard. They were both expert horsewomen, sitting astride the horses now, as Julia Linden-Barthorpe had shown them.

Esma dismounted from Elvara, a bay mare, and brushed leaves from her mount's mane, while Rowan slipped easily out of the saddle and led the black stallion to where Dearden was standing. Rowan had the clearest blue eyes and the bright winter sun caught golden highlights in her hair. A smile played on the strong features of her face, and in her eyes.

"That was good," she said, smoothing her hair. She slipped her hand around Dearden's waist. The stallion she had named Modig nuzzled up to her. She pulled two carrots out of her pocket and gave one to Esma for Elvara, and the other she gave to Modig.

"Jem, shall we go to the bank by the stream where we sat on the grass, and you told me some words of the Shakespeare?" she asked him in passable English with the Anglo-Saxon accent Dearden had come to know and love.

"We'll go later before the evening comes, my Lady Rowan of Maldon."

"My name is Rowan de Arden, not Rowan of Maldon," she corrected him with a mock-serious expression. After stabling the horses, they sat on the bench in the courtyard, the one Jem had painted when he was a child. On the day he came to de Arden Hall after learning he had inherited it he vowed to bring the laughter back to the old house, and he had in full measure. Life was calm now, after the Manhattan mission. His mind wandered and he thought of the Warwickshire Legends book with the chapter called The Golden Maid of Maldon, and now here she was, sitting by his side.

Her suggestion to go into the forest was appealing. They got some wine from the cellar and in the afternoon, well before dusk, they went into Leofwin's Hundred and drank wine on the bank of Shadow Brook.

Rowan was always fascinated to hear stories of the time they both now lived in, of Jem's childhood and of the House of the West Wind that brought them together. She had a thirst for knowledge that was almost insatiable, but Jem found it a delicious challenge to seek out and provide her with the answers. She, in turn, told him about her time in Heanton in the Arden and the affairs of the court, and about Harold Godwinson, her uncle who became king.

They came back after dark, their way lit by torchlight.

* * *

A number of weeks after the conclusion of the Manhattan mission, when the group of friends had returned to their normal lives, Dearden and Rowan invited them back to de Arden Hall for a celebration. Templestone was in one of the winged chairs in the great hall, a glass of whisky and dry ginger in his hand. Doughty, Matt Roberts, Leon Wynter and Julia Linden-Barthorpe were in a relaxed mood, and Red Cloud was in the other winged chair with Possum Chaser sitting at his feet. Esma was on one of the settees sitting close to Harry, and there was low music in the background. It was the time to tell stories, much as had occurred in the great hall over the thousand years since Leofwin of Mercia had given the instruction for it to be built.

The phone rang and Julia answered it. It was Trent Jackson.

"I've found something strange in the manual. It's a note, tucked between two pages. Whoever wrote it used a derivation of the alien script. That's why I needed Tim back here with me to work on the dating. The note was written far later than the manual. I have managed to translate a few of the words that have similarities to the language the alien race used to write the manual. It's a warning. I don't want to raise unnecessary fears, but you people must be very cautious around the Hub."

Julia re-joined the others as Dearden and Doughty were explaining what had happened to them in the storm drain. She decided to leave telling Dearden about what Jackson said until another time, after all, it was an evening of celebration and Jackson was uncertain about the contents.

"The light in the storm drain was strange, it was a kind of bluish colour," Dearden was saying.

"The colour of lightning," Doughty elaborated. "And there

was that high-tension smell we get around the Super Magnetron and the Hub, you know, ionised air."

"But you've never seen anything like what happened next." Dearden paused for effect. "Two great shadows were getting bigger on the wall behind us, and then two silhouettes, black as night with the light behind them in the tunnel came running toward us. We didn't know it was Jules and Tomahawk at the time. It was frightening, and you should have seen Raegenhere's face. He was petrified—"

"And there was the noise, the strongest storm wind you've ever heard, and Tomahawk's wolf-howl came out of the storm. It was the wildest place on Earth—"

"Tomahawk leapt from the tunnel with his teeth bared, he was demented, and Jules came running after him, brandishing Aelfrythsgiefu." Rowan smiled when Dearden mentioned the name of Leofwin's sword and Julia punched the air for effect as she recalled her entry into the storm drain.

"Raegenhere and the others didn't know what hit them."

"Come on, Mitch, I thought it was curtains too—"

"But then all hell broke loose," Doughty added.

Templestone settled further in his chair near the fire and the logs settled, sending a shower of sparks up the chimney.

"Harry," he said, when the laughter had stopped. They looked at Templestone, waiting for what was to follow.

"When did you realise you could use the hub to send someone to a different location?"

"It was at the time in October when Fengel and Beggs broke into the workshop and we shifted them back to 1063. It occurred to me that it would be irrational that the Hub would only be capable of temporal transfer. I needed to get one function working properly first, and the reason I chose the temporal one is because the residual current was already causing the timeshift to occur at the Hub. I began to experiment with the spatial function and that all came together when I shifted the table from the Hub over to the great hall."

"And scared poor Frieda half to death," added Dearden.

"That *was* unfortunate," Harry said. Frieda was in the great hall, invited to the celebration with her husband Gil. She could smile about the incident now.

The ones noticeable by their absence were Lloyd Perkins and his helper, Karl. They had disappeared without explanation. Afterwards, when she was clearing out their room, Frieda Heskin found a piece of paper with handwriting on it. It was under a chest of drawers, and it was part of a letter.

Theodore Uberatu sends his regards, and he thanks you and Lloyd for your help with the information.

The salutation that followed made clear the identity of Lloyd Perkins' helper, Karl. It said *I remain, as always Karl, your loving brother, Otto Fengel.*

"I wonder what turned Lloyd," Doughty ventured.

"Probably Karl Fengel persuaded him with the talk of easy money," Matt Roberts suggested.

"Could be," Dearden said. "But whatever the reason, he turned. I had my suspicions, but there was so much going on at the time I was suspicious of my own shadow."

"It was fraught. At one point I was about ready to abandon ship," Julia said.

"Perkins always made a pretence of not being interested in what we were doing," Templestone added. "That was suspicious in itself because the whole thing has been fascinating. How anyone could not be interested in what's gone on beats me. Anyway, Perkins is in the past now."

Wynter said, "But what about the future? What happens with the Hub now, Harry?" he anticipated an exciting future.

"We need more tests to prove the calibration beyond all

doubt. By the way, I can sense our tall friends in the Hub are about when I'm running some of the tests. I think they're monitoring our progress."

Red Cloud looked at Possum Chaser and she caught his glance.

"Do you think the Hub is a gateway to where they come from?" Julia asked.

"It's shaping up that way," Harry said, breaking into a smile. Esma looked at him and drew closer. They had begun to go out together on his Honda CX500 and she had chosen a flame red crash helmet.

"Well, my friends, this is a celebration of a job well done," Dearden said. He looked at the wall above the inglenook where the log fire was blazing. Aelfrythsgiefu, the magnificent jewelled sword of Leofwin of Mercia, hung in pride of place. The low light of the room reflected off the gems in its pommel and guard. Below it hung a Saxon hauberk, and a helm with a built-in nose and eye-guard. Julia saw where Jem was gazing.

"Raegenhere won't wear that hauberk again," she said.

"No, as far as he's concerned his life sentence *will* be life," replied Dearden. He looked at each of his friends in turn. "You know, there is *such* potential with the Hub. We've only had a small slice of the past thousand years but it has been the best time of my life." He reached for Rowan's hand "We must start a journal. What shall we call it?"

"The Saga of the Grid?" Rowan suggested, still in the story-telling mood and thinking of Beowulf and the Anglo-Saxon sagas. They agreed on the title. Doughty raised his glass and proposed a toast to *The Grid Saga*.

"The only thing is," said Dearden wistfully, "Where do we go next?" Rowan came close. Her answer surprised him.

"There are hands held out to us from the stars," she said.

"Yes, hands held out from the stars there most certainly are,

Rowan." She saw his eyes take on a distant look.

Red Cloud looked through the window. He stood and walked over to it. A movement outside had caught his attention. The moonlight shone on his face as he looked out into the night . . .

* * *

If we were to leave those in de Arden Hall to their well-earned time of relaxation and merriment and go outside into the night, we would probably hear the sound of a hunting owl flying above the trees of Leofwin's Hundred. We would hear the sounds of laughter, and turning to look closely at the old house we would see a window that extends to the floor, closed to keep out the cold night air. A Native American is looking out with a puzzled look on his face. The reflection of the log fire is flickering on the walls within.

Standing in the darkness outside, just beyond the light from the great hall, are three beings who are watching the people inside. They are very tall, of slender build and have a greenish tint to their skin.

"They are ready now," Lan-Si-Nu said to Thal-Nar and Fen-Nu, "They are ready to start their journey." The other two nodded their agreement. Lan-Si-Nu walked through the darkness toward the front entrance of the house, followed by the others. "We will give them the Key," he said. Opening the ancient outer door, he stepped inside and walked toward the great hall . . .

Afterword

In 'Leofwin's Hundred', the first book of 'The Grid Saga', it was necessary to alter some historical features and facts to bind the story together. Coventry Castle is one such example. I have placed it as thriving around the middle of the eleventh century and had it built by Earl Leofric of Mercia. In reality, Ranulph le Meschin, first Earl of Chester, probably built it towards the end of that century. Another alteration was the position of the bullion vault in the National Federal Bank of New York. I moved it from its true position in relation to sea level to enable it to be broken into from a storm drain servicing the financial district of Manhattan.

Most of the characters who step into the pages of the novel are fictitious but I have introduced historically accurate characters with whom I have taken liberties. That was the case with Leofric and Godgyfu (the Anglo-Saxon Godiva). I have placed events in their lives a few years away from the time in which they actually occurred, in the interests of the story.

Leofwine (who I have called Leofwin) was a Nobleman, an Ealdorman of the Hwicce. He was Leofric's father, not his brother as he is in Leofwin's Hundred.

The idea of a Camera Obscura, where, in Victorian times people would sometimes gather in an attic to gaze through lenses onto the outside world, figured highly in the idea that Dearden and his team were able to view the ancient world through a CCTV camera.

Nikola Tesla was a brilliant scientist who was way ahead of his time. I have used his project, that of picking up free electrical energy, as the method of powering the Hub. The method is proven. Tesla invented an aerial device, patented on the 21st May 1901. (US Patent number 685,957) describing it as an 'Apparatus for the Utilisation of Radiant Energy'.

Regarding the theme of the novel, who knows, in years to come there may be a group of adventurers who, with their intrepid scientific friend, appear in a different age because of discovering a naturally occurring phenomenon that enables them to transfer to different places through space and time.

The Forest of Arden is now very different to how it was in the Anglo-Saxon period of the story. However, in Warwickshire and the West Midlands of England, most of the remaining pockets of ancient woodland were once part of the Forest of Arden. At one time, it was huge. In folk memory, speaking of many years ago when the forest was largely untouched is the fact that a squirrel could leap from bough to bough in the great forest for the whole length of the county of Warwickshire.

These days, when walking in woodland and all is quiet, one can easily imagine the Forest of Arden as it used to be. In one of those quiet moments, we might even catch sight of Tomahawk Shahn of Offchurch loping past a great oak called Old Jack.

John James Overton,
The West Midlands of England.
2015.

About the Author

J.J. Overton is from Coventry, in England's industrial West Midlands. He served an apprenticeship as a precision toolmaker, studied mechanical engineering, and is a Freeman of the City of Coventry. He was a director of Grey and Rushton Precision Tools, and subsequently was involved with quality control, at industrial giants, Alfred Herbert Machine Tools, Massey-Ferguson, and Courtaulds Structural Composites. In later years, before devoting more time to writing, he was a self-employed stained-glass artist. His native Warwickshire, with its rich, and sometimes turbulent history, influences his writing. He is married and has two adult sons.

Thank you for reading this book. If you have enjoyed it please leave a review on Amazon and, if you could, on Goodreads as well. It only needs to be a few lines, and reviews really do help authors gain recognition in the current publishing marketplace, which is crowded with books. If you wish, you can connect with me on;

j.j.overton2@gmail.com

Thanks for that,
JJ

J. J. Overton

.

What happens after Red Cloud sees movement in the darkness outside Dearden Hall, and the aliens head toward the front door to give Dearden the key? Find out in the next book of The Grid Saga,

Second Pass

Here's a taster

1

2,370 BCE, THE LAND OF HAVILAH

The sounds of raucous laughter floated across from the city, lit by flaming torches and the light of the Moon. Ever since the time the ancestors migrated in ships down the River Pishon, one of the four great rivers flowing from the land where all things began, conditions had been deteriorating.

The Keeper, Sho'mer, was a wise man whose task it was to keep the records. He and the other wise men had discussed a light that had appeared in the sky in recent times. Instead of being low on the horizon, as it had been for many days, it was higher now, and growing in size. They talked with trepidation about what it portended.

Sho'mer's father and grandfather, who were both the record keeper before him, recounted stories from their younger years, but conditions for them had been gentle compared to today. Anarchy had become widespread, Murder and rape were rife, and few people could be trusted. The Keeper feared for the future.

Sho'mer, who was also a stonemason, went across the square to speak to the elder whose task it was to tabulate the progression of the light in the sky. When Sho'mer questioned him about whether he had any idea why the light was there, the elder said he was only interested in tabulating its progress, not the reason why it was there. Sho'mer, dissatisfied with the answer, and he determined to go in search of it further afield. One day, he was in conversation with some men from the desert who had arrived on camels. He heard that there was a man in a place far off who, with the help of his sons had been building a great vessel. So the story went, he had been building the vessel for many years and now the tides near where he lived were rising in their ebb and flow, and he had seen that, as the seas grew higher, so the light in the sky grew brighter. Word was that the old man insisted the First Cause had spoken to him.

Word of this man's activity was spreading everywhere but as people considered he was mad they took no notice of his warnings and laughed at his activities. He was telling people that, unless they changed their ways there would be a catastrophe. The people held him in derision and jeered when he walked amongst them in the marketplace gathering food.

Sho'mer was interested in what the man was saying about the light in the sky, so he gathered his meagre belongings into a bag that he hoisted onto his back and he started on a journey to find out for himself what was happening.

Eventually, after some weeks of travel over difficult terrain, he reached the place where the man was building the vessel. As he reached a hill near the coastline, he could smell the saltiness of the sea on a breeze that blew over the brow of the hill. The sea birds flying overhead sang to him of the deep ocean that he had never seen. He could hear its restless movement before ever he saw it, and he could taste its salt on his lips.

When he topped the rise, he crouched down and peered over the crest. Sho'mer saw the builders working on the strange vessel on the shore below. It was a busy but orderly scene. There were great piles of timber, trimmed of all branches, ready for use on a great box-like structure. A few younger men were doing the heavy work, lugging the timber to wooden scaffolding for lifting into position. There were large cauldrons suspended over fires some distance away from the timber, and from them, steam arose, and the smell of tar hung in the air. An elderly, heavily bearded man was standing to one side at a table, consulting a plan on a clay tablet.

Sho'mer heard part of the conversation as he approached. The old man was pointing out where a feature on the superstructure needed strengthening.

"That's the way it should be. It is how the voice I heard told me how to make it and we must follow what I have been told exactly so that we will survive."

The old man turned at the sound of a footfall.

"What brings you here, stranger?"

Sho'mer said he was interested in what was occurring. Since he heard about it from the nomadic travellers he wanted to help.

"You are welcome my friend, we have much work to do and, I fear, little time to do it." The old man looked up into the sky and shaded his eyes with his hands against the sunlight.

"See, it is happening just as we have been told." The old man pointed to the object in the sky.

He called for refreshments, which the wife of one of the younger men brought over, and he told Sho'mer to put his bag down, and sit and refresh himself.

* * *

Building work was nearly complete, and all, including the women, took a hand in applying the hot tar to the hull to make it waterproof. During those final stages Sho'mer, the Keeper, learned more about why the vessel needed building.

The family of the older man showed him great hospitality, and it did not take long for the old man to grow to love the Keeper almost as one of his own sons. In the evening times when they were sitting around a fire, the builder of the vessel would recount the progress they had made during the day. Sometimes he delighted to tell them how the proportions they had been given were important for the vessel's stability, and that they had adhered to the proportions rigidly. During those hours, Sho'mer carried on with his calling as keeper of records, writing the information on parchment with soot mixed with vegetable gum.

Eventually, a day came when the seas became fierce and rain lashed the land unmercifully. Torrents of floodwater ran down over the beach and into the sea in great gushing runnels. The elderly man said he had been told that it was time for everyone to board the vessel. Before they did, they stood firm against the tempestuous wind and looked into the sky through the wild weather, and saw that the light had grown into a great orb that was almost overhead. They entered the vessel along with the multitude of livestock bedded down on straw in many separate stalls on the different levels, reached by ramps, and then the heavy outer door shut solidly as if blown by a mighty wind, sealing them inside.

When a few hours had passed, they felt movement as the great vessel lifted from its building position and rocked with the movement of the wind and the water.

Sho'mer made a detailed record of the momentous voyage for the benefit of his ancestors. He felt compelled to continue writing while they were afloat, telling of the privations they faced, and their great joy at the first sighting of land after months at the mercy of fierce winds and mountainous waves.

After the vessel grounded, Sho'mer looked into the sky and wrote about the recession of the great orb, and about their life in the new land where there were lush vegetation and every commodity they needed. Sho'mer settled on the peaceful land and took as his wife one of the daughters of the old man.

He placed the words he had written in a cedar-wood box, and put in it the tools of metal that he used as a stonemason; a square, a set of compasses, and a mallet made of beech wood.

The generation of the voyagers passed with Sho'mer the Keeper's death. He was the last survivor of the voyage, and the box he left, with its contents, became revered by his descendants who, in the male line, also became the Keeper. In time, with migration and war, and rivalries of kingships that came and went, the cedar-wood box and its contents became lost. All that remained was the rumour of a sacred box and the account of a great deluge.

2

THE PRESENT DAY, 2009

The wolf, Tomahawk Shahn of Offchurch, stood abruptly from where he had been lying. He brushed by Dearden's leg and walked slowly to the floor to ceiling window where he stood still, ears alert, listening. He looked into the darkness, attracted by something outside. Dearden frowned at the unusual behaviour as Tomahawk, now full-grown and black, raised his muzzle high, and howled. The primeval sound from the Alaskan wilderness made the hairs on Dearden's neck rise in sympathy. Tomahawk edged closer to the window and sat alone, fixed on what he could see outside. The others in the great hall laughed at the performance, and apart from Dearden, Red Cloud and Possum Chaser, they carried on chatting against the soft background of easy music.

Red tapped Possum Chaser's shoulder. She looked up and saw him nod his head in the direction of the window where Tomahawk was sitting. She followed Red's gaze but could see nothing because of the reflection in the glass shining in her eyes from one of the table lamps. Red walked to the window and stood at Tomahawk's side, looking out into the night. The others in the room knew Red was a loner, so they took no notice.

Red often picked up what other people missed, and although he could see the topmost branches of the trees at the outer edge of the forest moving in a chill northerly wind that was springing up, he had also seen three tall silhouettes moving in the starlight. He kept his eyes on them as they walked slowly toward the house, one leading the way and two following. He turned to face Possum Chaser and nodded his head again just sufficient for her to see. From his clenched fist behind his back, he raised three fingers. She saw the signal and smiled in answer. They had talked through the possibilities of this happening. He returned to his seat and shifted it around. Possum Chaser clutched his hand tightly, and they waited, facing the door . . .

John James Overton
www.jjoverton.com
j.j.overton2@gmail.com

J. J. Overton

Follow Dearden and the rest of SHaFT
in The Grid Saga.

Nos Successio Procul Totus Sumptus.

We succeed at all costs.

J. J. Overton

Printed in Great Britain
by Amazon